ROOT CAUSE

ROOT CAUSE

The Story Of A Food Fight Fugitive

For Lucy + Daniel —
Think globally —
write locally !
All the Best ,

Jim

James W. Crissman

To order additional copies of this book, contact:
Xlibris Corporation
1-888-795-4274
www.Xlibris.com
Orders@Xlibris.com
90247

For my mom, Patricia Eells Crissman, 1926-2001:

a great cook, a talented artist, and mother of eight

with enough good humor and love for all.

ACKNOWLEDGMENTS

Thanks go to my early readers, Claire Yost, Vicki Fulkerson, and especially to Lisa Purchase; their eagle eyes for typos, sense of story, and frank opinions have been invaluable. Thanks also to Professor Judy Kerman and members of the writers' workshop who meet at her home for their astute input on several chapters. Thanks to Karen Brooks and the editorial staff at Dirt Rag Magazine for their mountain bike ride into the bright light of fiction from the murky murk of poetic obscurity. Thanks to my friend and vet school classmate Dr. Gordy Jones for sharing his world-class expertise on modern dairy farms. Thanks to the guys at Bader & Sons John Deere for their information on modern farm equipment; it is truly amazing. Thanks to my dad, Dick Crissman, and my brother John for keeping a rolling West Michigan farm and a beautiful herd of Angus cattle going for more than half a century; the farm has given me roots. And finally, thanks to my veterinary colleague and wonderful wife Jill for her unflinching support, encouragement, and love during the creation of my first novel.

CHAPTER 1

B ruce Dinkle's world had shrunk. He shrank it himself on purpose as an act of environmental conscience, but it fit him like a wool sweater after a hot dryer ride, and he seemed unable to pull it back over his head. He'd gone and shrunk his circle of food sources without fully thinking it through, reflexively wrapped himself around a very good idea—eating locally—as if the locavore lifestyle were a clam and he were an octopus. But of course it meant that he would never again enjoy eating anything as exotic as a clam or an octopus as long as he lived in Michigan. The market where the Dinkles shopped these days was definitely not super.

One hundred crow miles from home was the edge of the circle that Bruce had decreed as the ethical food boundary for his family. A hundred mile radius is the standard locavore limit—no matter that a third of the Dinkle family's circle was in the waters of the Saginaw Bay and Lake Huron. Luckily for Bruce, their circle just included the Hoppinhead Brewery up in Cadillac, the source of Peasant Sweat IPA, a hoppy and slightly bitter microbrew he depended on.

"Jesus, that was close," Bruce said after poking the pointy end of his old high school geometry protractor into his home in Bay City, Michigan, and swinging the pencil end around a map of the state. He took a sip of Peasant Sweat from his favorite beer glass.

"I see you just barely missed the Sonoma Valley by about twenty-five hundred miles," said Alice.

"Right, but I can stretch the circle over to Paw Paw for your wine—just because you're my wife and I'm such a nice guy."

"Who told you you're a nice guy? I've had better cough medicine than that stuff."

"It's not that bad."

"Boy, those are the words I look for in a wine review: *not that bad.* Whenever I read that, I go right out and order three cases."

"Well, if you don't like Michigan grapes, there are lots of good orchards north of Grand Rapids, maybe you could try apple wine, or maybe peach."

"Apple wine? Peach wine? Are you kidding!? Maybe *you* could drink weasel piss! But I suppose anybody who drinks something called Peasant Sweat would like it."

The ongoing domestic war made going to work not that bad for Bruce. And work was apparently where he had perfected his human relations skills. From his lowly slot in the hierarchy at the power plant, he'd watched enough of management in his eight years there to know that the corporate titans can usually maintain morale at a just-functional level by encouraging the peons to express themselves freely on a given issue, pretend to consider their points, and then announce the decision that, in truth, had already been made before the empathetic listening charade took place. He'd absorbed this process without consciousness, fully internalized the technique without awareness of the steps. It was as if an empty region of his brain had been waiting to receive the art of exasperating people; the toxic nucleus had seeped in unobserved and grown there like a tumor. He was aware that he pissed people off, but he had no idea how he did it. And he seemed blind to the fact that he was the ultimate victim of his own misery generation.

In the mirror he saw an athletic man. Facial asymmetries were confined to his left eyelid, which drooped a little after an eyebrow-lacerating sucker punch taken in a bar fight in college, and a rightward bend to his hawkish nose—a character mark acquired in a flying faceplant off his mountain bike on a tricky stretch of rocky upper-peninsula singletrack. The few gray strands in his brown curls were easy to miss, but the scars and early creases on his almost rugged face were enough to suggest a gravitas born of experience. He found his reflection reassuring, and apparently others did too, as he was often granted initial leadership in novel interactions, the way handsome men almost always are until they seriously disappoint the common prejudice. His blue eyes had a quality that appeared to the Bruce-novice to connect and engage, but his attention was divided. Alice, unfortunately, had married him while still in the novice stage.

Thus, his young family erupted in near mutiny when a year earlier he had sold their idyllic ten acre farmette on the Tittabawassee River near Edenville, Michigan, and paid cash for a small light blue ranch with a one-car garage in Bay City. But they somehow stuck together and became urban agriculturists. They shared a communal garden on a neighboring lot where they raised all their vegetables. A good share of their meat and all of their eggs came from the chickens they kept in the basement. Everything else came from somewhere inside the hundred mile circle. Bruce had become a strict locavore, so all the Dinkles became strict locavores to the extent he could hold sway: no coffee, no exotic spices, no tropical fruit, and no seafood except the walleye, perch, and smelt that came from the Saginaw Bay and the rivers flowing into it.

Alice worried about the dioxins and mercury.

"Maybe so, sweet things," said Bruce, "but eating locally makes a person feel connected and responsible for the local ecosystem. If enough people join the locavore movement, we can catalyze citizens to force the cleanups. People who get their food from any darn place they want learn to ignore the mess in their own backyard."

It was just the sort of speech that made Alice's temples pound, but they were solid points, she had to admit. Still, there were health warnings about the fish, and she hated feeding it to the kids.

After they'd moved to town, and against Alice's wishes, Bruce had sold the little black pickup and the old green station wagon with the bike racks on top. Bay City had no mass transit except Dial-a-Ride, so without a car they mostly got around by muscle power—on foot or by bicycle. "We don't need cars," he'd said, "I can bike to work, and you work from home anyway, and the kids can walk to school. It will be good for all of us."

To further limit their carbon footprint, they canned everything, even meat. Bruce was adamant that he didn't want a freezer to yoke them to the grid. "That darn thing hums away, sucking up juice like Anita Bryant, for what? We can put it all up in glass jars and save hundreds of bucks a year. We can probably put the kids through college on what we save. Plus, if the power goes out in an ice storm or a tornado, we've still got food instead of nineteen cubic feet of expensive compost," he'd said.

By American standards Alice was naturally inclined to tread gently on the earth, but she'd never had the true believer, bred-in-the-bones enthusiasm for causes that Bruce did. Before they were married she'd found his activist tendencies attractively assertive; the strength of his convictions added to his masculine allure, and she thought his purposeful spirit might rub off and make her a better person. She was proud of him back then. And although she had always wished he were warmer toward her, she was sure he would learn to empathize eventually. He wasn't stupid.

But over time and with the coming of children, her hope that Bruce would change faded. Her focus turned toward keeping the kids happy and the family together. She became more mother than wife, and increasingly let the sourest arguments with Bruce slide, even the chickens in the basement, as if ignoring were kinder than fighting. She understood the concept of a Pyrrhic victory, so went along to keep the peace. But lately she'd invented excuses for not coming to bed, which made her a two-books-a-week reader and a prolific crochet artist, since there was no television to watch—another energy-wasting casualty of the low carbon footprint regime. She arranged secret mid-day rendezvous with friends when Bruce was at work and the kids were at school. Not for sex—although she could have used some—but because she ached for variety in her lunch—and somewhere with a TV.

One appliance they did still have was a gas stove, the choice of good cooks everywhere. And Alice knew how to use it. She invented or modified recipes using the limited palate of local foods. Her yellow potato, leek, and fromage blanc frittata was delicious. Squash and zucchini pseudo linguine with goat cheese wasn't for everybody, but Bruce loved it. "Something for my old goat," Alice would say when she put a plate of it front of him. For that recipe, Alice had shrunk it to fit the circle by substituting garden-grown dried and flaked red pepper for black, apple cider vinegar for lemon juice, and wild hickory nuts for pine nuts.

But she suffered by confining their winter culinary palette to meat, eggs, dairy, dried beans, root crops, and home-canned vegetables. She missed year-round fresh produce and yearned for rice, nuts, olives, ocean fish, avocados, citrus, and a hundred other delicacies from outside their damn circle. And she thought she'd puke if she ate another pickled beet. Similar to the bar-fight sucker punch he'd taken years before, Bruce seemed unaware that he was living at risk for receiving a hurled rutabaga to the back of his head.

Using Bruce's imposed moral food framework, Alice wondered if it was greener to eat an out-of-season tomato grown in one of the local hot houses that took a lot of fuel to heat in winter, or one grown in the Mexican sun and hauled three thousand miles in a refrigerated semi. Probably neither. It's awfully hard to enjoy food when you have to consider the morality of every bite. At least tomatoes don't bleed, she thought. Local meat was good and plentiful, but that was a whole other ethical conundrum. In the moments when she identified most with Bruce's ideology and considered the ecological consequences of taking up the modern American allotment of space and resources on the planet, thoughts of ethical suicide flashed across her mind. So she tried not to think about it. Her husband was depressing the hell out of her, but she couldn't help thinking he was probably right.

Before they'd moved into town the previous spring they'd sold Alice's little Morgan mare, Tillie. Alice had cried when the new owners picked her up, but Bruce considered horses to be resource-wasting eco-disasters except as employed by the Amish, and was not sad to see the easy-going black mare go. With Tilly went her companion goat, Frank, a friendly castrated billy of mixed parentage. They kept their cat Calliope; cats earn their keep by killing mice. But they'd never owned a dog; Bruce considered them parasitic. He said people didn't own dogs; dogs enslaved people who were so pathetic that they would pay the high price of unearned affection in dog food and vet bills. He had once joked to a friend, "If I wanted to buy love I'd get a whore—they're a whole lot more fun and they don't follow you home."

Among the things that Bruce hadn't thought enough about until after they'd made the move to town was how he'd get the venison they'd come to depend on for their red meat. But he got so he could haul most everything with his bicycle and little aluminum-framed bike trailer, and he made it work. That fall he got slack-jawed stares from everybody he passed, but an especially gratifying mix of macho defeat and grudging admiration from overfed camo-clad guys in big four-by-fours who saw him pedaling back to town with his bow and a dead six-point bungeed into the little blood-stained bike trailer. Bruce felt exhausted, but proud. He smiled and waved to rub it in. Alice thought of the way that canning that much venison always made the house smell, and quietly gagged a little.

Bruce worked as control board operator at the power company's coal-fired generator. Despite his apparent managerial temperament and looks, his politics—formerly described at length on the tailgate of his old pickup truck, and now synopsized only briefly on the limited billboard offered by the frame of his bicycle—clearly indicated that he was not. Promoting local food, hemp, heirloom chickens, gay marriage, cryonics, microbrewed beer, Ross Perot, the flat tax, and the National Rifle Association were just a few elements of a wide-ranging bumper sticker agenda that was hard to make sense of. Walking to their cars one evening back when Bruce still had the truck, two upper management guys spotted it and wondered aloud what kind of wacko drove that beater. One said, "Not to worry; obviously he's armed and drunk and on our side." And they hadn't needed to worry; Bruce took pride in monitoring the boilers and turbines closely, both to keep Bay City and the surrounding area humming, and to minimize the inevitable pollution caused by burning carbon-based fuel. He rationalized that if he didn't do the job somebody else would, and they might not care as much as he did. And anyway, it was a job, and there weren't many of those. Still, it was long boring hours of shift work, and his attention drifted.

As a parent his duties came no easier. He sometimes saw his own children as baby birds with their mouths always open, never satisfied, always after him for some new toy or useless thing. Even the enjoyment he found in his roles as urban subsistence farmer and hunter faded as they came to seem more like chores instead of the quietly satisfying pastimes they had always been. The previous year's gardening had made his back hurt, and hunting had begun to feel like long hours of standing in a tree waiting to shoot meat.

The housework was divided in an egalitarian way: Alice cooked and did the laundry, Bruce had the floors and bathrooms. Consequently, the Dinkles ate pretty well considering the limited ingredient list, and their clothes were clean by farmer standards, but the floors were gritty and the sinks and toilets dingy at best. The house chores niggled at him, especially the toilets. When he sensed that Alice was at the end of her rope, waiting with deteriorating patience for him to get his damn jobs done, he would alternate his use of the two toilets in the house, and direct his urine stream at fecal stains stuck to the inside of the bowls. If he could successfully piss off the smears with his liquid waste jet, he felt he'd saved on cleaning products and done his job.

Often unable to sleep despite physical exhaustion, Bruce grew increasingly restless and depressed. He would lie in bed awake, stare out the moonlit window, and ponder a new life—something clean, some fresh start, somewhere without all the encumbrances. Simplify . . . simplify . . . unload, he repeated to himself. He would make his own way, alone, living close to the land and free. He had long envisioned how he'd get there—to unencumbered freedom—but the vision had changed without a car in it. In the old days, before he'd sold their motor vehicles, he had commuted to work in his little black pickup, and he would listen to NPR, only rarely drifting into the recurring, just-keep-going daydream. But the irritations that made him restless were nourished and kept close by the same warm mitten of routine and security that generated them. He needed to break out. He itched for a solo adventure—no, an odyssey. He would live by his muscles and wits. And, when he thought about it, he guessed he could be two states away before anybody missed him. Maybe halfway across Ontario.

But these days his pedaling commute on his old black mountain bike was without *Morning Edition* on the way in, and there was no *All Things Considered* on the trip home. He had little to consider but what was already rattling around in his head and the hard-to-read-in-the-dark intentions of the cars around him. It was dark going in and dark coming home from November through February. Even if he didn't admit that he hated the long dark winters, his body craved light. Of course he was fit as a greyhound from doing everything the hard way, but his rock-hard thirty-two-year-old body and the self-righteous strokes he gave himself just didn't compensate for his shrunken world. He hadn't used his skis all winter, even the cross-country ones, except once to get to the power plant during a blizzard when there was too much snow to bike. They never went anywhere beyond the range of their bicycles or Dial-a-Ride. The kids wondered why they couldn't just have a car and drive to the mall like all the other kids at school. They wondered why they couldn't have a TV. They wondered why they had to raise the chickens in the basement that made their house smell awful. The earnestness of the old man just wasn't rubbing off on them.

The hard routines, chronic fatigue, and family resistance slowly wore Bruce down. He walked out on the doctor who suggested that exercise was good for depression. He wouldn't have taken antidepressants anyway, because among the many things he didn't believe in, he didn't believe in big pharmaceutical companies. During the day he tried to lift his spirits with a local ginseng tea. His only nightly pleasure besides increasingly rare, dutiful, and uninspired sex with Alice was the Peasant Sweat from Hoppinhead. He guzzled Sweat and chomped locally made potato chips as if their ingestion were an act of solidarity with the locavore cause, wine and wafer, blood and flesh, nightly spiritual sustenance for true believers.

The just-keep-going fantasy became relentless. It was especially intense on gray mid-week mornings as he pedaled after disappearing tail lights on the Harry S. Truman Parkway while trying to avoid the deep pot holes and salty slush spray. Like a dying star, his obsession with running away grew in density and gravity even as it withered in scope. Now he dwelt on how far he could *pedal* before anybody missed him. He figured that eight hours of winter daylight might get him a hundred miles—somewhere near Lansing.

By then the cops might be looking for him, but maybe not. Husbands disappear all the time.

He knew now that he would go south—forget Canada. He craved heat. At home they never turned the thermostat over sixty-five. His rule. But he got chilled when he reclined too long in his reading and drinking chair, even with rag wool slipper-socks on his feet and his lap covered by layers of crocheted Afghans that Alice had made him as Christmas presents. Getting out from under the layers of heavy wool to get another beer was a major effort. By late February the just-keep-going thoughts became a brain worm. He'd never make it to spring.

The combined sense of responsibility and spirit of rebellion that spawned his environmental ethic spilled over to his feelings about his family. With his load of work, chores, and the self-imposed disciplines that he held as uncompromisable moralities in the face of society's self-destructive slide, happiness seemed irrelevant, a bourgeois indulgence, the province of children and the pathetically naive. He couldn't figure out just how happy a man was supposed to be. The noise and colorful plastic toy clutter made him short-tempered with the kids, which in turn caused a measure of self-loathing he blunted with the long-necked bottles of Sweat. He considered the craft brew a far more authentic and substantial beer than the mass-produced pilsners he had come to despise. Even choosing a beer had become morally weighty. He was sure that what simmered within him was only the quiet desperation that most men lived.

And if there was anything he'd absorbed from his study of ecology, it was that he was not special. The planet was crawling with billions of people chasing ever scarcer resources, and they all wanted what Americans had. He was trying to wean his family off all the waste and excess, but they resented him for it. The few people who seemed to admire him didn't live with him.

His internal monologue finally would not leave him alone. The day came. He had successfully driven himself past the breaking point. He packed a bigger lunch than was his habit, including two baked potatoes, a handful of shriveled carrots, and three wrinkled apples from basement storage, took a check book and a thick envelope of twenties that he'd accumulated in his desk drawer—money he'd skimmed over the winter from ATM cash withdrawals—snuck some extra clothes into his bike panniers, strained for a little more sincerity than usual as he said goodbye to Alice and roughed the kids' hair with his free hand, left for work, and just kept going.

CHAPTER 2

B ruce's chest fluttered as his legs churned out the first few blocks. A rush of adrenalin made him feel light; his bicycle raced with his mind. The weight of his plan could not slow him down because there was no plan but to go. Plan or no plan, going would change everything. This might be the last time to pedal past the coffee shop where he got his ginseng tea, might be the last time past the riverside park where they took the kids, could be last time past the home of a female co-worker after whom he had lusted, and, finally, there wasn't much chance he'd ever make the turn into the plant again at the stoplight where he might have seen his boss if he'd been a few minutes earlier. As he rolled through the decisive intersection his heart pounded in his ears.

Even under the dim street lights he had no expectation of anonymity here. On his bike he was a familiar sight to the morning commuters sipping from their steaming mugs as they peered through the small defrosted semicircles at the bottom of the wide windshields of super-sized pickup trucks and SUVs—big ass vehicles that appeared to Bruce to have no other job in the world than to haul their owners' oversized butts to work and back. Some would lay on the horn as they passed him, apparently just for the fun of watching him flinch. It was a wonder he hadn't been squashed by one of these half-blind blunderfucks.

Past the turn to the plant, he was suddenly out of place, a sweating fugitive. He could feel eyes on him, although actually there were few in the inbound plant traffic who noticed that the dim outbound bicycle light was Bruce going the wrong way—the wrong way in so many ways.

After a few miles the brief morning rush wound down, and there was only the open road with dawn seeping in, a paler shade of March gray with a cold east wind. He made his tacks south and west, favoring west for the wind at his back, working south for the eventual promise of warmth.

The rich flatland farms lay dormant all around him, a squared-up patchwork of rotting snow and half frozen dirt, fall-plowed and naked to the winds that howled unobstructed by trees or hills, winds that dusted the snow drifts caught in the roadside drainage ditches with dark topsoil, snowdrifts now half-melted, mud-stained, and poised to cloud the spring run-off. It was dead flat and fertile farmland, as productive and charmless as any on Earth. He didn't consider why he railed against what did not please his eye, why this agricultural plain needed to meet his personal aesthetic threshold, why beauty should trump efficiency in food production, but it irked him. He wished it all to be on a human scale, with messy edges and brushy fence rows and sweaty people coming close and touching each other, not these flat alienating plains tended by men in huge tractors with climate controlled cabs, always in touch by cell phone. Nobody was going to stop and chat over the fence with their neighbor here. And what had happened to the animals? He hadn't seen cow or a sheep or a pig in a field around here since he was a kid.

He guessed that the Saginaw Valley farmers were mostly Lutherans, everything neatly tucked away into tool sheds, the snow plowed clean from every driveway, two hundred-acre fields bordering on weedless bluegrass lawns with nary a bush or even a rail fence to mark the line between yard and field. Usually a few acres of bare trees remained in the center of the square sections, but in places he could look all the way across a mile of flat bare dirt and see a pickup truck moving on a parallel road. Every road was parallel or perpendicular. Only the big rivers—the Saginaw, the

Tittabawassee, the Cass, the Shiawassee—interrupted the square sections; the smaller meandering creeks had been straightened and ditched out deep after Michigan was clear-cut by men with axes and crosscut saws in the nineteenth century. He was astounded that this was accomplished in just fifty years with hand tools and horses.

The beaverings of sweating humans were unstoppable—so why couldn't more of them grow their own food? Why were they so out of touch with what kept them alive? Did they even realize that this was their only planet, and this their only life? Why had Americans grown fat, lazy, and stupid, bombing around in huge vehicles, stuffing food from grease-stained paper bags into their faces, and listening to bombastic blowhards on their radios?

Where the ditches weren't filled with rotting snow, he saw streams of clear water falling from black plastic drain pipes buried at regular intervals across the fields, clear soil-filtered water falling into the muddy drainage ditches that paralleled the road. Because of man's compulsion to meddle, control, and "improve," even the water ran square here. He looked forward to a climb, however gentle, out of the damned flatlands, some sign that the earth might wrinkle, that somewhere the physical world had native kinks a man might explore, a place where a watershed could follow its own course and he could walk a high bank. He couldn't wait to stand on the pedals, to sweat over the crest of a hill, and to tuck into a coast on the downside; so he stood and sprinted on the flat, pushed hard on the level to the next stop-ahead sign, and blew the stop. He longed for the challenge and reward of a little geography, land that didn't look like the flat bottom of the Saginaw Bay, a curve in the road to lean into, something around the next bend he hadn't expected.

Around noon the boss called. He pulled off the road and told the man he was home sick, and that he was sorry he hadn't called in. "I just forgot," he said as a pickup truck blew past.

"It doesn't sound like you're home and sick to me, Bruce"

"Yeah, well I am," he said, "but I think I'm starting to feel a little better. Maybe I'll see you tomorrow." Click.

Finally the land rose a little. The fields got a little smaller. Woodlands were occasionally allowed to grow right up to the road. His inner social critic ceased to rail on the sameness of it all and took up the cause of urban sprawl. Every rise with a pleasing view seemed to have sprouted a large home with a three car garage at the end of a long driveway. What would become of these rural castles when the price of gas rose to meet the real cost of fossil fuel? What would become of a society that valued isolation above community? He was oblivious to the irony of this last thought as he poured his energy into putting distance between himself and everything he was connected to.

That evening when he didn't come home, Alice called his cell. He didn't answer. She left a message: "Bruce, where are you? Josie has violin tonight and I need you to stay with Mikey. Call me when you get this."

Bruce listened to the message. It stabbed a numb part of his brain, and he noticed that he had less than a day of battery left. He hadn't thought he'd spend his skimmed cash re-accumulating all the crap he was running away from, but now he thought he needed a phone charger. There goes a twenty, he thought.

He found a truck stop just off I-69 east of Lansing. They didn't have chargers, but they had meatloaf and mashed potatoes and green beans. He didn't know where it was all from, probably Nebraska, Idaho, and California, even though they grow all that stuff in Michigan. He choked hard on his ideology and wolfed the long-hauled grub like a starved dog. He thought he could detect a hint of diesel in the beans. He remembered a Woody Allen joke about two women at a cafe. One said, the food here is terrible. The other said, yes, and so little of it. But there was a heck of a pile of it here, and he was ravenous. He ordered cherry pie, which of course turned out to be made with that glutinous canned filling, probably from Washington even though they grow tons of cherries right in Michigan. He ate it with ice cream, surely made from Michigan milk and beet sugar, he could at least feel sort of good about that. He had coffee too, and he was sure he recognized the mass-produced taste of Hills Brothers. He was pretty sure it wasn't shade-grown or fair-traded, but it was hot, wet, and cheap, and that would have to be good enough after a whole gray late-winter day of Michigan on a bicycle.

The waitress came over. "Warm that up for you, hun?"

"Thanks." He asked her where he might find a place to stay.

"Well, hun, there's nothing here in Perry except for Heb's, and I seen they got the no-vacancy sign lit when I come in. You'd have to go in a town for a room. There's a place on Grand River near campus. I'd guess it's about twenty minutes from here," she said, topping his cup and nodding west.

Bruce did the bicycle conversion in his head: that'd be about two hours of pedaling in the dark with snow flurries and a cold headwind. Christ. He leaned back in his chair and looked at Krystal. She seemed a little worn out, like him, but not too bad from the right angle. She was thin, with short wheat-straw hair and green contacts in round, close-set eyes. With the stenotic nostril slits in her somewhat flattened nose, she looked almost feline, like there might have been a cougar in the family tree. "I'm on a bike," he said. "Any chance you could put me up?"

"You don't look like no biker to me. You ain't dressed warm enough for a motorcycle. Where's your black leather?" she said.

"Not a motorcycle, a bicycle," he said.

"Good lord . . . let me get back to you on that, hun."

Bruce wrapped his fingers around his cup and gathered its heat while he waited for Krystal to think. He'd got her name from her tag. He had time to do some thinking himself. What was it that made him run? There was an element of tradition here. Although his dad hadn't actually left the family, he avoided it for the long days and over-time hours he supposedly spent working. Over the years he and his brother realized that there was probably another woman. They finally met her when she appeared in black and weeping at the old man's funeral; her name was Margaret. She told the boys they could call her Aunt Marge. Their mother, also a Margaret, but one who went by Peggy, was mortified, but she didn't weep at the funeral. Bruce guessed that it was not so much that she had been stoic; it was that she wouldn't miss the bastard. He guessed that she had done her crying years before. His dad had never taken him or his brother on the frequent out-of-state "hunting" and "fishing" trips he arranged for himself, even when school was out and they could have gone. It all fell into place then. He remembered the Robert Service poem his father had read to them as children, the one that starts with *"that night on the marge of Lake Lebarge . . ."*

and wondered if his dad had liked it simply for the line with Marge in it. It was hard to say.

Compared to Dad, he thought, at least he'd been loyal to Alice. He did feel good about that, but clearly his dick was meant for something besides taking a leak standing up. He was way past ready for the sex drought to end. And when he thought of his kids, he was pretty sure he'd been a better father than his old man. But he didn't think of his father without some sympathy.

His mother had been one of those sixties housewives who over-valued domestic perfection to such a degree that plastic slip covers protected most of the furniture, and the dominant note in the olfactory signature of the home was the scent of Lysol. He could see how living in a furniture museum might have driven his dad onto the streets looking for some interesting messiness. Similarly, chickens in the basement and dirty toilets may have been Bruce's rebellion against a childhood of microbial deprivation. But he could only rebel against his mother's specific behaviors as he recognized them; there was nothing he could do about the genes he got from her, a mapped but mysterious DNA code for a rigid black and white vision of the world. It didn't occur to him that the dull sawing conflict of his parent's marriage, between his mother's rigid expectation of an orderly world and his father's desire to feel the rough edges of freedom, was now entirely encapsulated within him.

His mother's genes may well have been the source of his discontent, the thing that predisposed him to be a man with a cause—a true believer—but genes could not dictate which of the universe of causes he would latch on to. If he hadn't become a locavore, he might have become a rigid ideologue standing up for or against any number of issues: it could have been abortion, gun rights, charter schools, creationism, female popes, cactus lawns, school uniforms, internet porn, water saving toilets, concrete roads, or teenage hairstyles. But of all the possible causes in the world, Bruce chose the local human food chain to lock onto and squeeze until his temples throbbed.

Krystal came back with the coffee pot and a few questions. She wanted to know how he'd lost his driver's license. He claimed he hadn't lost it. She said his story didn't make a lot of sense. Said she couldn't figure out why somebody would pedal a bike in the winter when they could drive. Said he didn't seem violent or perverted, which was more than she could say for her exes. Said she'd never taken a stranger home from work before. Finally she said, "I get off at eleven. You can throw your bike in the back of my truck and sleep on the couch. Just got to get you past my dog."

"What kind of dog?"

"He's a pit-rotty mix. His name's Bob Barker. He loves me, but he don't like men much."

Jesus, Bruce thought.

She kept his coffee warm, and he used it to wash down another slab of pie—gluey blueberry this time. They chatted when she wasn't busy until eleven finally came around. He got a box of Blatz from the gas station—they'd never heard of Peasant Sweat, but at least Blatz had a sort of proletarian cache—and threw the beer and his bike in the back of Krystal's truck. It was a fifteen-year-old, jacked-up F250 with tires that looked like they belonged on a tractor. It featured a large collection of banged-out dents, dents on dents, a few rust holes, and was brush-painted a faded orangish-red. She said she got it from her last divorce. Her ex had used it for mud bog racing and his construction job, but he'd lost his license for DUI and now rode a bicycle. Krystal told Bruce he reminded her of the guy, Jeff was his name, but without the mean streak—both of them skinny and tough and riding a bicycle and all. Bruce wondered how she could be so sure he didn't have a mean streak. He hadn't been in a fist fight since the one when he got his eye cut in college, but he sort of hoped he might still have one.

The truck made a hell of a racket when she fired it up. "Christ, what kind of mileage you get with this thing?"

"I try not to look, but about eight I think."

"Eight . . . fuck. How far to your place?"

"About twelve miles. Don't take long." She rumbled and roared away from the truck stop. The defroster cleared small patches at the bottom of the cracked windshield. Country music fought its way through frayed wires and bad speakers. A layer of Diet Mountain Dew cans covered the floor except where she kicked them away from the pedals, which she had to do repeatedly. He watched her drive while she lit a Salem and took a few quick drags. She said, "I shouldn't be doing this."

Bruce figured she spent everything she made waitressing on pop, gas, and cigarettes. "Well then quit," he said.

"No, not that. Taking you home. But I think Jeff's working down in Ohio this week, so I don't think we have to worry about him. I don't really know where the hell he's at."

"I thought you were divorced," Bruce said.

"I am, but the jerk still figures he's got rights with me. Got to get a restraining order."

"You think he's dangerous?"

"I know he is. He's the best deer hunter I ever met. He's hard to predict, and he could sneak up on a fishbowl of eyeballs. Plus he's mean as a junkyard dog. That's why I got Bob Barker."

"Jesus, it must have been fun being married to him," said Bruce, suddenly feeling like not such a bad husband.

"Yeah. A real blast."

Bruce went on thinking how much he disliked dogs and overly possessive men, and was urgently hoping he would not have to meet this mean dog of a man, when they pulled into a gray ice driveway. The truck's headlights illuminated a trailer the color of old snow except for the pink winglets riveted to the upper corners at one end, winglets meant to suggest a lightness and mobility denied by everything else in the picture: jumbled piles of unsplit wood, a charred rock circle, a snow-covered sofa, a rusted bicycle.

Bob Barker barked wildly from inside the trailer as they shuffled across the ice and got in. After a few minutes of Krystal yelling at him, Bob Barker finally stopped barking, but he continued a rumbling low growl with his hackles up, and he kept squeezing past Bruce to get behind him. Krystal scolded the beast, but it didn't matter much. Bruce could feel his own hair stand up when the dog got close. They slowly got used to each other. Bruce wondered why people with the least to protect had the meanest dogs and the most guns. Krystal cracked a beer for Bruce and offered him a glass.

"You're done waitressing for tonight, girl. I'll take it from the can, thanks."

She was touched by his sensitivity and good manners. She didn't see much of that in the men she knew. "Hungry?" she asked.

"Sure, whatever you got."

She brought out a bag of Cheetos, and they sat on the couch and watched Leno as their fingers turned orange. Bruce was too tired to wonder what sort of Day-Glo industrial batter spawned Cheetos. He conked out. She threw her comforter over him, turned down the heat, and went to bed.

He awoke in the middle of the night with a boner and a full bladder, and felt his way toward the bathroom in the dark. Bob Barker erupted and pinned him in the corner. Krystal tried yelling from her bed, but she had to get up and restrain the beast while Bruce peed. Her short nightie exposed tattoos on her otherwise attractive bottom that appeared to be a brief history of the men who had passed that way. Each apparently had a moment when he was special enough to warrant permanent inky remembrance on the lovely swell. She said, "Why don't you crawl in with me so Barker don't eat you?"

Bruce had no defenses, and wanted none; he shuddered in anticipation of the end of the sex desert his marriage had become as he climbed under the warm blankets. They let their fingers touch. Touch turned to stroke, stroke to explore, and soon Bruce was on a mission. He suggested additional more secular approaches, but Krystal apparently had a first-date, one-position rule. Besides, they were both exhausted. They awoke to banging on the door. Krystal bolted up and peeked out the window. "Jesus, it's Jeff," she said. "Get in the closet."

Bruce stood frozen in the dark among Krystal's clothes. The thin, smooth, feminine fabrics enveloped his bare skin as his nose filled with her favorite perfume mixed with stale tobacco smoke. He wondered briefly how his first extramarital dalliance could be going so far wrong so quickly. He was pretty sure that most guys managed to get laid without risking their lives.

She wrapped herself in a plaid flannel robe, answered the door, and tried not to let him in, but she had no more control of Jeff than she did of Bob Barker. He pushed his way through the door.

"We got done that job in Ohio, darlin. Joe dropped me off to see ya."

"I ain't your darlin. You got to leave."

"Well now darlin, last I heard it's a free country," he said, smiling as he removed and dropped his worn camouflage jacket. Bruce wondered why people who committed outrage so often couched it in patriotic terms. The voice seemed to Bruce to be too high for a tough guy, but with a menacing cigarette raspiness. Jeff faced Krystal with a wide stance, veiny arms jangling at his side, smile turned to sardonic grin. "Christ I sure missed your pussy down there bending steel in Ohio," he said.

"You're done with my pussy, asshole. I don't know who could give it to a jerk like you, but it ain't me. You got to get it somewheres else. Just get the hell out of here before I call the cops."

"I guess I'll get it the hell here, if here is where the hell I want it." Smiling to himself at the sound of that line and prospect of a little nookie, he pushed her into the bedroom and fell on her.

"Barker!" Krystal screamed.

Bob Barker lunged, clamping down on a generous hunk of Jeff's left buttock. Jeff rolled hard and swung his arms back to dislodge the dog. Bob Barker saw the opening, released ham, and dove for head. Jeff managed to bring his forearms in front of his face, but the dog bit hard and fast, shredding his left ear before clamping onto his wrist as he struggled and kicked from the fetal position. Krystal grabbed Bob Barker's collar and pulled him off, screaming, "Barker, stop!"

Jeff limped half way to the door, dripping blood, then turned back for a last stand, "I'll get you bitch!" he bellowed as he picked up a vodka bottle from the kitchen counter. He pitched it at Krystal. She ducked and it hit the wall. It was plastic and bounced.

Bruce bolted from the closet, naked, and drove Jeff toward the door like he was a football blocking dummy on ice. Bruce roared his rage: "You fucking bastard! Out! Out! Out!"

"Who the fuck is this?!" Jeff yelled as he stumbled backwards. Krystal let Bob Barker go. The furious beast joined the charge, slamming into the front door as Jeff frantically pulled it shut behind him.

Bruce found his pants, pulled the cell phone from his pocket, and punched 9-1-1. It was dead. Krystal found hers, and had the cops on the way in a few minutes. By the time the sheriff arrived, Jeff had disappeared, but it wasn't hard to find his blood trail in the snow and determine that he had run south. The sheriff called for backup, and the second car collared Jeff at a limping run about two miles down the road. Animal control came and took Bob Barker. Krystal cried and kissed him and stroked his big blood stained head as they loaded him into the truck. After an hour of questioning and filling out police forms, Bruce was free to go, but there would be a hearing on the incident and he would need to testify. He needed stay in touch.

For now, all Bruce wanted was to be gone. He lifted his bicycle from the back of the beat up pick-up, thankful that the truck was jacked up so high that Jeff hadn't seen it. He forgot to thank Krystal for the hospitality, but he told her to take care of herself. She kissed him on the cheek and told him she knew a good man when she saw one, and that he should go on home. She went inside and watched from the window as he walked his bike across the icy driveway.

As he reached the blacktop he swung his leg over and gave the pedals a little push. He hesitated, wobbled a bit in the middle of the road in a transparent moment of indecision, then pointed the handlebars south and stood on the pedals, sprinting hard over the first hill, racing to free himself from the vibrating fear that had layered itself over his depression and filled his head with noise. In less than an hour he was outside the hundred mile circle, and more out of touch than ever.

CHAPTER 3

Alice tried to call Bruce three times that evening after she realized he was missing. The messages she left on his cell sounded increasingly desperate. When she called Bruce's boss and learned that he had talked to Bruce earlier in the day, they both understood that Bruce intended to be gone: he was not sick, not late due to a flat tire, not a victim of the not-yet-invented criminal category of bicycle hijacker, not a hit-and-run accident victim swallowed by one of the deep roadside drainage ditches that made whole cars disappear from the Saginaw Valley: he was just gone—an adult runaway. Alice felt a curious mix of panic and relief. For several years she had imagined starting a new life, leaving Bruce to stew in his own juices while she got hers flowing again, but she didn't think it would start this way, or this soon. He was here yesterday, controlling everything in their life, and now, suddenly, he was gone. He just vanished down the road like hundreds of people do every day, each goner leaving dark voids in the lives of those to whom they were close, the shape of each void distorted by the awkward press of the peculiar parts of the leaver that had never conformed.

She put the children to bed, explaining that Daddy was late because of work. Then she called the police. She tried the County Sheriff's office number, but there was no one there after hours. The phone message instructed her to call 911. Not an emergency, she thought, and apologized to the 911 dispatcher as she explained her situation to the woman. No foul play suspected, they agreed. The dispatcher explained that when an adult runs away from home it's not a crime, and the police can't do anything until a crime is committed. Alice added that he wasn't exactly missing, she just didn't know where he was. The dispatcher joked, "Ma'am, I can't say I know for sure where my husband is tonight either." Alice forced a little laugh, agreeing that husbands could be a problem, and felt another flush of mixed emotions. She was on her own here. Finally the dispatcher recommended that if Alice didn't hear from Bruce within a few days, she should file for child support just to start that process. Failure to pay support was a crime they could collar him for, although it could be months before the court bureaucracy would fully activate in such a case.

Alice considered this. Apparently even on a bicycle in the dead of winter he could be in Timbuktu before the law would get involved. She crawled into bed but could not fall asleep. All night she mulled and turned the situation, alternating between anger at his leaving and excitement for the possibility of life without him. But she didn't cry. Alice could already feel the jagged void Bruce left in her filling, healing itself at an astounding rate, as if his removal had been surgical. She would mourn his loss no more than she would an excised tumor, and by four in the morning even the acceptance phase of her adjustment was truncated by the anticipation of freedom from the bastard. She would not just accept his loss, she would embrace it. It was an astounding change to make in less than a whole day, and she consciously considered that her emotions were in some way shameful, that the elation under her panic would not endure the harsh reality of her being left for no good reason to raise their children alone. She thought that it felt a lot like getting too high: if it weren't for her heart palpitations, the disorientation might be quite pleasant.

She stared blankly at the window as the winter sky revealed its first rumor of morning. The first pale gray blush in the southeast filtered through bare tree branches that divided the charcoal sky into angular shapes above their snow-covered neighborhood of modest single story homes. It would be an early March day so nondescript that the front page story in the local paper would concern a fender-bender on ice in which no one was hurt, but it was also a day in which she would make her debut as a single mother, and she was exhausted and still awake with her racing mind. Desperate for sleep, she conjured the most peaceful scene she could recall. It was the second week of May, the morning fog just lifted, the first week of summer break after her freshman year of college, final exams behind her. She was on Tillie, riding bareback in running shorts and a T-shirt. Tillie ambled a dirt path along the Manistee River, a clear, gravel-bottomed trout stream that sparkled in the light filtered through the sprouting new greenery. It seemed there was a warbler in every bush. A wood thrush sang like Maria Callus from the top of a tall white pine. The serviceberries were blooming, and patches of trilliums, violets, and trout lilies poked above the brown leaf litter. The smell of spring mingled with the mare's aroma, the sound of the running stream with her soft hoof beats. A whitetail doe and her two spotted fawns paused crossing the path ahead of them; they considered the horse for a few seconds, oblivious to its rider, then trotted into the brush. The intoxicating memory always calmed her. In a few minutes she was dreaming.

A smiling woman walked toward her and offered a hand. A rooster crowed in the distance. She took the hand and saw it was a man's hand, calloused and hairy with thick prominent veins and tendons. The rooster crowed again, this time closer. The sound gradually separated from the dream and Alice awakened. The rooster crowed again as he delivered morning cantilations for the first time in his young life. He continued to crow, again and again, so loudly that Alice thought he would wake the whole neighborhood. The rooster seemed proud of the quality and volume of his voice. All of the chickens were supposed to be hens. The crowing continued, the rooster's confidence growing. Another damn male who thinks he makes the sun come up, she thought. The simmering frustration of nine years of living with Bruce, a long sleepless night, the anger at being abandoned with their children, and a sudden raging sense of empowerment combined like bleach and ammonia—and she knew she could kill. She had seen Bruce do it, but for the first time she knew that she could do it too.

The children didn't need to get up and ready for school for another twenty minutes, and somehow the crowing hadn't roused them, though their dreams must also have been inhabited by the rooster. She padded down the basement stairs in her bathrobe and slippers, whispered softly to the chickens as she unlatched and entered their pen, and identified the young rooster by his growing red comb and wattles and the shining arch of his iridescent tail feathers. She cooed and stroked him gently as she hugged him close under her left arm. She felt the rooster's warmth, which was lovely and welcome in the cold house. The slender fingers of her right hand gradually spread as they slid over the top of the rooster's head and his lush dark feather cape. She curled her fingers under his jaw bones, and in one smooth motion tightened and jerked hard, pulling the young rooster's head away and bending it sharply skyward. She heard and felt a distinct crack as the rooster's neck bones separated. He instantly went limp under her breast. She felt warm blood flow from the bird's beak into her hand. She was shocked at how easy it was to kill the animal, how gently and quickly death had come, how it made her heart pound, and how intimate it was.

She hung the dead rooster by its feet above the utility sink with the bent wire of a shirt hanger, and snipped off his head with scissors between the separated neck vertebrae. His blood flowed out. She opened the faucet just enough for a stream of cold water to carry the blood away before it could clot, rinsed her hands, and left the water running for a few minutes while she contemplated her first personal slaughter and the blood dripped. The way the cold water joined with the warm red living blood and flowed to the drain, a confluence of life's most essential fluids, a small clear rivulet joined with the outflow of the dead bird's still-beating heart, captured her aesthetic sense and made her think that she might start painting again. Of course as a woman she had seen blood in water many times, but it had never before looked this beautiful. She also couldn't help but notice how, hung upside down that way, the rooster's wings naturally spread as if he were in flight, but he was flying straight down and brainless, which made her think of Bruce. She smiled through a tear and shook her head in sad but serene wonderment as she climbed the stairs, turned the thermostat all the way up to seventy, lit the burner under the tea pot, and went to wake the kids.

Josie rubbed her eyes awake and noticed her mother's robe, "Mommy, there's feathers and some poo on you."

Alice looked down at the place where she had tucked the rooster under her arm and saw a few gray downy feathers from its underside stuck with a bit of chicken shit to the faded blue terrycloth of her robe. Smears of blood made it look gruesome. "I killed one of the chickens this morning because it was a boy," she said.

Josie looked fearful. "Where's Daddy?"

"He didn't come home last night. I'm not sure when he's coming home."

Josie jumped up and ran to Mikey's room to see how far the male carnage had spread. Mikey opened his eyes wide as his sister gave her instant analysis: "Daddy's gone and Mommy killed a chicken because it was a boy and you have to get out of here! Right now!"

"Uh uh, I do not have to go!" said Mikey, instantly awake.

"Do so."

"Do not."

Alice appeared in the bedroom door and Josie began to scream for Mikey to run for it. Alice forcefully gathered the crying, struggling children in her arms and kissed them over and over as she laughed with tears streaming down her face. It took several minutes to calm and convince them there was not some testicular pogrom afoot in their home, and she loved them both more than anything in the world, and everything would be okay. And she really did believe it would be okay, but she had no idea how.

She made eggs and toast for their breakfast, put hard boiled eggs and shriveled home grown apples and carrots into their lunch pails, kissed and hugged them as they headed off on their walk to school, and returned to the basement to scald and pluck the rooster that would be roasted for tonight's dinner and featured in a pot of soup tomorrow. She felt like a pioneer widow in her urban basement while her goddamned Daniel Boone missing husband was out exploring the blacktop on his fucking bicycle.

When she finished with the bird she bundled up and got on her own bike, and pedaled to the bank where she opened new checking and savings accounts in her name, and transferred all but five dollars of their joint account's money into them. Because of their incredibly frugal lifestyle, the sum was considerable. Then she pedaled to the Ford dealership and with just a little haggling got a good cash deal on an Escape hybrid. She then threw the bike in the back of the new vehicle and drove to the grocery store where she bought staples and condiments and treats that came from outside the damn hundred mile circle. There would be oranges in tomorrow's lunch pails. There would be a fresh salad with the chicken tonight, and there would be rice in tomorrow's soup. The kids would taste apricot nectar for the first time at breakfast tomorrow. And from now on there would always be a bottle of a delicious oaky California Chardonnay in the refrigerator. They would drive to the movies on Friday night. She would shop for a TV on Saturday. Popcorn—they would have popcorn in front of the TV Saturday night! Her mind raced with culinary and cultural possibilities. Her renewed romantic possibilities hadn't even occurred to her yet.

CHAPTER 4

Bruce pedaled in a daze as the scene in the house trailer played over and over in his head. The lifeless late winter gray and snow-covered landscape offered little distraction other than the few small towns and many farms he passed. The roads he was on were all strange to him, made stranger by the old Door's song gone viral in his head: *People are strange when you're a stranger, faces look ugly when you're alone* .... And he felt dirty, as if he'd somehow been party to the violence instead of a helpful bystander. He felt disoriented by his emotions. His impulse to run only got stronger. His long-time preoccupation, thinking about where food comes from, gave his mind its only breaks from the cinematic replay of Krystal and Jeff and Bob Barker. If he'd had a specific destination you might say he was lost, but he didn't care where he was. He headed mostly south and a little west by dead reckoning, favoring secondary roads with decent pavement and light traffic, just laying down miles at the fastest pace he could sustain on his fat-tired bike, fifteen or so per hour.

He felt weak and suddenly aware of his stomach, which felt like it might eat itself if he didn't get food soon. At a rural intersection a road sign pointed to a town named Parma three miles on, so he turned that way, and although it was after noon he dreamed of a large breakfast. He coasted up to a diner called Martha's Kitchen with half a dozen pickup trucks parked outside. This would be where the local farmers come for lunch, he thought. He found a stool at the counter and gave his order to yet another waitress who called him hun, this one older and much larger than Krystal, more typical of the residents of a state whose demographic increasingly favored old and fat. He ordered a three-egg western omelet, hash browns, whole wheat toast, apple juice (maybe local, he figured), and coffee, and with all that got a pile of serving-sized peel-open plastic containers of coffee whiteners, honey, a medley of jams and jellies, as well as a selection of paper packets of salt, pepper, and various sweeteners depending on if you wanted to lose weight or not, which clearly most people in the diner should. Weighing the calories in the mountain of food and drink before him against the little paper packets of Splenda, he decided, what the heck, he'd put seventeen calories worth of real sugar in his coffee. Who knew where any of it was from.

A big man with an unruly shock of salt and pepper hair sat down on the stool next to him. "I seen you ride up on your bike out there. Isn't exactly bike riding weather we got today." His friendliness seemed a little forced, like he was investigating the stranger in town for the other men at his table, apparently the silverback males of Parma.

Bruce looked at the man. He appeared to be in his fifties and was wearing a flannel shirt and khakis with a yellow DeKalb seed corn jacket. The bill of a green John Deere hat stuck out of his jacket pocket. "Weather doesn't bother me much," Bruce said.

"Yeah, well, you start farming and you'll find yourself thinking about the weather like it was more interesting than sex—and maybe it is," he chuckled. "So where you from and where you headed?"

Bruce thought it was time to start creating that new life he'd been craving. "I teach college up in Saginaw. I'm on sabbatical for a year. Thought I'd explore the country by bicycle for a while. Mostly headed south. I'd like to get someplace warmer to work for a while. A farm, I'm hoping. I'm thinking about writing a book."

"Ah, jeeze, that's some job you get a year off. Book about what?"

Bruce had never been a teacher, or had a sabbatical, or thought about writing a book before, but the farmer seemed to be buying it. He thought fast: "Farming, actually . . . I thought I'd write about what farming is really like from a farmer's point of view."

"That'll fly off the racks!" Ray turned to his cronies and flashed a silly grin, raised his big arm high, and pointed a thick finger down at Bruce as he hollered across the room: "Biker boy here's writing a best-seller about farmers!" He turned back to Bruce, "My name's Ray by the way, Ray Vander Koop." They shook hands. Ray continued, "Cripes, folks don't even read the newspaper no more, let alone no book about farmers. People are dumber than donkey doo, ain't they?"

Bruce detected a note of insincerity in that last question, like the guy was checking him for wise-ass, know-it-all tendencies. It was a good interview technique but he wasn't fooled. He generally agreed that people were ignorant, but he wasn't going to say it. "Well, they don't read much off paper anymore, but you can learn most anything you want off the internet."

"Yeah, well that's a whole 'nother can of worms, isn't it. Looks like a whole lot of pornography and navel gazing to me. Eats up a man's time like days was peanuts and nights was beer."

Bruce smiled and said, "I think I've had that beer," enjoying the repartee and thinking that this was easily the most extroverted farmer he'd ever met.

Ray continued, "Why don't you come on and sit down at our table over there, I'll introduce you to some guys you might want to talk to—I believe you professors would call them research material."

Bruce was greatly relieved to free his mind from its preoccupation with the morning's violence. He happily accepted the invitation and moved his mid-day breakfast feast and a chair to the end of the table at the center booth by the windows overlooking the parking lot. This was clearly the center of power in Parma. He'd been in town for twenty minutes and already he was in the hot seat. Ray introduced him to the Mayor who also owned the gas station and a small oil distribution company, a pig farmer who had five-hundred sows on slats, a retired grocer who quit when his store burned down, which had been the only grocery store in Parma so now they all had to drive into Jackson, and Doc Voekle, the local vet. Ray gave them all a quick synopsis of Bruce's story as he knew it so they could all jump in on the quizzing. Apparently nothing interesting had happened in Parma for some time, and biker-boy was the day's entertainment.

The old grocer asked, "So how long's it going to take you to get far south enough? They's saying a snow storm's coming in later today. Supposed to get at least a foot."

"News to me. Kind of out of touch on the bike. Lucky I got knobby tires."

Doc Voekle weighed in: "Tires, schmires. You're going to succumb out there you get caught in this tempest on a bicycle." The doc seemed to like to sprinkle his speech with big words for their entertainment value. "You'll be taking shelter at the first farming abode you come to. Your luck it'll be Wanda the Goat Lady and you'll get swallowed up pecker first. Her billies will offer their eternal gratitude for a day off, though—just kidding. I think. Hey, you gentlemen ought to see her head billy goat, an old white Alpine named Moses. He's got horns the size of my arm, and she's got a wooden peace symbol hanging off his bell collar. About expectorated coffee out through my nostrils when I saw that one. I feel some kinship with the old goat though, being a peace loving senior herd sire myself."

Bruce sent a little apple juice out his own nose on that one, which stung as bad as beer going that way, but the belly laugh all around had the effect of adjourning the lunch, so the questions were about done.

Ray said, "Hey, I might have some farm work here for you, Bruce. Planting starts in less than two months and I could use another wrench in the shop. You any good with tools?"

"Seems like I spent my whole life fixing stuff. Where would I stay?"

"I can give you a roll-out couch in the farm office right off the shop. There's a coffee pot and refrigerator out there and my wife can feed you up a bit. She's a heck of a cooker. You look like you burn a lot a calories."

For the second time in as many days Bruce found himself throwing his bike in the back of a pickup truck, this one a big white late model Dodge Ram 3500 long bed king cab with dualies and a rumbling diesel engine.

Ray seemed to think it might never start again by the fact that he'd leave it parked and running for half an hour at a time. This was a pet peeve of Bruce's, but against his nature he held his opinion to himself for the time being. Ray said they had to run down to the implement dealer in Litchfield before heading back to the farm.

"How far's that?" asked Bruce.

"About twenty minutes. I need a barrel of bearing grease and some coulter disks for the planters. I'll get you started on that this afternoon."

The implement dealership was an eye-opener. Bruce had seen the big tractors out in the fields, but he'd never climbed up in one or seen the price tags. You could buy two average Michigan homes for the price of one these babies. Ray told Bruce he was sitting in a John Deere 8430, the most advanced row crop tractor in the world. He said it had a two hundred-fifty horse, nine liter turbo diesel engine, with cooled exhaust recirculation and an automatic transmission. And he said it got more than eighteen horse power-hours per gallon; it was the most efficient tractor ever made.

Bruce tried to work his mind around the stats, "Horse power-hours per gallon?"

Ray explained that that's how you measure efficiency in a tractor. It tells you how much work you can get done in an hour out of a gallon of diesel fuel. He said it's like miles per gallon in your car, but that farmers aren't out there just driving their pointless butts around in circles, they're pulling huge loads, doing work, so there needs to be a way to measure efficiency that takes into consideration what's being pulled.

Bruce suddenly understood that dumb and farmer aren't words that go together. "Sounds like you been drooling over one of these for a while."

"I quit drooling this year and bought this one. They should be dropping it off next week. If it works out as good as they say, I might get another one next year. Depends on corn prices."

"Ho-ly smokes. How big is your place?"

"We only got about a section and a half ourselves, but we lease a lot more. Farmers get old and quit and we buy up the leases on the crop land. We'll be planting about two-thousand acres a corn and another nine-hundred a beans this spring."

"So, I'm guessing you don't get your seed in little packets in the garden isle at Meijer's."

"Yup, you'd be right about that, Brucie," he said, and went on to explain that the seed would come by truck from Illinois in a couple of weeks. He said that since most of his land was pretty good, he'd be putting in about 30-32,000 plants per acre, and went on to explain that there are about 80,000 seeds per bag, so if you do the math, he'd be needing about eight-hundred bags. He calculated that high-end hybrid seed corn costs about four-hundred dollars a bag, so that would be about $320,000 just for seeds for the two-thousand acres of corn. And that wasn't counting the soy bean fields, or the fertilizer, fuel costs, pesticides, irrigation, drainage maintenance, harvesting, drying, storing, and land costs.

Bruce was staggered by the numbers and the complexity of the business. "How in the world do you figure your profit?"

"You don't. You just try to minimize your expenses and get a good price. It's all pretty much on faith. Every one of them numbers on the cost side is a moving target, especially fuel and fertilizer which are both oil based—and fuel is used at every stage. And my selling price isn't fixed either. I watch the futures markets all winter and try to fix a good price when I can, but it's all a gamble. Then there's the weather."

"You must spend a lot of time praying for rain."

"I ain't much on praying, that's my wife's area, but if it worked you'd need to meter it out real careful. You'd have to turn rain prayers into Jesus-make-it-stop prayers about every other week." He went on to explain that too much rain is as bad as not enough, which of course Bruce knew, but let him run. Ray said he ran irrigation on some of the lighter ground where he had those big sprinkler systems on wheels that pivot from the pump end. He said that his best soil down in the flat river bottoms was where he could get over two-hundred bushels per acre if everything went right, but that that land could go under in a flood, and then you're really screwed. If the rain comes at the wrong time or you get too much it can get too wet to plant, or drown the crop that's in, or you might have a bumper crop standing in the field, but it gets too darn wet to get it out of the field.

"Two years ago," Ray went on, "I had a beautiful corn crop down in one of my bottomland fields, but it started raining on Halloween night and it was standing in six inches of water by the start of gun season. We couldn't get in there with the combines 'til it froze solid in January, and by then the deer, with a lot of help from the turkeys and coons, had completely flattened a good ten rows by the woods and made a pretty good start on the rest of it. The hunters couldn't even get at the deer because they was all hiding in the standing water in the eight-foot-tall corn." He paused as he seemed to be considering the vagaries of the business. "You're just cutting your losses then—profits is kablooey."

While they talked, a fork lift operator put the grease barrel and the planter parts in the back of Ray's truck, carefully avoiding Bruce's bike. The operator said, "Good to see you got some spare transportation there Ray. You never know when them Dodges is gonna up and quit on you, and you'll have to walk. That there bike's good in-surance."

"I'm keeping my fingers crossed, Kenny." They jumped in the truck and Ray continued: "You can tell there's no big football game on today, Kenny's back on the pickup truck wars." Ray pointed out the windshield: "That's his old black F150 over there all chromed up with the Calvin pissing on a Chevy sticker in the back window. Makes you wonder if human intelligence is just an illusion, don't it?"

"Everybody needs somebody to piss on, I guess." Bruce agreed, and added that he was partial to the 'I heart my dog breed' bumper stickers himself.

Bruce was happy to be off the road and to know that he was going to have a roof over his head and a full belly for the night. The clouds were already getting thick in the southwest; it looked like the weatherman would be right this time. He liked the way that before a storm the clouds would build in the west while the wind picked up from the east. Weather "blowing in" as they say, but it's coming from one direction while the wind actually blows from the other. It would always force him to picture the jet stream and the storm spinning counterclockwise over the whole Midwest, and he could usually figure about where the center of the storm was relative to himself by watching the clouds and feeling the wind. Despite his earlier claim that the "weather doesn't bother me much," Bruce was like all bicycle riders, who focus on the weather almost as much as farmers—although they enjoy the good riding a drought offers. He figured that about now this storm was centered down in northern Indiana or Illinois, probably headed northeast toward the thumb, which would put Parma in the sweet spot on the north side of the low—big snow for sure he thought, and plenty of lake effect in its wake.

The heavy load in the back of the truck smoothed out its otherwise stiff ride, and he was beginning to nod off when they pulled into a wide gravel turn-around in front of several pole buildings and a large fabric-covered Quonset hut. A short distance away was a comfortable looking brick ranch with the remains of last summer's vegetable garden out in the back. It was Ray's home. A row of spruces marked the west edge of the yard and protected the house from the wind, which would be otherwise unhindered as it blew across a half a mile of open field, a field currently covered with bent corn stubble sticking through old snow. Behind the house was the original barn, a hundred-year-old, red, hip-roofed wooden barn with an earthen ramp up to big sliding doors that opened to the hay loft. Below the barn's peak, big white letters read: Vanderkoop Farms, Inc., Unit I. Bruce widened his eyes and thought, a corporate farm—the belly of the beast.

Ray backed his pickup through a roll-up side door on the biggest of the pole buildings. It was the size of a gymnasium, with tall sliding doors on either end, so that you could drive the biggest tractors and combines in one end and out the other. This was the farm shop. Ambient light came from rows of translucent panels in the roof and high on the walls. There were two identical corn planters and several big tractors including one fitted with a huge snow blower with three horizontal rows of snow augers, the others were fitted with wide snow blades and buckets.

Ray saw Bruce looking at the tractors. "I try keep Miguel and Leo busy in the winter plowing out the schools," Ray said. "And it's good for the tractors to run them once in awhile. Might put you on one tomorrow."

He followed Ray across the building to where Miguel was changing the air filter on an old John Deere 4020. "We use this old boy for smaller jobs—hauling wagons, stuff like that. Used to be considered a big tractor, but it can't pull none of the big field equipment no more. Equipment's so damn huge these days." Ray revealed his priorities by introducing the tractor before he introduced Miguel. "And this is Miguel. He's been working with us for, what, five years since you got out a Jackson, Miguel?"

"Seem like couple weeks the most. This is easy time, boss."

"Miguel's got some history he'll tell you about, I'm sure."

"Anyway that room over there in the front corner is my farm office. There's a fold out in there should be fine for you." They walked across the shop to where a fifteen foot square room had been framed into the big work space. Inside it was warm and there were windows facing the road and the house. Ray had a big old oak teacher's desk with a computer and an adding machine with a roll of paper tape coming out. In addition to the promised refrigerator and coffee pot, there was a microwave and a small TV. Ray said they moved it out there when they got the flat screen up to the big house, as he called his not-that-big house with his tongue firmly in cheek. There was a door to the outside, one to the shop, and one to a small bathroom with a cramped and slightly rusted sheet-steel shower unit.

Ray said, "The heat don't reach in there too good, but the pipes hasn't froze yet. If you get much stinkier, you'll probably want to use it."

They sat down and Ray explained the employment terms: minimum wage plus the room and work-day dinners, that's Monday through Saturday, which his wife, Deb was her name, would fix and he could eat wherever he wanted except in the house. If he wasn't going to be there for dinner, he should tell Deb. No smoking in the office or shop, and no drinking unless Ray poured. He looked at Bruce's ID and had him sign a few papers, and that was it; he was a farm worker—and a migrant one at that. He felt kinship with Miguel already. Ray had his hand on the door knob to the outside and said, "Talk to Miguel about getting started on them planters. I'm going in. Have a good night, I'll see you in the morning."

Bruce watched Ray walk the path up to the big house as the snow began to fall several hours ahead of the weatherman's prediction. The flakes were small, but there were a lot of them, and the wind had come up. Within minutes, snow snakes writhed across the gravel in front of the shop.

He got his bike from the back of the truck and unpacked his few things from the panniers. He checked the refrigerator and found an open pint of coffee creamer, a twelve-pack of Coke, and some horse vaccine. Must be a horse in the old barn, he thought. In a cupboard he found an open pack of generic chocolate sandwich cookies, a can of Maxwell House, and some coffee filters. He could easily subsist on Deb's dinners supplemented by cookies and caffeine until he got some groceries. But he still needed a phone charger. He could get a few things from the gas station convenience store in Parma, but he'd need to get in to Jackson soon. He glanced out the windows again. The gravel had already disappeared, and through the thick snow he could see only the bare outline of the spruce windbreak beyond the house. This would be a big one.

Bruce reported to Miguel, who gave him a quick tour of a pneumatic corn planter. Miguel showed him the pair of steel discs that push soil over each row of seeds and how they had worn down. He fork-lifted the box of coulter discs from Ray's truck to a spot near the planters, and gave Bruce the wrenches to replace them. There were two, twelve-row planters, so replacing forty-eight disks would keep Bruce occupied for what was left of the afternoon and most of the next day. As he worked he noticed the big white bins for fertilizer and the smaller bins for the seed corn over each row-planting unit of the planter. There were bundles of wires, hydraulic hoses, and vacuum lines all designed to deliver the precious seeds at precise intervals and exact soil depth with the right amount of fertilizer to help each grow up to be the best darn corn plant it could be. The central six rows of the planter were fixed, but the three outside rows on each side hinged and folded up over the top for transport, the upside-down components fitting like puzzle pieces into right-side-up parts. Even folded up that way the machine would be sixteen feet wide going down the road. Bruce managed to bark a knuckle in the process of changing the discs, but he found the task oddly satisfying. He admired the lengthening line of newly installed and perfect black disks as he sucked on the bloody knuckle.

When quitting time came there wasn't much doubt that Bruce needed a shower. His bare feet objected to the cold concrete floor of the shop bathroom, and he had goose bumps until he got under the generous stream of warm water and washed away the incredible day in layers: the outside layer of shop grime, the middle layer of bicycle sweat, and beneath it all a whiff of Krystal wafted up from his groin before it swirled down the drain. Dog tired, he'd just finished putting on his only change of clothes when he saw a bundled-up person carrying a cardboard box trudging through the now raging blizzard and half a foot of snow that already covered the path to the house.

"You must be Mrs. Vander Koop," Bruce said as he opened the door for her. Snow fell in from the door sill, blew in from the storm, and tracked in on her heavy boots.

"Call me Debbie, professor." She smiled and pushed back her hood revealing a cherubic, lightly freckled face and blond hair cut short and tightly curled into the doo widely known as helmet hair, hair completely unfazed by its recent scrape with the hood of her parka. "I brought you some dinner. You got pork chops, mashed potatoes, gravy, buttered corn, and bread and butter. And there's a big piece of carrot cake with cream cheese frosting for dessert, and there's a cold glass of milk in a plastic screw-top in there. And a course you can make yourself some coffee out here."

Bruce thanked her profusely and they talked about the storm and how nice spring would be if it ever came, and joked about how global warming sounded like a pretty good idea about now. Debbie said, "Ray says you're writing a book about farmers. I read a lot and write pretty good—I do the newsletter for the church—so if you want me to read some of it over for you, I'd be happy to do that."

"I might take you up on that. What sort of stuff do you read?"

"Oh, mostly the Bible and romance novels," she said with a little chuckle.

"It's all about love, isn't it?" Bruce said while keeping a straight face.

"Can't get to Heaven without it," she agreed.

She pulled her hood up and headed back to the house. The flying snow had a pinkish-yellow hue in the sodium yard light. Thick streams of flakes whipped across the yard. Bruce turned on the TV and sank into the couch with his meal. The weather news leaked over into the news-news. The newswoman explained enthusiastically how the low had intensified and schools had already cancelled for tomorrow, and that everybody should just stay home because this was a dangerous storm. The final news item concerned a woman who was saved from a rapist by her large dog, and that the man and the dog were both in custody, and that the dog was considered dangerous and might have to be killed. She added that an unnamed man who traveled by bicycle had been visiting the victim, and along with the dog had saved her from the rapist. Twenty minutes later the porch light came on at the big house, and Ray made his way out to the shed following in his wife's footsteps. During the time between the newscast and when he'd headed out the door, he'd had calls from most of the silverbacks at the diner and the sheriff. News travels fast in a small town.

Ray came in without knocking and stomped the snow off his boots. "So what's this I hear on the TV, Brucie? Sounds like you or somebody a lot like you had a damned exciting day before you come to our sleepy little burg. Was that you? They're making the guy out to be some sort of a hero." Sheriff Lennard Timmers pulled up to the workshed as Ray spoke. He came in stomping the snow off his boots. He brushed the snow from his badge and greeted Ray like an old friend before turning to Bruce.

"You the hero on TV? Got some ID?"

"About what? Just kidding—old joke." He pulled his wallet and handed his driver's license to the sheriff.

"You think this is funny?"

"It's been a slow day for funny," Bruce admitted, and added, "Am I in trouble?"

"Nope, we just wanted to get to know you a little better. We don't get a lot of bicycle riding hero strangers around here." He looked again at the license and read: "Mr. Bruce A. Dinkle." He looked up, "Initials B.A.D . . . . Are you *bad*, Mr. Dinkle?" The sheriff was smiling under the bill of his hat.

"I guess I was just in the wrong place at the right time, or maybe the other way around," he said, and went on to truthfully describe the events of the morning and night before.

Sheriff Timmers took a few notes and got all of Bruce's home contact information. He acted like it was an interrogation, like Bruce had done something wrong. It must be a dull community to be a sheriff in, Bruce thought. The sheriff continued, "And how is it you're on the road on a bicycle in the middle of the winter? You got family up in Bay City?"

"I'm on vacation. I go everywhere on my bike. I don't believe in cars. I got a wife and two kids up there."

Ray piped in, "Thought you said you was on sabbatical and writing a book about farmers."

"I guess I sort of made up the college professor part. But I think I might write the book."

"Best policy in a small town is to have one version of your story. Gets too complicated otherwise. Your wife know you spent last night with that woman?" Sheriff Timmers asked.

"I just needed a place to stay. I was lucky she put me up."

"So you left your family in the dead of winter to go ride your bike and sleep with strange women and John Deere tractors?"

"I might do that, Len," Ray piped in.

"Shut up, Ray," Timmers smiled and continued, "How long you thinking of staying?"

"I can't say. This looks okay for now. I need to learn more about where food comes from."

"That isn't hard: it comes from the grocery store. I expect you got grocery stores up in Bay City, right?"

Bruce was forced to explain the locavore movement. He told them all about eating only food that's grown locally and the hundred mile circle, and how he was sure it was the right thing to do, but that nobody in his family agreed with him, and that it finally got to him and he just left. In conclusion he said, "I guess I just got to see how it all works."

The sheriff crossed his arms and stared a Bruce for a long minute, repressing a smile and raising an eyebrow to indicate that he was cogitating as hard as he could on what he'd just heard. "Can't make this stuff up, can you?" he finally said.

Bruce straightened a bit while his mouth twisted to the side, a hint of a smile escaping his lips as he bit them. "It's all true," he said.

"Okay Bad Brucie, I don't think you're going nowheres on a bike tonight. Don't know if you're a hero or a crackpot, maybe both, but it's good to know where you're at. Welcome to Parma. I'm going back to the station, and I'm going to call your wife and confirm your story. I'll be checking in once in a while until we get to know you a little better."

Another inch had fallen while Bruce was being 'interviewed.' The sheriff spun his tires as he got back on the road and slowly fish-tailed away; his tail lights disappeared quickly in the thick snow.

"Okay, Bad Brucie, you might be the baddest dude I ever had working around here, and the weirdest for sure," said Ray.

"I'll take that as a compliment," Bruce smiled.

"I guess it is—congratulations on saving that woman—best story I heard in a while. You better get some sleep. I'll be out at five to get you started on a plow. My other guy Leo called in a bit ago, said he's feeling under the weather, flu or something, so this'll be your big tractor debut. I'll have you push snow in the junior high parking lot. Isn't much to hit there."

"Thanks Ray. Sorry for the trouble."

"So far you're more entertainment than trouble. Let's keep it that way."

CHAPTER 5

After their dinner of roasted free-basement-range rooster, Alice put the carcass and bones to boil and was adjusting the spicing of the stock when the phone rang.

"Mrs. Dinkle?"

"Speaking."

"Mrs. Dinkle, this is Sheriff Timmers down in Jackson County. I just wanted to let you know that your husband was present at an incident involving an attempted rape this morning, and I need to confirm a few elements of his story," he said, knowing he was giving Alice information that would be more upsetting in its incomplete form. There was nothing for the sheriff to solve, Bruce was not a suspect, and the perp was in jail, but the story had a lot of juice as the sheriff liked to say, and he wanted to know all of it.

"He what? Oh my god! A rape!? Oh my god! Did he try to rape somebody?!" Alice would have used an epithet more satisfying than the third person male pronoun to refer to Bruce, but the kids were listening.

"No ma'am, we don't believe he tried to rape anybody, but I'm trying to understand why he was there," he said, knowing that Alice would want to know that even more than he did. The sheriff went on give a sketchy account, stingy with details like cops always are, the better to catch someone in a lie. He didn't get to do a lot of interrogating down in sleepy little Parma, so he was relishing the notoriety of having someone in his jurisdiction who had been near a violent criminal and wanted to make the most of it. The story had been about half told on the TV news already, with video of Bob Barker in the pound and the reporter rhetorically asking if this hero dog ought to be euthanized. And there was more video of Jeff being taken into custody with his bloody left ear all but chewed off. Alice of course hadn't seen the news, since she didn't yet have a TV, and so had no idea that Bruce was being portrayed as a hero. But the sheriff wanted to make sure he knew more about the crime than anyone in Parma, so he could appear savvy and privy to the inside, birds-eye, low-down on the caper. He said enough for Alice to conclude that Bruce had spent his first night away from home with a strange woman. The wave of nausea she felt on hearing the story was oddly mixed with smug satisfaction that he was so instantly in so much trouble after abandoning his family, not realizing that Bruce's biggest problem now, by far, was with her.

"Jesus, he's as much trouble when he's gone as when he's here."

"Yes ma'am, I think I understand."

"You don't know the half of it."

The sheriff expressed his sympathy and went on to get confirmation of Bruce's story about leaving home on a bicycle and being a locavore and needing to find himself by studying farmers.

Alice's contempt almost burned over the phone line. "That's him. Is he still making people live on sprouted potatoes and boiled venison?"

"Can't say that he is, ma'am. But I thank you for your cooperation."

Alice stared blankly at the phone after she hung up, slowly composing herself before she turned to face the children.

"Mommy, what happened?" Josie asked.

"That was a man asking about Daddy. He saw a bad thing happen this morning, and they just wanted to check with me." Alice's instincts to protect her kids from the evil in the world were strong, but no match for youthful curiosity.

"But you said he tried rape somebody . . . What's rape mean, Mommy?"

"No, no, no, sweeties, he didn't try to rape anyone." For the second time that day Alice found herself calming, hugging, and reassuring the children while burying her own emotions. She read the children Dr. Suess's *Oh, The Places You'll Go* at bedtime while the phone took several messages from friends who had just heard the news and wondered if that hero was "her Bruce." She tried to get her mind around the yin and yang of the incident, and by the next day friends were stopping by with casseroles and cookies, and to offer congratulations to be passed on to Bruce if she heard from him, and to make sure they had all the slutty details that were adding colorful drama to their dull, gray, late-winter lives. Jazmine, a woman from whom she had once taken a yoga class called and offered her five free classes to help with the stress. Chad, a painter she knew from her visits to the Creative Outlet Center, offered to let her join his group of adult artists who put paint on canvas on Thursday mornings. She had the sense that half the town had just been waiting for Bruce to leave so they could get closer to her. Which was about right.

Alice's beauty was soft and unadorned. Her flushed cheeks and full lips needed no makeup, and the flash in her blue eyes and easy smile were only emphasized by their contrast with her daily uniform of blue jeans and a sweat shirt. She had been comfortable on the farm with the children and her daily chores with Tillie and Frank. There she floated through days and seasons, buoyed by her love for Mikey and Josie, caring for the farm animals, and her enjoyment of nature. It all seemed adequate to compensate for her growing difficulties with Bruce. Feeding hay and forking manure into a wheelbarrow were a twice-a-day, every day, fitness routine that didn't require wearing spandex. It kept her physically toned and emotionally grounded.

The chickens had been Bruce's job, but they added color to the landscape and the eggs were wonderful with their yolks standing tall and bright orange as Mexican igloos in the frying pan. Actually, everything on and around the little farmette had liked the chickens; the coyotes, foxes, raccoons, and the occasional mink all appreciated the odd midnight dinner of squawking chicken au feathers, or a lovely breakfast before sunrise of warm raw eggs en nest. The right farm dog to guard the birds might have helped, but that would have to be a dog without the taste that every other critter seemed to have for chickens and eggs, and such a dog would have required training and attention and a lot of dog food, none of which Bruce was willing to spend time or money on. And if it didn't earn its keep, Bruce said there was no point in having it. Alice had once told Bruce that since he could meet his own needs with one good hand and a gob of spit, she probably wasn't needed either. He could cuff his own damn organic carrot whenever he wanted as far as she cared. And more and more, that's just what he'd had to resort to.

But now he was gone, and as appealing as chickens had been in their farmyard, there was nothing appealing about the aesthetics of chickens in the basement. Without foraging out in the sunlight for greenery and bugs, their yolks had as gone soft and pale as store bought. And the chicken shit stink was almost as bad as Bruce's Aunt Marilyn's house; she was the aunt who hoarded cats and had sixty-four under her roof at one uncertain, hard-to-duplicate census.

At their little farm in Edenville they hadn't had a lot of visitors because it was a long drive and Bruce didn't make a lot of close friends anyway. But now that they lived in town and with the difficult husband gone, Alice's friends from the kids' school and her volunteer job at the library were already getting closer. Still, none of them stayed very long when they dropped by with their food offerings and to get the story on Bruce's adventure. It just stunk too much for most people to hang around. And it wasn't like you could cleanly walk away from it. Some of it went with you regardless of the power and durability of your underarm deodorant. The kids got teased at school for the way they smelled, although the teasers couldn't correctly identify the odor since they hadn't lived with their own personal housebound chicken flock. Instead, Mikey and Josie were teased for being bed wetters, and Mikey did still wet his occasionally, but Alice never let him go off to school in anything that would betray that embarrassing secret. It was clear to Alice that the chickens would have to go, and go very soon. She was taking control of her destiny, and it would be a destiny manifestly free of the embarrassment of personal indoor chickens from one shining coast of her basement to the other.

The easiest thing to do, she figured, would be to open all the doors and just chase them up the stairs, across the kitchen, and out the back door into the small city environment. Wild turkeys regularly ventured into town from the wooded flood plain on the other side of the river, and there were flocks of crows and pigeons in town, so she thought that a chicken ought to be able to forage around the city even in late winter without too much trouble. She considered driving them out to the old farmette on the Tittabawassee River, but she didn't have a cage that would fit in the back of her car, and she wasn't half crazy enough to put thirty loose chickens inside the brand new vehicle. Alternatively, she could slaughter them all in the basement, and then bone, boil, and can them, or buy a freezer to store them whole. Really, the latter was the only food storage option she would consider. She had found killing and plucking the lone rooster strangely satisfying, but the thought of the hours of blood and gore it would take to slaughter the entire flock made her a little sick, plus she wouldn't be able to do it until after she had shopped for a freezer and had it delivered, which might take days.

She wasn't willing to wait that long, so the next morning after the kids left for school, she opened the chicken-wire door to the basement coop, swung open the door at the top of the stairs, and using it and an old toddler fence made a sort of chute that would guide the chickens the short distance from the top of the stairs across the kitchen and out the open back door to what she imagined was their much longed-for freedom.

With the pathway cleared and all doors open, she went to the basement and gently began to shoo the birds toward the exit. But the flock immediately lost its flockness when she pushed it. They scattered like chickens. They did not recognize the stairs from the basement as their Stairway to Heaven, their Underground Railroad trestle to freedom, and instead dispersed mostly horizontally onto the food storage shelves and into the furnace room, the laundry area, Bruce's basement workshop, and the suitcase nook under the stairs. When Alice approached they either ran away or flew up to roost on the water pipes near the ceiling. Of course when a chicken or any bird is pursued, it jettisons any extra weight that could slow it down, so chicken shit bombs dropped with a terrorist's disregard for collateral damage. They would not be herded.

So she opened the egress window in the laundry area, and began, one at a time, to catch the birds and put them out the basement window, and from there they quickly disappeared. The house was getting cold from the open door and window. But the furnace was roaring and blowing full blast, and with all the chicken chasing effort Alice worked up a pretty good sweat. In twenty minutes she'd caught almost all of the birds and put them outside, which is about when the first chicken appeared at the top of the stairs, a fat Rhode Island Red hen she recognized as one she had just released. Then she heard a dog bark and scrambling and crashing sounds from the rooms above her.

She ran up the stairs and found the neighbor's chocolate Labrador, Muffy, in the living room with a chicken in her mouth, blood dripping into the carpet. A ceramic lamp was shattered on the floor, and there were terrified chickens blowing main ballast from every high perch, including bookshelves, stereo speakers, and the antlers of Bruce's trophy deer heads. Alice screamed and jumped up and down, which worried the dog and sent him out the door with the dead chicken dripping blood the whole way. She ran and slammed the door behind Muffy, gazed around wide-eyed at the chickens watching her from every corner of the house, and began to laugh uncontrollably until she almost cried, and then laughed some more, and finally collapsed to the floor exhausted, her sides aching. She lay there on her back for a good ten minutes, watching the chickens watching her, periodically breaking into a screeching, cackling, wet-eyed laugh like she hadn't heard from herself since the bravest man on earth, Tommie Roush, peed his pants on purpose while standing in front of his astounded fellow lunchroom eighth-graders and horrified parent-monitors to win a fifty dollar bet. Even the bettors caught hell for that one.

She decided she needed help and remembered that Chad the painter had said she should call him if she needed anything—anything at all. He had winked when he said this, which she thought was a little creepy, but she did need help, so she called anyway, and in less than an hour he was there. Chad was a thoroughly urban man, but he did have several qualities that would serve him well for this job; he was tall with long arms and large hands, had a calm demeanor, and he wore glasses that would protect his eyes from flapping wings and flailing chicken toenails. One by one he caught the hens and released them out the kitchen's back door as calmly and quietly as if he'd been a chicken thief his whole life. Then they went to the basement to release the leftovers from there, and found that all the chickens that had been put out the kitchen door had re-entered through the still-open basement window. So they cussed and laughed and caught them all again and tossed and shooed them out the window one more time. Then, after considering the clean-up job at hand, washed themselves up as best they could, brewed a pot of coffee, and sat down to think with a plate of oatmeal raisin cookies that had been dropped off that morning as congratulations on the missing husband.

"I've always kept a fairly neat house, I think," said Alice.

"This is a serious stain on your reputation—a lot of stains, really. You might not recover from this one," Chad laughed.

"Did you know that bird droppings have enzymes? This shit will eat the color off whatever it lands on. I not only have to clean it up, I'm going to have to repaint, and maybe recarpet and reupholster."

"Tomorrow is Saturday, let's have a work bee. We'll get phone numbers and email addresses for everybody we know and get them over here tomorrow morning. Maybe we can get that Oxy-Clean guy—what's his name?—Billy Mays, to come. We'll see how Oxy-Clean does on cock-a-doodle-doo-doo."

"Who's Billy Mays?"

"Oh yeah, you don't have a TV. You'll meet him tomorrow."

"Crap! There's a chicken in the window," said Alice.

And just then there were children rattling through the door as Mikey and Josie got home from school. "The chickens are on the roof and in the trees outside!" Josie said excitedly as she entered the house and looked around wide-eyed at the mess. "What happened?!" she asked.

"Mommy decided to set our chickens free, but they decided they liked it here, this being a heated, raccoon-free chicken coop with free corn. Turns out freedom isn't the most important thing to a chicken," Alice explained.

"*Freedom's just another word for nothing left to lose . . .*" sang Chad.

"Great song—wrong emphasis," said Alice. "It's more like, *chicken prison's a paradise with everything to lose*," she sang back.

"Maybe they just need to get used to being free," said Josie.

"Me too," said Alice, "let's go to the movies."

CHAPTER 6

I t was a short night. Ray came knocking at five with warm cinnamon buns and a thermos of coffee. Even if it wasn't part of the deal, Deb never let anybody go hungry. "Time to rise and shine, bad Brucie, we got a fresh fourteen inches of white stuff to push around. I'll give you a quick tractor lesson in the yard to get you started."

Bruce pulled on all the clothes he had and an old pair of pack boots Ray had lying around, and soon they were in the heated cab of a two hundred fifty-horse, middle-aged, four-wheel-drive Case tractor with a nine foot blade on the front. Ray demonstrated the hydraulic lever used to raise and lower the blade and another lever to change its angle for left or right snow delivery. He showed him the right and left brake pedals that could be used together by pushing one's foot in the middle, or used separately by pushing one pedal or the other to tighten the radius of a turn. He made the first pass across the farm yard while Bruce stood beside the seat.

"It's easy," Ray said, "you just got to plan for where you're going to pile the snow and try not to make any more passes than you need to get it there."

Ray traded places and put Bruce in the driver's seat. The many controls seemed awkward at first, but by the time he was finishing the lot, he had already shortened considerably the fumbling pauses with the blade controls.

Ray said, "The junior high and admin buildings is two miles down, then take a left on Maple and it's about half a mile on your right. Follow me. I'll go right past it and point to where it's at. Might as well leave the blade down for the trip, the county plows won't be down our road for a while. Miguel will take the other plow to the elementary school when he gets here, and I'll take the blower over to the senior high. Wait here while I get mine running."

Bruce enjoyed his coffee and a cinnamon bun in the warm tractor cab, while Ray fired up an even bigger machine with the snow blower. Ray pulled alongside Bruce, opened the cab door, and hollered above the idling diesels, "I'll take the right side of the road so's I can blow with the wind. You take the left."

In a blaze of headlights, flashers, and flying snow, they headed down the road. The blower blasted snow thirty yards off the south side of the blacktop while Bruce pushed a long row of it to the north side. Bruce enjoyed driving down the wrong side of the road burying mailboxes and plugging driveways as he went, while Ray pelted already snow-covered cars parked in front of houses well off the road. As they approached the Parma Public Intermediate School and Administration Building, Ray stuck his hand out the window of his cab to point the way for Bruce, and kept going.

Bruce stopped to survey the parking area, the details of which were more than a little sketchy under the deep snow. There was one snow-covered car left in the parking lot that he'd have to watch. He pushed the throttle forward and started in. His confidence and speed increased as he got comfortable with the controls of the big tractor and built small mountains at the edges of the lot. He imagined himself praised by the locals as a snowplow artist: "The way that new guy Bruce handles that plow, it's like ballet—a regular diesel dance," they would say. He smiled to himself and considered the feathery tolerances he could already shave with the huge machine.

As he neared the lone car in the lot he adjusted the angle of the blade so that no snow would spill toward it. He wanted the car's owner to be able to unlock and open its door without getting a flake on her shoe. He imagined she would learn his name and write him a personal note to thank him. A whole romance bloomed in his mind as he approached the car. In fact, he had imagined correctly that the owner of the vehicle was female, but that's all he got right. The blade skimmed the pavement a few inches from the car. The gap narrowed slightly as he passed, which caused him to lose his nerve and hit the brake. Unfortunately the right brake was the wrong brake. With the left tire still churning forward, the big tractor instantly pivoted around the stopped right rear, which drove the steel plow blade hard into the driver's door, nearly folding it in two.

The only thing to do was to finish the plowing and go back to the farm. In a last pass down the far side of the parking lot Bruce saw a fallen bicycle appear and disappear in the row of snow curling out the side of the plow. His fantasies of fame and adoration for his plowing skills were short lived.

Back at the farm he waited for Ray to let him know what happened and to make the necessary calls. But before Ray got back, Sheriff Timmers pulled up and motioned for Bruce to come and get in the squad car. The rancid smell of spilled coffee with cream explained the brown blotches on the seat fabric. He said, "Talked to your wife last night—don't think she's in love with you no more. Big Joyce isn't none too happy with you neither."

"Who's Big Joyce?"

"She's the Assistant Superintendant of the Parma Public Schools and a force of nature around here. She slept in her office last night and seen you hit her car. Figures you for a hit and run. You always this good with women?"

Bruce said, "It was still dark when I finished. The admin building looked like it was closed and my cell phone is dead, so I came back here to wait for Ray."

"I expect that's true, but Big Joyce wants your hide. I'm going to have to write you a ticket for leaving the scene just so's she don't come after mine."

Sheriff Timmers was finishing up the ticket when Ray rumbled into the farmyard with the big blower. He left it idling like he always did, and stepped down from the cab. "Bad Brucie still a hero, Len?"

"Yeah, but he done some damage to Big Joyce's Subaru. Just writing him a little ticket here."

"What the hell's her car doing at the school?" asked Ray.

"I don't know for sure. She's been sleeping in her office a lot lately. She says she's allergic to her cat, but I think she's got girl trouble with Rox." Chief among the sheriff's responsibilities was maintaining a high concentration of gossip in the air around Parma. It kept everybody entertained and they were happier to see him than citizens of other communities were to see their more conventional zipper-lipped officers. He had the low down or a theory about it for most every aberrant behavior exhibited by the residents of Parma, and a back story for a number of folks who seemed normal on the surface. It was a divide-and-conquer strategy that seemed to work for him—he'd been elected four times in the last seventeen years—though he probably never thought about it that way; personal motivational analysis and introspection weren't an apparent part of the sheriff's package.

"That's more than I can keep track of, Len," Ray said to the sheriff.

"This isn't fair. I'm going to fight this," said Bruce.

"Probably shouldn't. Isn't likely to go too good," said the sheriff.

When he left, Ray told Bruce what the sheriff had told him a year before: "Big Joyce once seen the local judge, Judge Heart, at a gay bar down to Detroit, and now she owns the guy. She don't give a darn because everybody knows she lives with Rox. She don't make no big deal about being a lez, but the judge, he's got a big secret that everybody knows, except he don't know that everybody knows. So if Big Joyce wants you to have a ticket, by golly you got one, Bad Brucie."

"I can see that Republican Family Values has really took hold around here." Bruce felt English grammar and any sense of reality slipping away from him. He felt a strong need to get back on the road, and soon.

"Yup. We got ourselves a com-munity here. Everybody knows everything about everybody else, and it keeps us in line so we don't go making spectacles of ourselves. Small towns work good that way," explained Ray.

CHAPTER 7

They had more cinnamon buns and coffee and spent the rest of the morning clearing the driveways and farm yards of the other three units of Vander Koop Farms, Inc. before heading to the diner. Doc Voekle came in stomping snow off his boots. "Got a couple calls up north of town, but got to wait for the plows. Snow at your place, Ray?"

"Nope missed us completely. Darndest thing. Deep snow all around us. We got daffodils sticking up, forsythia, robins, bluebirds, the whole dang shebang. Going to start planting this afternoon, just as soon as I teach Bad Brucie to drive straight."

Doc Voekle said he'd already heard about the new wrinkle in Big Joyce's Forester. "Kind of gave that door a camel toe crease, I hear. She ought to like that."

"Well she don't, and Bad Brucie's got his self a citation and a little fine for leaving the scene," said Ray.

"You don't want to get on Big Joyce's bad side, Bruce. I wouldn't fight it. Her bad side's like the dark side of the moon. You get back there you'll never see cerulean skies again," Doc said.

Bruce began to see that he was going to be out the hundred bucks, and there was no point to making it worse. Might as well cut his losses; he was falling into line. Doc said, "Ray, if you don't need him this afternoon, he could ambulate with me. I could introduce him to some more research material."

Ray said, "Well, I'm not sure what he's researching no more, but he can tell you all about loco-vores while you're driving around. Speaking a which, I think I need a pile a food a lot closer to me. My stomach thinks my throat's been cut."

They all had double cheeseburgers stacked with scab-like machine-made patties with melted-on American cheese on white buns with fries and iceberg lettuce salads with a couple of hard slices of pale juiceless tomato and a few well preserved croutons from a box. The low fat Italian salad dressing poured from the bottle like The Blob and tasted like vinegar and Metamucil. Bruce said, "You know, there's a lot to love about America, but this ain't it. I mean you think French wine, you think great. Iranian caviar: terrific. Italian pizza, Russian vodka, Spanish fly: all great. But American cheese?—this shit could gag a maggot."

It was the first they'd heard Bruce opine in a heartfelt way and they were mightily entertained. Ray said he liked the food at Martha's because the good old American cheese stuck his turds together so nice and the salad dressing made them real slippery so they shot out his ass like cannonballs. Doc Voekle told Bruce he'd better start ingesting and act like it's fine cuisine, or the waitress might stop calling him hun and pour hot coffee on his scrotum.

Of course he was hungry, and so he did eat it. The sun was just coming out as they left the diner and Bruce climbed into the passenger seat of Doc Voekle's traveling vet truck, making a space for himself by sliding a log book, a clip board, a bag of apples aside. "Let's go make the world hell for bugs," Doc said as they pulled onto the road.

"What?"

"Infections boy! There's critters out there been standing all winter in excrement up to their pizzles, suffering from antibiotic deficiency. It's our job to save their miserable lives. Load your hypodermics, boy! I want you to come out with both needles blazing! Here, want an apple?" Doc pulled one from the bag and offered it to Bruce as he sped down the snow-covered road.

Bruce read the bag. "Thanks. Michigan apple, eh? Fuji—I love these."

"That appeal to your loco-vore heart?"

"Sure does. Great apple," said Bruce as he chewed the first sweet juicy bite.

"Well, you'll get a gander at some more loco-vittles on the hoof in a minute." Ten miles later Doc dropped the truck into four-wheel drive and gunned it through the deep snow up to the door of a small steel pole barn behind an old farmhouse. They kicked back the snow from the door and got inside to find themselves face to face with two fat seven-hundred-pound Black Angus steers standing in manure so deep their heads almost touched the low ceiling and they could just about step over the stall boards to get down to where Doc and Bruce stood in comparative comfort, except for the choking air. The top foot of the mess was a liquid mix of feces and urine, and indeed the steers stood with their pizzles hanging in it. A woman and a boy came out from the house.

She explained that these were Jason's 4-H calves. She said, "We got them in here to keep them warm, but one of them's caught cold anyway." Jason looked to be about thirteen. He was off from school because of the snow. He stood quietly by his mother, shivering and looking sullen in a black hoodie with the menacing tattooed faces and gothic logo of a band called Skullduggery printed on the front. She turned and gave Jason a little shove, "Get in the house and get a coat on mister. I swear you ain't got the brains god gave a gopher."

"I'm not cold."

The air was steamy and thick with the smell of liquid cow dung and ammonia. Icicles had formed on the insides of the window sills from the condensation. The steers' long winter coats looked wet and slicked down on the few parts of their bodies that weren't armored with clinging balls of dried manure. One of the steers had thick ropes of pale yellow snot hanging from his nostrils and was breathing rapidly.

"Judy, they don't catch cold from the cold. They get pneumonia from breathing ammonia and being covered in filth. The bacteria live in their noses all the time, you just made it easy for them to get down to their lungs. They're range animals; they need to breathe clean air and walk on dry ground."

"But it's all snow and cold out there. You wouldn't want to sleep outside in this weather."

"I'd sooner freeze to death than lie down in this mess. Snow is fine. They're made for it. Healthiest place a beef cow can be in storm is in the woods like a deer. Barring that, out in the open is fine too. A three-sided run-in shed is nice for them in a storm, but they do just fine without one. This place is a gas chamber."

"What are you going to do?" Her voice quavered.

"I'm still trying to figure that out. I can't stand up in this pen, so there's no way to tie him up in there for me to treat him. Let's open the door and get them outside."

They got a grain shovel and a pitch fork and cleared enough snow and manure to swing the door open. The steers shot out into the fresh snow and blinding sunlight, coughing as they ran around the small outside pen. Steam from the deep manure rolled out the open shed door. Doc got a few things from his truck, including a rope halter and a throwing rope with a quick release, and he climbed over the fence. The going was tough with a good foot of boot-sucking barnyard mud under a thin frozen crust that kept giving way under his weight, all of it under the fresh foot of snow. He muttered, grunted, and struggled, but soon had lassoed the sick steer and wrapped the rope around a fence post. He handed the end of the rope to Bruce who was outside the pen, and told him to keep pressure on it, then, after pushing and snugging the steer up close to the post, he slipped a rope halter over its head and tied the lead rope to the post as well. Now he could release the lasso and the choking pressure on the sick steer's neck.

He listened to the steer's heaving lungs with a stethoscope, took its temperature, and confirmed his penside diagnosis of pneumonia. He pulled a hypodermic needle the size of a fence spike out of his shirt pocket and with the weight of his hips pushing the steer into the boards, leaned down and pressed low on its jugular vein with his left hand until the garden-hose-sized vessel filled with blood. Then he drove the needle right through the distended vein with a hard right. Doc appeared unfazed as the steer jumped and fought the rope. He slowly withdrew the needle a little until a stream of blood poured from it, then threaded it into the big vein.

He took a large brown bottle of an antibiotic solution from his coat pocket, connected it by a rubber IV tube to the needle, and stood with the bottle raised head high as the medicine poured into the bloodstream of the beast. "This is large animal general practice at its most elemental, Bruce. Great way to make a living, eh? You can see why it's so hard to get into vet school; everybody wants to do this," he said just out of his client's earshot.

When the drugs had been delivered, Doc Voekle said, "Okay Judy, I want you to leave this door open, and if you can let them into a larger area, you should do that—maybe run an electric fence around that grove of trees over there. I'll be by tomorrow and Saturday to follow-up."

Back in the truck Doc said, "People think that smaller is better, and sometimes it is, but just as often it's worse. At least the big boys know what the hell they're doing."

"Is that steer going to live?"

"Fifty-fifty."

"Will they make any money on them?"

"Those are club calves, so Jeremy's folks probably paid a premium price last fall from a good herd—I think she said they got them from Shagbark Farm up by Caledonia. But if the steer makes it, the kid'll get a premium price at the Jackson County Fair 4-H auction this summer, that's as long has he doesn't wear that dumbass sweat shirt and dye his hair blue to impress the bidders. He might've almost broke even if it weren't for this. It's no way to make money, but it's a good way to teach a kid a few things and keep him off the street. So far it doesn't look like he's learned to use a pitch fork, except maybe to comb his hair, but maybe he learned something today, you never know."

"How much will you charge him?"

"Well, that took us an hour. If I was to charge for my time like I should, when I add up this call and the two follow-ups, it would cost him about half of what the calf is worth. I can't do that to a 4-H kid, even one who looks like a punk."

"So you're pro bono on this one?"

"I've always been pro bono. You got something against a bono?"

"I think you just changed the subject."

"I did. You want to make the acquaintance of Wanda the Goat Lady? She's over on the South Branch of the Kalamazoo off Beaverhead Road."

"Will we be going past anyplace I could get a phone charger?"

"What kind of phone? Let me see it."

Bruce pulled the dead phone from his pocket. "Samsung, I think."

"I had one like that. Dropped it through the slats into the manure pit under a pig barn—decided not to dive for it. Got a whole drawer full of wall warts for phones we don't use anymore. Don't know why I collect them. I'll drop by the house and pilfer you one before I take you back to Ray's."

In a few minutes they pulled into Wanda's driveway as she was finishing pushing the farmyard snow with a little gray and red Ford 8N tractor. Doc Voekle said, "That tractor's as old as me." A wire-haired Jack Russell ran to greet them.

The farmhouse was built of field stone during the depression and looked like it could withstand a direct hit from a tornado. The Amish mason responsible for the home's exterior had laid up the stone in a peculiar and distinctive pattern using large, smooth, bushel-basket-sized stones, each encircled by a ring of apple-sized stones embedded in the mortar. The effect was quaint as a fairytale. Behind it was an old red wooden hip-roofed barn with a drive-up hay loft Wanda used for hay and grain and equipment storage. Her billy goats and young stock lived down below. There was also a newer, large, L-shaped red metal pole barn with a cupola at the peak featuring a brass billy goat weathervane, his curled horns lowered into the wind. Beyond the barns a series of small pastures divided by wooden fences and with a half-dozen large shade trees sloped away toward the river.

The farm sign said "Nanny Gate: Organic Goat Milk, Cheese, Kids, and Eggs"

"Goat eggs?"

"Syntax problem. She teaches biology at Albion College."

"Organic kids?"

"Got to do something with the boys. Can't run a goat herd on a husband and wife basis. She peddles them to Arabs mostly. They come all the way from Detroit to get them. You ever eaten barbecued kid? It's pretty good."

"No. We had a goat though, a castrated male, but we sold him with the horse when we moved to town.

"Who's we?"

"Me and my wife and kids. She had the goat to keep her horse company."

"You got a family?"

Before Bruce could answer Wanda got off her tractor and walked over to the truck. They got out to greet her. The little dog jumped on Bruce's leg with a ball in her mouth.

"That's Ishkabibble. She'll play ball with you till your arm falls off," she said brushing a little snow off her front, adding, "Heck of a dump, eh? About all that little tractor of mine could push."

"Looks like we timed it about right. I've done about enough slogging through the deep stuff for one day. I got a guy here I thought might like a tour of goat heaven. Maybe Ishkabibble could show him around."

She appeared to be a strong woman; not large, but square shouldered, and the glimpse of neck above the collar of her hoodie suggested a womanly muscularity. She had high cheek bones, clear blue eyes, buttery freckled skin, and a mop of curly auburn hair about half contained by a thick low pony tail. Even with the rest of her hidden under insulated brown denim coveralls she had Bruce's full attention. Her eyes ranged over Bruce in an overt, poker-faced way, like she was judging livestock. Her squinty direct method of evaluating one part at a time made Bruce think she might want to put him to work. Her gaze lingered a bit on his bicyclist's calves and quads where they stretched his jeans tight. Bruce felt self conscious, and unconsciously tossed the ball for Ishkabibble. When Wanda finished appreciating as much she could through his winter work clothes, she looked him directly in the eye. A wry smile told Bruce that she approved of the package. He hadn't been aware that there was a job here, but he sensed he'd just passed the physical.

"Where you been hiding this one, Doc?" she said.

The vet introduced them and said, "Bruce here's a drifter. Drifted into Martha's the other day on a bicycle looking for farmers to fill up a best-seller he's writing."

"No shit, you ate at Martha's and you're not in a cardiac care unit?

Bruce chuckled, "Yeah, no telling what's happening on the inside. I suppose I could die at any minute."

"Ain't that a fact. So you're a writer?"

"Not much of one, but I want to know more about farming. Your place is beautiful."

"Yeah, well, it's got *my* heart," she said, swinging an arm toward the barns. "But every farm looks beautiful under a foot of new snow. Come back in mud season. It's a little harder to love then."

Doc interrupted, "According to the most current weather prognostications, mud season will start in exactly two days. Hey," he added, "I got to get up to Gordon's to check on a lame horse. Wanda, how about I circle back in an hour or so to retrieve this gentleman?"

"Don't hurry Doc; I'll put him to work after I show him around."

As Doc Voekle pulled out of the drive, a BMW pulled in. It looked recently washed despite the mess on the roads. Two well groomed men in their thirties got out. Ishy ran to them with the tennis ball. "Wanda, you look fantastic in white," one of them said as he threw the ball down the plowed driveway.

"Well David, it's your lucky day, cause a snow storm's the only way you'll ever see me looking this virginal."

"Not the marrying kind, eh?"

"Put it this way: I've been in love with goats for just about half of the thirty-eight years I've been alive, all the while thinking a good man was just what I needed to help me out around here, but I never found one who could love me and love the goats."

"You ought to try Match.com, that's where I met Jeremy," said David.

"If they can match queers, they can match goat ladies," Jeremy added.

"There's an awful lot more queers than goat ladies in the world, and single goat men are rare as hens' teeth. And I don't want some damn born-again goat man who wants to be my shepherd," said Wanda.

"So why does it have to be a goat man?" asked David.

"You might not have noticed, David, but if you work with goats all day every day, you pretty much smell like a goat. Aren't a lot of men can get romantic in the face of that."

Bruce felt a twitch in his Levis. "Heck," he said, "I've always liked the smell of goats. Get too close to a billy, maybe it's a little strong while you're right there next to him, but the part that clings to you, that's just good musk to me. Makes me feel like Pan."

Wanda's knees nearly buckled.

"Oh my god," said David, "I think I just felt the earth move. Let's get our cheese and get out of here before these people burst into flames."

"Okay, we'll make it quick," said Jeremy. "We've got four guys coming over for dinner tonight. I'm making a crown roast of lamb with baked sweet potatoes and Swiss chard. I thought we'd have ruby port and wild Michigan hickory nuts with a little goat cheese for dessert. I think I'd like to get some of that Mont Saint Francis again."

Wanda stammered a bit as she struggled to regain her composure. A man who loved the smell of goats—holy shit! First she had to do business. "The Saint Francis sounds right: aged, rich, stinky, and semi-hard—should go well with the company," she joked.

"That's my Jeremy," said David. They all laughed.

Wanda continued: "You might want to offer a nice smooth Kentucky bourbon with that too—I like Old Fitzgerald or Bulliet. But if your friends aren't that bold, you might go for the Julianna: it's aged, but it's buttery with a mushroomy herbed rind. I'd serve a sauterne with that one. It'll knock you out."

"Don't worry about them being bold, Wanda, these boys will eat *anything*," Jeremy said.

David clutched his chest and rolled his eyes heavenward as he dramatized his approval of Wanda's culinary counsel. "You are a genius, Wanda. How much for a pound of each and a dozen eggs?"

"Forty-five for the Saint, forty-seven for the Julianna: that's ninety-two, plus four for the eggs, that's ninety-six dollars—I'll pay the governor."

David wrote the check while Wanda went to the house for the groceries. Bruce asked, "Where you guys from?"

Jeremy answered, "We're lawyers up in Lansing. We drive down about once a month to see the countryside and shop for things you can't get anywhere else. Isn't Wanda priceless?"

Two hours of driving for two pounds of cheese and some brown eggs, for which they dropped almost a hundred bucks—it was a little hard on Bruce's inner locavore. "Priceless, indeed," he agreed.

Wanda returned with the groceries. The cheeses were beautifully wrapped and boxed, the eggs in a reused carton. They left, and Wanda resumed leading Bruce's tour of Nanny Gate. They walked up to the old hip-roofed barn. The gentle rise of the earthen ramp to the hay loft was eased by the slope that fell away behind it—a rear walk out basement from a hillside barn. They entered the loft and stepped down the stairs, Ishy running ahead of them, to a row of wooden pens, each with a door to the outside and its own small paddock. As they descended, the almost choking smell of billy goat thickened the air. The first pen they came to was the largest and held about two dozen yearling does. "I'll be moving these into the main herd soon, then this pen will fill up with this year's kids." Several goats came to the fence and begged for attention. "The perky-eared white ones are Saanens, they're a Swiss breed, sort of the Holsteins of the goat world—high milk production, lower fat. The floppy eared ones are Nubians; think of them as the Jerseys of the goat world—high fat and protein, but lower production—good for cheese making. But, unlike Jersey cattle, they're also good meat producers. My Arab customers from Detroit really like them."

They walked a little further down the barn aisle. A large handsome dark brown buck with big white spots and long floppy ears stuck his Roman-nosed head over the fence. "This is my Nubian buck, Sadam." She explained that Nubians got their name from African goats that the English crossed with their native goats a hundred years ago. She said, "Don't turn your back on him; he'll break your leg."

The next pen held Slick Willy, the junior herd buck to the Nanny Gate Saanen's. "He's got a lot of potential I think. I'm using him on the daughters of Moses," Wanda explained.

"You're breeding Bill Clinton to Jewish girls?"

"And they like it," she chuckled. "And this is Moses, here," she said pointing into the last pen. Moses did indeed have a peace symbol hanging from his bell collar, just as Doc Voekle had said. He was larger and even stinkier than Sadam and Slick Willy. His horns had thick bases and extended in a wavy curve back past the muscular crest of his neck. His hair coat was long and shaggy from his neck through his brisket, and his thick dark stained beard hung down almost a foot. He shook his head and gave a low guttural bleat as Wanda approached, a greeting Wanda acknowledged with a soft bleat of her own, which caused Bruce to twitch again. "He's got a fifteen inch scrotal circumference. I've seen him breed a dozen does in a day—hell of a guy," Wanda said with pride and obvious fondness. Bruce was speechless. "Let's go see the mamas," Wanda added after a few moments of doe-eyed gazing at Moses.

The back of the big pole barn was open to the outside, allowing most of the herd access to a large barnyard area. Wanda explained that the lane from the barnyard had gates to seven pastures so that she could rotate them regularly. "Lucky seven," she said. Along one wall of the pole barn were a dozen small pens, several with a goat in them. "I've got these girls in the kidding pens. They're due any day." They walked slowly down the row of pens, Wanda looked closely at each doe, all of them with large pregnant bellies; a condition Wanda called "springing." A bluish membranous sac of fluid hung from the rear of one of the Saanen nannies. "Here they come!" said Wanda, "the first kids of the year!"

"Will she need help?"

"Probably not, but I'll show you the milk house and then we'll come back to check." Wanda took Bruce into the milking parlor, a cement floored room with six stanchions to hold the does while they're milked by machines just like the ones used for dairy cattle, except that these machines had cups for only two teats instead of four, to match the goats' anatomy. Stainless steel and clear plastic pipes connected the milking machines to the milk house, a room with a stainless steel bulk tank in which the milk was cooled, and a deep steel sink where they washed the milk-handling equipment. "By law, we have to cool the milk to forty-five degrees within two hours," Wanda explained. Next she walked Bruce into the cheese room where there were several vats as well as large pans and tools for working the curds. Everything was spotless. Bruce had a thousand questions, but Wanda said, "We better go check on that doe."

They found that the doe's water bag had broken and one tiny glistening white hoof poked out from her vagina. Wanda said she should check to be sure it was coming the right way. She got a bucket of warm water, a clean towel, and some liquid iodine soap from the milk room. She washed the rear end of the doe and her own arm, and slipped her hand inside. "The other foot's right there. But no head." She pushed her arm a little farther, halfway to the elbow now. "The head is turned back. Good thing I checked." She withdrew her arm. "You want to do the honors?"

"What, me? Put my arm in there?" Bruce was taken aback.

"Let me see your hands." Bruce offered Wanda both of his hands. She held them in hers, running her thumbs across the tendons and veins on the backs, then turning them to feel the muscular pads at the bases of his thumbs. "You've got strong hands," she said, continuing to hold them, "and long fingers, but not too thick. You should be a potter, but you'll be good at this. Take off your jacket, roll up your sleeves, and wash up." The doe strained with a contraction and let out a soft bleat.

Bruce washed himself and the back of the doe again, formed his fingers into a cone, and pressed his hand through her birth canal and into her uterus.

"There's legs everywhere!" he said.

"Twins probably—eight legs anyway," said Wanda, adding, "Concentrate on what's nearest the exit."

The kids' legs moved as he slid his arm past and found the nearest head, which was turned back toward its rump. He pushed a little further, almost to the elbow now, and wrapped his fingers around the nose of the kid to pull it forward. "Oh my god, it's sucking my finger!"

"Amazing isn't it? They know what to do before they're even born," said Wanda.

Bruce carefully pulled the head forward to align it over the front legs like a swimmer about to dive into the light. He withdrew his arm, and in a few minutes the kid was born. Doc Voekle returned from his horse call as the doe was licking the newborn, which was already trying to stand. He stood outside the pen admiring the scene. "Never gets old, does it?" he said.

"I can't believe I did that," said Bruce.

"You delivered that one?" asked Doc.

"He did," said Wanda. "He did fine."

"Life finds a way, doesn't it? Sometimes it just needs a little assistance," said Doc. "There's just nothing more satisfying than that."

"Come back tomorrow Bruce and I'll give you a quart," said Wanda. "Everything's been shut down for a couple of months, but we'll start milking this one tonight, and a dozen more are due this week."

Bruce said he'd love to come back, even as he was suddenly overwhelmed by a wave of parental longing when he thought of his own children. As they got in the truck Doc handed Bruce a cell phone charger that looked just like the one he'd forgotten to bring with him. "You must be anxious to call home," he said.

"Yeah. It's been a few days," Bruce said, dreading the conversation he needed to have.

CHAPTER 8

After Doc Voekle dropped him off back at Ray's, Bruce plugged in his new charger, confidently wrote a rubber check to pay the ticket for the snowplow incident from the account Alice had just emptied, walked it out to the mailbox, and raised the flag. Before he could shower, Deb walked down from the big house with his supper in a cardboard box she had lined with a red checkered dish towel. The Vander Koop's weren't Catholic, but they had a Friday fish tradition, so dinner was large helpings of deep-fried perch fillets, French fries, and creamy Cole slaw, with a big square of chocolate sheet cake for dessert, and of course the large screw-top container of cold whole milk. Bruce thanked her profusely and wondered how Ray had survived so long without a heart attack.

His appetite was off a bit as his apprehension grew over the call home that was so badly overdue. So he turned on the TV and paged through a recent issue of The American Farm Journal and read about the need for a government financed safety net for farmers. With his eyes on the farming article, the TV trying to sell him a Chevy pickup, and his fork on autopilot, he was adequately distracted from his personal problems so that the meal was mindlessly consumed by the time he got to the conclusion, which was that farmers need subsidies and protections so they don't go belly-up in a bad year, leaving us dependent on foreign food sources. He walked his dishes up to the big house, took shower, and generally tried to burn time while he waited for the phone to charge and for the dinner hour to pass back home in Bay City. He knew how much Alice hated phone calls at dinner. He picked up the phone and almost made the call, but figured that Alice was probably doing the dishes. He delayed again while he thought of her reading stories to the kids. Finally, in the hour between the children's bedtime and Alice's, he scrolled to her cell number and pressed send. She didn't pick up.

Bruce knew she heard it ring. She would be undistracted at this hour. He thought he had an idea of her mood by her silence, but he really had no idea. He left a message: "I thought I'd just call and let you know I'm okay so you don't worry about me. I'll try again tomorrow."

Actually, Alice was not worried about him, and had escaped her chicken shit bespackled house in the new car with the kids to get dinner and movie, and they were at that moment driving home from the theater after watching *The Little Mermaid.* Her cell buzzed in her pocket, but she was still getting used to driving again, it was dark, and she had Mikey and Josie with her. She listened to the message when they got home, whispered fuck you, and snapped the phone shut. She wouldn't have answered even if she hadn't been driving, and she intended to continue to ignore his calls.

While Alice took the kids out for the evening, Chad the painter contacted all of the people on the list they'd put together, and a dozen cheerful souls showed up the next morning for what his email invitation called a "hen party," advising that if you should lose your chewing gum while in the house, you should not under any circumstances put it back in your mouth. By noon the merry band of friends had disassembled the chicken cage and carried all of the lumber and chicken wire up from the basement and out to the garage, along with several heavy bags of chicken feed and the cylindrical galvanized steel chicken feeder. The broken living room lamp had already been replaced with one made by Chad's potter friend, Henry. And Chad, who had drawn a Billy Mays-style black beard on his face with grease paint, spent the morning using most of a case of Oxy-Clean he'd brought with him, spraying the blue fluid and energetically scrubbing away, all the while narrating his progress at the top of his lungs: "See this little yellow sundress with the chicken shit brooch?" he yelled, "Impossible you say? Watch this!" And he'd spray the miracle cleaner on the gray and white dropping, which would invariably make a big drippy smear before he finally scrubbed off most of it. Except for the glass, tile, and finished wood surfaces, none of it looked all that good when they were done, and the house would smell funky for months. By lunchtime the place looked about as good as it was going to, and they started spiking their coffee with brandy and devoured a box of bagels with a couple of tubs of cream cheese. Chad had the stereo turned up loud with the Talking Heads singing "... *this is not my beautiful house* ..." when a knock came at the front door.

A solid woman packed into a light brown uniform with a dark stripe down the outside of each leg—vertical stripes that were failing miserably at their slimming job—said, "Ma'am, I'm Officer Duncan from Animal Control. Are these your chickens out here?"

"They're my husband's, and we don't know where he is," she said.

"Could you give me his name and when you expect him home?" said Officer Duncan, not really asking a question.

"His name is Bruce Dinkle, Officer Duncan, and I don't know when he'll be home," then looking around and not seeing the children in earshot she added, "I'm hoping never."

Chad, standing behind Alice and feeling his brandy, said, "Dinkle Duncan?—is it that time of year already?" a quip that the officer seemed not to get, but that caused a little coffee spraying and choking from several of the more doggerelly inclined members of the cleaning party who knew the old verse, "... *when the frost is on the punkin', that's time for dickie dunkin.*" Officer Duncan wrote Alice a fifty dollar citation for keeping farm livestock within the city limits and gave her twenty-four hours to remove them. Alice succeeded in not laughing, accepted the ticket from the public servant, and thought just a little about dickie dunkin'.

Recapturing the chickens was not difficult. They merely opened the side door to the garage, filled up the chicken feeder that they had already put there, and made a little Hansel and Gretel style path of chicken scratch out into the still partially snow-covered yard. In a few hours all the chickens were happily inside the one car garage pecking at their feed and leaving chewing gum-like deposits on Bruce's stored hunting equipment. She closed them in. Getting them out of town would take longer, but she hoped that just getting them off the street would appease the officer while she found them good homes. Toward that effort she put ads in the Bay City Times and Saginaw News: "Free laying hens to good home: Aracanas, Barred Rocks, Rhode Island Reds. U pick up."

Chad helped with all of this, plus cleaning up after the cleaners. Alice pretended not to hear another whispered reference to dickie dunkin', but agreed that she would be at his painting class the next Thursday morning. She then loaded Mikey and Josie into the car and headed off to Circuit City to get a going-out-of-business deal on a flat screen TV, which turned out to be not that good a deal but she got one anyway. By that night they were enjoying popcorn, sliced apples, and chocolate milkshakes in front of the brilliant picture on the new set, while Alice flicked through the many cable channels in search of something the kids could watch. She discovered that *Family Guy* and *South Park* are cartoons that appeal to kids, but are apparently written for adults with adolescent tendencies. She might get back to these when the kids were asleep. She finally found *Sponge Bob Square Pants*. Mikey and Josie were happily mesmerized and slack jawed in front of the machine until bedtime, when they protested mightily against the tyranny of maternal discipline.

By the end of the week Alice could see that TV viewing rules were necessary but nearly impossible to enforce without offering competing distractions. It appeared that either she would have to become a soccer mom or the kids were headed for lives as lard-butted couch potatoes. Her own productive evening habits of sewing and reading were bound to suffer when she discovered *Weeds*, *E.R.*, and *Californication*. The new powerful seductress in the living room would require equal and opposite forces that she feared might not exist.

On Thursday morning after getting the kids off to school and watering the chickens, she dug around through cardboard boxes in the basement and garage until she found her paint brushes, palette, and a half-filled sketch pad from a class she had taken in college. She paged through the book and was suddenly face to face with a nude drawing of Bruce. There he was, sitting half sideways on the wooden square-backed desk chair that had come with her dorm room, his right arm draped across the chair back, his left leg languorously bent and turned out, his pubic hair and grown-up penis suggesting fuller maturity than did his skinny and youthful physique. She recalled reassuring him about the adequacy of his member and describing the anatomy of it during mildly inebriated love-making early in their courtship. She remembered pushing herself up on her elbows and pointing to their conjoined parts, saying, "Look, perfect fit, he goes in and out with not a bit of free space around him. I never had a wool hat fit better. Plus, he doesn't make me itch like wool." And he'd actually gotten better looking. The years since then had broadened his torso to a more full masculinity, and the structure of his face was improved as his milk cheeks finally thinned. But what was unchanged and struck her hard was the intensity and intelligence in his eyes. His eyes telegraphed the qualities that had so enthralled her, and she had captured them perfectly with her pencil. She smiled slightly to herself, pleased with her skill as an artist, but her smile was muted by disappointment that she had not predicted how those qualities would evolve. She searched her pencil lines for the asshole he would become, whispering to herself, "He must be sitting on it," as she snapped the sketch book closed.

The weather was finally breaking, so she put her art supplies into a small backpack and pedaled her bicycle to the studio where Chad taught his painting class. She found him to be an excellent teacher, concentrating on helping each student with the techniques they needed to realize their vision. Some students could not seem to get past the smudgy over-painting characteristic of the unsure and untalented, but Alice seemed to pick up where she had left off before the kids, with an observing eye, accurate lines, and intuitive sense of composition. She made half a dozen preliminary sketches that day for the painting she had seen in her mind's eye when she killed the rooster. In the sketches it was always sunrise, but the renditions ranged from fairly realistic through degrees of abstraction with elements of surreality, the rooster becoming the rising object on the horizon. In some sketches the rooster was sharp and life-like, in others he was a only a suggestion on the face of the sun. She considered the colors she might use for the sky, what the land should look like, if there should be a barn, if there should be people or other animals, finally feeling best about the starkness of a lone gray barn and a fence row of bare trees on a muted winter landscape at dawn.

Chad was impressed by her drawing and anxious to see how it might come to life with paint. He placed his hands on her shoulders and left them there a little too long. It made her uncomfortable. "When you told me what you had in mind I was afraid it would end up looking like a box of corn flakes, but this is good. Nice start," he said.

Alice fed on the compliment for a week, but wondered a little about his intentions. Still, how nice to know a man who pulled in the same direction. When she got back to her house there was another citation wedged in the door from Officer Duncan, this time it would cost her another hundred dollars. She pondered her options again, and decided that probably nobody read the newspaper want ads anymore and that she needed to get modern marketing for her flock of urban chickens. It was hard to imagine cyber-savvy chicken farmers perusing Craig's List, but some might, she reasoned. She put a price on their heads this time: a hundred dollars to cover the latest fine. She recalled her father saying that most people think free things are worthless.

CHAPTER 9

B ruce spent his Saturday morning in the shop with Miguel, finishing
replacement of the coulter discs, blowing compressed air through
the seed and fertilizer lines on the planters to remove any mouse nests, and
greasing every moving part on them and the cultivators used to prepare the
fields for seeds. By the afternoon the sun had melted most of the snow on
the roads, so Bruce pedaled out to Wanda's to pick up the goat milk she'd
promised. She was glad to see him and walked him out to the kidding pens
where he'd had the thrill of helping to deliver one.

Bruce's kid and its twin that arrived shortly after he'd left were nursing
vigorously, butting their mother's udder to stimulate milk let-down, sucking
frantically, and wagging their tails at a furious pace. Wanda said she gave
the newborns twenty-four hours to nurse before she started them on milk
replacer and began to milk their mothers. Two other does had kidded during
the night, each also with twins, and Wanda had moved six more does that
looked like they were ready to pop into the kidding pens. It was clear that
Moses and his buddies had worked fast the previous September. Bruce
helped Wanda haul fresh water buckets to all of the new and expectant
mothers. Then she broomed the dust and cobwebs off an old wooden
milking stand, and explained that they'd hand-milk the first few does to

freshen, which is the word farmers use to indicate an animal has given birth and is starting a fresh lactation.

Labor was a problem; her regular milkers who ran the milking parlor for most of the year were college students and were on spring break, so she didn't have anybody to do all that yet. Of course the training and recruiting process for student milkers was never-ending. Anyway, milking by hand was just easier for only a few goats. But in six weeks, with eighty does lactating, the machine milking parlor and a full workforce would be essential.

Wanda led the doe to the milking stand and up a wooden ramp onto its platform, put its head into the stanchion, and scissored it closed behind her ears. She put a scoop of grain into a feed bucket and hung it on the milking stand to keep the doe occupied while she milked it. Then Wanda washed and dried the doe's udder with warm soapy water and got a clean stainless steel bucket to catch the milk. Ishkabibble watched intently and whined a little, hoping Wanda would send a squirt her way. Wanda showed Bruce the milking technique. She squeezed the bases of both teats in the crotches of her thumbs to trap the milk, then wrapped her fingers around the teats from top to bottom to force it out. The first strong streams sprayed into the bottom of the milk pail and made a hollow metallic sound. She glanced at Ishy and said, "Squirt?" Ishy's ears perked and she opened her mouth. Wanda hit her little pink tongue from three feet away. Bruce caught on quickly and in a few minutes had squirted a gallon of rich pale yellow milk into the bucket. The aroma of the warm milk mingled with that of the nanny goats and the sweet and sour smell of the barn. It was as earthy and soothing as anything that had ever touched Bruce's nose. Wanda said that the milk was still considered colostrum, the antibody-rich first milk essential for newborns. And she'd give Bruce a quart, but would freeze the rest in case an orphan needed it.

"How much for a quart?" Bruce asked.

"Legally, I can't sell raw milk, but I was going to give it to you. For the people who want raw milk, which is all of my fresh milk customers, I sell them shares in a goat for fifty dollars a year, plus twenty dollars a week for its room, board, and labor. The milk is free. That way they own a goat and it's all legal."

"A loophole you could drive a milk truck through. Why the law?"

"The state worries about diseases, but I keep my goats clean and on nice pastures—totally organic—so I don't worry about it. Besides, heating milk destroys nutrients."

"Is that true?" Bruce asked, and didn't wait for an answer. "I didn't know that . . . Okay, I think I want to buy a share of a goat. I'll bring my checkbook tomorrow. Do I get to pick the goat?"

"I could give you a name, I mean your goat's name, but really, all the milk goes into the tank together. Anyhow, if something bad should happen to your goat, you wouldn't want to wait for a replacement, I don't think."

They strained the milk into a clean container and put it in a pan of cold water in the milk room refrigerator to chill. Then Wanda took Bruce to the house, she said to see the cellar where she aged the cheeses. Inside, the old house had the haphazard feel of a place occupied by a person whose life was focused elsewhere. There was a "Goat Breeds of the World" calendar thumb-tacked to the wall above the phone, and stacks of magazines, mostly *Midwest Goats and Sheep*, *Ruminations*, and *Goat Rancher*, along with a stack of Sanaan and Nubian registration papers, and books with titles like *Goat Cheeses of the Old World*. Several magazine and calendar pages featuring particularly fetching or inspiring photos of goats and chickens were cut out and masking-taped to the wall.

They made their way through the kitchen to the basement door that led down rough-sawn, wear-cupped, wooden stairs, and through a series of two doors at the beginning and end of a short tunnel that led to a food cellar. Wanda used the cool underground room for aging her cheese as well as storing root vegetables and wine. The cellar had been excavated and constructed several feet below the earth of her back yard. It was a living room-sized cavern with field stone walls and a concrete floor and ceiling. Varnished layers of red oak shelving covered the walls and glowed pinkish amber in the dim light of two bare, clear glass, low-wattage bulbs. Wanda lit a couple of thick vanilla candles and switched off the lights. She said it was far enough below the ground and isolated enough from the heated space of the house that it stayed a humid fifty-five degrees year round, the perfect storage conditions for everything from wine to winter squash to cheese. Bruce was beginning to sense that it was maybe a little hotter than that.

She took an old bottle of Port from the wine rack, pulled the cork, and passed it to Bruce. "Taste this," she said, without offering a glass. He took a swig from the bottle while she located a ripe round of the semi-hard Mont Saint Francis, cut a small piece of it, and held it above her head as she rolled it between her fingers, crumbling the stinky cheese into her hair. "Smell," she said, leaning her head into Bruce's chest. Bruce ran the fingers of his free hand into her thick curls, pulling the top of her head to his nose. He inhaled deep and long, and was hard before he could exhale. She took another bit of the cheese into her mouth, and pressed her open lips to Bruce's so they could taste it together. They kissed again, smearing the sweet wine and dissolved goat cheese into their faces as they frantically removed their winter work clothes and collapsed onto the pile of coveralls, blue jeans, and plaid flannel shirts, and fucked like goats, which is to say quickly and repeatedly. Wanda bleated and squealed "Holy Moses!" to announce her several enthusiastic orgasms. Bruce was astounded at his own repeat performances, which Wanda attributed to the 'hornigenic' goat acid pheromones in the cheese.

The next week went quickly for Bruce. During the days he worked at Ray's, trucking stashes of seed corn and fertilizer to the various farm locations and finishing maintenance on the tractors and equipment. At this point it was pretty much just an itchy wait for the fields to dry out and the soil to warm enough so that the precious seeds would germinate quickly when they finally put them in the ground. It would still be weeks before they could start. He and Miguel rapidly became good friends as they worked together.

Almost every evening, he pedaled is bicycle over to Nanny Gate to "help with the milking." He'd let Deb know that he'd be having supper with Wanda, and then he'd pedal home in the dark with his little LED headlight and tail blinker flashing, a fresh bottle of raw goat milk in his panniers, a smile on his face.

The new Vander Koop Farms, Inc., John Deere arrived on Wednesday. It needed nothing except to have its huge fuel tank filled, and Bruce got his turn at the wheel, driving it fifty yards from the shop to the diesel pump and back. The weather warmed; there was rain and a fog that lasted all day, and by Friday the snow was gone. Bruce attempted to phone Alice every day, but her caller-ID allowed her to avoid him. His messages got cut off against the sixty-second limit. He told her that he was working on a farm and learning a lot, but of course he left out the part about the attractive and passionate goat lady. He began to consider that Alice might not have him back, and all of the implications and possibilities began to crystallize. His guts churned a little. He massaged his own shoulders. Reconciling freedom and family, lust and longing, responsibility and adventure, made him hurt.

Miguel suggested on Friday that the weather and water levels looked like they would be pretty good for sucker spearing by Sunday and invited Bruce to join him. "Local food, amigo," he said.

On Sunday morning Bruce pedaled over to Miguel's trailer on Unit Two. Miguel's cohabitating girlfriend Doris stirred up some instant coffee before the two of them headed out for the river in Miguel's old, mostly blue but with a red driver's-side door, Chevy Impala. Since neither of them had a fishing license, they went to a remote spot at the back of Unit Three where the north branch of the Kalamazoo ran through a wooded floodplain. The lack of a license wasn't much of a worry since the only DNR officer in the county was focused on protecting the high value fish, bass and steelhead trout, from poachers. Law or no law, nobody cares about suckers; they're considered trash fish.

They parked in some trees off the road, and each tied a burlap gunny sack to his belt—actually that new fake plastic burlap—and each carried a devilish looking spear with a wooden handle the length of a man, and on the end a row of heavy barbed steel prongs, each the length of a beer can. They walked the last quarter mile through soggy woods to the water. Miguel wore his hip boots, and Bruce had a pair of knee-highs borrowed from Ray. The stream wasn't more than a dozen feet wide with a hard gravel bottom and short steep banks. The flush of the recent thaw had finally carried away the last of the snow and ice. Dead grass and debris hung high in the still leafless stream bank brush, unattractively festooning the high water mark with dried muddy streamers. The water remained a little high and cloudy, but it was clear enough to see into the faster current of the shallow gravel runs where the fish spawn. The holes at the bends remained dark water. They stood together at the top of the bank, maybe eight feet above the rippling stream, their eyes searching the bottom for fish. Miguel spotted a small group and said, "Stay here. You watch. Easy."

Bruce couldn't see the fish until he followed Miguel's finger and his description of the darkly mottled torpedoes lined up and nearly stationary in the current. When a fish moved Bruce suddenly learned to see them. Miguel walked downstream a half dozen yards before sliding down the bank and getting into the water. He shuffled slowly upstream, sneaking, stopping a body length below the fish. He raised his spear and brought it down suddenly and hard. Instantly there was a fifteen-inch scaly brown sucker flapping on the end, its mouth a thick lipped O, frantically blowing kisses from the underside of its head. He brought the fish to the mouth of the gunny sack tied to his belt and pushed it off the barbs into the bag. "Uno!" he yelled.

Bruce hollered back, "Got it!" and walked fifty yards upstream to find a pod of his own. He found a group of five drifting in and out of the current from behind a bushel basket-sized rock. A larger rock had its back above the surface a few yards downstream from the spot. Perfect, he thought. As he slid down the bank he heard Miguel holler, "Dos!" Bruce moved slowly like Miguel had, using the handle of the spear to test the depth ahead of him. The water was within an inch of his boot tops. He made it to the big rock with barely a cold trickle on his socks. He found a fish, and with his eyes locked on the target, raised the spear just as Miguel shouted, "Tres!" Bruce chucked and missed, nearly falling into the water as he reached out to avoid losing hold of the spear.

"Missed one!" he yelled back to Miguel.

"Aim lower!" Miguel yelled back. Bruce remembered reading somewhere about water refraction and bowfishing, so he knew what Miguel meant. A few minutes later, when the fish had resumed their positions, Bruce struck again, this time a little too low, but he managed to spear the sucker with one barb just a few inches in front of its tail. The flopping weight in his bag felt good. He stayed on the pod and speared two more with perfect hits in the next ten minutes before moving on. The earthy predatory nature of the pursuit made him feel primitive. He wanted to whoop. He dragged his fish bag through the current and scrambled back up the stream bank, grabbing brush and saplings to keep from sliding back into the water. He found Miguel and asked, "Up stream or down?"

"Don't matter. Nice hole two bends down," Miguel suggested.

Bruce found the hole and the run below it. There were several groups of fish in the current. He skidded down the muddy bank and grabbed a bush to stop him from sliding straight into the water. It took a while to find a shallow way in, but he finally did and slowly crept up on another pod which he decimated within a few minutes before moving toward the next group. He wasn't sure he'd ever had this much fun.

As he prepared to strike again, a much larger form came into view, a V-wake marking its upstream progress, its belly sliding over the rocks of the shallow run, its dorsal fin sticking shark-like out of the water. The fish seemed to move with predatory confidence; an alpha Piscean, Bruce thought, the daddy of all mother suckers. As it passed he raised his arm and drove the spear home in one smooth perfect motion. The big fish immediately yanked the spear out of Bruce's hand. He should have tethered the spear to his belt, but he hadn't. He ran through the current to retrieve the spear, filling his boots as he stumbled through the icy water. The fish went straight to the bottom of the hole at the bend. Bruce could see the tip of the spear's amber handle wagging below the surface. He was waist deep in the icy tea-colored water and off balance as he reached forward and down for the handle. He successfully grabbed it and attempted to pull the fish toward him, but only managed to upend himself into the deep water as all hell broke loose on the fish's end of the spear. Bruce gasped as he came up. He roared from cold shock as he expelled air from his lungs, forcing himself to breathe as his legs pounded for the bank, the fish pulling hard on his left arm. He reached for a bush with his right and pulled himself out. He swung around to an almost prone position, and anchored himself with a small tree between his legs. His back was against the steep bank, legs dangling on either side of the tree. With grunting effort he pulled the long spear with the large flopping impaled fish out of the stream. The hard yank, braced only by the tree between his legs, was painful, but he hardly noticed.

The fish bounced and flailed in the mud next to him. It was as long as his leg and almost as big around, dark green with rows of pale yellow markings and long toothy jaws big enough to swallow the suckers whole. Which of course was exactly why the big fish was there. Bruce recognized it as a northern pike, in the forty-plus-inch range he guessed. They both lay on the bank, near exhaustion. Bruce's chest heaved from the effort and the cold—mostly the cold—and he made a loud gasping sound as he forced himself to breathe. The pike flapped and flopped and flared its gills. It snapped its jaws as he wrangled the whopper to the mouth of the bag, in the process cutting his index finger almost to the bone on one of the fish's many long needle-like teeth. He ripped his jeans and poked his thigh half-an-inch deep with a spear prong as he pushed the struggling fish into the bag. He was still gasping and making raspy noises with each breath as he struggled to the top of the steep stream bank with the heavy fish bag and his spear. Miguel was just arriving, lured by the commotion: "What the fuck, Amigo?" he asked with deadpan calmness, surveying his water-soaked, mud-covered, bleeding, and breathless friend who had a hell of a flopping bulge in his sack.

Bruce acknowledged the question with an enthusiastic grunt, pointed the spear in what he imagined was the direction of the car, threw the fish bag over his shoulder—adding seeping fish juice to the back of his sweatshirt—and stumbled off as fast as he could, only once losing a boot in the deep boot-sucking mud of the flood plain, but then grateful for the lightness after he poured the water out and returned it to his foot. The empty boot felt so much better, that he stopped and drained the other one. Miguel caught up and corrected the direction of Bruce's flight by thirty degrees, and soon they were standing at the open trunk of the multicolored Impala admiring a good sixty pounds of speared fish, almost half of it in the one monstrous pike.

"Start this fucker, I'm freezing," said Bruce, his teeth clacking. True to his unflappable nature, Miguel let Bruce into the front seat of his automobile without protecting it from his filthy, bloody, and fish-beslimed friend.

"You look good, Amigo!" he said as he fired up the beast and drove out the two-track.

"Fuck yes!—I feel good!" said Bruce, shivering, hugging himself, rocking in his seat, and sucking blood from his finger.

Doris showed Bruce to their small bathtub where he could immerse all but his knees in hot water, while she took his clothes outside and rinsed the mud off with a hose before putting them in the washer. Miguel found him bandages, a dry sweatshirt, some pants, and a pair of Mexican sandals with soles made from old tires. Bruce tucked in the sweatshirt to try to fill the waistband, but he had to fashion suspenders from binder twine to hold the pants up, since Miguel's only belt had no holes in Bruce's wiry range. If Doris had owned a belt it wouldn't have fit any better, but anyway she always wore sweatpants.

"You look good, Amigo!" Miguel repeated when Bruce joined them in the kitchen. They worked together, gutting, scaling, and cutting off heads while they talked. "You ever smoke a fish?" Miguel asked.

"I tried once in college," Bruce deadpanned, "but I couldn't keep it lit." Miguel laughed and Doris joined in a little late. She cranked up a mariachi cassette on the boom box. They drank the better part of a twelve pack of Pabst Blue Ribbon and ate a bag of corn chips as they cleaned the fish and carried them to the smoker behind the trailer. Miguel had made the smoker from an old refrigerator. He put a hibachi with burning charcoal in the lower freezer compartment. From there a dozen holes drilled into the upper refrigerator part let the smoke flow around the fish before exiting the stack at the top. They loaded the steel racks with whole suckers and chunks of the big pike. Miguel stacked a few sticks of water-soaked applewood he'd kept from an orchard pruning job on the hot coals. He closed the doors, and in short order there was smoke drifting from the refrigerator's chimney.

"Okay, you come back tomorrow. We'll have smoked sucker—and pike, amigo!" Miguel laughed. They finished the twelve-pack and wolfed down a pile of Doris's bean burritos, Bruce got his clean and dry clothes back, and Miguel drove Bruce in an admirably straight line back to the farm where he fell into bed, his wounds throbbing, but as happy as he'd ever been.

The next night Bruce got Wanda to join him after the goat milking was done for a smoked sucker feast at Miguel's. Doris had boned and shredded the meat from several fish, then mixed it up with a can of corn, a ripe avocado, a few glops of mayo, and a long shake of habanera sauce. They rolled the mixture into flour tortillas and washed down a pile of them with another twelve-pack of PBR. Bruce kept his thoughts to himself about the distance the avocado and national brand beer had traveled to their mouths. Probably only the suckers were in the circle, but, hot damn, they were smack in the middle of it!

Doris told the story of how she met Miguel. She picked him from a list of prisoners looking for pen-pals because his crime didn't appear to be violent. Plus he smiled for his mug shot so she could see his teeth weren't that bad.

"He practiced his English by writing love letters to me," she said, "but he started using the F-word way too quick. I wanted some romance from a man. But he seemed awful sweet other than that."

"Girl's got a right to some romance," agreed Wanda.

"It get's horny in there. Not much romance in the pen, ladies," said Miguel.

Doris took a long pull on her beer can. "He told me my picture was pretty, though. That was nice," she burped.

Bruce wondered to himself how long ago the picture had been taken. He asked, "So what does it mean if somebody smiles for their mug shot? Does that mean, like, they're just as happy in jail as out?"

Miguel leaned forward and stared at the wall, "It means never let the bastards know they're hurting you. It means fuck you. Fuck you, I'm still Miguel and I'll still be Miguel when I get out of this hell hole." He slouched back into the sofa, looking suddenly detached.

Doris went on, "He got himself into Jackson because of a pot plant the farmer found behind his cabin at a migrant camp in a big orchard up north of Grand Rapids. The State of Michigan thinks sticking a marijuana seed into the dirt is a big deal. They made it a major felony with big fines and prison time. It's bullshit. Makes me want to cry. Since locking men up is big business for the state, the system works hard to keep the prisons as full as they can so the taxpayers is all happy and the guards has jobs. Otherwise who would give a damn about a dope plant."

"Prison time for growing one pot plant?" Bruce asked.

"Fuckin' nuts, eh?" said Miguel.

Doris said that as a migrant worker Miguel hadn't been at the orchard long enough to have grown the plant in the ground, but since the offending pot plant was itself in a plastic pot, the prosecutor claimed that Miguel had carried it with him from his August job which had been harvesting cucumbers in the Thumb, and before that it must have traveled with him through the blueberry, cherry, and asparagus picking jobs he'd had, all in different parts of the state. The old fart judge bought the prosecutor's story based on a farmer's testimony that Miguel was very good at growing things and had easy access to the plastic pots and fertilizer necessary for a healthy traveling pot plant. He threw him in the state pen at Jackson for the minimum mandatory sentence, which is four years.

"Minimum mandatory sentence of four years for growing one pot plant?"

"Fuckin' nuts, eh?" repeated Miguel. "That's Michigan. No money to educate people, but plenty to lock us fuckers up."

"The real charge should have been being near marijuana while Mexican," said Doris, finishing another can. She went on, "A justice project at the law school up to Michigan State—that's Cooley, I think—got onto Miguel's case. They got it overturned for incompetent defense and the lack of any good evidence that the pot was his."

"Jesus, they sent you up for something you didn't do?"

"I didn't say that," said Miguel, "but it still ain't right."

Doris went on, "You get in there for some minor little thing like this, you ain't nobody. Nobody's scared of you, nobody respects you, and you don't got no gang to protect you. Miguel got ass-raped—how many times?"

"Goddammit Doris, you don't got to tell everybody about that."

"People needs to know what's going on in them places, Miguel. Ain't no shame in it. Anyway he somehow got out of there without AIDS, so that's how he come to be my man."

"Ninety-nine to life," said Miguel.

"Oh, but I forgot to tell you he did get hemorrhoids and anal warts from it."

"Jesus Cristo, woman, I told you stop talking about my ass!"

"It's just the truth. I want people to know what happened to you."

"Want me to tell the truth about what your ass looks like? It's goddamn huge. Looks like a rock pile with a dirty sheet thrown over it."

"That's mean Miguel. I'm going to ignore it because I know you don't mean it."

"You don't listen enough to know what I mean." Miguel picked up his beer. "I'm going back to Mexico after the corn is in. I'm saving up. Probably November . . . I'm out of here in November. I had enough of this shit." He took a long draw from his can.

"No way you're taking me to Mexico," said Doris.

Miguel swallowed the beer in his mouth and wiped his chin on his sleeve. "Good," he said.

"We better go," said Bruce. "I'll see you at work, man."

"The sucker tortillas were really good, Doris. Thank you. And thanks for catching them, Miguel," said Wanda, doing her best to turn the conversation to a more civil note.

On the way back to Wanda's, Bruce said, "I figured Miguel did time, but I'd been wondering how he got his work card back after being in prison."

"It must be because his sentence got overturned. So now he gets to keep his cheerful but slightly mangled butt in the U.S. if he wants," said Wanda. "I sure can see why he'd want to go home. But what keeps him smiling?"

"Born happy, I guess," said Bruce. "One of the chosen few."

CHAPTER 10

Alice worked from home and had fallen behind on keeping the books for Hunter Sand & Gravel, a family-owned outfit that kept a couple dozen dump trucks and cement mixers on the roads around the Saginaw Valley. She needed to spend about four hours a day on the job, but her first week as a single parent had been a bust, work-wise. She had been busy, distracted, and stressed, and finding time to make art and watch the new television seemed critical for her sanity. But now procrastination was making the stress worse. She needed to just sit down and get the recent invoices and expenses organized and entered. Putting it off had fed on itself, and the growing onerousness of the task only bolstered her avoidance. The backlog was on the verge of overwhelming.

In Friday's mail there were several envelopes for Bruce that looked important. Looking beyond the six months or so that she figured they could coast financially, she was starting to fret about their longer-term security. So she tossed out all the mail that seemed likely to be charities begging for money. She opened the one to Bruce from the power company: he was fired. She had assumed it would be coming, but still it was a jolt. There was another from the bank, a notice of insufficient funds for a check written to the Jackson County District Court, another for a share of a milk goat to a Wanda Caprini. Alice steamed. But thinking about money finally motivated her to sit down and work. She made a fresh pot of coffee and spent the day getting Hunter Sand & Gravel's books ready for quarterly taxes. It was mind numbing but it worked to pass the time until the kids got home from school, and getting a good start on it seemed to loosen the grip it had on her chest.

When they came through the door Alice asked Josie and Mikey to go out to the garage and find some eggs before they did their homework. They would be having French toast for dinner. The kids cheered at the prospect of sweets for dinner and got right to the job. Mikey carried the egg basket and Josie flipped on the garage light, but there wasn't enough light to see behind the still-unpacked cardboard boxes or to the backs of the shelves where the chickens might lay them, so she pushed up the big garage door to let in the sunlight. Once again they were faced with the problem of free-ranging urban chickens, but with the outdoor light coming in, they found a baker's dozen eggs, pulled the big door back down, and opened the side door so the chickens could go back home when they were ready. While they were searching the garage they saw their dad's hunting bow, tree stand, and camouflage coveralls, all dappled with chicken droppings.

"When is Daddy coming home?" Mikey asked.

Josie straightened the eggs in the basket. "I don't think Mommy wants him to," she said.

At dinner they confronted their mom with this belief. She said he hadn't called and she wasn't sure where he was, but that she was sure he was okay.

"How do you know he's okay?" Josie asked.

"Grown-ups just know these things, sweetie."

Alice went on to say that she wanted Daddy to come home too, but wasn't sure when he was going to. In fact, her fingers had walked through the Yellow Pages that day shopping for a divorce lawyer. The kids ran to the living room and turned on the TV as soon as they finished their dinner. They had the remote all figured out already, so Alice started on the dishes. The phone rang. It was a woman from down state who had seen her ad for the chickens. They agreed that next Sunday early in the afternoon would be a good time. The woman would bring her own chicken crates. Alright, Alice thought, I'm dealing with a pro here. She felt just a little lighter as she pulled the plug on the sink drain and thought, I need a dishwasher.

The rest of the week went smoothly. Alice redeveloped the daily routine for getting Hunter's bookkeeping done. The only brush with excitement was that Officer Duncan stopped by again, saw the chickens still in the garage, and was about to leave another citation with a threat of arrest this time, except that Alice was able to convince her that the chickens were as good as gone. Maybe she would like to stop by on Sunday to help load them? Officer Duncan promised that she would be there to observe the outbound hens.

Alice visited the art supply store in town and picked up a dozen tubes of paint in the colors she had in mind, heavy on the reds and blues, and a car door-sized canvas. There was nothing small in her vision. That Thursday she started by painting the dawn sky, a dark blue-gray sky boldly streaked with pink and orange, and blood reds so thick and alarming that not just sailors would take warning, professional wrestlers might also quiver at the forecast. Chad told her that it was a brilliant start and that he couldn't wait to see what she would do next. And would she like to join him for a drink on Friday night?

Alice found a sitter, something she and Bruce had rarely done, put on her best jeans and a handmade sweater she had got from her Aunt Grace, kissed the kids and told them she'd see them in the morning, she was just meeting a friend, and went on her first date in ten years.

When she got to the bar Chad was not there, so she found two stools together, sat on one and put her purse on the other. She protected the seat for half an hour while she sipped a margarita and waited. Chad finally showed up dressed in his work clothes, which meant he was wearing his life as a painter on his color flecked jeans and sweatshirt. Under the paint smears the sweatshirt read: "Excuse me, you've mistaken me for someone who gives a shit." After Bruce, Alice thought, that might be a healthy sentiment. He asked her what she was drinking, and said he'd like one too. Chad's eyes were blood shot and he seemed stoned. Alice ordered him a margarita and got another for herself. She asked about his day.

He said he'd slept late but that he'd been painting most of the afternoon on his fence post series, and talked about the symbolism of the fence post and how a row of them strung with wire or boards was an obstacle to freedom, but alone and viewed from above they were circular, symbolizing universality, and how when planted in the ground they were grounded in the earth and yet pointed up into the universe and had additional meaning as phallic symbols. He said he was nearing completion of the painting series.

"I've completed seventy-four canvases. I'm thinking I'll go three-D to duplicate my vision on Mother Earth. I'm planning to place thirty-three organic cedar fence posts in the ground, one for each year of my life to this point, some shorter, some longer, some perpendicular to the ground, some leaning."

Alice thought they symbolized dead trees but asked, "Which of the thirty-three fence posts would symbolize your life now?"

"Well, I am now fully grown, so it would be one of the tall ones, but as an artist I fight the tyranny of symmetry, so for a number of years now I've seen myself as a tall leaning one, and of course from the phallic prospective, that's also the most suggestive of an erect penis, which mirrors the artist as a masculine entity."

Alice was flabbergasted. She was out on the town with a self-absorbed masculine entity. "So you have a dick like a leaning fencepost that represents your persona?" She covered her mouth to keep from spraying margarita as she snorked back a laugh.

Chad was less offended than he should have been, his pride in his as yet not fully appreciated fencepost-like member causing obliviousness to the comment on his personality. "I look forward to introducing you."

"I look forward to making his acquaintance," Alice replied with barely contained sarcasm, but feeling a little curious.

"Let's get a booth, I'm starving," said Chad.

Alice had to agree she was hungry, and so far Chad had succeeded in making her laugh, even though it was at him and not with him. She was entertained and in charge, a feeling she hadn't had with a man since before Bruce. Alice ordered a salmon Caesar salad and glass of Chardonnay.

Chad ordered a Kielbasa on a bun, a pile of fries, and a Budweiser, hold the salad.

They chatted amiably about the chicken problem and Alice's painting while they waited for their food. When it came they ate quietly, Alice because she was searching for words, Chad because he was stoned and ravenous. As he took the last bite of the sausage sandwich Alice asked, "So the phallic thing extends to the artist's diet?"

Chad was unperturbed by the question because it was true. He complimented her profusely on her awesome powers of observation and synthesis. In fact his predilection for tubular foods preceded his fence post fascination—he had always been a picky eater; hotdogs and macaroni were among the few things he would eat—but he explained the coincidence to Alice as a striving for artistic integrity. Alice didn't think she'd ever heard such a load of hooey, but could not help playing it out. She sensed that Chad was ready to make the next move.

"Come sit next to me," he said.

Alice could guess what was coming, but she slid in beside him anyway. He reached below the table, and she heard a zipper. She looked down and emitted a small scream, actually more of a medium-sized scream, sort of like when her brother had put a toad down her shirt when she was ten. Other patrons swiveled toward her with concern, but she managed to get most of her facial expression back to a forced neutral, except that her eyebrows wouldn't come down and she kept glancing at the fleshy cylinder.

She was again without words. Up until this point she had felt in control, but this required more cool than she could muster. She started to laugh uncontrollably, which at least had the effect on Chad of getting him to put it back in his pants. He had hoped for awe and worship, or maybe a semi-public hand job. Laughter wasn't what he'd hoped for. It had worked once before on a girl from art school. But it didn't work on Alice. She gathered herself and whispered to him, "Was that a penis? It looked like a penis, only smaller."

The waitress came over, "Will there be anything else?"

"That should just about do it," Alice said, "We'll take our check."

The waitress brought the bill and handed it to Chad.

"I hope you don't mind," he said, passing the check to Alice, "I forgot my wallet."

Alice took the check and looked at it. Where the waitress usually drew a little smiley face there were raised eyebrows and a big O mouth.

"No, I don't mind," she lied, "it's been a truly amazing evening." She shook her head in disbelief. With the tip, it was forty-three dollars she hadn't planned to spend.

"Could I get you to drive me home?" he asked.

"What? You didn't drive?"

"I think I got dropped off."

"You *think* you got dropped off?—Right . . . I *think* you better walk it off, bud. I've got a busy day tomorrow and I hadn't planned to entertain any masculine entities—or fence posts."

On the way home she again began to laugh, at first softly, then hysterically, and finally mixed with wet-eyed moans. She was saddened to realize that she wouldn't be going back to painting class, and saddened to realize that good men are indeed hard to find. Still, she was cheered by the speed with which she had weeded this one out, and cheered that it hadn't taken years of increasingly miserable cohabitation for this one's inner asshole to bloom. She decided to count it as a victory, like a politician who pleases his core constituency with a losing stand. She found herself wondering if there was such a thing as a normal man. And if not, how do you predict which kinks you can learn live with and which will become totally unacceptable? She decided that before she worked at getting a new love-life, she would concentrate on legally ridding herself of the old one. This freedom thing is tricky, she realized. And with two little kids it might not exist.

CHAPTER 11

Bruce spent the next week with Miguel and a couple of chainsaws clearing brush, small trees, and deadfall out of drainage ditches and fence rows around Vander Koop Farms, Inc. He had plenty on his mind already, and then he got the phone call he'd been expecting from Krystal. She said that Jeff's hearing on the attempted rape charge was scheduled for next Tuesday morning and that the court would be getting in touch with him.

It was good to be distracted by the hard physical work. But it was also good that it was made easier by the season: the vegetation was still leafless, the biting insects weren't out yet, and in the cool weather it was comfortable to work in the heavy canvas work clothes that offered protection from the thornapples, Russian olive, wild blackberry, and mulitflora rose. The only problem with this sort of work in the early spring is that poison ivy is hard for neophytes to identify. Only repeated victims cue instinctively on subtleties like the diameter of root hairs on the climbing vines, and learn to catch these details in their peripheral vision. Thus Bruce did not notice when he cut through several large poison ivy vines snaking up tree trunks, their insides wet with milky spring sap, which was then aerosolized by the whizzing chainsaw blade. A day later his face and neck and wrists—the only parts not covered by clothing—started to itch, and the day after that he had oozing blisters and one eye was swollen almost shut. Steroid shots or pills would have helped, but now that he was fired from his corporate job and had no health insurance, he wasn't about to go to the doctor for poison ivy, no matter how bad. Deb gave him a bottle of Calamine lotion, which mostly just gave the weeping sores the pink wash that serves to distinguish poison ivy victims from, say, burn victims or lepers out in the general public.

Knowing the cause of the malady and recognizing that it's not contagious doesn't have much effect on the revulsion others feel when they see it. People instinctively recoil from ugly, and that's the way they reacted to Bruce. Rivulets of serum leaked from his blisters, eroding crusty yellow paths in the pink lotion. The lymph nodes in his neck were swollen with their job of sending millions of white cells to attack any skin where the poison ivy sap had touched. He felt mildly sick and couldn't stop scratching in places where the reaction was just beginning to break out, like his chest and abdomen, where tiny bits of the poison ivy sawdust had sifted down under his T-shirt. The deeply blistered parts hurt too much to scratch. By Friday the infinitesimal amount of poison ivy juice that had been carried by sweat to the thin-skinned parts in his crotch began have its effect. Now he not only looked hideous, he was constantly pawing at his privates. The itch was intense and unremitting. His privates were swollen with edema, which gave them the manly girth that he'd always wished for, but he was in no condition to show them off. Even Wanda, a woman who loved the awful smell of billy goats, could not get past Bruce's swollen, scabbed, and oozing face. But there was no point in staying in his little room in the farm shop; he could be miserable in private or miserable in public, it really didn't matter. So he was at the diner for lunch with Ray on Friday when Doc Voekle ambled in.

"I see your immune system's declared war on urushiol," he said. Only he pronounced it with his comical cowboy accent, "you-roo-shee-all," as his way of softening the effect of his considerable intelligence.

"What the hell is you-roo-shee-all?" asked Ray.

"That's the bad thing in poison ivy. Get to your pecker yet?"

"I didn't think it showed," said Bruce.

"Don't have to. That shit's got peckerphilic molecules what homes straight to your underpants. Believe me, I'm a man of considerable experience with this particular ailment. Makes me want to itch my old boys just looking at you."

"It ain't had that effect on me," said Ray. "You getting light in your barn boots these days, Doc?"

They chowed down on Martha's usual low-residue-high-octane fare. Bruce's appetite was off a bit and he had to stop to dab the serum oozing from his neck and left eye more than once. He considered how good it might feel to press a handful of Cole slaw to his face, but instead concentrated on its sweet creamy flavor to distract him. They grow plenty of cabbage in Michigan, but he wondered where they got it in March. Doc said he had a herd health call out at Dykstra's that afternoon and asked Ray if he could spare his weepy-faced hired man. Ray said he'd probably scare the cows, but he might as well take him since he wasn't doing much but scratching anyway.

Bruce was amazed when they drove into a paved and striped lot with at least a dozen cars parked in front of the Dykstra Dairies milk production facility. A professionally-carved farm sign and a Holstein cow statue set in an artfully arranged cluster of boulders and evergreen shrubs announced that this was not your granddaddy's farm. The buildings were mostly pole barn constructions with white steel siding. The two largest, each maybe two-hundred yards long, were built on natural gentle hillsides, so that the roof peak lines followed the slope of the land. Directly in front of Bruce, the milking parlor building—you couldn't call it a barn—was faced with three stories of glass, behind which huge stainless steel bulk tanks and clear plastic milk lines were displayed. It reminded Bruce of his favorite micro brewery in Cadillac, with its big copper fermentation vat behind the storefront window, only on a much larger scale. They were greeted by a woman named Kathy dressed in blue coveralls embroidered with the farm logo and her name. She said the resident veterinarian was on vacation and thanked Doc for filling in.

They walked to an end pen inside one of the big buildings where ninety-four large Holstein cows with bulging udders had been gathered. The cows had freshened several months earlier and were now at the peak of their lactations. They had almost all been artificially inseminated about a month before and it was Doc's job to determine if they'd caught. The pen where the cows were corralled led into the gentle tapering curve of a working chute designed by Temple Grandin, a high-functioning autistic professor of animal husbandry with the uncanny ability to think like a cow. At the working end of the chute was a head gate to hold the cow while she was examined and treated, and a side gate where she would then be released. Kathy recorded the information on a hand held computer, which she would then download to the dairy's networked computer system, so that the cow's data would link to the radio transponder identification on her collar. Besides her health record, the transponder also let the computer system keep track of each cow's weight, her milk production, and even how many steps she took that day.

"Wouldn't it be nice if human medical records were kept this well?" said Doc.

"Yeah, but why the pedometer? This isn't a health club for cows is it?"

"No, but since the business of a dairy farm is lactation, it is a kind of a sex club. When the number of steps a cow takes goes up, that's a good sign she's looking for some action. It means she's in heat. It's time to get her inseminated."

"Man, I wish women were that simple."

"Well, yeah, they'd be easier to understand, but they wouldn't be near as interesting. Plus, unless you had a whole herd of them, you'd only get it once a year."

"I guess I better be careful what I wish for."

Behind the cow caught in the head gate was a small opening where the examiner could step in and out of the chute as each cow was moved into place. When a cow moved into the head gate, Doc stepped in behind her, lifted her tail with his right hand, and plunged his left, covered by a shoulder length disposable plastic glove, into her rectum. As he started each exam Bruce watched him pull several big armloads of feces from the cow's butt, pushing his arm elbow-deep inside each time in order to empty it before actually trying to find the pregnancy or diagnose any infection or malfunction of her reproductive tract. The few that were not pregnant had cysts on their ovaries or uterine infections; these he treated before the cow was released.

Doc explained that he could feel the cow's uterus through her rectum, and that by pinching it gently and letting it slip from between his fingertips he could feel the membranes that surrounded the still very small fetus inside. At just a few minutes per cow, it would be a long afternoon's work. Bruce helped to move the cows in the chute, but they moved easily, so it was easy to talk except when all the cows chose to moo in unison, or when Doc paused to concentrate on what his fingers were telling him. Based on the size of the pregnancy vesicle Doc could guess the breeding date to within a few days.

He told Bruce that on average, one of Dykstra's cows produced over twenty-two thousand pounds of milk in a year. Bruce did the math: Wanda had said that her Saanen goats, which were her best milkers—much better than the Nubians—averaged about two-thousand pounds a year, so he figured that one typical cow made as much milk as eleven top producing goats. And Dykstra milked close to three-thousand cows—to get the same amount of milk from goats you'd need thirty-three thousand of them! Seven average cows together produced more milk than Wanda's whole herd, and there was no dry period when the dairy shut down. Unlike a goat dairy, in any given month most of the cow herd was lactating. It was pretty clear to Bruce how a few huge dairy farms kept the whole state in milk.

"But how about all the antibiotics and hormones they get fed?" Bruce asked.

"Yeah . . . Well, if we have to treat a cow with an antibiotic for an infection, say in her uterus or udder—which are the common things—the milk has to be withheld a set number of days depending on the drug, until it clears from her system. Consequently, dairy farmers don't use any more antibiotics than they have to, because it means throwing the milk away, and they do everything they can to keep them healthy. It's not like feedlot steers that are fed a very high energy diet and need antibiotics in their feed to keep their digestive systems working. Dairy cows have to last for years."

"And the hormones?"

"Well, they only get one hormone, recombinant bovine growth hormone, and only in the declining part of their lactation, which is the only time it works."

"Doesn't that end up in their milk?"

"In miniscule amounts, yes. But so does the natural hormone, and you can't measure a difference. There's no increase in the total amount. The man-made growth hormone is made the same way as human insulin for diabetics, by genetically programmed bacteria, and they make exactly the same molecule as the cow does—a biochemist can't tell them apart. Besides, the growth hormones are all species-specific—the growth hormone that each species makes is enough different from the others that it doesn't have an effect except in the species that it comes from. The cow hormone doesn't have any effect on humans and vice versa, and anyway, growth hormone is digested in the stomach like any other protein. To have an effect, it has to be injected; it has to be given as a shot in the muscle."

"Still, organic milk has to come from healthier cows," said Bruce.

"Do these cows look unhealthy? . . . or, wait, let me ask you a different question—have you, or your wife, or your kids ever gotten sick?" Doc asked.

"Of course." Bruce sensed he was being set up.

"So if one of your kids had a bad ear infection, or your wife had a urinary tract infection, or if you caught pneumonia as a complication of the flu, would you expect your doctor to prescribe an antibiotic?"

"Sure."

"Well, if your family were cows in a certified organic herd, the dairyman couldn't treat you. Cows in organic herds are cows without health care."

"I never thought of it that way. But, well, they shouldn't get sick on a healthy organic diet, so they shouldn't need to be treated," Bruce countered, realizing his arguments were evaporating.

"Actually, they need more. To be organic, the crops they're fed have to come from fields on which no herbicides or insect control was used.

Consequently, their corn silage is about twenty percent chopped weeds, which really hurts their nutrition. So it's harder for the high producing cows to get enough protein and calories, and they're stressed. And of course it takes more acres of weedy corn to feed a cow."

"Maybe they should breed lower producing cows."

"That might work, but of course, either way the unit production costs rise. It's like driving a Hummer—it will definitely get you from point A to point B, but at what cost? Do you want to pay for moving yourself and a normal car, or, better, a hybrid car—or in your case, a bicycle—or yourself and three tons of pseudo-military equipment that says, 'I don't give a rat's ass about the environment?'"

"You're comparing an organic dairy to a Hummer?"

"I am." Doc gave a wry smile and paused for effect. "I have a classmate, a famous bovine veterinarian who speaks all over the world on cow comfort issues. Do you believe that?—there's a whole body of science on cow comfort—it's true. Anyway, he oversees the health of something like thirty-five thousand cows on a dozen big dairies like this one. He has one smaller unit with something like nine hundred cows that they run as a certified organic dairy to meet the demands of that niche market. When a cow in the organic dairy gets sick, they go ahead and treat her, but then they have to move her to one of the conventional dairies because she's no longer considered 'organic.' What do you think happens to that cow after they move her?"

"I'm afraid to guess."

"Her production level goes up about twenty percent, and the white cell count in her milk—that's the number of infection fighting blood cells shed into milk to counteract bacterial invasion of her udder—goes down by about half. And, it gets easier to get her bred. In short, she gets healthier."

Bruce was knocked back by this revelation. But he still had an ace: "Okay, suppose that's all true, you've still got the huge stinking lakes of shit that three thousand cows in one place make. How about all the air and water pollution from all that crap in one place?"

"That's been a problem in the past, you're right. But guess what—all that manure in one place turns out to be an advantage. My friend installed a digester system to trap the methane, which they burn in a huge engine that runs a generator that powers the whole dairy *and three hundred homes* in the area! The solid waste that's left after the digester—they bag that and sell it as potting soil. Unbelievable, eh?"

"That is incredible," said Bruce. "But you can't make me believe that factory farms are a good thing. I've read too much."

"I'd be lying if I didn't admit there was a dark side. There is. But dairy cows are lucky because economics strongly favor keeping them healthly and living long, so the dairy industry has done a lot of research looking at what makes a milk cow happy. Not that I've ever seen a cow laugh or open a birthday present," Doc chuckled.

"Anyway, it takes two years to raise a replacement heifer, and two or three more years before she reaches her peak milk production, so it clearly pays to protect that investment. It's not that big dairy farmers necessarily operate on a higher moral plane than other animal farmers, but the economics dictate that they better be good to their cows. I can't say the same for the mega beef feedlots, pigs on slats, or franchised chicken operations. In those places they push the critters to fat slaughter weight as fast as they can by getting them to eat as much corn as possible in crowded conditions that allow as little exercise as possible—it's hard on them. But I figure beef cows raising their calves on grass land probably get the best deal. That's exactly the environmental niche the critter evolved in. Some of those cows live over fifteen years; one makes twenty once in a while. Their calves that end up in the giant feedlots . . . not so lucky."

"But, all dairies aren't huge, so why not more small farms?" Bruce was afraid he already knew the answer.

Doc explained the obvious, that the economies of scale and technology made it impossible for the small dairies to compete. He said that the small dairies—and anything less than a hundred cows was considered small—the ones that are still in business are either what he called "sunset operations," so named because they would be going out of business when the current farmer died or sold out to the big boys; or what he called "lifestyle dairies" that were either passed down through generations or supported by jobs off the farm; or they were "niche operations," either Amish or focused on the organic market, which was supported by people who were willing to go out of their way to pay a premium price for their dairy products. Bruce figured that since Wanda supported her goat farm with her university job, and had inherited the farm and the start-up money, and because it was unlikely that anyone would ever buy it from her for its economic value as a goat dairy, that hers must be a sunset-lifestyle-niche dairy, which sounded pretty comfortable, but not much like a way to make a living. Doc told him the joke about the small farmer who won the lottery. His friends at the feed mill asked him what he was going to do with all that money. He said he figured he'd just keep farming till it was gone.

"But what about the damage to small towns from losing all those family farms?" asked Bruce.

"In the truly rural areas, you're right, little towns are dying for lack of an economic base, but for any place within commuting distance to a city, the bigger problem is urban sprawl—prime farmland growing up crops of houses. Plus the big box stores killing local businesses. We've built the whole environment up around the automobile, and it's entirely dependent on cheap gasoline to keep it going."

"Yeah, well, that's the reason I sold our little farm in Edenville—thirty miles one-way to work just didn't make sense."

"So your decision was based on economics, a little bit of sprawl pulling back in the face of high gas prices, and the change was awful hard on your family. Change is always hard. If everybody did what you did, a lot more rural small towns would die—and that's probably just what's going to happen as the price of gas goes up. And it will. I'm guessing you're about ten years ahead of the curve. They say the only constant is change, and these days change happens faster than society can adapt. It hurts a lot of people."

"So how do we stop it?"

"Beats me. I doubt that we can, and I'm not sure we know how. But eventually every trend changes. You can bet that the human population on this planet is going to hit its limit one of these days. And until it does, we're going to keep seeing other species going extinct to make room for us. We can try to plan and minimize our harm, attempt to control ourselves, or we can leave to Mother Nature to send in the Four Horsemen of the Apocalypse to put things back in balance, and eventually she will. Anyway, Americans generally regard social planning as government interference with their personal freedom and property rights, so even if we could figure out what was the best thing to do, politically it would be damn near impossible to do it. Best I can see it, a person just has to stay loose and be ready to adapt. But that doesn't sound much like a way to have a community, does it?"

"And that's why Parma doesn't have a grocery store anymore," concluded Bruce.

"And why you're on the loose," said Doc.

Against competition like the Dykstra Dairy, Bruce could see clearly that the future of farming was not small, as much as he wished it otherwise. It hurt him to consider small farms as only marginally relevant in the food chain. It went against his core and made him feel naïve and provincial, as if he were losing an important part of his mind that felt authentic and progressive. He had been sure that factory farms were cruel and inhumane, but he was having trouble finding the evidence on this place. He suddenly saw that big isn't necessarily bad, while it was confirmed that nature and economics are without conscience. His anchor was raised. It had not yet occurred to him that that's what love is for. With his face looking like a pizza with everything on it, and itching all over, he was already down. Now an important piece of his identity was slipping away. He needed a drink.

CHAPTER 12

H e didn't get one that night, but he did get another big Friday fried fish meal from Deb and some antihistamine pills that seemed to help the itch but made him sleepy. And he got a registered letter from the Lansing Circuit Court, subpoenaing him to appear the next Tuesday at Jeff's hearing for attempted rape. He tried again to call Alice, with the usual result. He left a message that he hoped everything was okay with her and the kids. He told her he had a bad case of poison ivy, but otherwise he was fine. Alice had listened to it twice before she whispered that she hoped he'd scratch his damn skin off, and snapped her phone shut.

The next morning he and Miguel kept busy by cleaning and reorganizing the shop. Miguel said he thought Bruce looked like he needed a dose of the "beeg city" to lift his spirits. He would pick him up and take him into Jackson that night. That afternoon Bruce pedaled the five miles over to Wanda's on the off chance he might get some, interpreting the itch in his pants as perhaps a double entendre. She said that even with his very attractive swollen pecker, his face had to stop oozing before he'd get any, but tomorrow she could really use his help on a road trip to pick up some chickens. He agreed to be there at ten.

Miguel stopped in to pick up Bruce just after dark. They drove the eleven miles into Jackson, the first time Bruce had ever been to the town. Near the old prison they found Miguel's favorite bar, a roadhouse called Lifers. Miguel's beater Impala looked right at home in the parking lot. He told Bruce not to talk to anybody and to try to avoid eye contact, that sometimes you had to fight your way in and fight your way back out, but usually it was fun. Lifers appeared to be the choice establishment for those who preferred to drink in public but lacked a pot to piss in. In fact Bruce arrived with a full bladder and quickly discovered in the men's room that a pot to piss in would be a major upgrade. There was a long trough-style urinal—the better for a shoulder-to-shoulder communal pissing experience—which a patron of the establishment had obviously misused for the solid excretory function, perhaps because the sit-down porcelain was plugged and overflowing. The stench was overwhelming.

The wall decorations contributed by artistically-inclined, felt-tip-pen-owning patrons did nothing to improve the ambience. Although the graffiti did serve to quickly inform novices that the clientele was both potent and versatile in its sexuality, as well as convinced of the superiority of white people. The thick smell of stale beer and cigarette smoke in the bar area seemed like sweet perfume when he exited the latrine.

Miguel leaned into the bar and was ordering a draft. Bruce wondered why anyone would seek out this dive on purpose if they could drink at home; but there was country music, a TV with NASCAR racing, and, he just noticed, a small linoleum-covered stage with a dancing pole. Men will tolerate all ten levels of hell for a glimpse of paradise. Any paradise. Bruce wondered where the off-stage area was, since the there were no doors or wall openings near the raised platform.

Just then the song changed abruptly. The bartender flipped on a color wheel and spot light that shined upon the stage. One of the three waitresses wiped her hands on her jeans and jumped up onto it, twirling once around the pole. The bartender announced her name as Starbright, and she proceeded not so much to strip as to undress, hanging her duds on a wall hook as she progressed in her disrobing. In between garments she would dangle herself suggestively on the pole, then stand up briefly to take off another thing and hang it on the hook. Bruce recognized the same Hane's cotton bra that Alice favored and ordered another beer.

Men put folded dollar bills in the young woman's cotton underpants—which seemed well designed to hold a lot of cash—before she finally doffed them for a brief final flourish which suggested that she generally shaved her pubic public-private parts, but hadn't in the past week or so, and was probably at the itchy stubble phase. This caused Bruce to paw at his own crotch, the itch being his main reaction down there. It took a couple of hours before all three waitresses had taken their turn to undress at the pole, and for Miguel to enjoy a lap dance and be ready to leave. The girls all evaluated Bruce from a distance and didn't even try to get him to buy them a drink. By the time they left, Bruce had gone through a pocket-full of tissues dabbing at his weeping face. And he'd steadily sipped down a dozen watery but cheap beers, plus a boilermaker bought for him by a fat, deeply pock-marked man with a magic marker in his pocket, who seemed to be the only soul in the bar who was interested in him. Bruce thought perhaps the man considered him a brother in epidermal distress. He was miserable, but at least he was drunk.

Consequently the morning was tough. He slept poorly; he awoke around three and never really got back to sleep, just tossed and half-dozed with a banging headache, churning stomach, and mad itching. But he had told Wanda he would pedal over to her place to be ready to go at ten after she finished the milking, so he tried to do that. He took a couple of aspirins for his head and antihistamines for the itch before he left Rays. There was a cold headwind that felt good on his face, but the hangover and the pedaling effort made him nauseous, and as the drugs kicked-in his vision strobed and he wobbled a bit on the road. A large black dog ran out at him, which caused an adrenalin rush as he sprinted away, and that helped with the drowsiness, but now he was seeing patterns of black lines, like he was looking at the world through a heavy wobbling screen door. He reached Wanda's place moving just fast enough to keep the bike upright, and nearly fell off as he dismounted. He leaned the bike against the milk house, braced himself next to it, and puked. Ishy ran to him with her ball.

"Dang, cowboy, you ain't looking that good," said Wanda.

Bruce spit the stomach juice from his mouth and wiped the strings of mucus that hung from his lips with his sleeve. "That's weird, I feel fucking awesome," he gasped. He bent down and threw the ball weakly. "Dogs never get hung-over, do they? That little pooch is relentlessly damn cheerful. I want her brain."

"You can sleep it off in the truck. We'll check the Yellow Pages for lobotomists later."

A few miles down the road Bruce started to sweat and feel nauseous again. "How about I bed down in the back?" he suggested. Wanda pulled over. The back of the pickup was still covered with wheat straw from the last time Wanda had taken a load of male kids to the slaughter house for the Arabs. There were some dry goat turds scattered in the straw, but the urine had long since evaporated, so the odor wasn't that bad. Using her emergency blanket, she made Bruce a cozy bed alongside the chicken cages.

As Bruce stuffed an old feed bag with the used straw bedding for a pillow, Wanda closed the lift gate and the hatch at the back of the cap. "Sleep tight," she said. The cool air, warm blanket, and the mild smell of goat excrement combined with the hum of the engine, and Bruce was out in no time.

Wanda had a local street map from her computer and good instructions, so she had no trouble finding the place. She pulled into the drive and glanced in the back as she got out. Bruce appeared to be sleeping soundly, so she left him undisturbed. Josie and Mikey came bounding out the front door ahead of Alice who greeted Wanda as "My chicken savior!" While the two women exchanged niceties, the kids ran to the garage and lifted the big door, once again setting the chickens free, which wasn't part of the plan to get them into Wanda's transport cages. Officer Duncan of Bay City Animal Control arrived as the chickens scattered across the yard. Alice yelled at the kids for opening the door, which awakened Bruce. He was sure he had heard his wife's voice. He cautiously raised himself to look out the window of the pickup cap, confirmed his worst fears, and resumed his lowest profile, pulling the blanket over his face.

Alice, Wanda, and Officer Duncan agreed that best thing to do was to put the big garage door back down, open the side door, and go inside for a cup of coffee while the chickens found their way back into the garage. Alice had made brownies for the occasion of the chicken exodus, and the women quickly became friends. Officer Duncan showed herself to be a prodigious trencher woman, consuming half the pan with two mugs of coffee. Wanda mentioned that her hot new boyfriend was sleeping in the back of the truck and soon they were talking about men.

"I pretty much give up on them," said Officer Duncan, adding, "My new best man-friend has batteries and a flexible tickler arm."

Emboldened by Officer Duncan's frankness, Alice revealed that her, "son-of-a-bitch husband ran off on his bicycle to learn where food comes from," and smiled just a little as she added that she could use a recommendation on a good vibrator herself.

Wanda's jaw suddenly dropped. "What's his name?" she asked.

"Bruce," said Alice, and picking up on Wanda's apparent distress asked, "You know him?"

The three women marched across the yard to the truck. Josie and Mikey sensed something was up, stopped chasing chickens, and ran to join them. Wanda opened the hatch and dropped the tailgate. "You under there, *Mr. Dinkle?*" she asked as she lifted the blanket from his blighted face.

Bruce groaned as he looked out, the leaky redness of his face gone to crushed beets. "Oh god," he said.

Alice slapped her hands to her face and screamed as she sprinted in place, pounding her feet into the ground, unable to find words.

The kids screamed, "Daddy! Daddy! Daddy!—What happened to your face, Daddy?

Wanda hung her head and walked in small circles near the truck, muttering, "You bastard, you fucking bastard."

Officer Duncan turned professional, urged calmness, and remembered her mission: "Let's just catch the chickens and get them out of here. Let's just get them *all* out of here," she said, looking at Bruce.

Wanda looked grief stricken, her face full of remorse. "Alice, I didn't know he was married. Honestly, I didn't. I am so sorry."

Alice slowly regained a little of her composure. "To hell with him. You can have him." Bruce felt the air between them freeze, as if it would shatter if he moved.

"Is Daddy coming home?" asked Mikey, looking to his mother.

"Not today . . . not ever." Alice walked away from the back of the truck to where Wanda stood, her head hanging, her hand wrapped across her brow. "I'm so sorry," Wanda repeated.

"Let's just get the damn chickens loaded and get you both out of here," said Alice.

The three women unloaded the empty crates together and carried them into the garage. Officer Duncan forced a cheerful narrative: "Okay, so there's what, thirty-one chickens? That's ten in two cages, eleven in the other. Okay, flip on the light there then Alice and let's catch us some chickens. Okay . . . you betcha. Okay, Wanda, okay . . . nice catch. That's one . . . ."

And over the next twenty minutes of flapping, flying feathers, and in-flight fecal bombs, punctuated by chicken cackles and women emitting high-pitched screams and curses, they scrambled over boxes, crawled into dark corners, climbed and reached from the top step of the ladder to the highest garage shelves and rafters, until, one by one, they caught every last chicken in the garage. Officer Duncan counted them in the transport cages. "Okay then, that's twenty-eight. Let's take another walk around outside."

The three women did a little walking tour of the neighboring back yards. They found one Barred Rock hen perched on a small branch twenty feet up in a tree. Officer Duncan looked around to see if any children were nearby, took out her service revolver, pulled back the hammer, steadied her aim, and shattered the chicken's perch with a single shot. The bird flapped down in full squawk: buc-buc-buc-buc . . . . Wanda sprinted under it, snagged it over her right shoulder, and tucked the hen into running position under her arm as she slowed to a jog and circled back to Alice and Officer Duncan. A neighbor on her back porch clapped, hooted, and yelled, "Go Blue!" and they all got their smiles back.

"Holy smokes, I've got Annie Oakley and Jerry Rice. Great shot. Nice catch," Alice laughed.

Meanwhile, Bruce had crawled out of his bed in the back of the truck, looking mangled, sick, and with just a few small goat turds stuck to his clothes. With the hangover vomit wipings on his sleeve he had a strong homeless street-shepherd aroma about him. None-the-less, the kids hugged his legs until he sat on the ground to face them. He looked at their beautiful faces and nearly broke down. Tears burned his raw face. He apologized and hugged them and apologized some more. Josie said, "It's okay, don't worry Daddy. Mommy got us a brand new car and a brand new TV."

Mikey added, "Yes, and we watch Sponge Bob Square Pants and have popcorn!"

"And the Discovery Channel and Jerry Springer!"

"Plus she's getting a dish watcher!" concluded Mikey.

Bruce pressed the heels of his hands into his eyes, shook his head, and groaned. He asked about school and teachers, if they were doing their homework, and what they were eating. He dabbed at his face with a tissue, soaking up tears and runs of still-oozing serum. They told him they had peanut butter and jelly, and yogurt, and apples from the store in their lunches, which he had to agree sounded pretty good. But he couldn't help thinking that only the yogurt and apples had any chance of being from inside the circle. They told him that Calliope the cat was fine, and that they had nice friends at school, and that since the chickens had moved out to the garage they didn't get teased anymore about the way they smelled. Their conversation was interrupted by a nearby gunshot. The kids moved behind their father and were quiet.

The women came walking back into Alice's yard, Officer Duncan holstering her weapon, Wanda with a black and white Barred Rock hen under her arm, all of them laughing until they saw Bruce. Wanda put the last hen into a cage. Officer Duncan told Alice that if the other ones showed up she should give her a call, but probably the raccoons or foxes or neighborhood dogs already got them. They loaded the cages into the truck while Bruce sat on the damp early spring ground looking morose. Wanda wrote Alice a check for the chickens and gave her a tentative hug. They wished each other luck.

Alice said, "Wait, I'll get his mail," and brought out a shoe box full.

"Where you riding?" Wanda asked Bruce.

Bruce stood up, keeping his forlorn gaze on the ground. A little mud stuck to the seat of his pants as he rose. "I guess I'll sit up front if it's okay with you," he said.

"Might as well. You've got a lot of explaining to do, my little goat boy."

Chapter 13

Bruce realized that a divorce was almost certainly coming. He felt it in his chest and it saddened him to a degree he hadn't anticipated. Even a loveless marriage has the comfort of its habits. It felt to Bruce like a broken addiction; the withdrawal made him ache. Heartbreak songs became poignant for him in ways they never had before. The country music on the radio in Ray's shop the week before had caused him to pause several times to take a deep breath and consider what was at stake. On the trip from Bay City back to Parma the radio played Bonnie Raitt singing "I Can't Make You Love Me" and Bruce's eyes welled up. He closed them and pretended to sleep so he wouldn't have to talk. Wanda saw the tear on his cheek and left him alone. He had thought the choice to go home to his wife and kids was still his, but now it appeared that it was not. He had passed through a one-way gate, like a raccoon into a live trap. There was no going back. The implications for his relationships with Mikey and Josie tripled the pain. Even if he got visitation rights, where would they visit him?

He spent Monday lounging and napping at Wanda's, trying to recover from the trip home and rest up for his bicycle ride to Lansing the next day. The poison ivy eruption was still less than a week old; new patches of blisters were still popping up here and there and the oldest sores on his face had barely begun to heal. He crusted up one of Wanda's pillowcases with dried yellow serum from his leaky skin. Wanda told him that he was still too ugly to get laid, but she gave his crotch a pat and called him goat boy when she said it.

Jeff's attempted rape hearing was the next day, and Bruce had been ordered to appear. So today's agenda was to gather enough emotional and physical strength to pedal to Lansing. Wanda had to teach at Albion all week and couldn't drive him. He called Ray to let him know what was up. Ray generously told him to take his time to recover; they were still a couple of weeks from planting, and Miguel could do most everything until then. Bruce figured that since the hearing wasn't until the afternoon, that with an early start the sixty miles should be pretty easy even in his ragged state.

And it would have been, had it not been for the weather: intermittent cold rain and a gusty north wind in his face. He worked like hell to maintain twelve miles an hour. He was forced to stop at a gas station to warm his feet, try to dry off a little, and refuel. Luckily the gas station attendants were amused by the miserable looking bike rider who bought neither gas nor snacks. Bruce stood outside the men's room door and washed down the peanut butter and jelly sandwich he'd packed with a screw-top jelly jarful of raw goat milk.

By the time he arrived at the courthouse, the rain had found a number of ways under his rain suit. He was wet, chilled, and bedraggled, and also a few minutes late, so he had to go straight into the courtroom. He sat a few rows back on one of the hard wooden benches and dripped. On the way to his seat he surveyed the room and saw Jeff in orange coveralls and shackles, his hair cut short, his left ear mostly chewed off. Rows of fresh purple suture holes lined up on both sides of the new scars on his face. Jeff glared at Bruce and forced a short derisive laugh, although in his maimed and shackled state his attempt at aggression seemed pathetic.

Finally sitting down, Bruce took the opportunity to take off his shoes and wring the water out of his socks. He was twisting his second sock, in the process of leaving a dinner plate-sized puddle on the courtroom's hardwood floor, when he was called by the prosecutor to testify. Bruce approached the bench on water-wrinkled bare feet. His hair, newly freed from his bike helmet, was wet and matted in rows that matched the helmet vents, his face a bright shade of red from weather exposure and the rash. The oldest poison ivy patches on his face and neck had begun to form brown scabs and crusts. The rain had softened and turned parts of the scabs a translucent white with the red base of the sores showing through, while the newer blistered lesions had resumed oozing serum in the warm courtroom. The effect was almost as revolting as Jeff's dog-pruned ear. But there was a patch of thick wool carpet in front of the judge's bench that felt terrific on Bruce's still-numb toes, which caused a hard-to-interpret expression of sudden pleasure to cross his face. The judge asked if he should understand Bruce's appearance as hostility toward the government's case or contempt for the judicial process. Bruce assured him that no such disrespect was intended. He glanced over at Jeff and saw a sneering chuckle. The judge called for a ten minute recess to allow Bruce to replace his footwear, dry his hair, and generally attempt to make himself presentable to the court.

Krystal had already testified before Bruce got there, accurately describing Jeff's aggressive entry into the trailer and attempt to force sex on her. Jeff's court-appointed defense lawyer had questioned Krystal about how it could be construed to be an attempted rape if Krystal had opened the door to let Jeff in, and added that his client had never even unzipped his pants. The defense attorney suggested that the only crime was the assault by Krystal's dog on an innocent man who wanted only to talk with his former wife. When the hearing resumed, the prosecutor asked Bruce to explain what he had witnessed at Krystal's trailer, which he did.

Jeff's attorney cross-examined: "Mr. Dinkle, so is it not true that you in fact saw almost nothing, and that you were hiding in the closet and bare naked during the conversation between Ms. Galet and my client, her former husband?"

Bruce hesitated slightly. It was the first time he had heard Krystal's last name. "Yes, but . . ."

"Mr. Dinkle, did you not in fact join in the assault on my client by the complainant's vicious Pit Bull-Rottweiler crossbred dog, one Bob Barker?"

"I was only helping to get him . . ."

The defense attorney interrupted, "Your Honor, the defense contends that the sight of Mr. Dinkle bare naked in the company of my client's former wife is a provocation that no man could reasonably be expected to graciously ignore. And further that the assault and maiming endured by my client is already excessive punishment for the imagined crimes of my client. I move that the case be dismissed."

The prosecutor pointed out that the presence of Mr. Dinkle in the closet, bare naked or not, was unknown to the alleged assailant at the time of the assault, and so was not provocative, but rather allowed the defendant to believe he could commit his intended crime with impunity.

The prosecutor's argument was solid, but Jeff's defense attorney and his chewed-off ear had caused enough sympathy to sway the judge toward leniency. They released Jeff on two thousand dollars bond. He got a number of probation restrictions and an electronic tether, and a trial date was set for a month later. Krystal finally had the restraining order she needed, but she feared it would do little to protect her, especially now that Bob Barker would not be at her side.

As they left the courtroom, Krystal asked Bruce if they could have lunch together. They couldn't afford a real restaurant but found a nearby Burger King. The bicycle ride to Lansing had made Bruce ravenous. He inhaled a Whopper, large fries, and a quart of full-sugar red-label Coke while they talked. He imagined the factories behind this food, all the miles the various ingredients had come to end up in his belly. He wondered why, with all the petroleum backing this meal, local fare wasn't the cheaper and preferable option. He thought of what he'd look like if he ate this stuff all the time and didn't ride a bicycle everywhere. He knew there was little chance that any of this came from inside the circle, except maybe the potatoes, and probably not those either. Then he wondered how his own efficiency compared with a car. How many calories did he have to eat to pedal a hundred-twenty miles? And how would that compare with the energy in the five or six gallons of gasoline he had saved? Of course he also had to consider the fuel used to grow, process, and transport the food. Besides that, his body had basal caloric needs even if he never got out of bed. He imagined the fireball that would result from putting a spark to five gallons of gasoline and figured he wouldn't use anywhere near that much energy pedaling from Parma to Lansing and back, plus his heart would be the stronger for it. Clearly an accurate calculation was complicated, but there was no doubt that traveling by bicycle was far better for the planet. He felt good about that. Krystal was absorbed with her own problems and could only see that Bruce's mind was elsewhere.

"I don't dare go home with Jeff on the loose," she said. "Let's go visit Bob Barker."

"He's still in the pound?"

"Yeah, they decided not to put him to sleep, but they got him on rabies quarantine for a month—two more weeks to go. After the story was on TV there was all kinds of people marching up and down the sidewalk out front of the pound. They was waving "Save Bob Barker" signs. One sign said: "Kill Bob Barker? The Price Ain't Right!" And anyway a pound guy told me they wasn't going to kill no hero dog."

It was starting to seem like some sort of odd date. Bruce wasn't at all interested in seeing Bob Barker, the dog terrified him, but his week of too-ugly-to-get-laid, poison-ivy-induced celibacy was plenty to pull him toward Krystal. He sensed he had a chance. He threw his bike in the back of her truck and they drove to the Lansing Animal Shelter. The desk officer led them back through gray hallways to the dog cages. The racket of two-dozen barking dogs bouncing off the concrete walls was deafening. Bob Barker barked louder than any dog in the place. When he saw Krystal he stopped barking and began to wag his thick stump of a tail. Krystal got down on her hands and knees and cooed and baby-talked to the beast while she scratched his muzzle through the wire. Bruce stood back and couldn't help admiring her rear.

"I'll pick you up just as soon as you're free, Barker. Yes I will. Yes I will," she babbled through the cage door.

"Any relatives you could stay with till they spring him?" Bruce asked, feeling a little impatient.

"I got a sister in DeWitt," she said rising to her feet, smiling coyly, apparently aware she'd been ogled, "but Jeff knows where she lives and would find me. Besides, it would give her more trouble, and she don't need no more trouble."

"What kind a trouble?"

"Men. Ain't it always men?"

"It isn't always easy to be good. We do our best," Bruce said. "How about a safe house, one of those women's shelter places?"

"Maybe, but I can't live there forever. Anyhow, I've about had it with this town. I want to get out of here."

Bruce had an idea; he pulled out his cell phone. "Hey Wanda. Bruce. You want to hire Krystal to work on the farm?" They discussed the prospect. Wanda said she'd consider it but she couldn't have Bob Barker around the goats or Ishkabibble. Krystal would have to find her own place where she could keep the dog, but until Bob Barker got sprung from the pound she could stay at the farm and try out the job. They drove back to Krystal's trailer and packed a suitcase and a few garbage bags with her things.

"I still got some of them Blatzes in the fridge," she said.

Bruce thought he saw a wink with her smile. "Sure," he said.

They sat on the couch and drank the beer while Bruce helped Krystal consider what steps she had go through to sell the trailer and move. She stroked her fingers across his inner thigh as she tried to think, which instantly clinched Bruce's personal list of things that needed to be done. The poison-ivy-imposed deprivation of the last week had agitated him and given his nether parts a hair trigger. He was grateful to have Krystal pull it.

They fell into bed, this time without the late-night exhaustion or first-date, one-position limit. Krystal kissed Bruce's face—scabs, crusts, and all—and made love with all the enthusiasm she could muster. Bruce's pent up sexual energy overcame potentially wilting thoughts of the other women in his life and how he had just managed to complicate his fucked-up life even more. "God I'm an idiot" thoughts alternated with "Jesus this feels good" thoughts. Predictably, the horny thoughts beat the shit out of the guilty ones, and they came together in a sweaty frenzy of groans, oaths, and screams.

Afterward, as they lay in bed and talked, they figured that Jeff probably wouldn't make his move on his first day out of the clink, so they decided to spend the night in the trailer. They tried to eat everything in the fridge, which wasn't much, just some hot dogs, Velveeta cheese, and a jar of pickles. Krystal worked on her large supply of Diet Mountain Dew while Bruce gulped away at the Blatz, which had a dulling but further dis-inhibiting effect on his libido. Consquently, the after dinner sex was even more creative, prolonged, and intimate, if harder for him to remember. Bruce thought of the old Mormon polygamists and wondered how one man was supposed to keep more than one woman happy. He was going to need a steady supply of goat cheese and womanly understanding, both of which he feared were rare commodities. Still, it was a happy problem, he reasoned.

In the morning they wasted little time loading Krystal's stuff into the truck. They would come back for the rest if the job worked out. Bruce tried to direct Krystal along the same roads he had used when he'd made the trip on his bicycle two weeks before, but missed a turn. They ended up finding their way to the I-127 expressway and were in Parma in less than an hour, even with a stop for gas, coffee, and an airtight box of little powdered road donuts. By ten o'clock they pulled into Nanny Gate. Krystal squealed with delight when she saw the fairytale place with the field stone house on the little hill, the grass just beginning to green, the pasture fences lending a reassuring sense of order to the land as it rolled away toward the river that ran through the woods at the back of the farm. Wanda heard Krystal's old truck rumble in while she was cleaning the milk house and came out to greet them.

"So, you didn't get the bastard locked up, eh?" said Wanda.

"I'm afraid he's back on the street, but at least she got a restraining order," Bruce said before making the introduction.

"I am so excited to be here," said Krystal, "I feel safer already. And I love animals."

"Well, I hope this works out," said Wanda, "I could sure use some steady help. The student's schedules are just too darn erratic." She paused to survey Krystal's thin but fairly sturdy frame. "Let me see your hands," she said. Krystal looked a little surprised, just as Bruce had been when he'd gotten the slow once-over from Wanda on their first meeting. Wanda took Krystal's hands in hers. Her fingers were a little bonier than would be expected for her age, her veins clearly visible, nails chewed short. She had moved her wedding band to her right ring finger some time ago; the pale indentation that had been visible on her left ring finger was no longer discernible. Her hands were clean, but with pale brown stains at the tips of her cigarette fingers. Wanda confirmed by pulling Krystal's left hand to her nose and sniffing deeply. "No smoking in the barn or in the house. Can you live with that?" she said.

"Yeah, no problem."

"And this guy is mine," Wanda added. "You okay with that?"

Krystal hesitated and looked at Bruce, who was staring at the ground. "I didn't know that," she said.

"Yeah, he's a pretty good, hard-working guy, but he leaves stuff out."

Bruce kicked the ground as he turned away, shook his head, looked skyward, and muttered inaudibly, "Christ, I can't believe I get myself into this shit."

"He's a goat boy," Wanda said turning to Krystal, "they have other redeeming qualities."

"Yeah, I guess they do," said Krystal.

Bruce wanted to change the subject. "Can we just get this stuff unloaded and show her around?"

"We could, but it's a woman's job to make a man squirm once in awhile—and you're looking a mite squirmy about now. Rash is looking better though," said Wanda, raising her eyebrows and elevating one hand above her hair, pretending to crumble something into it. Bruce wondered what the limits of the goat cheese magic were. He remembered in college a friend explained the boom-bust sex cycle by saying that women can smell if a man is getting it, and that if you are it makes them want a piece of the action. The irony, that women then expected the man to offer exclusivity rights, seemed to be one of the great cosmic jokes, but one that was only funny at a distance. He hoped that Wanda and Krystal would somehow see the fun in it. So far the hostility level was manageable.

They got Krystal's stuff into the upstairs extra bedroom and gave her a quick tour of the farm. Then Bruce biked back to the Vander Koop place. As he pedaled, his mind chewed on what might happen next, now that he had put these two women together. He wondered if having two girlfriends would be worse than one from Alice's perspective. Probably no worse, maybe better because it doesn't show commitment, he thought. But it was hard to imagine that this would go well.

CHAPTER 14

There was another bicyclist on the road to Parma. One with a gun in his pocket. His buddy had dropped him off at the trailer just minutes after Bruce and Krystal left. He found Krystal's change-of-address card in the mailbox and put it in his pocket. His rusted bicycle was still there, leaning against the trailer. He broke the back door window with the help of a charred rock from the fire ring, reached inside, and let himself in. He found the 3-in-1 oil, went back out and squirted some on the bicycle chain. He worked the links loose and got the crank and the wheels spinning. There was just enough air in the tires to get to a gas station for more. He stuffed his pockets with the food Bruce and Krystal hadn't finished, lit a cigarette, and guzzled the last Blatz. He found his tin snips and cut the tether off his ankle. On his way out he flicked his burning cigarette butt onto the bed sheets. He smiled at his cleverness, thinking how hot that little bitch was in bed and how much hotter her bed was about to get. With his fingers blackened by the bicycle chain, he left prints everywhere, but what the hell, the place was about to go up in flames.

The woman working at the gas station would remember seeing the man on a bicycle when he pulled in to get air and use the restroom, but he was wearing a knit hat pulled down low so she couldn't have seen that he was missing an ear. It was the next day before the police came by to ask questions. From what she recalled they could not be sure it was him, and they didn't know where he was going. Had they noticed the Michigan map book on the sales rack with greasy fingerprints and the Jackson County page torn out, they might have figured it out.

He was already miles away when the first smoke from the trailer rose above the trees. No one noticed it at first. It wasn't until a woman drove by and saw the flames that anyone knew there was a problem. It was another ten minutes before she got to a phone, and fifteen more before the fire trucks got there. By then, only the twisted metal frame of the trailer remained, and Jeff was in the next county. He found a stand of pines near Williamston and slipped in unnoticed. He spent the day hiding there, sleeping on a bed of pine needles. Arson inspectors found the broken window and the melted remains of his electronic tether. The police issued warrants and bulletins. They called Krystal to let her know that Jeff had violated his probation and that they were looking for him.

The weather had turned nice and the moon was just past full, good enough to bike at night. He couldn't go fast pedaling in the near darkness; potholes were a danger, as were passing cars, and barking dogs that might alert their owners to his presence. He slipped off the road and hid in the ditch or woods every time he saw headlights. That night he spotted a small brown shingled house with no garage and no cars parked in front. He rode his bike around the back, got off and peered in the windows using a flashlight he'd stolen from the gas station. It appeared that no one was in the one bed he could see. He used the rock trick again, breaking the window and turning the latch on the door. There was baloney, white bread, and cans of generic store-brand cola in the refrigerator; he loaded up his pockets and began to make a meal to eat on the spot.

An old man's voice called from an adjacent room, "Who's out there? . . . I got a gun . . . Who's out there? . . ." Jeff didn't answer. He finished making the sandwich, adding a knifeload of Miracle Whip before closing the bread. "I got a gun . . . Who's out there?" the quavering old voice repeated. The voice reminded him of his grandfather.

Jeff chewed and drank as he stood in the dark kitchen, smiling. He put the unused food back in the refrigerator. His feet crunched the broken glass as he walked to the door to leave. "It was the one-eared baloney bandit. I got a gun too. Go back to sleep, old fart." He laughed at his own cleverness. He found a newspaper on the kitchen table, wadded up a couple of sheets, and stuffed them into the hole in the broken window to keep out the cold. He felt virtuous as he pedaled away, quiet and nearly invisible in the night.

He made good time, and late that night he found Beaverhead Road. He rolled to a stop in front of Nanny Gate a little after three in the morning and spotted his old truck in the driveway. He lingered a bit to study the buildings and the lay of the land. In the moonlight he could see the pasture fields falling away behind the barn, beyond that a dark line where the woods started near the river. Ishkabibble heard Jeff's bike tires crackle on the gravel shoulder and began to bark from the screen porch. Both women awakened. Jeff resumed pedaling. They listened, concerned, but Ishy stopped barking and they went back to sleep.

Jeff used his flashlight to study the map. There was a bridge a couple of miles down the road that would get him across the South Branch of the Kalamazoo, and it appeared that there was State-owned woodland on the other side. At the bridge he had his first chance to size up the river. The water was black and sparkling under the full moon as it rushed under the bridge. It wasn't more than twenty yards wide at that point, and the ripples told him there were rocks not far under the surface. It would be wadeable. He resumed pedaling and took the first turn on a road that paralleled the river on the other side from Wanda's farm.

Two miles down he found a sandy two-track that headed into the woods at what he figured was about the right place. His tires rolled quietly on the packed dirt. He was relieved to be off the road and out of sight. A group of deer crossed the trail just in front of him. A doe snorted loudly as he passed. A half-mile down the two-track he found a turn-around and a fire ring. He could hear the river flowing below him. The bare trees cast shadows and glints of moonlight winked from the current.

A flock of Canada geese honked overhead. He looked up and saw a winged silhouette pass the moon; its shadow rushed across him. It made him feel superstitious, but he didn't know if it was good luck or bad. He walked his bike a short distance into the woods, made himself a bed of leaves and gathered more leaves over himself for a blanket. He slept a couple of hours until dawn when he was awakened by the soft rustling of a raccoon scurrying back to its tree, passing only feet from his head.

He used the leaves to hide his bike, and made his way down the steep bank to the river. He urinated in the water and waited a few seconds for the current to carry the foam away before he knelt and drank from his cupped hands. He climbed back up the high bank to use its vantage points to search for the farm as the sun rose. He walked a quarter mile upstream and down, peering across, looking for what he imagined the back pastures of Nanny Gate might look like. As he looked for the farm he scouted for a shallow rapid where he might cross.

From above a deep bend on the high-bank side he could see that the woods were thin across a narrow flood plain on the other side. With the trees still bare, he could just make out an open field and maybe a fence row beyond, and a red hip-roofed barn on a hill beyond that. He hiked a hundred yards back upstream to where the water widened and several large rocks rose above the fast current.

He found a stick to probe the dark water ahead of his feet, put his pistol and matches in his jacket pocket, wrapped the jacket around his head like a turban, and tied it with the sleeves. "I'll be a fucking Indian," he said to himself as he stepped into the cold early spring water. He breathed hard as he waded across, the water first just to his knees, then his thighs, then a deeper hole near the far bank. When it reached his crotch, his waist, and finally his chest, he groaned and forced himself to breathe. He was almost there. He grabbed a bush and pulled himself out. He shivered uncontrollably.

He gathered some wood and built a small fire. Wanda and Krystal were in the barn milking by then, and did not see the smoke. But if they had, Wanda would have guessed that it was local teenagers who had had a beer party and smoked pot and slept over at the campfire spot on the other side of the river. Jeff took off his clothes, wrung them out, and hung them on sticks around the fire. He squatted close to the flame, warm on one side, freezing on the other. After fifteen minutes he realized that it might take hours for his clothes to dry, so he put them back on, still wet. For a few moments they were still warm from the fire, but it didn't take long for his jeans and quilted flannel shirt-jac to feel clammy and cold again.

His best bet was to keep moving, let his clothes dry on his body. He bounced and ran in place close to the fire until he warmed a little. He found a big spruce tree near the back edge of the pasture. It had a wide cape of branches all the way to the ground and offered perfect cover. He climbed it slowly, keeping the trunk of the tree between himself and the barns.

He watched for almost two hours from the high vantage point, occasionally climbing up or down a few branches just to move. He edged around the tree to feel a little of the sun. He saw figures going back and forth between the barns. A group of goats started down the lane toward him, but turned into the first pasture where they spread out to nibble on the fresh green shoots. A car pulled in. People got out and met someone, then left. A tank truck came from the elevator with a load of bulk feed that they blew through a flexible steel pipe into the barn. At his distance, the loud racket of the feed blower was less than the hum of mosquito in his ear. He could see a small person with a pitch fork and a wheel barrow cleaning the pens under the hip-roofed barn. He thought it was probably Krystal. All the daytime activity told him to wait until dark, but the waiting was driving him nuts, and he was hungry.

He walked back to the river and waded into a shallow rocky stretch. He turned rocks with one hand, while the other was positioned just downstream to catch the crayfish he dislodged. He collected four, putting them in his jacket pocket as he caught them. The pocket squirmed as he climbed out of the water. He put the live crayfish on the dying coals of his fire for a few minutes before nudging them back out with a stick. He broke the tail off of each crustacean and scooped out the meat with his thumbnail. Delicious, he thought, but he was still hungry.

He decided to try for frogs and went back down to the river and walked the bank. There weren't many, but he caught one good sized green frog by distracting it with his left hand and making a lightning grab with his right. Then he stumbled upon the nest of a pair of Canada geese, and from them stole two eggs while they honked, pecked, and beat on him with their wings. He added the big goose eggs to the coals.

He took the frog out of his pocket and whacked its head on a rock, then used his knife to cut the skin around its waist. He pinched the edge of the cut skin and pulled down hard, depantsing the frog all the way to its toes in one smooth yank, then used his knife to finish cutting off its legs at the pelvis. He sharpened a short forked stick and pressed it into the ground at the edge of the fire, then propped another stick, this one long and green, in the fork, its small end just a few inches above the fire. He secured the butt end to the ground with a rock. Then he straddled the frog's legs over the end of the long stick, so that its skinned toes were just above the coals. The dry sticks he added to the fire made only thin tendrils of smoke that drifted away on the rising breeze as the day warmed up. He felt content with his woodsman skills as he watched a turkey buzzard circle above. It was a fine day to be outside.

The frog's legs were done in ten minutes. They were good, but he thought they needed salt. He let the goose eggs rest in the coals for a good half hour, turning them every few minutes. He was disappointed and slightly nauseated when he cracked the first one open and found a nearly-ready-to-hatch gosling. The remnants of the yolk, criss-crossed by tiny blood vessels, clung to the baby bird's abdomen, its neck curled back, everything cooked and fixed in the shape of the egg shell. He peeled the yolk from the bird and tasted it. Pretty bad, but he ate it anyway. He pulled off a leg and tried that. Its muscles were thin and the moist down-covered skin nearly gagged him when he tried to swallow it. He spit it out before he puked. He tore back the skin over its tiny breast, hoping for at least one good bite. He got less than that.

He added a little more wood and blew it into a flame. He cracked the second egg, peeled the shell away, and skewered the gosling on the frog-cooking stick to let the fire burn off the down and crisp the skin a little. He ate this one with the skin on; it was better, and the liver was at least one good bite, but it still didn't add up to much. He couldn't bring himself to eat the bird's bones and guts the way a fox would. He was still hungry. The goats were a temptation, but he didn't dare walk out into the pasture in daylight. He tried to sleep. He considered whacking off to pass the time and ease the tension, but he wanted a full load for Krystal before he killed her. Then he whacked off anyway, imagining her fearful and compliant as he stroked himself.

Finally the light began to fade and he dozed off. He awoke, cold, and in pure darkness. Clouds had come in and he felt a few rain drops hit his face.

He did a few pushups and ran in place to warm himself before he felt his way to the back pasture fence. Once over it and in the pasture he moved quickly. It was easy to cross the series of fences separating the pastures since the goats required neither a tall fence nor barbed wire. In a short time he was behind the old barn. The barn blocked the view from the house, so it was safe to turn on his flashlight. He climbed into the pen with the young stock. The goats all ran as one to the part of the enclosure farthest from him, bleating and running to the back of the pen as he entered the barn. No barn windows faced the house; the light was safe. He felt secure, though it might take a while to get used to the strong billy goat smell.

He found half a cup of coffee on a shelf in the feed room. Jeff remembered Krystal's habit of leaving unfinished drinks around the trailer and knew he was in the right place. The cup was printed with a laughing bearded billy; in a comical font it said: "Do it with Goats!" He drank the cold coffee as he walked up and down the barn aisle, considering this advice and his best ambush lair. He liked the position of the hay feeder inside the first billy goat pen, and he liked that the big polka-dotted goat with the floppy ears lacked horns. He could hide behind the feeder and be unseen by a person coming down the stairs from the hayloft entrance above. After the crime he would sneak away across the fields the way he had come, cross the river, and be away on his bike before anyone found Krystal's body.

He turned his search to food. Had he known about the milk house and cheese room in the other barn he would have gone there and gorged, but he'd never been on a dairy farm and he didn't know how they worked. He found a bowl of dry cat food. He ate a handful; the kibbles had a nice crunch, but they were bland and fishy. Better than goose embryos, he thought. He found the water faucet and filled the coffee cup, drinking it dry twice and refilling it before slowing to sip as he looked for a place to bed down. A small stack of straw bales made the best bed he'd had in three days. As the rain became steady he felt snug and warm in the barn.

At first light he took off his jeans, removed his underwear, then put his jeans back on and left his fly unzipped. He figured it was like clicking the safety off; he wanted the rape to be seamless, no fumbling. He fingered his gun, a cheap snub-nosed 0.22, a Saturday night special. He spun the chamber. Six rounds—one should be plenty. Not much of a weapon, but more than adequate to kill with a shot to the head, and not that loud. Using his jacket for a silencer, the sound wouldn't carry beyond the barn. He climbed into Sadam's pen and took his position, crouching behind the hay feeder, waiting for Krystal to come to clean the pen like he had watched her do from the tree the day before.

The wait was long. Sadam stamped his foot and paced the far wall. At one point the goat hunched his back and urinated on his own beard. A fresh wave of gagging billy goat smell washed over the area. Finally he heard the big hayloft door slide open above him, then footsteps on the wooden loft floor, then coming down the stairs. Krystal was singing to herself. He recognized her voice. Ishkabibble bounded down the stairs in front of her. She got her pitchfork and a wheelbarrow and started on the young stock pen. Jeff hardly breathed, waiting behind the solid wall between the pens. She picked out a dozen forkfuls of wet straw and wheeled them out to a manure pile. Then she broke open one of the straw bales on which Jeff had slept, not appreciating that it hadn't looked so packed and smooth the day before. She scattered a few sheaves of the bale in the pen. Ishy loved to bark at the straw as it was scattered. Krystal laughed. She put the fork in the wheelbarrow and rolled it to the next pen—Sadam's. The little dog had learned not to go into Sadam's pen. Krystal kept her eye on the heavily muscled goat as she entered the enclosure. He gave a low bleat and stamped his foot. "It's okay, big boy," she said as Jeff quietly rose up behind her and pointed the revolver at her head.

"Morning, darlin. Drop the pitchfork and don't make no sound." His voice sounded calm and assured. "I still got a mighty hankerin' for your pussy, and I don't guess you'll be siccin' your goddamn dog on me this time." Ishkabibble saw the stranger, barked twice, and got her ball for him to throw. Jeff pulled out his flaccid penis—he probably shouldn't have jerked off if this were to be a decent rape. "I come a long way for this," he said, "I think I'll start with a little head, darlin. Lemme see them tits." Jeff made an upward motion with the gun barrel to indicate that she should pull her sweatshirt over her head. He waved the piece at her bra, "Come on, let's see them twins, darlin." He wagged his cock at her with one hand while he kept the muzzle of the gun pointed at her face. "On your knees, cunt. You know what to do."

She got down. He held almost all the cards, but she contained her terror. She took stock. She knew this man.

He stepped toward her and shoved his still flaccid member in her face. The gun barrel pointed at her brain, his finger on the trigger. "Suck on it, darlin." She took it in her mouth. He dropped his head back, grinned at the whitewashed rafters, and groaned with satisfaction. He was thinking how worthwhile all his efforts had been.

Sadam made a quick and silent charge: three hops then rearing onto his back legs so that the full force of his two-hundred fifty pounds in motion coalesced behind his thick head bones. His knobby skull hit Jeff mid-thigh with a loud crack as his femur broke in two places. His arms flew out and he fired a wild shot into the barn ceiling, the 0.22 report like the echo of his breaking bone. The revolver fell from his hand as pain shot through him. The blow knocked him hard into Krystal. She reflexly bit down to keep his growing penis from going deeper in her throat—actually she bit a lot harder than pure reflex would explain. Jeff collapsed on the straw with a roar that was almost a scream, his leg bent at an odd angle, the base of his instantly deflated penis pumping blood.

Krystal kicked the gun away and grabbed her pitch fork. She wiped Jeff's blood from her lips with the back of her hand, and looked straight into his eyes. Fear was suddenly leaking through his defiance. If he still didn't understand that the tables had turned—that Krystal was a human being to be reckoned with—he was about to.

"Suck this, you fucking bastard," she said flatly, as she plunged six long goat-manure-encrusted pitchfork tines into his chest, pinning him to the dirt floor of the goat pen. A scream formed on his lips, but no sound came out.

CHAPTER 15

I n the wake of the police and the ambulance that carted away the not quite expired Jeff, reporters swarmed Nanny Gate. They dug for every smarmy detail on Sadam the cantankerous billy goat and the little lady with the pitchfork who together took out an armed rapist. It was the lead story for a whole day on all the cable news outlets, and follow-up stories lasted almost a week before Krystal got knocked out of the twenty-four hour news cycle by a woman on fertility drugs and welfare who had a litter of babies that would have made an Irish Setter proud. There were videos featuring gushing reporters standing outside Sadam's pen, rattling on about the hero billy goat that was the second animal in as many weeks to save Krystal from her monstrous former husband. Wanda closed the big goat in the barn to give the reporters better access. The muscular, spotted, floppy-eared buck stood in the straw at the back wall of his pen and stomped his feet. Bruce was interviewed to get a recap of the previous rape attempt in the trailer. He balked at first, since he thought Alice and the kids might see it, but the lure of his moment in front of the cameras won out.

Reporters also drove to Lansing to get pictures of Bob Barker in his rabies quarantine cage. He barked and growled ferociously and lunged at the cyclone wire. Most who saw the video wondered why such a dog would ever be released. Lured by the media frenzy, the retired game show host Bob Barker flew in from Palm Springs. A worshipful flock of animal rights activists materialized around him. He looked dapper in his dark blue suit, white shirt, dark tan, and gleaming silver hair. He talked to the press about the plight of innocent animals while keeping a safe distance from the slathering beast. Mr. Barker paid the tab for his namesake's month-long rabies quarantine and opened a fund in his name, writing an oversized TV check for the first thousand dollars to guarantee the dog's long-term care. The TV exposure for Bob Barker's Endowment Fund for the Study of Animal Rights boosted funds coming in to that charity, but it appeared to be a zero sum game for celebrity animal causes, as donations dwindled to a trickle for the Doris Day Animal League.

From the Ingham County pound, reporters drove out near the village of Perry to get pictures of Krystal's burned out trailer. There was no one there to interview, so reporters created their own narrative at the scene. The fire hadn't spread to the jumbled woodpile or the weathered potato brown couch that squatted next to the charred and twisted metal frame of the trailer. A poetically-inclined chubby reporter looked straight into the camera and said with all the gravitas he could muster, "I'm standing here in front of the incinerated wreckage of what was once the home of an innocent diner waitress, a modest trailer home set idyllically in the Central Michigan woods, now ravaged by domestic violence, a home that now, tragically, appears to be a super-sized all-starch meal of baked potato, French fries, and a platter of charred aluminum noodles. And that's how it looks to me from here. Jason Smarkly, Channel-Five News."

Police sniffer dogs found Jeff's bike in the woods across the river from the farm. They shot close-ups of the remains of his campfire at the back of the farm with the crawdad heads, frog bones, and goose egg shells with the half-eaten goose embryos scattered around. And they interviewed the old man whose house Jeff broke into to get food: "He seemed like he might be a pretty nice guy if you was to get to know him. He plugged the back door window with a wad of newspaper where he'd broke it with a rock, and all he took was food. He didn't seem like no rapist to me, just hungry."

Fox News ran an NRA editorial suggesting that liberals would now want to force the registration of pitchforks and goats, and that nothing in The Constitution could protect farmers from the threat of the nefarious bleeding hearts. They printed up bumper stickers that said, "When Goats are Outlawed, only Outlaws will have Goats." Their major implication was that all this could have been avoided had Krystal been packing a 0.38, which of course would trump a 0.22 in a shoot-out at the billy goat corral, especially if it were a semi-auto with a big clip. Bruce wondered why they didn't jump harder on the pitchfork angle as well. He figured the billy goat imagery must have been as devilish as the NRA dared get, and that evangelical gun nuts probably determined that the Satanic implications of a pro-pitchfork-rights campaign would send an unpalatable message to their army of Christian soldiers. None of the news outlets came up with an editorial angle on the hero billy goat's name, Sadam, although a few Unitarian ministers updated sermons on prejudice and not judging a book by its cover.

Several of the army of reporters showed up at Martha's Kitchen to get local reaction to the incident and some lunch. Ray was unrattled by a microphone stuck in his face—he'd always hoped to have a chance to voice his opinion on the news, the subject didn't much matter. But he had to admit that he hadn't yet met the pitchfork girl. Still, he mustered an opinion: "One of my hired men, Mr. Bruce Dinkle, already had to help save her once already. She seems like she needs a lot more saving than most of the gals around here. But I'm glad she come to Parma to get saved this time, even if it was by a goat." He smiled broadly and asked the cameraman, "How was that?"

Doc Voekle added with his typical eloquence, "The women of Parma are not to be trifled with, and any man would do well to respect their independence. The measure of fear that the strong women of Parma rightly engender in evildoers is exceeded only by their feminine charms and beauty, virtues that the men and even the animals of this community are also ready and eager to defend."

Big Joyce wasn't sure that Doc's remark wasn't sexist, since what did beauty have to do with anything and why would a woman need defending anyway? When the reporter got to her table she had a prepared statement: "We will be asking Krystal to speak to the Women's Defense League. Clearly, the pitchfork hasn't been fully appreciated and is under-utilized as a weapon of self defense. As long as women have the thing that men will kill for, women need to have all lethal forces at their disposal."

Ray and Doc elbowed each other, chuckling about man's unquenchable desire for what the big lesbian was prepared to protect with lethal force. Ray cupped his mouth toward Doc, "There's more than enough of that woman to wilt me without no pitchfork."

"Three hundred pounds of bad attitude would sure as snot put my boy into deep hibernation. He'd curl up like a dead chipmunk. Couldn't resurrect him with an electric cattle prod," Doc whispered back.

"That works? What setting?" asked Ray. Laughter erupted around their table. Big Joyce glared in their general direction.

Other news stories spun off on the dairy goat business, organic food, and raw milk. Within twenty-four hours Wanda was inundated with customers who wanted her products. She sold out of everything. She renamed Nanny Gate's oldest and stinkiest cheese, the Mount St. Francis; the new labels would read "Sadam's Pitchfork." Almost half of Nanny Gate's milk output was diverted to production of the newly named cheese. Over the next week Wanda got inquiries about the availability of the cheese from dozens of gourmet shops around the Midwest. Wanda decided not to sell any of the doe kids born that year, but to add them all to her herd and bump her total up over a hundred milkers.

Jeff would spend a month in intensive care with a breathing tube, chest drains, and an IV line. His treatment was distinguished from the other desperate cases on the floor primarily by the shackles that secured him to his bed, and by the armed guard outside his door. The nature of his wounds—dirty round punctures—caused significant but manageable blood loss, mostly from the tine that pierced the right ventricle of his heart. He still had serious medical problems after resolution of the life-threatening heart puncture, collapsed lung, and infection by several kinds of bacteria from the goat manure left in his chest. One tine of the fork had pierced a spinal disk and gone all the way through to the cord. He wasn't completely paralyzed, but he'd never walk without a cane. Orthopedic surgeons screwed a steel plate to the pieces of his shattered femur. X-ray images were leaked to the internet and went viral when people noticed that the skin staples showed in the radiographs—not just the two dozen used to close the long incision over the plate on his thigh bone, but also the seven stainless steel clips used to close the bite wound at the base of his penis. The soft tissue shadow of the repaired organ on the radiograph suggested that he would be an acute right angler in the future. It probably should have been sutured by a plastic surgeon, but the medicos took a "good enough" attitude toward the felonious phallus. Overnight, the image became a metaphor for anything bent. David Letterman referred to a corrupt Republican Senator from Ohio as, "crooked as a chewed weenie."

Of course becoming an overnight celebrity caused the biggest changes for Krystal. Nothing in her hard life had prepared her for this. Fear and emotional trauma followed by fame and adoration spun her on her heels. Leno, Letterman, Oprah, and Jerry Springer all wanted her on their shows. Publishers offered to connect her with ghost writers and dangled six-figure advances on the book. A company that made purse-sized, designer dispensers of self-defense spray wanted her to endorse a line of products they would call Krystal Mace. She needed an agent, but she had no idea how to pick one. Bruce and Wanda helped her to think things through, but their only advantage was a little emotional distance; they had no experience with celebrity either, although Wanda's farm had once been featured in the accent section of the Jackson News.

But what Krystal did feel sure about was that she would settle in Parma, at least for the time being. With her experience in the diner business, and with Martha getting on in years and thinking of retiring, she briefly considered buying the diner. But in just the few days she'd worked on the farm she had learned to love the feeling of it, and Wanda was proving to be a real friend. On the farm it felt like space opened up around her. She could breathe deeply and walk the pastures with a long open stride she could never use in the diner. She could even break into a run if she wanted. She could throw bales, fork manure, haul buckets, use her all her muscles and feel sore but satisfyingly spent at the end of a hard day. She felt bigger and natural and good, like quitting smoking would be easy and her life could change. Wanda said she could stay at the farm as long as she wanted, and relented on the Bob Barker issue, saying that if they could build a secure kennel, the dog could live at the farm when he got out of quarantine. The Bob Barker Trust Fund meant the price of a kennel would be right.

The three of them, Krystal, Wanda, and Bruce, walked the grounds of Nanny Gate together, considering a site on which to build Bob Barker's new home. Ishy followed Bruce with a tennis ball; she had come to favor him for his strong throwing arm and willingness to throw again and again. Ishy had become an exception to Bruce's general dislike of dogs, a crack in his dog dogma. She more than earned her dog food in her role as comical sidekick.

In the brushy fence row that sloped back toward the river from the north end of the old hip-roofed barn, Krystal noticed a little home-made table built on fence post legs buried in the ground. It had an attached seat, so it looked like a quarter of a picnic table. There was a partially overgrown path down the fencerow beyond it; the path went a hundred yards down the slope to a dump-truck-sized dirt pile. In front of the mound a tattered black rifle target barely hung on by rusted staples to a shot-up piece of weathered plywood nailed to two short fence posts.

"What's this?" Krystal asked.

"Looks like a shooting range. Hadn't noticed it myself," said Bruce.

"Oh yeah, my dad used to shoot a lot," said Wanda.

"NRA type?"

"No, he wasn't paranoid enough for the NRA—not one of those guys who worried about the feds taking his guns away. Funny thing is, the feds didn't, but his daughter did. I sold most all of them after he died. He had a big collection—everything from AK-47s to muskets."

"Did you ever learn to shoot?" asked Krystal.

"Yes, I did. He sort of made me and Mom. I got pretty good at it, better than her anyway, but it never was fun for us like it was for him. It was just boys making big noises as far as we could see."

"You want to teach me to shoot?" asked Krystal.

"You want to add guns to mean dogs and pitchforks? You're going to kill somebody yet, girl," said Bruce.

"I don't know," said Wanda. "I might . . . maybe someday. I only kept one gun, it's .225 mag with a scope. It's a hell of a varmit rifle. I can take a woodchuck at two hundred fifty yards with it. We could fire off a few rounds sometime—as my dad would've said. But if you're thinking of protecting yourself, you probably want a handgun. I sold all my dad's handguns. I didn't like having them around. I don't think they make you any safer."

Krystal considered how a gun might have changed the events in the trailer with Jeff and figured Wanda was probably right. She'd either be up for murder or shot with her own gun. Just as well the dog had done the dirty work, but still she wished Bob Barker would have killed the bastard before he came to Parma. Of course the two assaults had turned fate in her favor.

"It's better to be lucky, I guess," Krystal concluded.

They continued walking and finally settled on a little-used patch of lawn off to the side of the dirt ramp up to the hip-roofed barn. Wanda said it would be nice to have a little less grass to mow anyway. Bruce was given the kennel building task. He drew up a plan and a materials list one evening after work at Ray's. In his mind he modeled the construction after the chicken coop he'd built on the old farmette in Edenville. Thinking about it caused a pang of regret. He used Wanda's truck to gather the materials for the small outbuilding. It would have a tall hinged door under the peak and a round dog-door under a shed roof at the side, giving Barker access to a generous outside pen. Barker would have options to be inside, outside under cover, or outside in the sun. With the window facing east, the lucky dog would have his straw bed in a morning sunbeam on those days when the Michigan clouds parted. It would be a virtual doggie palace thanks to Bruce and the Bob Barker Trust Fund.

Bruce found an Amish saw mill operator who specialized in white cedar. From the Amishman he got rough sawn framing lumber and planks, as well as fence posts for the outside pen. From the lumber yard he got red shingles, a variety of nails and staples, and a roll of six-foot dog fence. He got an old four-pane window from a salvage yard. For two weeks Bruce worked nights and weekends building a handsome rustic cedar home for Bob Barker. Personally, he had not warmed to the big dog, but he certainly had to Krystal and Wanda, so he threw himself into the project to please the women. He dug footings and mixed concrete to fill piers at each corner of the structure. After anchoring the corners and framing in the floor joists he decked the dog house with two-inch-thick tongue-and-groove boards. He built a handsome front door with two X-braces, top and bottom. He fashioned a beefy sliding wooden lock to secure the door. He used rough-sawn cedar one-by-eights for board and batten siding, nailing it vertically on the two-by-four frame, along with narrower strips of cedar nailed over the cracks between the boards. He draped the circular dog-door from the inside with overlapping red carpet squares to baffle the wind.

They debated about whether to pour concrete for the outside pen, but decided to use a thick layer of crushed limestone gravel over sand so that urine would drain through. He buried the bottom six inches of the fence in the crushed limestone to prevent Bob Barker from digging his way out. In the second week of construction, now late April, the first really warm days of spring arrived. Daffodils bloomed, the grass seemed to grow overnight, and working in the afternoon sun Bruce peeled off his sweat-soaked T-shirt, baring blindingly white skin for the first time that year. The last of the poison ivy sores had finally healed, and he knew that despite his near albino whiteness he looked pretty good.

Wanda and Krystal stood together, arms draped across each other's shoulders in the easy way women friends do. They admired Bruce's physique and handiwork as he measured and cut and nailed with uncommon skill and efficiency for a man who didn't make his living that way. Wanda claimed the best paintbrush skills of the three, so took the job of painting in red letters "Beware Bob Barker" over the door in a cartoonish hillbilly script. It was a prime example of the wood butcher's art. Krystal bought stainless steel bowls for food and water, a big bag of premium dog chow, and a lidded metal trash can to store the dog food in. When Barker was finally sprung from the dog slammer, which would be that Monday, they would be ready for him, they thought.

In the meantime, with the new kennel finished and Krystal's impending wealth, a little celebration was in order. When the milking was done that night, and the goats all fed and tended, the three of them made a simple but fine Sunday dinner of lemon roasted backyard chicken, new potatoes sautéed in butter and chives, stir-fried asparagus, a spring green salad with Kalamata olives and fresh goat cheese, and a bottle each of a Washington Chardonnay and a California Pinot Noir. Bruce commented that the wine and olives had come an awfully long way. The women told him to shut up.

The chicken, goat cheese, butter, and chives were all in-season and local, or from just the next growing zone south in the case of the asparagus and rhubarb. The flavors from near and far melded and danced together like the ingredients were in heat and their mouths were mating grounds for pleasure. Krystal especially was unaccustomed to such gastronomic ecstasy and let a drop of the mingled juices run down almost to the tip of her small chin before she caught it with a finger and moved it to her tongue. They were enjoying the food too much to speak. Bruce couldn't help thinking that this little compromise on his locavore dogma was awfully tasty, but he kept it to himself. Wanda got up and put on k.d.lang's languorous album of smoking songs, *Drag*.

There hadn't been time to bake a dessert, but with stewed rhubarb over vanilla ice cream, no one complained. Several times during the meal they stopped to toast each other and express their mutual admiration. Somehow the early jealousy between the women had evaporated; it seemed that the sharp corners of the triangle had melted into a circle; generous affection spread between them. The safety they felt with each other drew them closer until hormones surged and urges became irresistible. There was no negotiation, no awkward propositioning, they simply arose as one, holding hands around the circular table, and slow danced into Wanda's bedroom. Their lovemaking was generous in every combination; everyone's needs were met, everyone's fantasies were exceeded. They fell asleep together, Bruce sandwiched between two women who were at least temporarily infatuated with him and with each other. He couldn't believe his luck and had no idea how to make it last.

The obvious pitfalls and potential snags of the new arrangement fluttered his chest and churned his guts when he awoke at dawn to the buzz of his cell phone alarm under his pillow. He was at first surprised by his situation, then uncertain as to how one properly expresses affection for two women simultaneously and without revealing favor. He had already failed miserably with the standard allotment of one woman per man. Even with the legal and social structure of marriage set up to protect his family, he hadn't been able to deliver Alice enough attention and respect to keep it going. Now there were two women whose warm skin was pressing him under the covers, and he was still married to Alice. It would be complicated, he could be sure of that. Even the problem of which of these sleeping women he should crawl over to get to the bathroom, which was an urgent need, seemed to be a minefield. He slowly curled himself straight up in a sit-up movement and gracefully continued into a headfirst roll over the footboard. Wanda glimpsed his hairy behind as it disappeared over the end of the bed and skooched herself sleepily across the void until she re-established skin contact. Bruce did a quick once-over with a wash cloth to quench the lovemaking aroma, and was out the door in minutes, pedaling his bike back to Ray's to be at work by seven-thirty.

CHAPTER 16

With the field edge clearing done, the soil warmed and the muddy areas dried, field prep for planting was about to start. Miguel would circle the fields pulling a huge chisel plow, churning and aerating twenty-four-foot-wide swaths of ground, burying last year's cornstalks and turning the earth a rich dark brown. Bruce would follow with a wide disc harrow that would smooth and further pulverize the seed bed. They used the two biggest tractors that Vander Koop Farms owned, both huge four-wheel-drive machines with tall and wide dual tires front and back. They had climate-controlled cabs with sound systems and walkie-talkies so they could listen to the radio and keep in touch. It was exactly the sort of impersonal mechanization of farming that Bruce had railed against, but here he was, feeling quite connected to the process and the people involved. He felt proud about how much food he was helping to grow, although he knew that none of it would end up in a farmer's market or as fresh produce. And even though his thoughts turned often to Alice and his children, they were poorly formed thoughts, and the work nearly fully occupied his attention. He had become a dutiful cog in the industrial machine, just as he had been at the coal-fired power plant.

Ray said he'd let Bruce and Miguel get a couple of days ahead before he and Leo started planting. After that, Miguel would be the supply guy, shuttling seed, fertilizer, and diesel fuel. Bruce would then alternate between pulling the chisel plow and the disc harrow, covering each field first with one, then the other. His job was to prepare three dozen fields ahead of Ray's planters. Deb would show up at the field entrances with lunches and dinners through the whole process. Wet soil packs together and becomes hard and airless, so significant rainfall could stop them—a frequent event in the spring. Thus, while soil conditions were right, they worked as long as they could.

By noon of the first day Bruce and Miguel had earned loyal followings of seagulls. The birds apparently sent out scouts from their home on Lake Michigan, looking for fields being tilled. Now hundreds of the graceful white birds swooped and landed directly behind the implements, a dancing, dappling, white shadow above the freshly turned soil as the gulls feasted on thousands of suddenly exposed earthworms. The cacophony of the birds' excited screeches carried as far as the roar of the big tractors. Bruce observed that some of the locals apparently loved to see the fields worked. They would stop their cars or slow at the field edges, wave to him, and watch the big equipment crawl across the fields, changing the land's color, spouting black exhaust, hundreds of sea gulls hopscotching each other in a great winged white wave. It was as sure a sign of the season as the changing leaves in the fall.

The planting weeks went pretty well for Bruce, despite being chronically sleep deprived and exhausted. Most nights after work he had just time to shower and crawl into his bed at the farm shop, sleep five or six hours, and get right back on the tractor; but every third day he felt compelled to satisfy other needs and would get Krystal or Wanda to come pick him up. It made for short nights, but he came home satisfied and resupplied with fresh raw goat milk. It was after one of these nocturnal triangular conjugal visits, with the scent of both women still on him, that he rose for work so tired that his vision strobed and he staggered a bit.

On the tractor he drank coffee steadily, slapped his stubbled face every few minutes, and harmonized with the big diesel engine at twenty-five-hundred rpms, belting out songs like Credence Clearwater Revival's *Joy to the World* at the top of his lungs. But during a groggy intermission between the few songs to which he knew the words, and while taking a break from the invigorating self-administered dope slaps, he fell dead asleep at the controls of the three-hundred horse tractor as it pulled its wide chisel plow straight across the blacktop of Perkins Road. Luckily there was no appreciable roadside ditch where this happened, so he didn't flip or get the tractor stuck. A motorist saw him slumped in the cab, head bobbing and heading straight into the road. She stomped on the brakes and laid on her horn as Bruce passed in front of her. The plow ripped a wide swath of pavement to bits, and continued a few yards into somebody's lawn. The car horn, the loud cracks of the buckling blacktop, and the bucking tractor did finally wake him up. Thus he didn't knock down any yard trees or the small house in front of him.

The residents of the house were terrified to see him coming toward them across their yard, and relieved to see him stop. Fortunately, the man of the house was in a particularly good mood, having been watching the start of game-two of a twi-night double-header as the Tigers beat the living snot out of the Yankees. Curtis Granderson had just smacked one over the right field fence with two on when they heard the diesel roar and cracking pavement and looked up from the TV. The man, his wife and kids, and a couple of baseball buddies all ran out of the house, beer and pop cans in hand, and had a good laugh at Bruce's expense. Bruce appeared dazed as he climbed down out of the cab, held his face in place with both hands, looked around, shook his head, and repeated over and over, "Oh Jesus, oh fuck, Ray's gonna kill me."

Sheriff Timmers showed up fairly quickly with sirens screaming and flashers flashing, and had to think hard about just what the tickets should be for. Finally he said he'd arrested plenty of drivers for being on the road plowed, but Bruce was the first perp he'd caught for plowing the road. He decided the citations would be for failure to yield since he had crossed in front of another driver, plus non-malicious destruction of public property. The homeowner declined the opportunity to press charges as long as Bruce would rake and reseed the damaged lawn, which he did after finishing the nearby fields the next day.

Ray put Miguel into Bruce's tractor and got it back in the field, then drove Bruce back to the farm to sleep. "What's the deal, Brucie?" Ray slapped the dash of his pickup to get Bruce's attention, "Deb's coffee ain't doing it for you? We got twelve-hundred acres to go. I can't have you crapping out on me." Bruce apologized, staggered to his bed when they got back to the farm, and fell asleep until the next morning when they started all over again.

Ray's buddy on the Road Commission said the road was slated for repaving later in the summer anyway, so they'd smooth it over with gravel for the time being and the repairs "wouldn't cost him nothin'." The forgiving nature of these people was not lost on Bruce.

Delayed only by that glitch and a couple of moderate rains, they planted almost three-thousand acres in three weeks; every seed in the ground before Memorial Day weekend, which came early that year. Not counting the cost of owning or renting the ground, between the corn and beans, Ray had buried almost a million dollars in the dirt around Parma. To break even, yields would need to be good and prices near record levels. But from that moment until the fall harvest there was little or nothing he could do to tilt the odds in his favor. Ray said it was all up to the weatherman. He could stir his coffee with Doc and the boys down at the dinner, and he could shoot the bull with anybody else with time on their hands. But he would keep one eye on the sky as he waited and watched for the crops to germinate, grow, and mature.

After that there would be the even bigger effort of getting it all out of the fields, dried down to a storable moisture level, then augered into the big steel storage bins or delivered to the elevator where it would be loaded on box cars and transported to his contract buyers. Deb of course left it all in the hands of God, but on Ray's advice she would be non-specific and ask the Man Upstairs simply for a good crop, lest The Long Bearded One overshoot for or against rain. And of course it would help to bump prices up if He would maybe drown a few hundred-thousand acres of river bottom corn in Iowa and Illinois, and maybe scorch a patch of soy beans the size of Connecticut in Brazil.

Deb also prayed that one of their three children would come home and take over the farm someday soon so that she and Ray could eventually retire. Ray suggested to his wife that she might want to target those divine requests especially at their son Ray Jr., and maybe it would help to lobby him directly on the phone rather than through the heavenly ether since Ray Jr. probably wasn't necessarily tuned to that station. Ray Jr. was their eldest, a decisive young man with good business sense and a laconic unflappability that suits the modern farmer's job description, but Ray Sr. had been unable to lure him into the family business.

Ray Jr. had acquired sophisticated urban tastes and the ability to make easy money after changing his major from crop science to finance at Michigan State. He was now a Chicago commodities broker putting his farm background to profitable use. But he had little interest in actually working the dirt himself. Ray Sr. consulted with his eldest son about crop futures when making his planting and contracting decisions, and he hoped to draw him in with the lure of ownership someday. But Ray Jr. had learned to love the rich complexity of urban culture, and he'd married a fashion-conscious city girl, an ambitious high-heeled beauty in the advertising business who didn't have a down-home bone in her gorgeous body.

Still, Ray Jr. was a better bet to keep the farm in the family than their daughter Sarah who was currently paying her rent by violin busking on the streets of Seattle, or their son Mike who moved to Los Angeles to paint gas tanks and fenders on custom motorcycles. Sarah lived a financially precarious day-to-day existence, coaxing classical music from her violin in public places, collecting her rent a quarter or a dollar bill at a time as they were tossed into her open violin case. The immediacy of the relationship between her performance and its rewards ironically allowed her to live in many ways more grounded than her father the farmer, so she was happy enough, and she was very good—good enough to have a fair shot at making it into the Seattle Symphony someday. Ray and Deb worried plenty with the sketchy information they had on their Left Coast offspring, so it was just as well that they didn't know all the other details, like that Mike had also attempted to cash in on his rugged good looks in the Los Angeles porn business.

To that end—hoping to bring their eldest back home—and with summer upon them and the crops all in, Ray and Deb's main focus turned to getting ready for the Memorial Day bash they'd put on for the town every year for the last nine. A tent, a stage, a band, tables, barbeque, pot luck, drinks, lawn darts, horse shoes—the whole shebang had to come together in a few days. There were last details to arrange and a lot of work to be done. It was a chance to once again make Parma look as attractive as possible for Ray Jr., in their probably futile parental quest to lure him and Sonia back to the simple life on the farm. Of course it was not a simple life, but an interesting life that the younger generation craved. They would not be disappointed.

CHAPTER 17

Bob Barker was about to be sprung from dog jail, so Krystal had to drive her old mud-bogging beater to Lansing to retrieve the beast. Based on the advance on her book deal and the talk show appearances, she had ordered a new truck, but she wanted a color and trim package that wasn't in stock at the local dealer. Thus, she didn't have it yet, so she had to drive the old jacked-up, banged-up, gas hog to Lansing one last time. She was anxious to be rid of the rumbling eye-sore and had already spotted a local salvage yard where this last vestige of her ex could be disassembled for parts. She imagined the son-of-a-bitch seeing it there when he went to the junk yard for a used ear—what would he get? Naugahyde? Chrome?

The caged month had been hard on Barker. All he wanted was to run. He heaved himself into the choke collar as Krystal struggled to lead him to the truck. She fought to restrain him with one hand, while she opened the creaky truck door with the other and coaxed him inside. On the ride back to Parma he kept vigil out the passenger side, barking at most everything, and giving the full show of fangs and growls to any men in passing vehicles. She stopped to get a burger and had to block him with her elbow from lunging across her lap to get at the freaked-out kid tending the drive-through window. With Jeff sure to be in prison for at least fifteen years, she wondered whether this unguided muscle of a beast really made her any safer. Probably not, she thought.

But they made the trip without serious incident and Barker seemed pretty happy with his new digs. He did jump up and put a foot through the window though, which resulted in a lacerated paw pad. Doc Voekle made a house call to stitch it up. He had to put the dog under for the minor surgery because Krystal wasn't strong enough to restrain him for more than a few seconds. But a few seconds was enough to get the pentabarbitol into his front leg vein—he didn't even seem to notice the needle going in—and knock him out for twenty minutes. Ishy brought Doc a tennis ball and pressed it into his leg as he sutured Bob Barker's foot. "Would somebody please throw the ball for Ishkabibble!" Doc laughed as he quickly tied a neat row of silk sutures in the big dog's paw. Ishy had already figured out that she should keep her distance when Bob Barker was awake, but in her experience Doc was usually good for a couple of tosses. Krystal got ball throwing duty while Bruce screwed a sheet of heavy steel mesh on the inside of the broken window before Barker woke up. The steel gave an incongruous maximum security touch to the otherwise rustic charm of the structure. But the incident worked out well enough; the blood loss and anesthesia hangover slowed the dog down for a day while he got used to his new surroundings.

Big Joyce's Women's Defense Club invited Krystal to ride their float with Bob Barker and Sadam in Parma's Memorial Day parade. The Women's Defense Club float would be with the other non-profit organizations near the end of the middle of the parade—after the high school band, the politicians, and the local businesses that put banners on the sides of pickup trucks with their logos and phone numbers, but before the streamer-adorned bicycles and finally, bringing up the rear, the local wannabe cowgirls and cowboys on their impeccably groomed steeds tacked up with silver-trimmed show saddles.

It would occur to Bruce that darn few of the costumed cowpokes in their spit polished Western finery had ever touched a cow, but, then again, in the information age almost no one sees the animals alive, or even the vegetables in the field, that provide their food. One can get the information with a bit of digging, but it comes free of real understanding. Bruce thought that perhaps instead of "cholesterol-free," or "trans-fat-free," food products should be labeled "context-free." He wondered how many of the parade onlookers could trace the path from the thousands of acres of corn and soybeans that were now sprouting around Parma, to the paper bags and plastic cartons filled with the fatty fast food they consumed while riding in their increasingly corn-powered vehicles. He didn't completely understand it himself.

The big box home improvement center where Bruce bought some of the materials for Barker's kennel—they'd put the local hardware out of business years before—gave Krystal a shiny new six-tine pitchfork to carry in the parade and to keep; in exchange they would get their name on the float. The actual fork she had used to skewer Jeff to the barn floor was being held as evidence by Sheriff Timmers. Bruce and Wanda knew the sheriff well enough to suspect that he intended to keep it as a souvenir and prop for telling the story of his most exciting day on the job ever. Krystal told Big Joyce she'd agree to be on the float if Bruce would be allowed to ride with her, since he'd helped repel Jeff's first rape attempt, and besides she might need him to help to restrain the animals. Big Joyce wasn't real happy about having a man on the float, especially the one who had caved in the side of her Subaru, but Krystal's assertiveness had blossomed through her recent ordeals, and she had become capable of issuing the occasional ultimatum herself. Either Bruce would ride the Women's Defense Club float with her, or she wouldn't do it.

A news item about the upcoming parade in the local weekly newspaper, the Parma Post Intelligencer, listed the parade participants and included a special note about the Women's Defense Club float and who would be on it. Very few of Parma's residents had met Bruce or Krystal, or the now famous animals, so it started quite a buzz around town. The item made the TV news in Jackson and a few other channels around the state, which is how Bruce learned he would be riding the float when he caught the eleven o'clock news on the little shop office TV before he collapsed onto the roll-out after a long day on the tractor.

He called Krystal the next day from the cab of the tractor. He had to yell above the engine roar. "What do you mean I'm riding Big Joyce's float?! Did it ever occur to you that I might not want to? Why didn't you ask me?"

"I just want to give you the credit you deserve," she said. "Besides, I might need some help with them animals, and I want everybody to know how cool you are."

"I'm definitely not cool, and I've had all the publicity I want. Please don't make me do this." Bruce was jolted by the embarassing thought of Alice seeing him in the news yet again. Then he guessed wrongly that probably it wouldn't make the news all the way up in Bay City. Alice had seen it already.

"It's already been in the paper. I had to fight Big Joyce to get you on, and if you love me you'll do it."

"Who said anything about love?" Bruce yelled above the engine noise.

"Call it what you want, but if you ain't doing it, we ain't doing it."

It was the ultimate ultimatum; Bruce was well and truly pussy-whipped, and responded smartly to the threat of withdrawal, although he might regret missing his chance to reduce the complexity of his romantic entanglements. The irony of being bribed with sex to ride on the Women's Defense Club float only occurred to him later as he told the story to Miguel during a field lunch in Miguel's multicolored rust bucket Impala. Miguel spattered the inside of the windshield with a little well chewed ham salad on hearing the news, and he passed the story to the boss at the first opportunity.

All of which is why, when the Memorial parade day came, the sidewalks and streets of Parma were more jammed than usual with paraders and onlookers ready to cheer and whoop for their friends and family, and especially for the feisty new girl in town with the pitchfork. It was a lovely warm morning with a refreshing breeze, but with the promise of heat, humidity, and a stiff wind later. The weather was supposed to hold for the parade though; no thunderstorms or tornado watches were expected until well into the afternoon.

The citizens were in a festive mood and the weather gave them something to talk about: "Hot enough for ya?"

"Praise Jesus for the breeze!"

"You think it'll rain?"

"Garden's in. Let it pour," were staples of the conversation at the side of the street.

So were, "I come to see that gal with the pitchfork," and, "Me too, and that goddamn ear-eatin' dawg."

As the breeze began to pick up the parade animals got jumpy. The horses got all wired up and prancy, and they put more apples on the road than usual, a lot of them jettisoned before their time and thus not fully dehydrated or easily forked. Exceptionally juicy, high colonic, still-green horse fruit splattered the pavement after the well formed road apples had dropped on the first block of the parade route. Luckily the horses came last and no one had to march in their semi-solid exhaust. One onlooker nodded toward the mess and said, "A couple a days ago that was a bucket a water and a bale a hay—worth four bucks. Now it ain't no different from what we get from Washington."

Doc Voekle gave Bob Barker a little acepromazine tranquilizer for the event. Actually, he gave it to Wanda, who gave it to Krystal, who packed it into a bit of goat cheese curd before letting Barker wolf it down. Sadam got a little too; Wanda mixed a small measure of the medicated granules into his feed. So when the parade was assembling on a residential side street just south of downtown Parma, Sadam stayed bedded down and sleepy in his little patch of straw in the front of the float, while Bob Barker sat tied to the back rack of the hay wagon, panting and looking alert, but absorbing the sights with a good deal more equanimity than was his normal undrugged nature.

Krystal stood by the dog, scratching his ears with one hand, holding the new pitchfork in the other, handle on the wagon floor, tines skyward, looking like American Gothic gone badly awry. The label on the pitchfork indicated that it was a professional model. Krystal figured that the high quality designation was aimed at her as a paid manure forker since few women ever went pro at man forking, although she was making a bundle from her singular moment in the man-forking biz. She wondered briefly what distinguished the professional manure slinging tool in her hand from an amateur model, then remembered to warn the bicyclists swarming behind her to keep their distance from the dog.

Miguel drove the tow vehicle, which was Vander Koop Farms, Inc.'s oldest tractor, a 1939 Model HN John Deere row crop tractor with a single front tire, like a big green tricycle. Ray was at the parade assembly site to start the tractor, which was done by spinning the flywheel by hand. The ten horsepower, two-cylinder engine came to life with a distinctive, hesitating then quickening pop-pop-pop-pop that thrills the heart of every old farmer who can remember the Model H series from their youth, which is to say all of them. Distinct puffs of black exhaust issued from the stack with each cylinder firing.

The wind was coming from behind the float, causing the billy goat stench to be blown toward the tractor. Consequently, Ray evacuated the area for the downtown heart of the parade route as soon as he got the tractor running. He didn't really want his buddies to see him with the float anyway. On the tractor seat, Miguel was anxious to get moving so he could turn the corner onto Main and get the wind in his favor. Bruce of course didn't mind the smell, and sat on a straw bale next to Sadam, scratching the goat's shaggy neck and stroking his stained beard; the same beard that Sadam habitually urinated on to increase his powerful scent.

Big Joyce was at the center of the hay wagon seated on a small throne built of plywood by the women in her self defense group. It was painted flat black with white silhouettes of women kicking and punching attackers. This year the throne painting had been revised to include a woman spearing a man with a pitchfork. Big Joyce wore her karate outfit with the black belt she had earned when she weighed a hundred pounds less, and a Brunhilde-style horned helmet over her dyed, short cropped, tightly permed, brassy auburn hair, prompting a few onlookers to comment that the helmet was redundant. She kept one hand on a large plywood sword, point pressed to the wagon bed. Then, when the parade finally got moving, Big Joyce waved to the crowd with her free hand, pausing frequently to toss hard candies to women along the route, and to adjust and re-adjust her way-too-tight karate tunic. She tried to smile, but it was nearly impossible for her to raise the corners of her mouth through the deep facial grimace caused by the goat stink. She'd never before experienced the billy goat odor at close range, and she found it overpowering.

Bruce watched her face redden and a lurching suppressed gag reflex periodically ripple through her flesh. He also worked to strangle his own convulsions, only his were of laughter. Between dry heaves, the large horned woman sent Bruce a full ration of disgusted looks as she watched him stroke the odiferous goat. The crowd did not share Bruce's and Big Joyce's restraint; they both laughed and gagged freely as the float passed.

Krystal had grown tolerant of the smell, but like Big Joyce found that with both hands occupied—one hand on Bob Barker's collar and the other holding the pitchfork—she couldn't really wave at all. She could pump the pitchfork into the air in a celebratory way, but that seemed a little too triumphant, so she let go of Bob Barker and waved with her free hand.

A lone thunderhead began to darken the southwest sky several hours ahead of schedule. They were passing under the one stop light in town at Main and Maple when lightning caused a rumble loud enough to be heard over the cacophonous parade. Bob Barker snapped to attention and began barking—the tranquilizer apparently wearing off. A teenage boy weaving and winding with the decorated bicycle contingent rose to the challenge presented by the fearsome beast and circled close to the wagon. Bob Barker lunged and growled, fangs bared. Krystal yelled, "No!" which worked the first time, but the next time the kid circled close Barker heaved himself through a gap between the boards of the hay wagon's rear rack—the rack to which he was tied on a short leash.

The leash and spiky choke collar functioned as a hanging noose. Bob Barker's hind feet barely touched the ground as he struggled madly to breathe. Before Bruce could react, mesmerized as he was by his goat-stroking job, Miguel, fully attentive and raised on Mexican streets where dog smarts were required, cut the throttle, jumped off the moving tractor, and sprinted to Barker's aid. He muzzled the flailing dog with one hand and lifted him with the other while Krystal quickly untied the leash. Miguel returned Barker safely to the wagon bed amid cheers from the crowd, cheers that sounded as if they came from a group of people with allergic sinusitis, and accompanied by minimal applause, since most people were using at least two fingers to pinch their nose. One of the exceptions was a kid who clapped wildly and whistled through his fingers after he had stuffed hard candies into both nostrils.

The tractor had continued moving slowly, though temporarily driverless, during Miguel's heroic deed. Bruce let go of Sadam and fairly flew off the wagon, then scrambled up the back of the tractor and into the driver's seat where the only familiar control was the steering wheel. He kept the tractor creeping straight ahead through the downtown crowd for thirty seconds, which it probably would have done on its own. After Miguel accomplished his canine heroics, he sprinted back to the tractor and followed Bruce's scrambling route up the back of the old machine. As Miguel arrived back at the tractor seat, Bruce vaulted forward and out of the cockpit, brushing the deep tread of the slowly turning rear tire with his jeans, nearly getting himself run over as he landed, and then jogged back to the float and gracefully jumped aboard. Those who saw it judged Miguel and Bruce to be both brave and stupid, but it all looked a little like a circus act designed to delight and horrify the crowd.

As Bruce arrived back on the wagon he heard a child's voice from the thick, flag-waving, nose-holding crowd of amazed onlookers: "Daddy!" screamed Josie.

Josie and Mikey ran toward the wagon. Alice let go of her nose and snatched them back from the rolling tires and the dangerous animals. Bruce was nearly speechless to see them. He beamed and said their names, but he dared not leave his billy goat tending duty until the end of the parade. Wanda was just one storefront further along the route and saw what was happening. She trotted to the wagon and jumped on. "I'll take over. Go see your kids," she said. Bruce wished she hadn't done that, since he had no idea what to say to Alice. He knew he looked ridiculous on the float and smelled worse. Alice would be merciless. The last time he saw her he had been afflicted with a nasty case of poison ivy and a puking hangover—and now this. There was no chance that he could maintain even a shred of dignity. Then again, he wasn't sure he wanted to go home yet anyway. He missed his kids, but he hadn't had this much sex since he and Alice were in college. Plus he still wanted to maintain the illusion—or delusion, he wasn't sure which—that he was on some sort of quest to learn where food comes from.

Mikey hugged his dad's leg while Josie hugged his waist with one arm, the other on nose duty. Alice cupped her hand over her face, tears rolling down her cheeks, half laughing, half crying. "Jesus, you stink," she said.

"That ain't a nice thing to say about Jesus." Bruce forced a small laugh at his small joke. "Anyway, I kinda like it. Good thing, cause it doesn't wash off that easy." He was trying his best to accommodate Alice's tone.

"I'm filing for divorce," she said.

"I was afraid of that." He was surprised that tears suddenly welled up. Without letting go of the kids, he blotted his eyes with the shoulders of his 'Get your Goat' T-shirt. "When can we talk?"

"Call me tonight after I get the kids in bed—say about ten. I'd hoped we might go to lunch, but you can't go in a restaurant smelling like that."

"You haven't been to Martha's Kitchen," he said, attempting to lighten things up. "Anyway, we're having a big barbecue and a town party at Ray's this afternoon. I'll get cleaned up. I'm sure Ray would love it if you came." He looked at his kids and didn't want to let go of them. "How does a big farm picnic with a band sound, kids? And there's a swingset!"

Bruce was surprised that Mikey and Josie seemed less than enthusiastic. The friction between Alice and him had apparently made the children unsure. "It sounds okay," said Josie in a soft voice. Mikey looked at his sister and nodded.

Alice considered the offer. She thought about putting the kids back in the car and having to buy them another fast food meal on the way back to Bay City, where they would likely spend the rest of the day in front of the TV unless she forced them out the door. She was confused about what was best for the kids. She saw that Bruce seemed glad to see her, that he was upset about the divorce. "I might . . . we'll see," she said.

CHAPTER 18

For the fifth year running, Ray hired Delbert Delmore—everybody called him Farmer Del—a colorful character from up near Grand Rapids who ran a eighty-brood cow Aberdeen-Angus beef and breeding stock operation. His job was to barbecue beef and play recorded blues during the band breaks at Ray and Deb's annual Memorial Day bash. Over the years Del had made some friends down in Parma, so he enjoyed the job, but it was a side business for him. Ray hired Farmer Del as much for the personality and music he brought to the party as for the delicious beef he cooked.

With the planting done, it was a good time for a crop farmer like Ray to relax and throw a bash; not so good for Farmer Del who had a hundred acres of hay to bale in the next month using marginal old equipment that was prone to break down at just the wrong moments. So Del was a little preoccupied due to twenty acres of alfalfa hay laying cut and windrowed and ready to bale in the field, and he didn't want it rained on. Wet hay can't be baled until it re-dries, or it will rot, and may even spontaneously combust. When cut alfalfa finally dries after being rained on, many of the leaves will have fallen off, and the hay will have lost much of its nutritional value. Cattle will eat moldy, stemmy hay if they're hungry, but poor nutrition means slower gains, which of course means lower profits. So Del was wishing he hadn't made the commitment to cook beef for Ray for the little money that was in it. His antsyness expressed itself as inattention and distractibility, the latter split between cloud watching, chatting up the more attractive women of Parma—fancy heifers he called them—drinking beer, and looking for a chance to slip behind the barn for a few tokes.

But summer wasn't all fun and relaxation for Ray. He had to keep track of plant diseases, infestations of weeds and bugs, and tend to any irrigation needs—most of which he could do nothing about anyway, since ninety-five percent of his corn ground didn't have a well or stream nearby. And he did still have to spray the Hoedown-Ready corn and soybeans with the Hoedown herbicide that the seeds, produced by the same corporation, are genetically engineered to resist. But if the growing season went well—and so far it looked pretty good—there wasn't much else to do for the next few months except mow the grass, tend the backyard vegetable garden, and flirt with the waitresses down at Martha's.

Ray did plan to make a summer project of building a screened-in gazebo with a hot tub behind the garden in the back corner of his lawn where it butted up against the field corn. He liked the idea of a cold beer and a hot soak with Deb while they listened to the corn grow on a hot July evening—sort of a middle-aged version of watching the midnight submarine races out at the Thornapple Lake boat launch like they'd done when they were high school sweethearts. But for now, he was focused on celebrating the start of summer. Half the town was invited, and it looked like most of them showed up.

While the bash was getting underway, Wanda and Krystal took Sadam and Bob Barker back to Nanny Gate in Wanda's truck. Miguel drove the antique John Deere with the hay wagon back from the parade to Ray's backyard. The wagon and a few straw bales were then pressed into duty as a stage for the local bluegrass band, The Parmones. The lingering whiffs of billy goat disturbed the band and the few fans who liked to get right up close and touch the stage. The band members themselves had passed the point some decades earlier when young fans were anxious to get their hands directly on them, but the persistent goat aroma repelled the crowd further from the stage than usual.

The years had only improved The Parmones' music though, and some people thought they played their most heartfelt set ever. Perhaps this was because of the earthy caprine bass note in the atmosphere, or maybe because tornado weather sharpens the senses, or maybe the reasons why a band puts on an uncharacteristically great show are magical. Probably it was because the fiddler and the banjo player had been laid off over the winter when the car parts manufacturer that had employed them went belly up, so they spent a lot more time practicing, and the hard-times bluegrass lyrics came straight from the heart.

Back at the shop, Bruce used up all the hot water taking a twenty-minute shower; he lathered and scrubbed three times over and used a stiff brush on his fingernails. After that, only the most sensitive noses could sniff him out from more than a body length away. But inside that circle the residual billy goat pheromones were not subtle—intrusive and troubling as a bass solo. Only Wanda felt the urge to get close to him, which didn't help with his need to have an important conversation with Alice. Mikey and Josie and Ishkabibble found each other and played fetch with a tennis ball. They met other kids and played on the swing set that Deb had bought for the hoped-for grand children who didn't seem to be coming. Deb was happy to see it getting some use, and Alice was proud to see how easily Mikey and Josie made friends. Alice thought about how much the kids would enjoy a dog like Ishy. Bruce excused himself from Wanda and found Alice at the edge of the crowd. "I didn't expect you to come, but I'm glad you did," he said.

"You smell like something came on *you*," she said. "Anyway, I did it for the kids."

"Doc Voekle says it's caproic acid—essence of billy goat. I used half a bar of soap in the shower, but it doesn't come off that easy." Bruce raised his eyes from the ground and glanced at Alice, his head still hanging. "But I'm guessing you're probably not here to tell me how I smell."

"You're right. I'll try to tell you straight: most of me is glad you're gone, but a little part of me wishes you'd made at least a little effort to come back.

Honestly, there wasn't much chance I'd have taken you. Maybe I'd just like the chance to reject you back, just to get even." Alice paused, "What the hell—why should I wait?" She let it out, "Screw you!—don't come home!" She looked down and scuffed the grass with her running shoe. Bruce followed her gaze and was reminded what great legs she had. Alice crossed her arms. "The kids really miss you," she added.

Bruce said, "I still care about you a lot, but I don't think I could come home even if you said you'd have me. It's been a long time since you were in love with me. I feel like a dog that broke his chain and I can't make myself come home right now. I can't work for the goddamned coal plant anymore, and I can't live with a woman who doesn't love me. I wasn't put on this earth just to be tolerated. I'm doing better here." Bruce felt that he'd articulated his position rather well, considering his own words were surprising him.

"Jeeze that's just great that you're doing better, Bruce. I'm really happy for you," Alice said with all the sarcasm she could muster. "And you know what, mister? I'm a lot happier without you too!" She slugged at her beer. Swallowing soothed the lump in her throat and calmed her racing heart while she came around to the big question. "So, mister happy man, what are we going to do about the kids?"

"Christ, I know. It's the worst part. I think they could visit me at Wanda's this summer, I'm sure they'd like the farm, but then I don't know. I want to stay and help get the corn in this fall, but after that I just don't know."

"What do you mean you just don't know? You're just going to keep running? What's going on in your head?" Alice swiveled away and then turned back. She stamped her foot and squealed softly. "You're such an asshole," she said, almost whispering to the ground, doing her best not to have an emotional breakdown in public.

"I'm learning first hand where food comes from—most of the world's calories come from the corn and soybeans we're growing. I'm seeing the future. I'm close to something important here, and it's important for me to understand it." Bruce's little speech seemed defensive to himself, and he sensed that it seemed trivial to Alice. But in this rare moment of considering his motivation he wasn't sure of his own sincerity. He was having trouble distinguishing between a solid rationale and a self-serving rationalization.

And he had no idea how to move history backwards, to transform industrial farms into small farms that grew real food and could support families, or how to move city people back to the land and teach them all the skills a farmer has to know. "And I don't like what I'm seeing," he said. "There has to be a better way."

"And so you walk away from your kids in a quest for the perfect food source? You've got to be the biggest damn jerk on the planet. You want to find out where your fricking food comes from?—who gives a shit?! Where do you think kids come from?! Parents, goddammit! They need parents! Two parents! I just can't believe I ever loved you." She stumped away in tears, gathered the kids, and left.

Ray saw her and was going to introduce himself, but caught her wet red eyes and angry gait from a distance, and thought better. He'd ask Bruce about it later.

Wanda approached Bruce, "How'd that go?"

"Shitty. Is there is a good way to break up?"

"You should feel shitty; you've got kids. And I feel like it's partly my fault."

"You *are* making it easier—and I thank you for that. But it's not your fault." Bruce sipped his beer and changed the subject. "Did you guys get the critters back to the farm okay?"

"Yup we did. Sadam just staggered into his pen and bedded down. He's still high I think. But that damn dog, he's back to fully wired. Good thing you barred those windows. That one's gotta stay in jail. He's a lifer I think."

Meanwhile Miguel had arrived at the party without Doris and was looking for Krystal, who'd been flirting with Farmer Del over by his big cooker.

"So how do you know when your meat's ready?" Krystal asked.

"Darlin' if you don't know by now, I can't help you." He laughed and raised the steel lid on the big black rotisserie. "Actually, you press it like this," he said as he poked a finger into a large chunk of beef round, browned and mostly covered by a rind of dripping fat. "When it starts to get firm, it's ready. It's about like men, only you can use your teeth."

Miguel joined the conversation just as Del and Krystal shuffled to the other end of the cooker to avoid the shifting smoke. Miguel stayed where they'd been; he liked the smell of the barbeque smoke when it hung up in his thick black hair—even better than the smoked sucker when it snagged up there.

Farmer Del greeted Miguel as an old friend, "Pickin up a cover scent for the hooch, Miguel?"

"Never touch the stuff no more, Delfino." Miguel liked to Latinize names even when there wasn't a Mexican name to match. "You still going light on the weed killer in the back forty?" he asked.

"Not really, but the damn sprayer gets clogged up sometimes for no good reason. You wouldn't believe the shit that comes up in the spots it misses. Weeds the size of Christmas trees. Sometimes I just got to burn em."

"A little bit at a time rolled up in paper, eh?"

"I can help you burn some a that," Krystal caught on.

"You got too much people here to get all red-eye high," said Miguel.

"They think I'm half crazy anyway," said Krystal. "You got some with you, Farmer Del?"

"I always come loaded, darlin. Shall we?" Del made an inviting gesture with the hook of his arm and stepped toward the old barn.

"We shall," said Krystal, taking his arm, and added, "You coming Miguel?"

"No way Jose. I ain't ready to get sent back to Mexico just yet. Got to make more American pesos before I go. Anyhow, Sheriff Timmers is here. Be careful, man."

They wandered toward the back of the big lawn, a practiced casualness and goofy nonchalantality about their gait and hand gestures. Wanda spotted them and read the over-acted innocence from a distance. She took Bruce's hand, "Come on Brucie, we're going to blow away your sorrows." They caught up with the sauntering escapees. "Hey Farmer Del! Hi ho the dairy-o!"

"Wanda the Goat Lady! Dairy-o, fairy-o—ain't getting me around no herd of cows with four tits I gotta pull twice a day."

"Machines, Del. Milking machines—great invention."

"It's still more work than I ever want to think about. I turn my eighty black mamas out to pasture, the rain falls, the sun shines, the grass grows, the babies suck on tits like nature intended, and I sleep till I want to get up—it's fat city."

"Farming's nothing but a long rock in the old chair, eh? You headed behind the barn?"

"Thought we might have us a little appetizer," he said.

"As I remember that works pretty well. What did you eat last year?—a gallon of potato salad and the whole darn rhubarb pie I brought—not to mention enough beef to feed a third world nation," said Wanda.

"My truck rides better when I flex the springs a little. Takes a big man to get a smooth ride out of an F350." Del crouched and did a gliding moonwalk for a few steps, looking remarkably agile for a forty-something with farmer's back and Dunlop syndrome.

"You haven't changed," Wanda laughed. "Hey, Del, I want you to meet Bruce—Bruce Dinkle, he's the other new guy in town besides Krystal. He's kind of a locavore on the lam."

"Smells like a locavore on the goat—just kidding, Bruce—sort of. The hell's a locavore?"

Wanda explained the idea while Bruce nodded agreement, adding, "Just trying to live responsibly on the planet." He sensed his earnestness was not in tune with the party mood, but then neither was his heart after his talk with Alice.

"Well, I'm about to set fire to a little home-grown irresponsibility. It makes a nice contrast with barbecued responsible beef and Wanda's responsible rhubarb pie."

"Everything goes with my pie," said Wanda, smiling broadly.

Del raised his eyebrows and was momentarily speechless. He reached in his shirt pocket for the joint and lit it as they arrived at the paddock behind the old barn. As it made its first circle of the group, Deb's horse Bogart came to the fence. Del offered the old gelding a hit. "Why the long face, dude?" he asked. The horse nickered and Del tried to hold the smoke against a laugh, which was impossible. The joint circled the group a few times and they'd just heeled the roach into the sod when Deb came around the end of the barn.

"Hey Delbert, I hope you're not smoking dope," she said. "This isn't Michigan State twenty years ago. Sheriff Timmers is here and he will bust you if he sees it. Anyway, please don't do it. We don't need any more sad stories like Miguel's around here." She lightened her scolding by adding, "Plus, I won't be able to keep you guys off the dessert table."

"Hey Deb. You got it. Hate to have to shoot the sheriff. Meat ought to be about ready anyway. I'll see if we can head off the rhubarb pie stampede with some juicy Angus beef. It should slow them down a little."

"You do that. You didn't feed the butt to Bogart, I hope."

"The roach? Nope, no dope to Bogart. We did not Bogart that joint."

So while continuing to assess the western sky and the local heifers, and after sucking down a couple of quick beers and lifting his spirits with a little home-grown, he unloaded the beef from the turning spits a little sooner than usual, hoping that he might still get some baling done when he got back to the farm, since nothing good was going to come from hanging around Ray and Deb's. Either his hay was going to get rained on or his libido would—probably both.

Despite the shortened spit time, there was not much risk associated with the bloody rare beef. It had never been on antibiotics and had been grass-flushed on pasture for a week before slaughter, so almost no chance of a bad *E. coli*. He forked the first roast onto a big oak cutting board and flashed his long carving knife over the steel a dozen times in a few seconds. The lightning strokes of the blade toward the hilt of the honing steel looked like an excellent way to fillet an arm, but the move was practiced and no blood was shed. The glint of the sun on the blade and the unmistakable raspy steel-on-steel sound were all the dinner bell necessary to bring the nearest twenty people to the serving table.

The Parmones got down off the hay wagon and Farmer Del took a few seconds to cue up the tunes he had planned to go down with the food: Coco Taylor singing "Wang Dang Doodle," the "Hungry Women Blues" from Sapphire and the Uppity Blues Women, "Red Beans" from Professor Longhair, Barbecue Bob singing "Barbecue Blues", "Gimme a Pigs Foot and a Bottle of Beer" by Betsy Smith, and "Take out the Squeal (If You Want a Meal)" by Earl Jackson. It was a masterful blend of blues, beef, and beer. Ray had put out two iced kegs of Bell's Oberon, a delectable summer wheat ale brewed just down the road in Kalamazoo.

The beef was choice Black Angus and was steak-tartar quality; everybody who liked their red meat truly red thought the taste and tenderness were exceptional. Those who liked it more done got the heels. Del served the medium-and-beyond eaters silently, considering them dim-witted ciphers, figuring that anybody who wouldn't tolerate a little blood with their beef wasn't worthy of their meat. He wasn't much of a reader, certainly not of modern poetry, but the phrase—*worthy of our meat*—popped into his head without ever having read Wendell Berry's prayer-poem asking for just such worthiness. And while the poet-farmer and the farmer-chef-blues disc jockey might have had different criteria for what made a human carnivore worthy of their meat, both would argue for the virtue of being intimate with your meat while it was alive and acknowledging that it died for you. Who could waste meat that died for you? To Farmer Del—at heart a sentimental man who loved his cows—a little red juice running down one's chin was simply a mute admission that we are fellow animals and thanks are due. Others, of course—the vegetarians and those of delicate sensibility—thought it was gross.

Wanda and Krystal huddled with Bruce and Miguel and juggled plates of food and beer glasses while compelled by the music to bounce in place as they devoured the delicious beef with a selection of baked beans and salads: potato, pasta, green—and green Jell-O with marshmallows. Miguel didn't appear to be suffering for his lack of a buzz. Bruce forced himself to bounce to the beat along with his friends, and so appeared oddly unaffected by the emotional interchange with Alice. But his natural distance from his deeper emotions was failing. He wasn't fully engaged with the pleasant sensations of good food, his new friends, and multiple intoxicants. Michigan beef, Michigan potato salad, Michigan beer, Michigan weed: he should have been in locavore heaven.

Ray approached the stoned eaters accompanied by a tall well-dressed thirtyish man and a dark-haired, olive-skinned woman of startling beauty. Miguel recognized Ray's commodities-broker son and city-girl advertising designer daughter-in-law. She used her husband's arm to steady herself as she teetered across the deep green lawn in peek-a-boo toed, sling-back wedges. She wore beautifully tailored, olive drab, linen safari shorts and a matching jacket over a clingy silk designer blouse in a color the manufacturer called African Sunrise. Bruce would have called it orange, but was mostly straining for a glimpse of the curvy loveliness behind her third unfastened button. Her snake-skin purse matched her shoes; the jade and gold earrings matched her necklace, and there was more gold at her wrists. Alarming red lipstick matched her fingernails and toes. All men within eyeshot were functionally lobotomized and drifted toward her unconsciously.

Ray Jr. wore Ray Ban Wayfarers, a monogrammed white oxford cloth button-down dress shirt, designer jeans, and woven leather Italian loafers; no belt, no socks. He'd rolled up his sleeves two starched turns to reveal vacation-tanned health club forearms and a square-faced Cartier wristwatch, the one with the leather band for weekends. His light brown hair was boardroom perfect despite the humid breeze.

Ray Sr. made the introductions all around: "Sonia and Ray, this is Wanda, Krystal, and Bruce." He went around the circle again saying a few words about each person in a display of gracious manners, the likes of which none of them had ever seen from a farmer. Ray Sr. was clearly on his best behavior. The parents were putting the full court press on Ray Jr.; their strategy was to connect him and Sonia to everyone they could in the community, in hopes that relationships might be sparked and they might reconsider the charms of rural life. Since they couldn't imagine what kindred spirit Sonia might find in Parma, they decided to take a shotgun approach in hopes that she might be attracted to the aggregate charm of the village, if not the specific charmers.

"Commodities broker, eh? So tell me what happens to all the stuff we're growing here," asked Bruce, knowing that he already knew at least part of the answer.

"Well, I doubt you want me to list the thousands of things that get made from corn and soybeans."

"Yeah, not the thousands," said Bruce, struggling against his high toward a rational conversation with a straight person, "but I want to hear your version of the big picture."

"Okay—the big picture. Well, let's see, the lion's share, a little less than half the crop, still goes to animal feed for cattle, pigs, and chickens. And a little more than a third goes to industrial processing for everything from ethanol, to latex paint, to compostable bioplastics."

"How much goes just for ethanol?—How much food are we burning up in our cars?"

"I'd say about a quarter of the U.S. crop ends up in gas tanks. But there's a huge by-product—distiller's grains left over from making the ethanol—and that mostly gets fed to cattle."

"How much goes for high-fructose corn syrup?"

"Yeah, sugar . . . well, as I recall, we're successfully fattening up humans in the over-developed world with less than four percent of the crop."

"So how much corn is that?"

"A lot. Let's see, for round numbers, figure the whole U.S. crop this year will be something under twelve-billion bushels. They'd predicted higher, but a hell of a lot of prime Midwestern corn ground in Iowa and Illinois has been underwater for most of the planting season. So the futures price is way up, which means less will go to animal feed, which means higher prices for anything that comes from an animal that gets fed corn—which is all of them, from cows, to catfish, to penned salmon out in the ocean—or any food that has corn by-products in it, which is a big share of everything else. And if the prices of all those things go up, some consumers choose other foods, and so the prices of those other things get pushed up too. But let's see, back to your question, for round numbers on the HFCS, four percent of twelve-billion is what, almost half a billion bushels dedicated to sweetening up darn near everything we eat. At fifty-six pounds per bushel, that's what, about twenty-eight billion pounds of corn. Makes you feel kind of hefty just thinking about it, doesn't it?" Ray Jr. smiled.

"It does. My belt feels suddenly tight." Bruce realized he had a font of knowledge with a calculator in his head right in front of him. "So how about the beans?" he asked.

"Mostly oil. Three quarters of the fat that slides down America's throat comes from soybeans—it's the vegetable fat that's in everything from corn chips to mayonnaise to fried chicken—something like seventeen-billion pounds. But more and more we're burning that for fuel too—biodiesel. But it's been hard to predict where that's going—maybe nowhere. The EPA just said that biodiesel from soy doesn't meet greenhouse gas emissions requirements, so those subsidies may end. Of course the more we burn crops for fuel, the more forests we have to cut down to grow enough to run all those engines *and* feed the six-billion people in the world—*nine* billion by 2050. It's nuts."

"It's not sustainable is it?" asked Bruce, thinking he might corner Ray Jr. on this one.

"I don't know. I mean, for how long? Not forever, that's for sure. The thing is, the way we make food is incredibly efficient in terms of energy use. The big tractors here pull implements that could prepare the average vegetable garden in a few seconds. What's the typical backyard vegetable garden like my dad's, maybe thirty by sixty feet? You have a disk harrow that's thirty feet wide, you go the length of the garden in what, about four seconds? Include a pass with the chisel plow before that, and you've spent, what, maybe ten seconds preparing the ground? Compare that with a rototiller or garden tractor in terms of energy use per acre—let alone labor—and it doesn't come close to the efficiency of the big diesels in big fields. Then you start adding up trips to the store for seed packets, fertilizer, plant sets—all the stuff that we get to the fields by the semi-load—and really, if you look at the economics of it, the only reason to garden is because it makes you happy to eat food you grew yourself."

"And it's better for you," Bruce said confidently.

"Maybe, but I doubt you could measure the difference. You'd be hard pressed to find data that says people who grow their own veggies are healthier than people who eat store-bought veggies. The unhealthy thing is to not eat veggies, and if they're more expensive, like the organic ones, people will eat less of them. Vegetables are already expensive calories; and the organic ones are a lot more expensive. French fries and corn chips are cheap calories. Ask Doc Voekle about that. He knows all about food toxicology and nutrition."

Bruce rifled his brain for data to support his argument. He wondered if it had been only an article of faith. Finally he said, "Yeah, is there anything that guy doesn't know?" and then added, "Well, at least I know home-grown tastes better—I know you can't beat that argument."

"You're right on that one. I wouldn't even try. You can pick riper fruit when it doesn't have to be trucked. I'll take a fresh-picked backyard tomato every time."

Bruce was relieved to win a point. "So, okay, what's going to happen when we run out of oil?"

"You're right on that too. We're screwed. We've got what?—ninety percent of the population living in cities being fed by a small group of old farmers—less than one percent of the population, average age about fifty eight. Did you know that we've got more people in prison than we've got farmers in this country?

Anyway, as the cost of fuel goes up, and it will, we'll have to find new ways to grow all the food, and it will all get more expensive. Petroleum gets used at every step of the process: tilling, planting, spraying, harvesting, drying, transporting, processing, distribution—everything. Even the nitrogen that gets used to fertilize corn—anhydrous ammonia—even that's made from from natural gas.

These days the only people moving to the country just want to live a 'country lifestyle' within driving distance to their job in town. They couldn't grow their own food if they had to. They might have a little vegetable garden, but you'd be hard pressed to find one who still knows how to can a tomato, let alone one who contributes diddlysquat to the general food supply. Gas burners are all they are."

"I didn't expect a Chicago commodities broker to be an environmentalist."

"I don't know that I am. I could rail on against the system that feeds me, but what would we replace it with? I think it's fine that you want to grow your own and buy only local food—personally it would drive me nuts.

I like my green salads in the winter. But the point is that if big agriculture were to suddenly break down and we had to depend on large numbers of people to grow enough for themselves and a few others, there would be mass starvation until the earth got down to a human population it could sustain. I mean it would take that kind of apocalypse to get people to move back to the land in a serious way, lots of people focused on food production. And how are you going to move all those people back to the land when it's all owned by big corporate farms? It would take a revolution—I mean a real violent revolution to get the land back. But I guess revolution is a natural part of an apocalypse."

"So you're agreeing with me that the system we got now isn't sustainable?"

"Yeah, I mean that's pretty clear if you think in terms of present consumption levels of everything, then extrapolate for growing world population, shrinking oil reserves, and American farmland turned into suburban housing developments. Add climate change to that and you've got a recipe for disaster."

"Man, I didn't expect to hear this from a guy who pulled up in a Mercedes."

"You don't get where I am by being stupid. The whole job of being a commodities broker is to look at the future. You don't make money buying and selling crop futures if you can't make predictions."

"So why the hell don't you try to change the future?" Bruce was getting angry at the man's arrogant complacency.

"It's pissin in the wind, Bruce. What am I going to do? Go to third world countries and make them to stop having babies?—actually, Sonia and I give a lot to International Planned Parenthood. But do you think we could get New Yorkers to become subsistence farmers? It's all just human nature working through economics and politics. Everybody wants to minimize work and maximize pleasure in their life. I'm no different."

"But you've got more money than God; why not put it to good use?

"Well I'm not Bill Gates, or even close. But you do know that vaccinating for childhood diseases in the third world means faster population growth, don't you? However, if you educate people, especially women, they'll limit the number of children they have, but more will survive, and they will raise their living standards, so you've just increased demand and consumption, and probably decreased the number of subsistence farmers. So we knock down more of the Amazon to grow more food for all these new consumers, and where are we? You get a four-wheel drive economy, four-wheel drive food production, four-wheel drive health care—everybody jumps in the big human truck until it gets overloaded and stuck in deeper mud. Every time we increase food production—the first green revolution, and the new one based on genetic engineering—the population grows until we once again don't have enough. Right now there is plenty—more people in the world suffer from eating too much than too little—but that won't last. So, Sonia and I enjoy life—plays, sports, concerts, museums, books, a nice place to live, interesting friends—and we're going to ride it out as long as we can."

The smug callousness of the argument flabergasted Bruce. "You might be the most depressing person I've ever talked to."

Sonia piped in, "No . . . no . . . actually, he's a lot of fun for a Democrat."

"I would have guessed Republican."

Ray Jr. said, "Nah, Republicans are about denial. They start with answers and try to make the world fit their ideology. You have to start with questions. Politics is like science, only harder—you have to work without control groups. Not that the Donkeys don't have their delusions, too. Anyway, it's all games. Tilt toward the light when you can, tell the truth when you think you see it, and try to enjoy this life. You're not likely to get another."

"I'll drink to that," said Krystal, raising her glass to the handsome man.

"I don't know how you figure you're tilting toward the light," said Bruce feeling his anger rise. "I'll just drink."

"Me too," said Miguel.

Wanda sipped her beer and said, "I gotta get going. You guys stopping by for some cheese before you head back to Chicago?"

Sonia said, "Yes Wanda, that would be great. Maybe tomorrow afternoon? What was the funny new name for the aged one, Sadam's Pitchfork? I want to try some of that."

Bruce was reeling with frustration. The breakdown with Alice, and now this. Nothing was as simple as he wished it to be. It was plain that mass food production wouldn't be reverting to a human scale anytime soon, at least not without a social and economic cataclysm. If Ray Jr. was right, and he suspected he was, people are incapable of doing the right thing until they are forced, even when the right thing is clear. And the right thing wasn't clear. It was maddening. At least there was still a place in the world for a small goat dairy. As he was thinking this the southwestern horizon was darkening, and Bob Barker was making gravel fly.

CHAPTER 19

W anda headed back to Nanny Gate to supervise the milking and work with some of the developing cheese curds. She told Krystal she could stay on at the party since the new girl Eva Green was working that afternoon. Eva would be a sophomore at Albion College that fall. She showed an interest in cheese making and planned to spend her summer working on the farm. Wanda didn't mind leaving the party—a dark cloud line, still low on the western horizon, suggested that the picnic bash had less than an hour to go anyway. She left Bruce still talking with Ray Junior. He had been doing his best to absorb the commodity trader's take on global food, energy, and population into his mildly intoxicated brain.

Wanda was glad to see Eva's old Honda Civic parked near the milk house and was about to go look for her there. But when she stepped out of her truck she heard the sounds of goat distress—long, panicked bleats—from behind the old barn. She ran across the yard and around the far end of the barn. As she passed Bob Barker's kennel she saw a deep dog hole in the gravel; Barker had tunneled all the way under the buried fence.

She shifted gears into a sprint. She found Barker at the back of the grassy paddock chasing the young stock. From a distance she could see that several of the small goats were on the ground and not moving. Even from that distance she could see blood on the white ones. Ishkabibble ran to the edge of the paddock and barked, but didn't dare challenge the killer. The big dog kept the fenced herd running and scattering. When they would regroup, he would run at them again. He dove for the haunch of any goat who slowed to his loping pace, bringing it down easily, then diving for its neck and shaking the life out of it before going on to kill another. Wanda screamed, "God damn it!" as she pounded for the house. The sky was darkening rapidly. Thunder rumbled in the distance.

She banged through the doors to the front closet where she stored the one rifle she had kept from her father's collection. She flew out the door with it, slamming a clip of Remington .225 magnum cartridges into the underside of the stock. She worked the bolt and chambered a round while still running, reached the top of the small hill at the side of the barn, dropped and skidded into a sitting position, propped her left elbow on her knee, and brought the walnut stock hard against her right shoulder. The dog and the remaining goats were all the way at the back of the paddock, close to a hundred yards from where she sat—the distance at which she had sighted-in the rifle the last time she'd shot it, years before. She found the dog in the scope and waited for a clear shot. With the high-powered optics she could see his lolling tongue, see strings of blood tinged saliva hanging from his mouth. There were wide red smears on his face. He was panting and there was a dog smile on his face.

Bob Barker paused briefly in his marauding; he watched the flock regather—now broadside and in the clear. She put the crosshairs in the center of his chest and squeezed. Nothing. The safety, dammit, click the safety. She glanced away from the scope and down at the breach to find the safety and click it off. In that second Barker resumed his chase; he was in full charge and about to sink his fangs into the tender leg of yet another of the young goats. Ishy continued to bark wildly. Wanda rushed the shot. Barker stopped, surprised by the sound and the puff of dirt where the bullet struck the ground just beyond him. The report bounced off the line of trees at the back of the farm. He turned to look in the direction of the echo. Wanda racked another cartridge into the chamber. The ejected brass shell case smoked in the grass next to her hip.

Barker now faced directly away from her, not an acceptable shot at an animal you intended to eat, but it would do just fine for this. A Texas heart shot, she'd once heard her dad call it. No goats in the way. She steadied the crosshairs on the asterisk of his anus and squeezed. The bullet traveled the length of the big dog at four thousand feet per second, mushrooming as it ripped through his guts, his liver, a bit of his lung, the base of his heart, the arch of his aorta, and out through his windpipe with a spray of blood. He hit the ground instantly, gone by the time he arrived there. Ishy ran to the dead dog and continued barking.

Eva heard the shots and came running from the milkhouse. Wanda dropped the rifle and sat holding her knees to her face, crying and cursing. She struggled to compose herself.

"Eva, Eva . . . god damn that dog!" she sobbed. "We have to call Doc Voekle."

Wanda got the vet on her cell and told him to hurry. The two women jumped the fence into the paddock and ran to help the injured goats. It was worse than Wanda had thought. Barker had started inside the barn. There were seven dead inside and four more outside. Of the nineteen still alive, it was hard to tell which were stained with their own blood, and which with the blood of their slaughtered penmates. The survivors were agitated and hard to approach. Wanda decided to clear the inside pen of casualties, then herd the others into the barn before the storm hit. She and Eva sobbed as they pulled the dead goats outside and threw them over the fence. They ran to the back of the paddock again and collected the dead ones there. Flies and yellow jackets had already discovered the blood that stained the grass around the carcasses. The storm was getting closer, the wind rising. Ishy licked at the puddle of blood around Barker. Wanda dragged two of the dead, one with each arm, to the fence and threw them over onto the pile. Eva cradled the dead goats in her arms as she carried them one at a time to the pile. Eleven.

They herded most of the survivors into the barn and left Bob Barker cooling under the darkening sky. The storm had organized and gathered itself into an ominous, rumbling, greenish-blue-black wall cloud during its unobstructed flight over Lake Michigan. The first jagged bolt of lightning streaked to the high ground on the far side of the river. There was less than a second delay before a loud crack and earth shaking thunder. Water began to fall, first widely-spaced grape-sized hailstones that appeared to jump from the ground like popcorn and sounded like hammers on the steel barn roof high above them. Then a foggy gray curtain flowed across the pastures. Suddenly it was pouring rain and hailstones, then for a minute only hailstones the size of golf balls pounded the roof, the sound almost deafening, hailstones jumping from the grass, hailstones piling up below the eaves, more lightening and crashing thunder, now pouring rain, a magnificent summer deluge, washing the blood from the grass and from the dead, carrying life's red fluid back into the earth.

Two wounded goats remained outside. The hail subsided. The women ran out into the downpour to retrieve the last two and were instantly soaked to the skin. Wanda took a late-falling ice ball to the forehead and was bleeding. Rain water drained from her thick auburn hair and thinned the blood oozing from the bluish-red goose egg on her forehead. The confluence of blood and water flowed into a pale red streak down the central valley of the soaked T-shirt plastered to her chest that said: "Animal Farms: Where Manure is Piled before it Hits the Fan." As the roof-hammering din subsided, a faint wail rose above the sound of trees bending and flailing in the storm and the white noise of wind-whipped rain hitting the old barn. It was the tornado siren in Parma. "Don't worry about it," Wanda said.

They caught each of the young goats in turn, examining them for tooth punctures and lacerations. It became apparent that few of the surviving goats had been wounded. For the most part, if he caught them, he killed them. There were only three that had felt the big dog's teeth and still managed to escape. Wanda lifted them over the side of the pen into the barn aisle. She sent Eva to the milkhouse for iodine, and had a moment to herself. It was raining so hard now that Bob Barker was invisible where he lay at the back of the paddock. The faint sound of the siren in Parma persisted. Sadam gave a guttural bleat and raised his head high over the solid wall of his pen. A beautiful walnut-brown iris surrounded his rectangular pupil. He gave her a look she read as defeat. She looked fondly at the old buck. She said, "You couldn't save them, could you boy."

Doc Voekle announced himself from the top of the barn stairs. "Wanda," he yelled, "How bad is it?"

She could not find the strength to raise her voice to answer until he got closer. "Bad for the living, dead for the dead," she finally said when he reached the small wooden gate from the barn aisle into the pen.

"That's it, isn't it? Death is dead for the dead. The rest of us just have to deal with it." He paused and assessed the three injured goats in the aisle. "Got any sort of a surgical suite we could set up? Cosmetic tissue approximation whilst kneeling on these arthritic old knees is getting tough."

She pulled a milking stand into the aisle and opened a small blue tarp to cover the dust and chaff on its platform, then carried a straw bale for him to sit on. One by one Wanda and Eva brought the injured goats to the vet. He cleaned the wounds and gave each a shot of tetanus toxoid and another of a broad spectrum antibiotic. The two more severely injured animals got a small dose of sedative before he numbed the areas around their larger wounds, cleaned and debrided them, and sutured them closed. Wanda admired Doc's sinewy hands as he closed the jagged lacerations with neat rows of silk, laying on surgeons knots with speed and precision, leaving just enough slack to allow for swelling. He left the smaller tooth punctures open to allow any infection to drain. Ishy stood by with her ball, ready to play as soon as Doc was. Bruce and Krystal arrived as they were finishing up.

"I shot your god damned dog," Wanda said matter of factly, avoiding eye contact.

"Oh my God! What happened?! Did he do this?"

"Who left the kennel door open?" Bruce asked.

"Yes, he did this. And nobody left the door open. He dug his way out of that fancy little pen you made, Bruce. You know, this place was pretty nice before you two came around, and I think it will be nice again when you're gone. Let's make that fresh start now. I can't trust a person who would own a beast like that anyway."

"He saved my life," said Krystal, "I couldn't just let them kill him."

"Well I could, and I just did, and now I want you the hell out of here," Wanda said, still unable to make eye contact.

Krystal put her hands over her face and cried.

"Ah, geeze, Wanda, we all agreed that we didn't need concrete for his run. And now he's dead anyway. Can we just try put this behind us," Bruce said, once again failing to appreciate important emotions.

Doc Voekle interrupted, "If I can offer my perspective, you young folks were getting along pretty well before the dog, and even in spite of the dog, and I suspect you'll do even better now that he's gone. Give this a little time." He paused in the process of packing up his black case. "There's a lot of grief here. I think maybe you should consider a memorial service to help work through it. I would even offer to officiate."

"That's a good idea. I could help," said Bruce.

Krystal stopped sobbing. "Would it be for Bob Barker or the goats?" she asked.

"Nobody's praying over that damn dog on my farm," said Wanda.

Doc said, "How about we don't cogitate too much about what we're praying for just yet. I don't think that dog's soul is apt to levitate too far above the ground anyway. Maybe we can start to think more along the lines of remembering what these animals meant to you all, and why we all get so upset when something like this happens." The old vet took on the aura of a sage. It had a calming effect on everyone. The rain slowed to a patter.

"Maybe . . . maybe okay . . . okay," said Wanda.

"I can cook for the wake," offered Bruce. "Does Wednesday night sound alright?"

"If no emergencies spring up, I can do that," said Doc.

"Done," said Bruce. His cell phone rang. "Miguel, what's up? . . . Oh Jesus . . . Oh no . . . Yeah, I'll be right over." He snapped the phone shut.

"What?" asked Krystal. They all looked at Bruce.

"Ray was running around trying to get things under cover before the storm hit. All of a sudden he threw up, and then fell down holding his chest. The ambulance just took him to the hospital in Jackson."

"By God, life looks tenuous today, don't it?" said Doc. "I've got to go see him. He's one of the good ones." Doc mumbled softly to himself as he finished gathering his bottles and instruments into his black case and stainless steel bucket, and was silent as he carried his equipment out of the barn to his truck.

Wanda gave Krystal a brief side-hug. "I didn't mean it," she said with unconvincing sincerity.

Bruce felt suddenly alone. He thought of Alice and his children. He wrapped his arms around the tearful women. "Let's be strong together," he said, "I've had enough coming apart for one day."

CHAPTER 20

D eb held Ray's hand as the siren wailed and the ambulance sped down I-94 headed for the emergency room in Jackson. The morphine was kicking in. Ray had always heard that heart attack pain was like an elephant's foot on your chest, but he thought it felt more like a tractor tire. He'd never tested the weight of an elephant, but his mind flashed to the time when he'd let his little brother Jack run over his foot with a tractor. The ground had been wet and soft, and the twelve-year-old Ray had placed the toe of his high-top canvas basketball shoe strategically between the deep lugs of the big rear tire, so no bones were broken. But the weight of the thing had surprised him, and it hurt a lot, although he didn't let on; he had just grinned and claimed, "It wasn't nothin'." Privately he figured it wasn't worth the quarter, but it sort of paid off in little brother adulation in the short term, until Jack decided to try it too. Jack went and stuck his little foot right under the tire lug and broke three bones.

"Whose darn fool idea was that?" their father had said, looking into the backseat while driving too fast to the hospital.

Ray was near tears and took the rap: "I did it a few weeks ago, Dad, but I didn't know Jack was going to do it. I didn't even see him stick his foot under there."

"Well now you went and got your little brother's foot broke. If brains was dynamite, you two couldn't blow your nose," the old man had said.

Ray figured that was the first time he'd ever been inside a hospital, forgetting he'd been born in one—the same one he was headed to now. Since then he'd been back to the hospital for the births of his own kids and to be with his parents in their final illnesses, a heart attack in his dad's case, colon cancer for his mom, but he hadn't been there for himself since they cut his umbilical cord. It wasn't that he hated hospitals or doctors or anything, he just didn't need them. Healthy as a horse. His eyes were closed and he looked almost relaxed on the stretcher even as the medic worked to start an IV and wire him to the electrocardiogram machine. Ray lifted the oxygen mask from his mouth, "Good play up till now, eh Mrs. Lincoln?" he whispered.

Deb squeezed back a tear and blotted her eye with her shoulder as she patted the big hand she held so tightly in hers.

The medic said, "Just lie still Mr. Vander Koop. Don't try to talk."

Ray waited a minute before lifting the mask again and saying to the medic, "Did I ever tell you how much I love this woman?" Deb leaned down and kissed his forehead.

"I can see that, Mr. Vander Koop. Please just lie still and keep your mask on, sir. You need to conserve your strength. I want you to have a chance to love her for a lot more years."

Deb stared at the green lines tracing across the monitor above her husband. She didn't know what they meant. The medic said that all the data was radioed straight to the emergency room docs. They would be ready for him.

Ray lay still for a few moments, his eyes closed, then lifted the mask again and said, "Ray" he said. "Call me Ray. I'm a farmer." He paused. "Crops is all in. We did the big party. Looks like I get the summer off."

"Shhhshhh," Deb gently attempted to quiet him, then after a few moments added, "Good thing Ray Jr. is here for the weekend. We're going to need him."

"I bet he didn't bring no work clothes," Ray said with a faint smile.

"He can't fill your boots," she said, "but at least they fit him."

The ambulance screamed up the exit ramp and into town. Traffic parted. They ran every red light and stop sign. Ray appeared to doze off. Deb looked up at the screen. The green lines suddenly looked chaotic. She folded into herself, "No, no, no," she squealed and then began to pray under her breath.

"We're here," the medic said.

The medics off-loaded Ray in a flash and rushed him at a dead run through the big doors and into the emergency room where the code team was waiting. A medic applied the metal paddles to his big chest and shouted "Clear!" while the gurney was still rolling toward a curtained space. Ray bounced on the table. The line on the green screen resumed rhythmic highs and lows; the peaks and valleys suddenly looked orderly. People in pastel colored scrubs surrounded him. The ER staff rushed to prep him for the cardiac cath lab, medicating his pain to zero, cutting off his clothes, starting a second IV line, adding leads to the EKG, surgically preparing the site in his groin where a catheter to would be threaded up his femoral artery to his heart. In less than ten minutes he was ready to go.

After watching the flurry of activity, Deb could only wait. The atmosphere was whispers and discretion. Finally the cardiologist appeared in the waiting area. He showed her the images of her husband's heart. It was a big heart like she knew it would be. The doctor said the size was normal for a man his size, but he pointed to places where the blood flowing through Ray's coronary arteries was squeezed down to the size of pencil leads. He pointed to one artery that was blocked completely. He said they were taking him directly from the cardiac cath lab into surgery for a quadruple bypass.

Deb thought of all the delicious food she had lovingly prepared and served to her hungry husband over the last thirty-six years and felt as if she might throw up. The two of them had always agreed that a heart-healthy diet was a sort of sissy urban affectation, a diet for couch potatoes, not the way a hard-working farmer eats. A man farming three thousand acres grows a lot of food and is entitled to eat a lot of food, and she made darn sure he got it. Besides, Ray was healthy as a horse and he loved his wife's cooking. Deb got her German culinary heritage from her mother, who got it from her mother, who, she said, "got it from God." In the last generation they had

Americanized, super-sized, battered, buttered, refined, and sweetened that German heritage until it was nothing but a delicious, sweet, salty, greasy, high-caliber bullet to the heart. The only thing that could have made it worse was smoking cigarettes, and he'd quit those just two years before.

Every morning it was bacon and eggs with buttered white bread toast and jam, unless it was pancakes with sausage, or waffles with whipped cream—and more sausage. At lunch it was off to Martha's Kitchen for a cheeseburger, fries, and a slab of pie. Dinner was a fatty beef pot roast or thick pork chops or fried chicken or chicken fried steak, or battered and deep fried fish, all served with thick gravy over creamy mashed potatoes. Even the vegetables were creamed: the green bean casserole, creamed corn, creamed onions, scalloped potatoes; the food fairly slid down his gullet with hardly a chew. There was no food on earth that could not be made richer with more cream, or more butter, or a handful of crumbled bacon, or all three. And there was no meal that you could call a meal without a generous serving of fatty corn-fed meat. Almost everything was better washed down with a cold glass of whole milk, and there was nothing that could not be made more scrumptious with a thick glaze of butter and sugar. And then there were all the old family desserts: flaumen kucken, Schaum torte, rhubarb custard pie, peach cobbler, chocolate cake; and now the modern, even richer desserts: Snicker's torte, seven layer bars, Death by Chocolate—all gaggingly sweet and irresistible as sirens on the shores of the sensory rich passage to Ray's belly. Every day the rich food added hundreds of unburned calories as he sat in the cabs of the big tractors or in his office drinking coffee and sinking his choppers into Deb's warm cinnamon buns drizzled with buttery sugar icing and fretting the weather, the crops, and the farming business. It was a wonder this hadn't happened years before. Healthy as a horse.

Ray Jr. and Sonia arrived in the waiting area. "How's Dad?"

Deb gave them the details and finally asked, "How are we going to run the farm without your dad?"

"I guess we can muddle by for the summer with Miguel and Bruce, but they'll need experienced help to get the crops in this fall if Dad isn't back in action," said Ray Jr.

"We're not moving to Parma," Sonia said to her husband.

"Ah, you'd like it fine here, sweetie. I hear that Saks is moving into the empty building next to Martha's Kitchen," he answered.

"And pigs are flying south in Vs," she smiled.

Ray Jr. smiled at the predictable response from his wife. He was glad to not have to take the full rap on himself for not moving back to the farm.

"So what are we going to do?" Deb asked.

"I can make decisions from Chicago and just drive up here occasionally for face time with the men. Which of the guys do you think would make the best foreman, Mom?"

"Well, Miguel's got the most experience, but I don't feel comfortable putting an ex-con Mexican in charge. Bruce might not stay around very long, but I think he's pretty bright, even though he messes up a lot. I think we could get him to stay. He's writing a book on farming, you know. Leo, we hardly see him anymore except to drive truck during the busy times. He's getting awful old and he can't type, so he can't do email and he'll just mumble your ear off if he calls you. I think it's got to be Bruce," said Deb.

"Why not you, Mom?" asked Sonia.

"Yeah, well, I guess that women's lib thing just sort of passed me by. I always helped Ray with the books, but I've never drove the tractors, and I couldn't even tell you where all the fields that he's got rented are even at. I've always just been the wife and mom, and since you guys all grew up, I been busy with the church newsletter, keeping the house and all that . . . and cooking for your dad." Deb broke down again thinking about the mountains of food she'd put in front of the big man.

"You've done a lot more than that, Mom," said Ray Jr., a sentiment echoed by Sonia.

"Maybe . . . but I don't think I can face this alone," said Deb.

"You won't be alone, Mom," Ray Jr. promised.

Over the next couple of days Doc Voekle visited Ray twice in the hospital and assured himself that his friend would live to once again sit with him to drink coffee and flirt with the waitresses at the diner. In his spare time between farm calls and hospital visits, he busied himself trying to compose a service to remember Bob Barker and the dead goats. But he was having trouble getting past, "Dearly beloved, we are gathered here . . ." so he stopped by the Lutheran church to see his pastor, a man he didn't see that often, the Reverend Roger Revson—everybody called him Rev Rev, both for his name and his love of NASCAR—for some advice. Rev Rev's black Camero parked in the church lot was festooned with bumper stickers, one warning that there was only "one way," another proclaiming that he hearted his wife with the call letters of a local religious radio station, and a white window sticker with the single digit "3", indicating additional reverence for Dale Earnhardt, Sr., who died in 2001 after hitting the Daytona Speedway wall at a hundred fifty miles per hour in his souped-up Chevy and a loose seatbelt. Rev Rev's advice was that animals don't have souls, so there would be no point in performing such a service.

"It's not for the animals—they're dead—it's for the people. I'm thinking maybe you've got a memorial service designed for human animals that I could adapt?"

"I couldn't allow the Lord's sacred words to be desecrated in that way, Cecil. We don't think of people as human animals; we are God's children—children in his image. You're going to have to go it alone on this one. God bless you."

Rev Rev issued the blessing as a dismissal that Doc more or less ignored. He was disappointed in the holy man's insistence on religious dogma, and got a little testy. "I guess I forgot we all look just like God in the mirror."

"It's not about looks. It's about being human."

"Right," Doc said. "Anyway, I'd still feel a lot more abundantly blessed if you'd offer a little pastoral assistance at this juncture, Rev Rev," forgetting that everybody called him that, but nobody called him that to his face.

Rev Rev's jowly face reddened a bit, as he almost accomplished a practiced look of ministerial serenity. "I think I'm going to leave you to tend your own flock on this one, Cecil. Come see us next Sunday, and I will take the opportunity to remind you what God says about our relationship to the beasts of the land. You've given me a good idea for a sermon, and I thank you for that."

"Happy to be of service, Rev." And with that Doc was out the door, certain that he wouldn't be attending that sermon.

So Doc turned where all modern intellectuals like himself turn for any kind of advice these days: The Internet. He Googled "animal memorial services," and hit the mother lode. There were services for the animals of Christians, the animals of Jews, and the animals of Secular Humanists. There was even a prayer for grieving children attending the flushing of a goldfish. If a cat has run away from home, the internet has comforting words already on file, just fill in the cat's name. If an old milk cow, say the beloved 99-874, has expired, and the rendering company is about to winch her into the truck, there are perfect healing words waiting in cyberspace. If a deer gets smucked by a car in front of your house and there are swarms of flies on it and the poor doe is stinking to high heaven and you dig a deep hole to put her in, there are words waiting to provide spiritual comfort to you and your family before you send her under. Doc scrolled through the pages and wondered what he could use. Did Bob Barker really have a "beautiful loving spirit, kind eyes, and unconditional love, like an angel"? Bob Barker didn't fit his conception of an angel—maybe a black angel of death, but not the smiling cherubic or virginal kinds that people liked to imagine.

At least there was the poetry of Ecclesiastes: "To everything there is a season . . . ," he could probably use that, but he knew that the power of words was in the specific details and images, so he would have to compose something original and moving for the occasion. He had planned to use the power of a deadline to goose his creative juices the night before the service, but he was called out to a calving and didn't get home until after eleven. His wife Mattie made him a pot of coffee and brought it in his favorite mug as he sat down in front of his computer. He thought a bit about how to start, got blocked again after typing "Dearly beloved" on the screen, got up to get his brown bottle of Maker's Mark. He poured a little shot in his coffee as Mattie headed off to bed without him.

Immediately after he volunteered to cook for the wake, Bruce's brain turned to thoughts of what he would serve. With a dinner menu fully in his control for the first time since he'd left home, he didn't want to waste the opportunity to cook using all local ingredients—to finally serve the fruit of his convictions to his new friends. Suddenly the pile of dead goats looked to him a little less like a tragedy and a little more like a local food resource. Unseen, while Wanda and Krystal collected themselves from the debacle and started the evening milking, he sorted through the newly dead and found three fat ones with hind legs apparently unlacerated by the dog's long canine teeth. He lashed the three good ones—maybe seventy-five pounds of goat kid—with binder twine to the metal rack over the rear tire of his bike, and headed back to his place at Ray's. Luckily, there were no passing cars treated to the sight of Bruce pedaling down the road with the bloody load, but Miguel saw him roll into the farm yard with the bounty and shook his head.

"What the fuck, amigo?"

"It's hot. We gotta get these kids field dressed and chilled, ASAP," said Bruce, skidding to a stop and straddling the bike to steady its heavy load.

"Pronto. The word is pronto. You sound like asshole when you say ASAP," said Miguel.

"Right. Pronto. Get your knife."

"Get my knife?" Miguel laughed, "I always got knife. You think I hang with gringos without no knife?"

"Okay, where should we do this, pronto?" Bruce asked.

"Tall grass behind the tool shed. I follow you."

Bruce peddled his load behind the building, untied the goats, and laid them in the grass. Field dressing the little ruminants was just like doing a deer, only easier. In a few minutes there were three gut piles. They carried the carcasses inside and hung them in the shade while their blood drained. It wasn't nearly cool enough to age the meat, so they went straight to work, first skinning, then cutting the meat from the bones and trimming away any bloody tooth punctures.

"What are we cooking, amigo?" asked Miguel.

"I'm thinking stew. I know a recipe for venison stew. It should work fine for this."

"More meat than you need for pot of stew. One kid would make maybe four big pots."

"I suppose that's right. You want one?"

"Si. We'll roast it over fire—muy bueno."

"Oh yeah, good idea. Let's do that for the wake."

And so they didn't bone out the last kid. Bruce dug a hole and buried the gut piles, skins, and bare skeletons behind the tool shed. They put the boned meat in a plastic garbage bag, and the whole carcass in another, and drove the bounty over to Miguel's trailer. They put the small scraps of muscle from the neck, belly wall, shanks, and ribs through a hand meat grinder clamped to Miguel's kitchen table. "Burritos cabrito—muy buena!" said Miguel. The rest they left in larger chunks for other culinary delights, and froze it all.

"So what else on the menu?" asked Miguel.

"Spring in Michigan: that would be asparagus and rhubarb."

"I'll give you some dried morels to add to the asparagus."

"Fantastic! And potatoes from last fall . . . potato salad. I'll have to find a recipe for the asparagus and morels. I think I'll have to make a rhubarb crisp—Alice never taught me how to make a pie crust. With the goat, that should be plenty."

"So what will the ladies think when they see cabrito over a fire?"

"They're going to think: mmm-mmm, I'm hungry!"

"No wonder you got girl troubles, amigo. You better cook it here."

CHAPTER 21

Animal funeral day landed on a Wednesday in the first week of June, a day that glided in like a bevy of prom queens on skateboards. The lawns and trees around Parma were emerald with new leaves. Irises of every color spread their petals like the hussies of the flower world they are. Purple clamatis busied itself entwining and blooming. Annuals blanketed their beds; impatiens, pansies, and petunias in every yard. Hostas spread their giant variegated leaves, violets winked along wooded paths, wild dogwoods under tall oaks flashed terraces of white petals. Every living plant was renewed with fresh greenery and half of them were in blossom. An abandoned field over the fence from Nanny Gate was overrun with Russian olive—acres of it dressed in dusty pale green foliage and millions of small creamy blooms—a brushy, thorny, invasive alien bush with an utterly intoxicating scent. Drivers stopped and rolled down their windows just to vacuum the perfume into their noses. Wispy horsetails in the stratosphere promised a colorful sunset. They would hold their service that evening as the gentle breeze fell to a whisper and the sun inched toward the horizon. It was one of those Midwestern summer days when a goat pasture in the warm, well-watered mitten of Michigan would be a finalist for the most beautiful place on earth.

In the cool of the morning, after his now routine quick breakfast of granola doused in goat milk, Bruce pedaled his bike down the pasture lane, one hand on the handlebars, one balancing a long-handled spade on his shoulder. Ishy ran beside him. On a small rise in the back pasture, the one nearest the river, he dropped his bike and dug two deep holes, one for Bob Barker and another larger one for the massacred goats he hadn't salvaged for food. That they would be dining on a young goat killed by Bob Barker was a detail Bruce hadn't yet revealed to Wanda or Krystal, but he failed to see why it should matter.

In any case, he got right to the job; he outlined the holes with the shovel blade and carefully lifted squares of sod and topsoil to one side. Earthworms panicked in the sunlight and writhed their way back into the dark sandy loam. Below the sod, except for a few glacially rounded granite stones that jarred his whole body when he jumped on the shovel blade and hit them, it was easy digging down through the moist, cool, iron-stained sand. The gritty smoothness of it pleased him. He liked the way the rounded steel shovel blade slid easily into the golden soil under the pressure of his booted foot, the pleasant heft of earth lifted and tossed. It was as if the shovel had been invented to give a man pleasure. Ishy barked at each shovelful as he threw it. He dug down and down with the spade until the tangled roots of the pasture grasses brushed the reddish brown hair on his belly. His muscled torso, still much too white to withstand a day in the summer sun, glistened with sweat. Stinging drops of salt water trickled into his eyes. He squinted and wiped them on his sweat-slicked arms without much relief. He kept digging, alternately squeezing one eye shut and then the other. When the hole was deep and wide enough, he placed a hand on the sod on each side, pushed down hard, and vaulted out, landing on his feet beside the grave. Ishy stood on the tallest dirt pile and barked her approval. He was still an athlete.

Before he left Wanda's, Bruce pulled a thick bundle of rhubarb stalks from a patch on the sunny side of the milk house. He used his pocket knife to cut off the elephant-ear-sized toxic leaves and pressed them to the ground around the remaining stalks for weed control. He bundled the pink stalks with a couple of rubber bands, and pedaled them over to Miguel and Doris's trailer where he planned to cook most of the big meal. They were both at work, so he had the place to himself. He found the baggie with Miguel's stash under the brown saddlebag lid of the ceramic donkey table lamp, rolled a joint, and took a few lungfuls. The heat of the day began to seep into the trailer. He was sweating. Dang, that's good weed, he thought. He undressed and threw his work clothes into the washer, took a cool shower, rinsing away the salt and dirt from the grave digging. He felt fantastic. And since he had no other clothes, it was getting hot, and he was alone and pleasantly buzzed, he thought it would be interesting to cook in the nude.

He took the goat carcass from the freezer to thaw, and, after considerable cupboard and drawer banging, located the bowls, pans, cooking utensils, and all the ingredients he needed to make the rhubarb crisp. He remembered watching Alice make it and the fight they'd had over cinnamon, a spice that comes from Sri Lanka—not even in a thousand mile circle. The sour bright scent of rhubarb rose from the oak plank on which he chopped the stalks. He gathered the cut rhubarb into a large bowl, added corn starch, brown sugar, and an egg, and mixed it all with his bare hands. In another bowl, he mixed the crisp topping of rolled oats, flour, more brown sugar, and canola oil. The combined smooth and grainy textures fell through his fingers and he suddenly became aware that cooking could be as sensual as eating. He realized a little of the pleasure he had denied Alice. He imagined the pleasure that others would take in the meal, and smiled. He gave Doris' lazy-Susan spice rack a spin and found the cinnamon on the second trip around. He filled a teaspoon with the fragrant ground bark from halfway around the world and sprinkled it in. Then he tossed in a little ground nutmeg—more new ground for a strict locavore. He mixed it all again, then buttered the baking pan, and impulsively used the residue on his fingers to butter his arms. He spread the chopped rhubarb mixture in the pan, covered it with the topping layer, and as he slid the pan into the hot oven, apologized silently to Alice.

It was time to start the fire.

Stepping into the bright sunlight of Miguel's backyard, Bruce stopped and relit the joint. Squinting through the tendrils of smoke seeping from his nostrils, he checked the visual lines from the road to the yard and decided that clothing was optional here too, since the small gaps in the trees, bushes, and tall weeds offered only a quick glimpse to any passing car. Except that there were emerging thistles, sharp gravel, and a little broken beer bottle glass around, so he left his boots on.

He expertly laid in newspaper, sticks, and dry splits of oak and maple inside the stone fire ring behind the trailer. Squatting at the edge of the stones, he struck a match to the newspaper. He felt the unmown grass brush his parts hanging low in the heat. He felt aboriginal—never mind that Michigan's true aboriginals would never have set fire to last week's edition of The Parma Post Intelligencer. The local small town paper would have been a mysterious and possibly sacred object. Aboriginals certainly would have first clipped the colorful coupons for the beef flank steak 'On sale this week only!' in the butcher's case at the supermarket in Jackson. But the ancient people wouldn't have recognized most of the foods at all. What the hell are Ding Dongs? Fritos? Cherry Coke Zero? Assorted lite lunch entrées? They might have searched the paper for a deal on bulk jumbo white oak acorns, but quickly determined that they wouldn't find those in the grocery store during the wildflower moon. They would wait patiently for the acorn ads in the newspapers that came with the geese-flying-south moon. Or they might have called it the moon of falling velvet for the whitetail bucks whose necks began to thicken about then. The Native Americans had been locavores who lived fully in the season. Bruce had come along just two centuries too late.

In a few minutes bright orange flames jumped shoulder high and Bruce was forced to retreat a few steps. He located the section of galvanized pipe that Miguel had left for him to use as a spit, and the baling wire he'd left to tie the goat carcass to it. He walked into the edge of the woods behind the trailer and used Miguel's ax to cut a couple of saplings to make forked supports to hold the spit over the fire. In only his work boots and with the ax over his shoulder, his hands still smelling of butter, sugar, cinnamon, and nutmeg, he felt deliciously primitive and dangerous. A patch of stinging nettles had already grown waist high at the edge of the yard. It brushed and lit up his thighs as he walked back to the fire with the green forked sticks.

The first yellow jackets of the summer were showing a lot of interest in the sugar residue on his hands. He waved them away. He wished he had set the spit supports in place before he'd lit the fire—it was hard to get close enough with all the heat. The blaze was so hot that he decided he needed to get his pants on for protection. His pants would feel good pulled on damp and cool after the cold rinse cycle in the washing machine. He left the blaze and sauntered back to the trailer. The fire and the rising heat of the day relaxed him; he felt cavemanly as he glanced down on his dangling parts that bobbed cheerfully with each stride in the bright sunlight. He wondered if they could sunburn. He opened the screen door and grabbed the knob. It wouldn't turn. He slapped himself where his pocket with the house key would have been if he'd been wearing pants.

"Crap!" he whispered loudly to himself. He listened for traffic before scurrying around to check the front door. Also locked. Damn! He put his hands on his hips and looked at the sky, shaking his head in "Why me?" disbelief. He couldn't even call Miguel since his cell phone was sitting on top of the washing machine. That's when the mailman, actually a mailwoman, quietly coasted to a stop with half a pound of junk mail and the power bill for Miguel's mailbox. Bruce heard the gravel crackle under her coasting approach and forgot to cover himself as he turned. She deposited the mail, closed the box, and her mouth fell open as her eyes briefly connected with Bruce's hairy danglies. After a surprised squeal, she managed a weak smile and a friendly Midwestern wave as she pulled away, but then decided the sheriff might want to know about this, and dialed 9-1-1 at the next mailbox.

"I seen a naked man with an ax trying to get into Miguel Rameriez's trailer," she told the dispatcher. "It doesn't look like nobody's home."

Bruce felt some relief at the friendly gesture he'd observed from the mail lady as she drove off, but the feeling would be short lived. He scurried back to the privacy of the back side of the trailer, and was struggling to get the air conditioner out of the bedroom window so he could crawl in through the hole, when he heard the stove timer go off, indicating that the rhubarb crisp was done, and almost simultaneously the siren of Sheriff Timmers's squad car, indicating that he was also about done.

He lifted, twisted, jimmied, and yanked hard on the AC unit. It gave suddenly and scraped and pulled the hair on his chest and belly as he wrestled the machine out of the window. A family of wasps that had been gluing a paper nest on the underside of the unit with hornet spit and orneriness buried their stingers repeatedly in his groin area. His entire front side was on fire. He dropped the machine on the ground, groaned and cursed, but had no time to waste, so used it for a step up to the window. He managed to scramble about halfway through the sharp-edged aluminum window frame before the Sheriff came trotting around the end of the trailer, Smith and Wesson thirty-eight drawn. His professionally trained eyes surveyed the crime scene in a heartbeat. He observed the blazing fire, the newly cut forked sticks, and the ax. He recognized Bruce's bicycle and he knew instantly just whose hairy butt it was hanging out of Miguel and Doris's trailer window.

"Mr. Dinkle! . . . baaaad Brucie," he said, "why do I know it's your pink butt and naughty parts I see hanging out the window of one of my voting citizens who is not you?" He kicked the ax to the ground from where it leaned against the old picnic table. "It's good to know you went and put that ax down, or I might have had to put another hole in your back end. You're a hell of a fine target you know? Nice little bulls-eye you got there."

Bruce yelled into Miguel and Doris's bedroom, "I was getting ready to cook a goat and locked myself out." He hoped he yelled loud enough that his words would ricochet off the bedroom walls, back past his bare butt, and out the tight-fitting window frame to the sheriff.

"If I had a dime for every buck-naked pervert who told me that one, by God I'd have me a dime," the sheriff chuckled. "Why don't you just back your bare-assed self back out of that window. And please try not to snag nothin important. I don't want to have to call no ambulance to stitch your mangled parts back on. I think you and me need to have us a little mano-a-mano here."

Bruce struggled to back out of the sharp-edged aluminum window frame. He further scraped and shaved his already painfully abraded and hornet-stung frontside as he wormed his way in reverse. It was especially hard because there was nothing inside the trailer against which he could push back. Finally he got his feet on the ground. He covered his burning, stinging privates with his hands and turned to face the sheriff. Some of the scrapes on his bright red chest and abdomen were oozing a little blood.

"Guess you're one perp I don't need to frisk," he laughed. "I think I won't ask you to put your hands up. There's things a man can't unsee."

"Guess not. I locked myself out and my clothes are inside." The stove timer continued to beep.

"What's going off?"

"I got a rhubarb crisp in the oven. It's going to burn if I don't get in there."

"That ain't all that's going to burn if you don't get you some clothes on, Mr. Dinkle. You got Miguel's phone number? We better get in there."

Sheriff Timmers called Miguel. He dropped his work mowing Ray and Deb's lawn—not usually his job, but with Ray in the hospital he needed to help out around the Vander Koop's house—and bombed right over in the multicolored Impala with the house key. Bruce pulled the crisp out and his pants on. Everything was slightly burned but salvageable. The sweet aroma of the baking covered up the dope smell pretty well. He was doubly glad he'd added the spices. Bruce thought he might sweeten the sheriff up a bit with a slice of the warm dessert.

"Can I cut you a piece of rhubarb crisp, sheriff?"

"First you better make me believe you ain't trying to bribe me."

Actually, the bribe disclaimer was a formality. The sheriff wasn't a threat for more than a verbal warning after the rhubarb crisp aroma hit him full on the nose. If there had been hot rhubarb cooked into a crisp, a pie, or any other sweet baked-good of any sort coming out of the oven at the domestic calls he'd made during his law-enforcement career, he'd still be looking for his first arrest. He was a rhubarb junkie and there was no twelve-step program to get him over it. Best a man could do to get through it was to brew a strong pot of coffee to wash it down, which is what Miguel was doing in solidarity with his friend's predicament, along with breaking out a carton of vanilla ice cream. Bruce served up the crisp while Miguel poured coffee and they ate mostly in silence while the coals burned down to the perfect level for cooking a goat, and until the sheriff composed a little lecture:

"You know I could write you a ticket for public indecency and you'd be ever-after classified as a sex offender? You couldn't be around no kids and you'd have to register with the local authorities wherever you lived at. You'd even have to go up to all the neighbors around here, door to door, one by one, and introduce yourself as the local pervert so they'd know to throw stuff at you when they seen you pedaling that silly ass bicycle a yours down the road. They'd run your butt right out of town, and it wouldn't be pretty."

"Can I get you another slice, sheriff?" Miguel asked.

"Yeah, I guess you could. Just one. Then I got to be going."

By the time the sheriff polished off his second helping, he had what he wanted: a bellyful of rhubarb crisp and another good story, both of which were a lot more fun and a lot less work than arresting the citizens he was pledged to protect. He left in a rush of handshakes and smiles and promises to keep pants on, and Bruce got right back to the cooking. He got the goat on the spit with Miguel's help, and once he had it secured and balanced so he could turn it, and he could see that the hot coals were doing their work, he got to peeling and boiling a pile of Yukon Gold potatoes, potatoes grown in his home county back where Alice and Mikey and Josie lived, which was a little more than a hundred miles away since he'd run away from home, but he let it slide. He was pretty sure there were no fresh in-season starches from Jackson County available in the grocery stores except for the month or so when the sweet corn was in, so he went just a little outside his current hundred-mile circle for the potatoes.

He'd got some Michigan onions from the supermarket in Jackson too, but as for the other fresh vegetables for a potato salad—celery and sweet red pepper—they were imported this time of year and he wasn't ready to compromise that much, so he left them out. Later in the summer there would be fresh Michigan celery and sweet peppers, but for now the only local vegetables were the fresh stalks like the asparagus and rhubarb, and those that had been stored from last year like the potatoes and onions. He substituted corn oil for olive, and just closed his eyes and bought the mayonnaise since he had no idea how to make it. God knows where it was from. And he gave it a good grind of black pepper in the same spirit he'd used the cinnamon. He was softening up a bit.

The recipe he had called for sea salt. This had become a pet peeve of Bruce's. Wasn't all salt sea salt? Where did the salt snobs think all the salt deposits came from that were now under Detroit? Anybody who's attended a non-fundamentalist high school knows that there were once inland seas here, seas that evaporated and left millions of tons of salt now deep underground where it's been waiting for hundreds of millions of years for Detroiters to dig down and discover it, and then haul it up to shake on eggs—or spread on roads to accelerate the rusting of the cars they made so that people would have to buy more cars—which was a grand and virtuous cycle for the auto industry—but, to the point, Bruce wondered why anybody would want to sprinkle the salty residue of a modern ocean on their food, contaminated with God knows what, when you could sprinkle it with an ancient evaporated sea with nothing more frightening in it than a little petrified prehistoric fish sperm? Petrified fish jism or modern industrial pollution?—easy choice. He poured a little iodized store-brand salt into his palm, tossed it into the potato salad, gave it a stir, stuck it in the refrigerator, and called it done.

CHAPTER 22

W anda wouldn't let Krystal help her lift the dead goats onto the flatbed trailer to tractor them to the burial site. She wanted feel the full weight of her loss, compelled to wallow in her pain. And she didn't help Krystal lift Bob Barker either, because she just didn't feel like it. The dead mutt weighed more than Krystal—the bitch could just struggle with him herself. Any sort of pain she could cause Krystal was justified. In the warm summer sun, two days of waiting for burial had been at least a day too long. The carcasses stunk, and maggots were already hard at work performing the soupy part of the dust-to-dust routine. Still, as they loaded and unloaded the big shot dog and the pile of mauled goats on the down-wind side of the holes, they couldn't help but notice that the goat count was off.

Krystal questioned, "I thought there was supposed to be eleven?"

"There were," said Wanda, "Maybe coyotes dragged a few off?" She was genuinely puzzled. "I don't know," she added.

"Yeah, probably. I lost a nice cat to them damn things once. There wasn't no coyote going to get Barker though."

"Anybody else had a shot him besides me, you'd never know what happened to the bastard. Farmers around here use the three-S rule: shoot, shovel, and shut-up. I suppose it's the same everywhere. Can't have crazy-ass killer dogs roaming free where there's farm animals—or little kids for that matter. I heard of a woman with a couple of Bull Mastiffs—huge dogs with heads the size of bushel baskets—killed seventeen of her own sheep and two lamas while she and her husband were at work. She had to shoot her own damn dogs. Dogs like that will take down kids on bikes, too. Happens all the time."

"I don't guess she *had* to shoot them. Damage was already done."

"Yeah, well, it's like keeping a loaded gun for burglars in a house with a man who's a mean drunk. Like most Americans, you're worrying about the wrong problem. Just bad judgment. A mean dog's a loose cannon—unpredictable—doesn't make anybody any safer."

"You ever seen the dog whisperer? I bet he coulda turned Bob Barker around. I shoulda called him," said Krystal.

Wanda said, "Krystal, you seem like a sweet person, but for some dumb reason you collect meanness around you. You needed yourself a husband whisperer way before you needed a dog whisperer."

Doc Voekle'd had a couple of regularly scheduled herd-health calls that day, which required him to shove his arm into the rectums of a good hundred dairy cows. In addition, he'd castrated a dozen backyard pigs, dehorned three big Hereford calves that should have been done months before—a real bloody wrestling match—pared out a sole abscess deep on the underside if the dinner plate-sized hoof of a twenty-five hundred pound Angus bull tied to a fence post—a dangerous, back-breaking job—and put ten stitches in the forehead of a headstrong gelding that had banged himself on the top edge of the door of a horse trailer. In between, on his lunch hour in his little one-room clinic, he'd seen a cat with ringworm and a dog that was scratching himself raw due to a flea allergy. He was exhausted and a little hung over. But he'd finished writing his slightly inebriated thoughts in the wee hours and they were folded in his shirt pocket.

By seven the western sky was beginning to color up and the southerly breeze was becoming indecisive, falling to shifting whispers of summer flowers, unless you happened to be standing northerly of the not-that-recently-departed pile.

Doc Voekle arrived right on time in his vet truck. He peeled off the fourth pair of blood and manure-splotched coveralls he'd gone through that day, pulled on a string tie with a Petoskey stone bolo in the shape of the Lower Peninsula, and worked it under the collar of the still mostly white western shirt with pearl snaps he'd put on that morning. He pushed his big knuckly fingers back through his thinning hair before crowning himself with his favorite straw hat, the old beat-up one with the turquoise chip hat band. He figured it gave him the aged cowboy-philosopher-at-a-special-occasion look he was after, and it helped him to slide the short distance into that character. He hadn't had time to change into his dressy lizard skin cowboy boots, and he sure as hell couldn't have worn those toe-crushing cripplers to work in all day—he'd have been in a wheelchair by now. And he wished he'd had time to shave and clean up properly after the day he'd had, but he'd washed his hands and splashed water on his face to erase the specks of blood and manure. Anyway, there'd be plenty of cover scent at the gravesite.

Miguel and Doris arrived with Bruce in the back seat of the old Impala. The feast, including the barbecued goat, the potato salad, and the remaining half pan of rhubarb crisp, was all packed into one hot and one cold Thermos chest in the trunk. The six of them, Wanda, Krystal, Doris, Miguel, Doc, and Bruce, walked down the lane together, making small talk about the beautiful weather, the chances for rain tomorrow, and generally avoiding the subject at hand.

When they arrived at the gravesite they sniffed and shuffled in unison around to the upwind side of the deceased. Doc pulled the paper from his pocket and turned to face the small group.

"I guess we should just start in, then?" he asked, looking to Wanda for agreement.

"I guess so," she nodded.

Doc cleared his throat and unfolded the paper. There was a round bourbon-spiked coffee stain on its corner. He began to read: "When somebody dies, folks sometimes feel bad if their feelings are mixed, if they are what college professors call, ambivalent. None of us is feeling ambivalent about these poor goats, they were innocent as any critters can be, but there's a pile of mixed feelings about that dog."

"The diminutive goats—they just got their numbers tattooed into in their ears a month ago—they never had a chance to grow up and have kids of their own, or have the pleasure of Wanda pulling on their tits twice a day with her good strong hands. Never got to run and eat grass in this beautiful pasture. It would have been a fine goat life. It'll be hard to miss them though, because we hardly knew them. But they would a got names and developed little goat personalities, which are better personalities than some people can lay claim to. Rev Rev down at Parma Lutheran claims animals don't get to go to Heaven because they aren't in possession of souls. I don't know how he figures he knows that, or anybody could know that, so I recommend a policy of generally letting them in."

He went on, "Personally, I won't feel all that useful in Heaven if they don't have some nice farms with red barns and white fences on rolling green pastures with some good-looking critters like these little goats here for me to keep vaccinated and wormed. I'm especially hoping for a calico cat in Paradise to keep the mice down around the house and to sit in my lap while I read James Herriot of a winter's evening. I understand a cat in Heaven might have to be declawed so it doesn't catch too many song birds. There's bound to be some rules to keep Heaven running smooth, like I'm sure it does. But maybe cats will train better up there, I don't know. But by God, if they're going to call it Heaven, there's going to have to be a lot of birdsong to keep all us dead folks cheered up. Although I expect we won't need turkey buzzards in the sky above Heaven, since everything lives forever up there, and how could there be sky above Heaven anyhow. Plus, there shouldn't be much carrion, especially since folks are bound to drive slower there, since what's the hurry, so not much road kill. But there'd sure better be warblers in the bushes and maybe a wood thrush at the top of a big white pine outside my door. Just wouldn't be Heaven without songbirds. I think I'm going to like that."

He cleared his throat. "But Bob Barker . . . Bob Barker . . . he didn't have a number tatooed in his ear; he had himself a name, a great name. And he sure as hell could bark. People are always telling me about their dogs: "Don't worry Doc, his bark's worse than his bite." Well that just wasn't true about old Bob Barker. He had a bark as big as the Hound of the Baskervilles and a bite to match, and it worked both ways, both good and bad. The few of us folks standing here tonight will always remember that he killed a bunch of little goats, but millions of people who only saw him on the TV news will always remember that he saved Krystal here from being raped—chewed the bugger's ear off and then ran him off with a little help from Bruce, here. Bob Barker had what all of us have in us: some good, some bad. He had a heaping helping of both, and he didn't have a filter on it. If he felt it inside him, it was coming out. And when you're as strong as that big dog was, by God you can make things happen."

Doc slowed toward the finish: "Maybe a dog like Bob Barker can teach us all something about honesty and acting on our true feelings—maybe honesty and integrity aren't all they're cracked up to be. Maybe kindness is more important. Maybe we don't need to act on every feeling. Maybe we ought to all train ourselves to sit, stay, and even heel and fetch once in a while. Maybe the integrity that comes from acting on our every conviction can throw us out of whack. Maybe sometimes it's best to just sit and shut up. We all got to get along. I wish I knew how to make that happen—but I just don't know."

This was the point where Doc had more or less passed out from whisky and exhaustion while writing the night before, and it seemed as good a place as any to let it go.

There was a moment of silence in the goat pasture. There had been the expectation of a single word, "Amen" to end the service. Even Unitarians don't end their services with "I just don't know." Maybe they should, but Bruce felt the void acutely and said the word without thinking. "Amen," he said, and the others gently mumbled the same. I just don't know. Amen.

Bruce suddenly felt doubt seep into his choice of a main course. But as always he found at least temporary respite from sustained thought in hard physical work. He and Miguel pulled the work gloves from their back pockets, and together lifted and dropped each little goat and finally Bob Barker into their graves. Then they all filed past the holes and each tossed in a shovelful of dirt. Wanda pretended not to notice that she had included a good sized rock in her shovel, and landed it squarely on Bob Barker's head. Apparently she wasn't quite over it yet. Krystal on the other hand was moved by the service, and cried as she tossed dirt on the little goats, and began to sob when she did the same for Bob Barker. "I am so sorry," she quavered. She felt sorry in so many ways, both for her dog and what he had done. Doc Voekle put his long arms around Krystal and Wanda and began the walk up to the house. Doris stayed back and watched Bruce and Miguel fill the graves in a flurry of shovel work—ensuring that no live animals would fall in with the dead—and neatly replace the sod. After a couple of rains, it would be hard to locate the spot.

"Maybe we could plant an oak tree on the graves," Krystal suggested.

"The goats would eat it," Wanda said.

"How about a cross?" Krystal suggested.

"That might work for the Saanens, but I suspect the Nubians, being from Africa, are probably Muslims," said Doc.

"I guess that's why the beards," said Wanda.

"Never thought of that," said Doc. "Course the Saanen's got beards too. Maybe all goats are Amish."

When they got to the house, Wanda spread a red checkered cloth on the picnic table under the big white oak in her backyard, and set it with her best silverware, cloth napkins, and wine glasses. Bruce and Miguel weren't far behind. Bruce hurried into the house to cook the asparagus with several bunches of spring onions and the double handful of dried morels that Miguel had given him. Later in the summer the edible plants would be roots and fruits, but this early it was all stalks—asparagus, rhubarb, green onions—and morels, the queen of the local fungi. He rehydrated the morels in hot water, briefly boiled the asparagus and onions, then drained and quickly sautéed the whole mess in butter. The aroma in the old farmhouse kitchen was rich, smooth, and round as mother earth in a leotard, barefoot and pregnant.

Bruce brought the asparagus out to the picnic table to "oooohs" and "ahhhhs" all around. Wanda uncorked the wine while Bruce got the coolers from the trunk of the multicolored Impala and took out a cold six-pack of

Peasant Sweat—he'd finally got the Parma gas station quick stop to carry it—and the potato salad to more murmurs of approval. Finally, after placing a large cutting board, a big fork, and a long sharp knife at his place at the table, he opened the cooler containing the barbecued goat. He had glazed it with a hot spicy barbecue sauce that violated the hundred-mile rule at least half-a-dozen ways, and it smelled fantastic. He lifted it out carefully and laid the headless carcass on the cutting board, "Voila!" he said, attempting to make the sale.

Wanda groaned, "Oh God . . . you didn't."

"My provisional diagnosis would be that, in fact, he did," Doc Voekle confirmed.

Miguel attempted to bolster his friend's case: "Muy bueno! Cabrito! In Mexico this is *very* special!"

Krystal started to cry. Doc reached his arm around her shoulder, "It's okay, I'm sure he didn't mean anything by it," he said.

"Wanda already hates me because Barker killed the little goats . . . and now you want to . . . you want to feed them to me! You want to make me eat the dead goats my dog killed! Bruce, you asshole, I can't believe you'd do this to me! I hate you!" She extricated herself from the picnic table, turned away, and began to sob.

Bruce attempted to defend himself. "Doc's right, I didn't mean to upset anybody. I just wanted to feed you all the best local food I could. I thought it would be special."

"There's a hell of a lot more meaning in food than where it comes from, Bruce. I can't believe you did this, either," said Wanda, "but jeeze it looks awful g . . ." Her attempt at peacemaking came too late.

"You want your food local? I'll give you local food up-close and personal, you goddamn meathead!" Krystal screamed as she turned, charged the table, and grabbed the barbecued goat by a rear leg and swung the entire carcass in a high round-house, landing its rib cage hard down over Bruce's shoulders as he ducked and covered, and was splattered with barbecue sauce. The leg disarticulated from the body at the hip as it hit him, leaving Krystal with a more manageable-sized club in her hand with which to pummel Bruce. The remainder of the detached goat landed on the table between

Wanda and Miguel. Wanda pulled a small bite from the torn rump area and laid it on her tongue. Bruce rose slowly from his defensive crouch, his hands positioned to protect the side of his face nearest Krystal. Showing remarkable ambidexterity, Krystal deftly switched the goat haunch to her left hand and delivered a wicked meaty left uppercut, catching Bruce square on the chin with the bare head of the goat's disjointed femur, opening a small cut and sending him backwards into the table where his left hand sank deep into the big bowl of potato salad between Doc and Miguel. They dabbed with their fingers at the spattered food on their clothes, tasted it, and began to chuckle. They looked at Wanda who was chewing the first bite of goat, and all three nodded their approval to each other. Doris took the cue and began to shovel a large portion onto her own plate. That no one else was taking Bruce's offence terribly seriously took some of the fight out of Krystal.

"I say call the fight for Krystal on a technical knockout—call it a TKO in round-one! The fight goes to the little lady with the tasty left hook," said Doc.

"You guys don't think this is creepy?!" Krystal asked, incredulous, her cheeks wet with tears, the goat haunch back in her right hand.

"Yeah, a little, but it's awful good, honey. Why don't you just have a seat," said Doris.

"Let me pour you a glass of wine," said Wanda. "I don't hate you, but I guess I've been slow to get over it. I think I am now," she said smiling. "I'm sorry I was mean to you. And I'm sorry I had to shoot your dog."

"And I'm sorry I upset you with this food," said Bruce, in one of the few apologies of his life.

Doris lifted her considerable bulk slowly from her seat while balancing her plate with the potato salad in the center of her palm. "And I'm feeling awful bad about not having nothin to feel sorry about," she drawled as she calmly and squarely landed a generous serving of the cool starchy side dish on the side of Bruce's face, filling his ear with mayonnaise, bits of chopped onion, and a soft cube of boiled potato.

"What the hell was that for?!" Bruce screamed.

"The broken air conditioner and the big mess you left in my house," she said, and added, "also so's I could have something to feel sorry about, too."

"Before we dump and smear all this good food on each other, perhaps we should request a blessing upon it," Doc suggested, hoping to restore a little order.

"Good idea," said Bruce, dabbing the blood from his chin and digging the potato cube from his ear and eating it.

"It looks like professional wrestling meets The Food Network here," said Wanda, "Guess we might as well bring in the 700 Club, too."

"Don't you people take nothin serious?" asked Krystal.

"In my experience, we all take too much, much too seriously," said Doc, "but I think we went and got some of that seriousity aired out just now." He paused for a moment of silence, then continued, "Dear Lord: If you were watching us just now, I know that you know that we got us a lot of sorry people down here using the good food you've blessed us with as weapons, which we all know is wrong. It's bad to waste a potato, and it's a lot worse to waste a goat. We all know that. There's a lot of hungry people in the world, and right now I'm one of them, and I expect there's others here at this table on this beautiful evening, an evening that you yourself made from scratch, whose stomachs are growling just like mine is. So we ask your forgiveness, and that you please don't choke us with a piece of gristle, even though we sure know that you could. Amen."

And even though Amen is only a word, and there are precious few closures among the living, they all answered in unison: "Amen."

And it was good. It was real good.

CHAPTER 23

Ray was expected to be up and about, pushing his IV stand up and down the machine-waxed beige linoleum floors of the cardiac ward, within two or three days after the transplant of clean veins from his leg to the outside of his big heart. But he wasn't coming around that fast. His attitude wasn't the problem; he said he hated being cooped-up in the hospital, and he seemed highly motivated to get out. Although he had had some very warm vague fantasies concerning the young nurse who gave him his sponge bath—gauzy thoughts, it should be stipulated, that were unaccompanied by any outward evidence of arousal—not surprising given the diameter of the red rubber hose that someone, he had no idea who, had threaded up his shriveled penis and into his bladder. In any case, the dose of the narcotic pain killer in which his exhausted brain soaked made get-up-and-go ambition seem as curious and alien a quality as green skin. Coincidentally, he had overheard Sonia saying to her mother-in-law that, in fact, green was his skin color, and he didn't look long for this world.

But it wasn't his time, and he was a man with things to do, so he attempted to think about the farm in his waking minutes. He tried to think about all the jobs that needed to be done. The crops were all in, so there really wasn't that much. The Hoedown-Ready soy beans and corn needed to be sprayed with the broad-spectrum herbicide for which they were genetically engineered to be ready, lest the weeds take over. And the planting equipment needed to be cleaned and stored. And the vegetable garden needed weeding occasionally. And more than ever he would want to get that screened-in gazebo built out in the gap in the backyard spruce windbreak at the edge of the field with a gurgling hot tub into which he and Deb could sink up to their necks and listen to the corn grow. It would be perfect for his convalescence if he could just get it built. All these things didn't add up to much of a job list, given that they had the whole summer to get them done. But neither could he quite form them into action items, let alone concrete plans, in the face of the drip, drip, drip of a narcotic pain killer that had him fading in and fading out like a far-away radio station full of interference and long periods where static noise and strange dreams completely buried the signal.

Miguel, of course, being in his fifth year on the farm, knew the important seasonal routines and had already blown out the planters' seed and fertilizer lines with compressed air, and had parked the big machines inside the back door of one of the steel-sided tool sheds the day before. And, with Bruce's help, he'd hoed and weeded the Vander Koops' garden, as well as his own, just that morning. Miguel had a big garden plot, maybe thirty by a hundred feet, behind his house trailer. Two weeks ago, he'd transplanted the seedlings he'd started in his cold frame in the early spring. He put in three kinds of tomatoes, broccoli, red cabbage, two varieties of egg plant, onions, sweet red bell peppers, and three kinds of hot peppers—including fiery hot habaneras. Plus he'd planted the seeds for corn, beans, peas, summer and winter squashes, pumpkins, melons, radishes, Russian kale, spinach, and lettuce; all of which had now poked their tender first leaves up and out of the rich ground.

Before he planted he'd borrowed a trailer from Ray to haul a couple of loads from Bogart's pile of well-rotted manure to his garden spot. He buried a couple of shovels-full of the compost under the spot where he would carefully plant each set. But horse manure wasn't the only secret ingredient that made his garden the best in Parma; his real edge came from the wooden outhouse he'd hammered together at the edge of the woods, where he would sit facing the trees with the door wide open and an eye on the squirrels and squawking blue jays, with his work pants piled around his ankles. Every spring he shoveled out from under his outhouse and into his wheelbarrow a year's worth of peppery Mexican feces. He wheeled half a dozen loads of this brown gold into his garden and immediately rototilled it into the soil, always on a warm late April day when Doris was at work. After the night soil was tilled in, it took a day or two before the smell faded—longer if you were standing right in the garden—but a generous load of Bogart's recycled waste added simultaneously worked as a pretty good cover scent for the unsuspecting and untrained nose. So the roots of Miguel's vegetables wended their way down into a mother lode of nutrients, and sprang forth with fruits and greenery like nobody else's in town. Ray wasn't much of a vegetable eater, so his backyard garden wasn't as diverse—sweet corn, potatoes, and tomatoes, with just a couple of hills of Howell melons—big sweet cantaloupes developed just a few counties away—and then four rows of Indian corn and half a dozen hills of pumpkins for the third grade art class at Parma Elementary to carve Jack-o-lanterns and decorate their school room for Halloween. A farmer at heart, a garden was still important to him.

So Ray needn't have worried too much about the farm in those moments when the narcotic haze thinned, but he did worry, and on the third day after surgery, the morning after the animal funeral at Wanda's, when his wife returned from breakfast in the hospital cafeteria he tried to tell her about his concerns.

"Ah whaaa di moe summm . . . ," he said from the side of his mouth.

"What was that sweetie?" Deb's eyebrows rose.

"Whaaas maa shooofff mahnnnn . . ." The right side of his face looked relaxed and pulled across to the left side. That side suddenly looked panicked.

"Oh, God baby . . . oh God . . . where is the nurse button?! . . . oh god . . ." She found the button and punched it, then ran into the hallway to scream for help. The first person she saw was Doc Voekle ambling down the hall toward Ray's room.

"What's up, Deb?" he said, radiating calm concern.

"It's Ray. He can't talk. I think he's had a stroke! We need a doctor right now!"

Nurse Amy was already waddling toward them, herself an adipose encased victim of the countless plates of cookies brought by grateful patients and those who thought their loved one would get better care if the nurses had a steady supply of chocolate-filled goodies—briberous bonbons she was powerless to resist. At age thirty-six she was less than a year from full-blown type-II diabetes and her first dose of glucophage. But besides her nose for chocolate, she could sniff out a real emergency and could tell this was one, so she waddled as fast as she could, jiggling and huffing as she came. A bit of her midriff roll bobbed and flashed below her smock as she leaned into the turn, knocking Doc with her left hip and the door jam with her right as she rounded the corner into the room, completely winded. She pressed out her lower lip and exhaled hard, blowing greasy brown bangs into a rooster tail.

"Whaddawegot here?" she said as she got as close to the bed as her bulk would allow and pulled Ray's lopsided face in line with hers with its soft landslide of chins. "Tell me your name, Mr. Vander Koop."

"Whaaaaden mmmnaw."

"Don't worry Mr. Vander Koop, I'm getting the doctor for you." She quickly put the wheels in motion to deal with the clot that had broken loose and gone to his brain. It had come from his plaque-encrusted aorta after it had been disturbed by the clamp the surgeon had used when they had stopped his heart to transplant the new vessels. It was a relatively rare but perhaps the most feared complication that could happen to a cardiac bypass patient. Ray's luck had just run out.

Deb sat in the chair next to Ray, rocking, praying, and crying. The old vet stood next the bed with one hand holding his old friend's hand, the other on Deb's shoulder.

He said, "You're a strong man, Ray . . . You're going to beat this." He said this because he didn't know what else to say. Truth was, with a bad heart and a large piece of his brain dying for lack of oxygen at that very moment, there was a good chance he wasn't going to beat it. If he lived at all, it would likely be months before he could talk again, and he would probably never have the intellect and decision-making power to run the farm again.

The stroke team quickly mobilized and headed for Ray's room. They could not fight the clot with drugs; he was already fully heparinized—his blood was a thin as it could get. There was only one thing to do: fish out the clot with a wire. They readied the instruments for the cutting-edge procedure as Ray rolled with his full complement of hanging bottles, IV lines, catheters, wires, monitors, and loved ones toward the CT scan lab. There they would locate the clot, then send a long thin tube with a miniscule sheathed corkscrew on the end up his left common carotid artery and northward toward its target. It was a dicey proposition that would lead to a small artery in the middle of his head that should have been feeding Ray's brain blood—a job it had quit doing twenty-seven minutes before. It would be an amazing show of technology whether they pulled it off or not, and in the face of a lifetime of accumulated crap in his arteries, it was a long shot.

The doctor would visualize the tip of his instrument on a computer screen and expertly guide it toward the blockage. After a surgical cut-down to the left common carotid in his neck, an assistant injected dye into it, then cross-clamped it and inserted the long instrument. The dye in Ray's carotids showed they were as plastered with plaque as his heart, making it tough to thread the instrument through and pull it back with the clot corkscrewed onto the tip without dislodging even more gunk that would be carried to and stick right back at the same or another branch point. The wet art of medicine, the practice in the practice of medicine, the unsettling messiness of desperate cases, had become plain.

Doctors individually learn peculiar ways to ignore the panicked feeling and press on with the procedure at hand, or abort and launch some other emergency protocol, anything but emotionally acknowledge that a life that had recently been so vital, a person so loved and indispensible, was slipping away on a raft of cascading complications. The medical team had a plan and they were in execution mode. The doctor, Yao Za, an Asian man in his thirties who had not shaved in days, but you couldn't tell because of the surgical mask, emitted humming sounds like a race car accelerating, up-shifting, decelerating, down-shifting, braking, through a series ever smaller arteries. It was as if he were driving a race course that starts on I-75 at Flint and ends on a deer trail in the U.P. Dr. Yao Za leaned into his computer screen: "Errrrrrrrrr—unh" (rapid acceleration toward the head, upshift) "Bumbumbumdebumbum—unh" (deceleration, downshift, dive into internal carotid toward brain) "eeeeeeeee" (braking, tires squawking into Circle of Willis) "errr—bumbumbumdebum— errrr—bumbumdebum" (the sound of soft acceleration and deceleration around the circle), then a rumbling ululation; his tongue flapping lightly on his lips as he rolled his idling racer into the left middle cerebral artery and his target.

For Dr. Yao Za it was a video game. This is how he got his distance, how he was not pulled into the panic. He made a small cheering crowd noise as the tip of the instrument reached its mark. With a couple of movements he unsheathed the corkscrew and wound it forward another centimeter, then began making the squeaky sound of a corkscrew turning into a cork. Finally he gently pulled the long instrument back, making similar engine sounds but lugging a bit under the load, eventually pulling almost a foot of tube out of Ray's body, then a cork popping noise as the end emerged with the clot. He held it up and pulled down his mask to reveal a huge smile, like a child might show off his first little perch that had swallowed a worm under the dock on a summer afternoon. He mixed metaphors like they were college students and he was beer—race cars, wine bottles, caught fish—so it was good that he hadn't chosen writing as a career, but he had gone off to medical school a brilliant video game addict and had been transformed into a miracle worker.

Doc Voekle hugged Deb on the other side of the observation window. Ray Jr. and Sonia had just returned from a restaurant breakfast and were puzzled to find Dad and Mom missing from Dad's room. Miguel and Bruce were also headed to the hospital, as they had been informed that three days after the bypass would be the first day Ray might take visitors other than immediate family.

Bruce could hardly wait to get to the hospital, not because he was so anxious to see Ray, but because finding a toilet had suddenly become urgent. His guts rumbled and cramped.

"You got to stop at this gas station, man. I got to get to a shitter."

"Just another mile to hospital, dude. You make it."

"I don't think so, man. Pull in!"

Miguel swerved into the Clark station, causing the big Impala to list hard to the outside of the turn as Bruce opened the door and was nearly thrown out. He stumbled a bit then moved fast—you couldn't call it a run with his knees and butt cheeks clenched together. He hobbled like a woman in a long tight skirt.

"Which way to the bathroom?" he squealed at the clerk who was busy with a customer.

"Just a sec, hun, I'll get you the key," she said, giving her full attention to a personal check transaction with an elderly woman standing in front of Bruce as he winced and danced from one foot to the other. A pants explosion was imminent.

The old woman finally finished with her careful handwriting and began to strike up a conversation. "I haven't seen that Maxwell boy in church for months. Is he still sweet on that pretty Terpstra girl? She's such a beauty," she said, clearly savoring a moment of human contact.

"Nah, I think she dumped him, Helen. I hear she thinks she's too good for him. But, I also heard that he got in trouble for . . ."

Bruce yelped, "Eyeegeeze!"

The clerk flashed a concerned and apologetic smile, and slowly reached over Helen's head with the men's room key, which was fastened by a short length of electrical wire to the sawed-off handle of a busted windshield squeegee. It could have doubled as a numchuck.

"Here you go, sir. It's around the back." She motioned in the direction Bruce should go when he got outside.

In his haste he grabbed the key but missed the gesture and guessed wrong, reaching the air hoses around on the north side but no crapper. His legs parted a little as he pivoted to reverse direction, which was the only breach of anal security necessary for the first watery brown squirt to sully his whitey-tighties. He did his speediest duck walk back across the front of the gas station, at one point stepping off the sidewalk to avoid a customer entering the building, another move that allowed another squirt. He was blanched, wide-eyed, mouth agape, as he speed-waddled toward his only important destination in life. He jammed the key into the lock and wiggled it . . . and wiggled it . . . and finally it turned as another squirt came. And now he felt it running down his leg. The door opened at last and he lurched toward the toilet, pulling his pants down as he stumbled and pivoted onto the launch pad. The sensation was exquisite, like being eviscerated through his rectum. Everything poured out of him with a fetid stench. He gasped and groaned and reached back for a mercy flush. He caught his breath and grabbed a wad of toilet paper to begin to clean his underwear and the inside of his jeans. Another wave of cramps, another jet of pure liquid flew from his ass. Miguel appeared in the bathroom doorway, which Bruce had failed to close.

"You don't look so good, man."

"Holy shit, man . . . I can't go see Ray like this. What the hell is this?"

"Evacuaciones."

"Big goddamn word for the shits. I think I need a doctor."

"They got lots where we going."

"Shit, I don't have any health insurance."

"That's what emergency room is for, amigo. They got to take you."

"It's just the shits, man, it's not like I got hit by a truck."

"You *look* like you got hit by truck, man, and then they backed up over your ass. Let's go, amigo." Miguel gestured toward his old Impala, then hesitated, "You need any help?"

"Like you're going to wipe what's left of my burned out ass?" Bruce's light chuckle was interrupted by another vice-like cramp that doubled him over. More liquid sprayed into the bowl. "Ahhhhhhhhhggh . . . oh God!" Yet more liquid. "Jesus fuck! . . . Okay, I'm going to try to get my shit together here, and we can go find a doc."

Miguel closed the bathroom door while Bruce undressed, dropped his underwear in the trash can, and rinsed his jeans in the sink. He was shaking. He pulled his wet pants back on and did his best to clean up the mess, but it was hopeless, and the stench of his soiled underwear in the wastebasket was not fixable. He left the key in the door and walked gingerly to the car, his face ashen. He suddenly felt chilled and had the urge to throw up.

"Oh my God, what is this?"

"I told you, dude, evacuaciones. Cursos. The shits. I'll get you to doctor, pronto, amigo."

Miguel dropped Bruce off at the E.R. and parked the car, while Bruce met a triage nurse who seemed remarkably unfazed by his odor, but wasted no time getting him admitted and into a conveniently assless hospital gown, a process interrupted twice more by intestinal purging—and now puking. The fucking one-eighties. His shirt was soaked with sweat. By the time he was in a bed in an isolation room, he was too weak to stand. The doctor gave him oral rehydration fluids that looked suspiciously like blue Gatorade—but undoubtedly a hundred times the price—and said he was the second patient that day with a similar presentation. Her communication was interrupted by the rapid the return of the blue fluid from its very brief stay in his stomach. She said they'd start an I.V. since he couldn't keep the liquid down, then they would do a fecal culture, and, in the meantime, until they figured out what this was, fluid replacement was the best they could do.

CHAPTER 24

M iguel found Deb, Sonia, Ray Jr., and Doc Voekle in the waiting area on the cardiac floor. After getting the bad news on Ray, Miguel reported on Bruce.

Doc Voekle said one word that nobody understood: "*Campylobacter.*"

"What?" was the question on every other face in the room.

"Fill us in Doc," said Ray Jr.

"*Campylobacter jejuni.* Stressed goats comingled with chickens—unpasteurized milk—I wager he's got Campylobacter enteritis—dollars to donuts.

"I'm still not getting it, Doc," said Ray Jr.

"Most chickens carry the bacteria, goats often do too, especially if they're with chickens. The whole goat herd was stressed by the dog attack, and stress weakens their immune system. A few does then shed the bacteria in their milk, and the milk isn't pasteurized. Voila—we've got an outbreak. I better go speak with them. There might be more cases. It'll take them too long to figure it out if I don't." He headed out the door.

"How does that guy know so much?" Sonya asked.

"Born with a hell of a brain and he decided to use it," said Ray Jr. "You ever see his office at the vet clinic? Books floor to ceiling—thick ones—hundreds of them, all the way around the walls, except for a small north window looking out at the grain elevator, and an old oil painting of a flock of Scottish sheep on the wall in front of his desk. Never saw a better place to think. Even the sheep look like philosophers."

As they spoke, a coed named Eva, smelling faintly of goat, presented herself with acute explosive diarrhea to a nurse practitioner at the student infirmary at Albion College. She was told to go home and drink Gatorade. A four-year-old boy from Jackson, a fragile asthmatic boy who was given goat's milk because of a cow's milk allergy, had profuse watery diarrhea with streaks of blood in it and was being treated at home by his single mother with homeopathic remedies and an astringent herbal tea said to cleanse the intestine. A vegetarian English professor at Albion, his wife, and two teenage daughters were desperately arguing for the next shot at the only working toilet in the old house they were remodeling at the edge of campus. And a retired third grade teacher and health food devotee from Litchfield, a sweet but persnickety old woman who was on an immunosuppressive drug for rheumatoid arthritis, was unable to rise from her bed where she lay sweating in a fetid pool of blood flecked diarrhea.

Wanda felt a little "off" herself, but needed to just shake it and get her goats milked, since her student milkmaid Eva hadn't shown up for work that day. She had no idea the volume of shit that had hit the fan, or the force with which it would be blown back at her.

Doc Voekle arrived in the E.R. and asked to see one of the physicians. The desk clerk handed him a clipboard. "You'll have to wait your turn sir. Just sign in here and the triage nurse will see you when your turn comes." She turned away before he could protest. She was a large woman with golden helmet hair and the don't-screw-with-me demeanor of a cop who'd seen everything. She'd learned her people skills at her previous job where she earned her Christmas bonuses by denying patient claims and rescinding coverage for pre-existing conditions for a large health insurance company.

Doc called her back, "I'm not sick," he said, "I want to talk to an E.R. doc about one of your patients. I think I can be of service."

"Are you a doctor, sir?"

"Yes, I'm a veterinarian."

"We don't treat animals here, sir. I don't think we can help you."

"I don't need your help. You need mine. Does the word zoonosis mean anything to you?"

"No, but I'm sure it does to you." She drummed her fingers on the counter and gave Doc a look of contempt at the edge of exasperation. "Our doctors are very good and very busy sir, and they don't need to be bothered by horse doctors. We have sick *people* here that need their attention."

"Do they pay you to be obstructionist or just ignorant, ma'am?"

"I'm calling security, sir. They can help you."

"Jesus . . ." Doc muttered as he pretended to walk toward the exit, then pivoted and walked straight back to the patient area. He saw a woman in a white coat with a stethoscope hanging around her neck studying a computer monitor. He waved to get her attention.

"Hi, I'm Doc Voekle, I'm a veterinarian, I have some information . . ."

As he spoke a very large black security guard with biceps the size of footballs approached him from behind and squeezed his arm in his giant right paw, "Time to be going, old man. We can't have you back here without authorization."

The woman in the white coat interrupted. "Lewis, take your hands off that man. Who told you that you could treat this man like that? Never mind—I can guess. Just let go of him Lewis. We're having a professional consultation."

Lewis reluctantly let go of Doc's arm, a little disappointed that he wasn't going to get to do any bouncing that morning.

"Quite a defensive line you got there, doctor," Doc Voekle said.

"It takes a good sense of the playing field to get past them. You must have played some ball. Most people don't get past the line of scrimmage." The physician, an athletic woman in her late forties, quickly sized up Doc, appreciating the aging face of hard physical work and intellectual challenge. She could see he was a man at ease in his skin: calm, engaged, still pretty good looking for a guy on the back side of sixty, apparently unfazed by his run-in with the front desk, and wearing a gold band on his left ring finger. Damn, she thought.

"Been dodging cows my whole life. Keeps you light on your pegs if you can just get your geriatric bones out of bed in the morning. Anyway, I wanted to talk to you about one of your patients, a Mr. Bruce Dinkle."

"Before we get to that doctor, I'm Georgina Bottoms," she said, extending her hand accompanied a broad smile. "Of course I can't discuss any of my patients with you, doctor . . . I'm sorry, I didn't catch your first name."

"Everybody's been calling me Doc for so long, sometimes I forget. Cecil, as I recollect. Cec Voekle. Nice to meet you, Georgina." He fiddled a little with the pen in his pocket, embarrassed by the feminine attention.

"Anyway, I wasn't going to ask you to divulge anything, confidential or otherwise, doctor. I don't know how much history you got, but I wanted to let you know that Bruce Dinkle drinks unpasteurized goat milk. There are a number of customers of Nanny Gate Dairy—that's a goat farm about ten miles west of here—anyway, there's a bunch of folks around the area who ingest raw goat milk from there. She pedals shares in her milk goats to her raw milk customers in order to skirt the legal problem of selling it unpasteurized. Awful nice folks, but they got this cockamamie notion in their mushy brains that milk's healthier drunk raw. I wonder if a few days of intestinal purging might not disabuse them of that misapprehension—clean their guts out right up to their cerebral cortex. Can't tell them a damn thing. Anyway, there's a good chance its *Campylobacter jejuni*, although of course it could be staph or a number of other things. They've got chickens free-ranging with the goats, so there's plenty of opportunity for fecal contamination. Just thought you'd want to know."

"Good to know, Cec. I expect you saved us a lot of sleuthing. Thanks, Doc." She smiled and added, "By the way, that was Leila the Linebacker who tried to stop you from coming back here. I apologize for her. Thanks again, Doc; I owe you one. Maybe a glass of wine sometime."

"I'd enjoy that Georgina, but I doubt my wife would approve."

And so the outbreak was solved before it was apparent to anybody else that there was one. Reports of the disease were emailed and phoned-in from physicians and nurse practitioners to county health officials in the area who quickly confirmed the common source. They put out a bulletin to all of the health providers in the area. Then they got a list of Wanda's customers to alert each of them. And then they shut down the dairy. After taking samples for bacteriology, the State Health Inspector opened the valve at the bottom of Nanny Gate's refrigerated bulk tank and drained a hundred gallons of rich goat milk into the septic system.

The single mother, Maxine Jurek, the one with the very sick little boy, Amos was his name, was too preoccupied to check her emails or phone messages. She was busy scanning her authoritative compendium of herbal remedies to find what was "good" for diarrhea with blood and cramping. She ran her finger down the alphabetical list looking for treatments she might already have on hand: amomum fruit, angelica root, astragulus, aurantium fruit, bamboo shavings, bupleurum, cimicifuga, citrus, coptis, corydalis tuber, immature orange peel, licorice, peach kernel, platycodon root, pulsatilla, and rhubarb. She underlined the things she had on hand, citrus, licorice, and rhubarb, with a pencil, then went to her garden and pulled half a dozen stalks of rhubarb, hurriedly chopped them into a sauce pan, and put them on the stove with a little water to simmer with a whole chopped lemon—the hardest, greenest one in the bag, peel and all. She poured in a shot of Ouzo (a left-behind from her ex) for the licorice in it, knowing the alcohol would cook off. She wished peaches were in season so she could add a chopped peach kernel, but with three active ingredients, all organic except the Ouzo, she was sure it would work. She didn't allow sugar in the house, so she sweetened things for herself and little Amos with stevia, a sweet powdered herb she got from the health food store.

After the mixture cooled a little, she tasted it and decided to add a pour of goat milk to meld the flavors. The milk curdled instantly in the acidic mush, which gave the mixture an opaque granular appearance, the color of yellowed Pepto Bismol. She tasted it again and declared it not that bad. Actually it was vile, but she had long ago parted company with self-honesty in favor of fanatic loyalty to the Church of the Contrary Intuition. A shrink would have another name for her condition, something incorporating paranoia and delusions, but he might not be able to name the yellowish pink concoction with the goat milk curds, lumps of lemon rind and strings of rhubarb that she was about to foist upon her child.

It was roughly the pH of battery acid, which was only part of the reason that only moments after she goaded her little patient into swallowing a spoonful and leaned in close to stroke his fevered brow, it came back like a spinning pink boomerang, a sour liquid projectile straight into her face. It managed to foul the hemp-upholstered, organic-cotton-filled futon and her batik dashiki, and it completely dissolved the cruelty-free blush on her cheeks. The acidity of the vomit in her eyes blinded her. She screamed and ran for the bathroom, struck the door jam with her forehead, and collapsed on the floor. She looked like a rag pile. Amos heard the crash, opened his eyes, and saw his heap of mother lying very still and quiet. In his small sickly voice he cried for her to get up, "Get up Mommy!" but she didn't move. He used the little strength he had to crawl to her. He tried to shake her arm but he was too weak to move it. He got her cell phone from her pocket, opened it, and dialed 9-1-1.

In a quavering voice he told the dispatcher, "Mommy's on the floor and I can't wake her up, and I don't feel very good."

"That doesn't sound good, honey. What is your name?"

Amos accurately gave his name, his mother's name, and their address, and help would be instantly on the way. It was the stuff of happy endings, the sort of heartwarming story tacked on at the end of the local TV news to leaven the nightly barrage of horror. But Maxine Jurek came-to just as Amos was closing the cell phone, discovered that he had called 9-1-1, and called them right back to cancel the emergency, explaining that she had just fallen asleep after staying up all night with her sick little boy. The dispatcher got a good laugh and they agreed that kids today are amazing with the new technology.

CHAPTER 25

Ray found himself swimming up to a light, swimming up through warm aquamarine waters. It seemed it should have been salty, but it wasn't; the taste on his lips was fresh. His stroked in slow motion up through the crystalline water as if it were thick as honey. Slowly up, and up, he patiently stroked through the sparkling goop. He picked up speed through a school of large silver fish . . . salmon . . . fresh water . . . it must be Lake Michigan . . . I remember it being colder. He continued swimming up . . . up and never wanting for breath . . . stroking toward a small circle of light . . . kicking like a pearl diver rising from the green depths . . . a single violin playing Mendelssohn, a heart breaking melody that filled his throat with tears. The light . . . the violin . . . the gliding up . . . *Heaven*, he realized . . . I'm swimming up to Heaven. I was right. I'll have to tell Deb. It is on earth. Heaven is right here on earth. And I'm almost there . . . from wherever I was. His body glided slowly up between long strokes, soaring in water like a ray (he dream-smiled and thought, I *am* Ray) with the music and water flowing over him. Now light spread across a wide swath above him, waves rippled on his ceiling. Aquamarine gradually faded to crystal clear, and above that, blue sky, silver glints on the waves. It would be a sunny day in Heaven . . . it doesn't take a weatherman to know *that* . . . he smiled to himself. His farmer's concern about the weather was coming back. But more importantly, who will be there? Would there be a diner like Martha's? Will angels call me hun? The music swelled; he could hear the tiny scratches of fingers touching strings. Sarah . . . Sarah is here in Heaven! . . . I thought she was in Seattle. He cried to think his daughter would be in Heaven. He missed her. He wondered how she got there . . . what had happened to her? An accident? No . . . no . . . if Heaven is on earth, then she's alive. And now here he was . . . he had arrived . . . Heaven . . . . His head broke from the heavy water into thin air. Just like that. A small gasp, no struggle, no need to dry off—simply transported from the water below to the land above.

Dr. Yao Za pulled his penlight away from Ray's eyes, tucked it into the pocket of his scrubs, and stepped back to observe his patient. Ray looked past him, his vision gauzy, and thought, yes, yes . . . there she is . . . Sarah . . . he could see his beautiful daughter right there . . . Sarah . . . Sarah, playing her violin like an angel. And Mike . . . Mike the prodigal son home from California . . . and Ray Jr . . . . and Sonia . . . and Doc . . . even Miguel . . . and right next to him, Deb, she's holding my hand . . . I can see her . . . my wife . . . my beautiful wife . . . she's so beautiful . . . I must tell her she's beautiful and we live in Heaven. They all beamed at Ray as he surfaced. Nurses and visitors beamed in the doorway, drawn by Sarah's violin.

Dr. Yao Za said to Deb, "I think he's going to be okay. But he won't be himself right away. The drugs will make him a little goofy, but they'll wear off in few hours. And the ointment in his eyes will make his vision blurry for a little while. We'll just have to wait to see how quickly and how much his brain can heal itself."

Deb watched Ray's eyes fill with tears as they scanned the room flooded with friends and family and golden evening light. "Good morning, sunshine," she said, stroking his head.

"Hi," *Ha*, he whispered, "Heaven," *Heben*.

"I know," she said, kissing his forehead. "I live here."

While Ray had been swimming up to Heaven from the nether world of anesthesia and hypoxic brain injury, Bruce was getting his escaped bodily fluids replenished. And Maxine Jurek continued her incompetent medical care of her little son Amos with a righteous sense of mission, the same impulse that caused her to refuse his childhood vaccinations and opt for home schooling. She was not the religious fundamentalist variety of home-schooler, so she planned to teach him about evolution some day, but she might as well have been a Young Earther—she understood biology at about the same level a cow understands grass, her notions of cause and effect every bit as simple as "because God said."

If Amos survived her medical ministrations, he would still have to overcome her lesson plans to make a success of his life. But if he did, somehow, and if he became a writer, he would have a clear shot at a best-selling memoir that would share shelf space and a Dewey decimal number with all the other books written by victims of crazy but well-meaning mothers. The odds of growing up weren't looking good though; he was slipping in and out of lucidity and mumbling incoherently, which prompted Maxine to rifle through the pages of her herbal remedy compendium for herbs that support the brain. She couldn't find anything that matched Amos's symptoms; most of it claimed to be "good" for senile dementia and Alzheimer's, so she called her friend Latrina Fisher who owned the health food store in Albion. Latrina gave her a very bad idea mixed with some very good advice: "I think you've done all you can, Maxine. I've got some *cerebrum compostium suis*, and I could bring it over, but maybe you should call a doctor."

"But they would stick needles in my little Amos. He hates shots even more than I do."

"I always feel better after a good cry, Maxine. Maybe he will too."

"No! Western medicine is evil. It breaks everything down into little parts and objectifies them and doesn't look at the whole person. And then they treat you with poisons—did you ever read the list of side-effects that comes with a bottle of pills from a big drug company? You said it yourself—you told me you don't trust doctors either. The last time I went to a gynecologist he talked about my vagina like it was a third party in the room. Well, maybe the fourth, since there was a nurse to keep him from trying anything, which I'm sure he would have if he'd had half a chance. Anyway he said I should stop with the rosemary and peppermint douche, he said it was irritating my tissues and that womanly odors are desirable, but I tell you what, he irritated the hell out of me. What the hell does he know about womanly odors? Men! I told him . . ."

"Maxine, maybe you should forget about womanly odors and call a doctor. This might be serious for little Amos," said Latrina.

"No. Bring over that cerebrum compost . . . composite . . ."

"*Compostium. Cerebrum compostium suis*: powdered pig brain with other secret ingredients. I'm not sure it will work, Maxine. It's really excellent for Alzheimer's, but I'm not sure here . . ."

"Well how will we know if we don't try it?"

"You really want to experiment on your little boy?"

"It's not an experiment. Herbal medicine is ancient, you know that. How could it be thousands of years old if it didn't work?"

"This medicine isn't herbal, it's homeopathic. It absorbs homotoxins. It hasn't been around so long."

"Still, a long time."

"I suppose. I'll be right over," Latrina relented.

Latrina arrived shortly. She ran up Maxine's driveway with her large cotton shoulder bag sagging under the weight of a half-dozen jars and bags of herbal and homeopathic concoctions.

"I came as fast as I could. Where is he?" Latrina's chest heaved. She looked flushed.

"He's sleeping. I don't think we should wake him."

"What happened to your face?"

"I ran into a doorway."

"Was that bastard husband of yours back?"

"No, really, it was a doorway. Carl's screwing some slut in Jackson, so he's been a little nicer. Men—that's all they think about. It won't last when he sees the settlement I've got drawn up, though. I'm taking him and his little wayward dick to the cleaners. He'll be sleeping in his truck when I get done with him."

"You're one tough broad, Maxine."

"Thanks, sister. Can I make you a cup of chamomile?"

"No thanks, I think we better go check on him."

"Yeah, I guess we should. I hope we can get him to keep this stuff down. How do you give it?" Maxine asked.

"In a pill or mixed in a drink. Either way is fine. Milk is good."

Maxine poured a small glass of raw goat milk from the glass jar she kept in the refrigerator. Latrina opened two capsules of the powdered pig brain into it, and stirred. It smelled goaty, piggy, and a little off, but it was medicine.

"This is going to work, I can just feel it," said Maxine.

"I hope so. Let's wake him up."

They entered Amos's darkened bedroom. It smelled of vomit and diarrhea with hints of citrus and goat. Latrina leaned over her friend with a hand on her shoulder, as Maxine knelt next to her son and gave him a little nudge. She spoke in the soft, high, sing-song voice parents reserve for small children, extra high since it was for a very sick small child. "Amos . . . it's your mother . . . I've got something to make you all better," she crooned. Amos didn't respond. She gave him little shake. "Amos . . . it's your mother . . . wake up Amos . . . I have something for you to drink, Amos . . ."

Still nothing.

She shook him a little harder this time, and in a fuller voice, "Amos, wake up Amos."

He remained limp.

The seriousness of the situation was getting through to Maxine. She fairly screamed, "Amos! Wake up Amos! Amos!" and pulled the rag-limp boy upright, shaking him vigorously. His head lolled and his eyes rolled back under half-closed lids.

Latrina already had her cell phone out and was punching in 9-1-1. "Stop shaking him Maxine!"

"He won't wake up! Who are you calling!?"

"9-1-1—who do you think?"

"Amos just called them a few hours ago when I bumped my head. They're going to think I'm an idiot."

"You might be Maxine. We have to get this boy to a hospital or he's going to die."

"But don't you believe in what we're doing?" Maxine asked.

"It's time to stop believing and start thinking, Maxine." It was the first chink in the evidence-free armor of alternative medicine that Latrina had admitted to a customer since she'd opened her store twenty-two years before.

The ambulance arrived at full wail. A female paramedic ran with Amos in her arms like he was football. She tried to start an IV in the vehicle but his veins had collapsed. She couldn't find one she could hit. They'd have to get him to the hospital for a venous cutdown. They screamed down the potholed back roads to I-94 and into Jackson at close to a hundred miles an hour. Maxine sat by her son in disbelief and uncharacteristic silence.

Dr. Georgina Bottoms met the gurney. "Does he drink raw goat milk from Nanny Gate?" the doctor asked Maxine.

"Why . . . yes, yes, it's totally organic . . . no toxins in it and no nutrients destroyed," she answered, confused by the question, adding, "How did you know that? Will he be able to get it here? That would be great."

"That would not be great," the doctor said as a scrub-clad team rushed around Amos. They quickly intubated him to increase his oxygen level and protect his airway from vomit.

"Why are you doing that? He can breathe fine," Maxine protested.

"Would somebody please show Mrs. Jerky to the waiting area?" asked Dr. Bottoms.

"It's Jurek—Ju-rek. I can't believe you people know what you're doing. What does oxygen have to do with diarrhea? I don't think I should leave him with you. Where did you go to school, doctor?"

Dr. Bottoms raised the ante in a calm voice. "Someone call security please," she said, as she quickly prepped the cut-down site, focusing hard on the task at hand.

Lewis, the large black security guard with the football-sized biceps, appeared shortly. He gently took Maxine's arm in his huge hand. "Let's go get you some coffee, ma'am."

She attempted to jerk her arm back, but it was futile. His fingers more than encircled her arm—fingers as thick as her son's forearms. "I don't drink coffee, you big pig! Coffee is poison and it exploits *your* people."

"Ma'am, I'm not sure who you think my people are, ma'am, but whatever you prefer to drink, ma'am, you can't be in here right now. They're trying to help your son, ma'am, and they can do it better without you here." Lewis noticed the fresh goose egg on Maxine's forehead and the two black eyes developing below it. "I'm going to take you to a safe room, ma'am, where you can talk to a nice person who can help you," he added.

"I don't want a god damn safe room and I wish you'd stop ma'amming me!" Maxine struggled and argued all the way to social services where there was indeed a very nice person who listened well enough to determine that Maxine did not need protection from a violent man, but that her son desperately needed protection from his mother.

There were limited infectious disease isolation facilities at the Jackson hospital, so as soon as little Amos was hooked up to a full kit of tubes, pumps, and wires in the E.R., they assembled the components of a pediatric intensive care bed in the same room as Bruce, with just a curtain between them. Bruce's nausea was under control and the diarrhea had let up a little; with fluid replacement, a drug to stop the retching, and an antibiotic that usually works against *Campylobacter*, he was getting better quickly. The no-visitors restriction in the infectious ward meant that Bruce's only friends were the television and the nurses, who weren't very interested in chatting while they tended to his new desperately ill roommate. He tried the TV, but couldn't decide which was worse, the commercials or the programs. When Bruce felt another round of intestinal purging gurgling and cramping his guts, he had to get his own isolated self off to the bathroom, pushing his I.V. stand ahead of him, happy to have at least something to hang onto to steady his almost buckling knees. He was miserable, but at least he wasn't on a ventilator like his roommate.

Dr. Bottoms entered the room. "How are you feeling tonight, Mr. Dinkle?"

"Better . . . not right, but better. When can I get out of here? I don't have any health insurance, and I'm guessing this is costing me more than a Motel-6."

"You're making good progress, Bruce. I think we should be able to get you out of here tomorrow."

"How come you put this little guy in here with me?" Bruce asked.

"Because he's got the same infection that you've got, only a lot worse. You both drank the same unpasteurized goat's milk. It made a whole bunch of people sick around here. There's another woman they took up to Lansing in critical condition. You know, it was a big step forward for public health when Louie Pasteur figured out more than a century ago that heating milk to a hundred and sixty degrees Fahrenheit kills bacteria without curdling it—right up there with water chlorination. Why wouldn't you want to take advantage of that?"

"Pasteurization destroys nutrients."

"Where do you people get this crap? Actually, right after man learned to make fire, he started cooking his food. Or maybe it was right after he put a fork in an old wildebeest that couldn't outrun an African grass fire and declared it delicious—who knows? But cooking was a big step forward. Cooking starts the protein breakdown process and makes it easier to digest—you get *more* nutrients from cooked food. You believe in fire?—or is that just too darn modern for you?—sorry, I'm out of line on that, Mr. Dinkle—I'm sorry. I'm just very upset about this boy—pure ignorance that he's here—pure goddamn ignorance that you're both here."

"Is he going to make it?"

"I don't know. But if he does, he'll probably have permanent damage."

"What would be damaged? It's just diarrhea."

"Jesus, you people always yammering-on about holistic this and holistic that, complaining that doctors don't look at the whole person. I'll tell you what, it's just a little more complicated than "the head bone's connected to the neck bone." He's got an infection that has him so dehydrated that he went into shock—cardiovascular collapse—his blood pressure dropped to the point that his organs, especially his brain and kidneys, weren't getting enough blood. We may get most of him back, but we may not get his brain, and if he still has a working brain, he may not have working kidneys. He may need a kidney transplant. It's not *just* diarrhea, you d—" Dr. Bottoms caught herself. There were tears in her eyes. "Oh God, I'm sorry, and I should not be talking to you about another patient. I apologize. I'm sorry. But dammit!—three-hundred years after the dawn of the Enlightenment!—the

Age of Reason!—and we're going fricking backwards! It makes me crazy! This kid should not be here—there was nothing!—nothing!—not one damn thing fundamentally wrong with him except that he's got a mush-brained mother who believes in powdered pig brains and snake oil!" The doctor tried to compose herself. "Oh God, I'm sorry . . . If I get myself fired, at least you'll know I cared enough to say something." She walked out without waiting for a response. She was afraid what she might say next.

Bruce was speechless anyway. Clearly Wanda had led him and her other customers astray with her scheme to skirt the law prohibiting the sale of raw milk on the pretext that it was more nutritious. But there was so much *virtue* in her small farm and in local food production. He could see that his locavore ethic could be separated easily enough from the raw milk issue, but there was no dividing Wanda. There were even moments when he thought he might be in love with her, but now she had done this horrible thing. She hadn't meant for it to happen of course, but here was the predictable result. And here he was flat on his back in the hospital, racking up medicals bill he'd never be able to pay with his part-time minimum wage job, and sharing a room with a child who might die because of her negligence. All he had were questions: How is a person to live responsibly? Where is the moral path? How can a person tell if he's on it? Or does a man just have to slash his way through life's undergrowth by dead reckoning? Must a person try to fix every wrong he comes in contact with? How did his earnest attempt to fix one problem lead to so many others? Who should pay—who *would* pay—for this mess?

A woman with an unruly mop of auburn hair and a blue chambray work shirt appeared in the window of the door to the isolation ward. She looked exhausted. Her eyes were red and wet, and when they met Bruce's eyes, she blew him an uncertain kiss. Then she turned away and doubled over, her face buried in her hands. She convulsed with sobs and her thick curls fell all around.

CHAPTER 26

I n her lawyer's dark plywood-paneled office, shades drawn against the first ninety-degree day of the summer, Alice stared at a legal form glaring back from a small pool of light under a halogen desk lamp. She leaned forward in her chair and signed her name on the black line labeled 'plaintiff'. She had thought she was prepared, even anxious, for this day right from the moment Bruce abandoned the kids and her, but the power of the act took her by surprise. It was a simple stroke of the pen that thousands of married couples use to uncouple every day in America, and yet she was devastated. Of course it wasn't final yet—there would be a series of miserable meetings before all the custody and financial issues were settled—but it was clear to Alice that eventually, probably by summer's end, it would be final. So little of what had gone wrong between the two of them was her fault, she thought. None-the-less, feelings of regret and remorse, sorrow and sadness, came over her in waves and stuck in her throat as she and her lawyer worked to draft a divorce settlement across his wide black walnut desktop.

He was Robert Cruzer of the law firm Keillor, Cruzer & Gomer, a jowly graying man in a well worn gray suit and green tie patterned with diagonal rows of Mallard ducks flaring their wings to land—that critical live-or-die, hunter-versus-duck moment, machine-embroidered on silk, and repeated down the broad slope of his chest and belly. His demeanor—smooth but curt, matter of fact, seen it all before—was troubling to Alice. He'd spent a large part of his career defending criminals, and it had given him a low opinion of people. She believed she could feel his disapproval oozing onto her, though he himself was on his third marriage. Actually, when he gazed on Alice, in all likelihood his thoughts were the same as every other man who appreciates a beautiful woman. She wasn't a criminal, but she was about to be a divorcee. She had never thought she would be a divorcee. She never wanted to be one. *Divorcee*—the word sounded tawdry. It sounded like loser. She felt her knees wobble when the she stood to leave. She looked unsteady.

"Can I get you anything, Alice?" Robert Cruzer asked.

She wished he wouldn't address her in that familiar way, him being a party to the dissolution of her family, a witness to her ugliest chapter. What would she have him call her? Mrs. Dinkle? Clearly not. She decided she would reclaim her maiden name: Freeman. Never had her family name meant so much to her. She had thought it comical when she gave up Freeman for Dinkle, her girlfriends had teased her about it, and she laughed with them at the time, but the rush she felt knowing that now she would get her name back blew in with so many emotions—defeat, shame, pride, sadness, anxiety, anticipation, freedom—it was almost overwhelming. Alice Patricia Freeman. "Can I get you anything, Alice?" he had asked—like they were old friends. She couldn't find the assertiveness to correct him—not even close. But she managed a little dig: "Um . . . no thanks . . . *Bob*," she said, and walked out of the dim air-conditioned office into blinding sunlight and the heat of a withering day.

The next day, a heavily tattooed, buzz-cut, fat man drove an old brown Oldsmobile too fast into the farmyard of Vander Koop Farms, Inc., Unit One. He raised a little gravel and a dust cloud as he swung the old car around to face the exit, as was his learned habit. He got out with a thick manila envelope and a sixty-four ounce mug—an ice bucket really—of gas station pop, leaving the car door open and the motor running. Miguel was cleaning the nozzles of a big self-propelled crop sprayer in the farm shop. The tall sliding door was wide open to catch the little breeze. He came out to meet him.

"I'm looking for Bruce Dinkle, are you him?"

"No, he's stinkier than me." Miguel grinned and added, "He's in hospital with the shits,"

"The shits, eh?" The man paused to slurp from the bucket, "I bet he shits when he gets this! Yup, he'll shit for sure! He'll shit his brains out!" The man had a big laugh at his own cleverness, adding, "What hospital's he in?"

Miguel's instinct to protect his friend suddenly kicked in. "I ain't telling you, man."

"I'm an agent of the law, mister . . . what did you say your name was?"

"I ain't telling you that neither."

The paper server took his first good look at Miguel who was wiping his hands on a rag, causing his forearms to ripple—a little thick in the middle . . . unflinching eye contact . . . an old hunting knife on his belt. "Alright, I'll be back in a day or two and I'll be looking for a little more cooperation."

"And we be looking for *you*," Miguel said cheerfully.

Wanda drove her pickup to the hospital the next noon to get Bruce and bring him back to Nanny Gate to convalesce for a couple of days. He felt drained, literally. His guts were still sore and his appetite was off, but he could finally keep a little bland food down. Dr. Bottoms had said he would be back to normal in a few days. Wanda said she would make him chicken and rice soup. It sounded good. He decided not to mention that rice isn't grown in Michigan. Wanda looked tired.

"How's the farm?" Bruce asked as they drove.

"Terrible. They drained the bulk tank. Eva isn't back yet—she got it too . . . . I don't know if she's coming back. I got a touch of it myself. I feel like hell, and I'm having to do all the milking and then pour it all down the drain. It's killing me. Everybody at the college read about it in the paper, and I'm having trouble just doing my job. It's hard to teach when you can't focus."

"I'll try to help with the goats, but I still feel weak, and there's things I got to do out at Vander Koop's too, what with Ray being down. His kids are all in town though; maybe they'll help out." Bruce sighed deeply. "What's Krystal up to?"

"I don't know . . . She's out driving around in her new truck more than she's working the last few days. I saw it parked over at Ray's shop yesterday afternoon. She must've been seeing Miguel about something," said Wanda.

"Yeah, I noticed she was hanging with him at the party too . . . and Doris wasn't there either . . . Huh? . . . I wonder if they've got something going? So what's her new truck look like?"

"Kind of trashy nouveau-riche. She got a black Chevy three-quarter-ton, small box, four-by-four with tinted windows and headlight covers, chrome wheels, pin stripes—all that macho glam stuff. Looks like a back-country pimpmobile to me, but she's so full of don't-fuck-with-me since she stuck that fork in Jeff, I'm afraid she might be growing balls."

"Can't blame her. The truck's got to replace Bob Barker for intimidation. I bet she looks hot in it, though."

"She looks like she's got a sugar daddy in a trailer park."

"You jealous?"

"Not really."

"You know, I bet if you took off the chrome and the tints and the stripes, and sandblasted off the clear coat, it could pass for a Mennonite truck. It would look darn near organic with those bulging rear fenders—old fashioned, kind of like gram-paw used to drive—just the thing for selling goat cheese and brown eggs at the Farmer's Market." Bruce felt himself smile for the first time in days.

Wanda was in no mood for joking. "I can't sell the milk or the cheese now, and I'm not driving a thirty-five thousand dollar truck that gets twelve miles-per-gallon just to sell free-range eggs, even if they are four bucks a dozen."

"Just kidding. What are you going to do to get the dairy back up and running?"

"If I'm still in business, we've got to sanitize everything, get the milk tested a bunch of times, and get a pasteurizer—or send it all to a milk plant that has one—but of course there's no goat milk truck to pick it up. I can't risk this again."

"What do you mean, "if you're still in business"?"

"You don't think there's lawsuits coming? I'm pretty sure Nanny Gate is totally screwed—and me with it. It's funny . . . you know how when people die, they say 'poor old so-and-so, he *bought* the farm,' but when you go bankrupt, you *lose* the farm, which for me is like dying. Maybe it's like Doc said, Heaven's bound to have nice goat pastures—so maybe I'll get to rock back in my chair on a shady front porch on a goat farm in the sky. Of course, if my milk kills Amos Jurek or the woman they took up to Lansing . . . Hazel Springer . . . what a sweet lady . . . then maybe Heaven isn't where I'm going."

It was the first trace of religiosity that Bruce had heard from Wanda. "You buying that Heaven stuff? I didn't figure you for it."

"Yeah, well, maybe not, but I can tell you this, I've got a little Hell going right here on earth about now." Wanda blotted her eyes on her sleeves so she could keep driving, but they filled again, half blinding her, and she began to sob. She violently squeegeed her tears with the backs of her hands. Suddenly she cranked the wheel onto a dirt two-track and drove a short way into a dense woodlot. She looked desperate.

"Why are we stopping here?" Bruce asked.

"I want you to fuck me." Her face was wet and red, her mouth pulled down at the corners like there were hooks in it.

"You want to make love right here? Right now?"

"How could you *make love* to me? How could anybody love me?—I'm a crazy-ass goat lady who *kills* people? I want you to *fuck* me! I need so bad to feel something besides pain! Just fuck me!" She struggled with her jeans and panties under the steering wheel.

"Wanda, this isn't right . . . Besides, I'm so weak I can hardly walk, and my guts still hurt . . . I don't think I could do it if I wanted to."

"Goddammit Bruce, you better."

Bruce couldn't remember ever turning down sex before, but this felt like something else. Like consent from the ineligible. Like asylum rape. He was confused and horrified. He slid next to her on the truck seat, put his arms around her, and hugged her as hard as he could in his weakened state. Wanda sobbed deeply. The tears wouldn't stop. Bruce held her close for a long time as she cried it out. He pulled her smell into his nose. He held her so long his arms hurt. He noticed the bandage where the I.V. line had been in his arm and wondered whether a person could dehydrate from tears. Maybe not, but when a farm dies, it takes a farmer with it.

The healthy Vander Koops, Deb and her three kids and daughter-in-law, had a pow-wow over breakfast in the hospital cafeteria that morning. They weren't really kids of course, but Deb had them fixed in her mind from the time when they left home, and somehow expected them to stay the same. In essence of course they had stayed the same, but that essence had bloomed a world far away from the big farm and the small town. There are a few city kids who sense that they're farmers at heart, move to the country, and soak up every last bit of farming know-how and culture they can find; and then there are busloads of country girls and boys who can't wait to get away from their podunk town and cut loose in the big city. One group yearns to be around normal folks anchored to the land and community, the other has a desperate need to express themselves in a place where they can disappear in the crowd and won't be judged by narrow minded people. Either way they're bound to be disappointed when the fantasy turns out to have a nasty case of crotch warts, but every one of Ray and Deb's three kids had opted for the concrete on the other side of the fence, and they weren't interested in moving back home.

Sarah had taken Bogart to the county fair from the time she was old enough—nine was the age to join 4-H—until she graduated from Parma High School. She enjoyed it well enough—there's hardly been a girl who didn't love a horse or wish she had a horse to love—but the violin was her other love, and the country music station that was always playing in the horse barn at the county fair was a big hint to Sarah that these weren't her people. Her parents were simultaneously proud and bewildered by the girl.

Like all parents with kids who fly far from the nest, they had theories as to where those off-type genes came from. Deb had a brother who was good in math, and that often goes with musical ability, and she'd sung in the church choir herself, so she figured it was *her* musical genes that had come through. Ray said maybe, but that *his* charm, good looks, and outgoing personality were what made her a soloist. He would always assume a snooty expression, inflate himself, tuck an air violin under his chin, and give it a few strokes when he made this claim. Always good for a family chuckle. Like all the best parents, they had given their daughter the wings to fly—and she'd gone and used them. Deb envied her friends who had managed to keep their daughters close to home, but she didn't know how she could have done that without breaking Sarah's spirit.

Deb said, "Sarah, you used to drive tractors. How about you take a break from playing Seattle train stations and spend the summer in Michigan? I bet you'd get a better tan than you would out in the rainy northwest."

"I wouldn't bet much on a Michigan tan, Mom. And please don't ask me to do that. I've got try-outs for the Seattle Symphony next month, and I'm booked to play with a cellist friend for six weddings this summer. Plus I've got a cat. I can't just leave; it's my home now."

"The symphony will still be there, a solo cello is fine for a wedding, and you could bring your cat. I couldn't have him on the furniture, but he'd love to spend the summer out in the barn with Bogart."

"*She* . . . my cat's a *she*, Mom. She's a calico and her name is Pizzicato, everybody calls her Pizza Cat. Anyway she's an indoor cat. Please Mom, don't make me do this."

"I can't make you do anything, Sarah—God knows we both know that—I was just hoping. You can't blame a mother. You could leave Pizza Kitty with a friend."

"Mom!"

"Okay, okay. How about you Mike? What's your excuse?" Deb assumed defeat with Mike before she started.

"Don't need one, Ma. I'm just not doing it." He also could have said that he couldn't do it because of weekly meetings with his probation officer as the result of a little skirmish a couple of months before outside a bar in

East L.A., but he wasn't prone to explaining himself. The punchee had made a disparaging remark about a paint job on a tricked-out chopper parked there, unaware he was talking to the guy who painted it. Mike had just adjusted his attitude a little. The kid had carried a chip since he was old enough to lift one. Sometimes it seemed like a security blanket he used to keep the world away. He just liked a lot of distance. Ray Senior's grandfather on his mom's side had been a hard man to get along with that way. You'd think that trait would have disappeared after being diluted by three generations of sweet people, but there he was, a sour apple, and L.A. hadn't done much to sweeten him. Not a real bad apple mind you, you wouldn't be afraid to have a beer with him, although you probably had best be gone before the tenth.

It had started with a bit of dyslexia, and although it was never diagnosed, it caused Mike to fall behind in school early on, and he never really recovered. His defense against the judgment he felt from parents and teachers was emotional distance; he dug a moat around himself and stocked it with attitude. He took to wearing black in junior high and fell in with the Goths, who were glad to have him, although they were a little suspicious of his athletic good looks until he got some piercings and tattoos. He spent most of his free time doodling and drawing fantasy characters. Ray and Deb fought against his antisocial behaviors, but comforted themselves with the wishful thought that it was just a phase. Adolescence is just a phase of course, but it leads to adulthood, and patterns have a way of sticking.

So now he airbrushed motorcycle gas tanks with adult fantasy scenes that caused parents to shield the view from their children when they passed his art work parked on the street. And he had tried to trade on his good looks by dabbling in porn. He had almost everything he needed for success in the sex biz: a good physique and natural extroversion from his dad, and he got a kick out of shocking people; but that most critical part for a porn actor, impressive as it was in dimension, retained just enough Midwestern reticence to be unreliable in front of the cameras, so he stopped applying for parts because he wasn't getting them anyway. But he'd made some friends in the business, especially among the porn women who found his on-camera shyness endearing, so he got invited to their parties—and he sure as hell wasn't going to find *that* kind of action in Parma—so he wasn't coming home.

"Alright Mike, I know better than to fight you too. But I am glad you come home to see your dad though, I really am, sweetie."

"Thanks, Ma. It means a lot," Mike answered.

"So that leaves you, Ray, and we've already had this talk. What are you thinking, now?" Deb asked.

"What am I thinking?—I'm thinking we've got a pretty good man in Miguel. I know you're not crazy about him being a Mexican and an ex-con, but he knows the farm and he works hard. Bruce trips over himself about once a week and I have no idea what he's planning to do next. If he throws in with Wanda he's going to be on the losing end of the stick. She's bound to lose her farm in the aftermath of this diarrhea outbreak, and he's going to get cleaned out by his wife in the divorce if that goes through, and he doesn't seem to be doing a darn thing to stop it. Of course, he and Wanda would be two pretty smart hard-working people to have working for us, and lord knows they're going to need jobs."

"Seems like a lot of jumps ahead, Ray," said Deb.

"Yeah, how do you figure you know all that, big brother?" asked Mike.

"I watch and I listen, and my job is seeing the future," said Ray Jr.

"Of corn prices," Sarah added. "What makes you think you've got a crystal ball on Wanda and Bruce, Ray?"

"I don't really, I've just seen what happens when people dedicate themselves to an idea with big blind spots. Sooner or later it comes back at them."

"You've dedicated yourself to unsustainable agriculture. I've heard you say yourself that it won't last forever," said Sarah.

"Yeah, but we're saving up for when it all comes down, which won't be tomorrow, anyway. Wanda's horizon's a lot shorter. In business it's all timing. In fact, we could do her a favor and buy her farm. It would make good corn ground. That neighbor of hers—Rogers I think—the one with all that Russian Olive running all over his place—put that piece together with Wanda's farm and it would make one worthwhile-size cornfield—maybe a hundred acres."

"You think she'd sell?" asked Sonia.

"It might be good if she did before her assets get frozen," said Ray Jr.

"Where would we get the money to buy it?" asked Mike.

"Oh jeeze, Mike, the bank loves Dad, it would be easy," said Ray Jr.

"Yes it would, but is this really the time to grow the farm, with Dad being down for who knows how long?" asked Deb.

"Mom, I'm kind of warming up to idea of running this place from Chicago with just Miguel and Bruce up here, and maybe Wanda. And I'm betting that Dad will be back up and running things in six months," said Ray Jr., adding, "I could get an agent working on putting deals together as early as next week."

"I can't believe how fast you business guys run," said Sarah.

"He's just like his dad, only on steroids," said Sonia, adding, "You should live with him. It's like being tied to a freight train."

"Out of my league," said Mike.

"It scares me to death, Ray, but I if you think you can run it, that would be great. I'm going to have to do a lot of praying," said Deb.

"What you going to pray for, Ma?" asked Mike.

"I don't know. Your dad always said I needed to be careful about praying for rain or we might get a flood."

"Maybe you should wait and see the business plan Ray takes to the bank and you could use it for a prayer outline, Ma," said Mike.

"Mike, you are such an asshole," said Sarah.

"Visiting hours are starting," said Deb, "Let's go upstairs, kids."

CHAPTER 27

Life for Wanda had become a sort of sentence. She needed Krystal's help with milking since Eva was out with the diarrhea, but Krystal was more out than in, and anyway she mostly avoided Wanda since the food fight at the animal wake, even though they'd kind of made up. So the Sisyphean task of milking eighty goats twice a day and then dumping the milk down the drain was all hers. For his first couple of days out of the hospital Bruce was only a little help, driving the old Ford tractor with a few bales of straw bedding from the hip-roofed barn down to the milking shed. Wanda did the real work of loading the bales, throwing them into the goat pens, breaking them up, and spreading them around. Bruce was improving, but was still pretty useless, and his weakness was another reminder to Wanda of the havoc she had wreaked. So she was just as glad to see him go when Doc Voekle stopped by. He stood outside the kitchen screen door as Wanda and Bruce sat at the table spooning up Wanda's chicken and rice soup.

"I've got a sheep call up north of here and then I need to meet the State Vet at some dump with a bunch of hungry horses. Want to come on a couple of interesting calls, Bruce?" Doc asked.

Wanda wiped her mouth. "Take him," she said before Bruce could answer.

"I guess I will then."

"I'll wait in the truck then—let you finish your lunch." Doc cleared the passenger seat. Bruce walked out to the truck slower than his usual near trot, and got in. "How you feeling, Bruce?" Doc asked as they pulled out. "You look a lot better."

"Maybe not as better as I look. Still dragging my ass, that's for sure. And Wanda's really tore up bad about this. She's having to work her butt off and then dump all the milk, and of course she's worried sick about Amos and that other woman in the hospital up in Lansing—I forget her name."

"Hazel Springer. I take care of her cat."

"Right. You heard anything? Are they going to make it?

"I'm pretty sure Hazel's going to be fine from what her sister told me this morning, but Amos is in kidney failure. They've got him on dialysis—I expect they're looking for a donor."

"Oh, God, that's awful." Bruce was knocked back by the news.

"Yeah . . . he doesn't have any brothers or sisters. I don't know what he's got for cousins. I'll bet that one of his parents will come through, though," said Doc, adding, "Anyway, to change the subject, I thought I'd take you out on a sheep call. There aren't many sheep in this part of the world anymore. A shepherd's a rarer bird than even a goat lady these days. You'll get a kick out of old Luther. He's got biblical delusions, I think."

They turned onto a dirt road and drove over a few rises to find Luther Yarnell's place tucked between small glacial hills. A short gravel driveway led to an old two-story farmhouse. Behind it was a gray barn with a rusted steel roof, and a sway-backed combination corn crib and tool shed that housed an old red Farmall row crop tractor. Luther's tractor shed would have fit easily in a corner of the machine shed at Vander Koop Farms, Inc., Unit I. Doc and Bruce were greeted by a gray-muzzled Border Collie who approached the truck at a walk while informing Luther with a couple of matter-of-fact barks that intruders had arrived, but that they didn't look too alarming. Doc gave the old dog a biscuit from his pocket and a scratch behind the ears.

"Hey Barney, how you doing boy. You seen the boss?"

Barney turned toward the fieldstone and shingle farmhouse and barked once more. Luther Yarnell emerged from the house slowly, the way a hermit crab exits his shell. He wore bib overalls, thin to the point of disintegration around the knees. Sparse shocks of white hair randomly pierced the air above his head. His skin was pale, transparent, and cracked like parched earth. His voice had the quavering raspiness of a musical saw. "I believe I fell asleep, gentlemen. I thank you for rousing me. What sort of a shepherd takes his repose in the forenoon? A very old one, I venture. It's got so it startles me every time I wake up. Dreams are a pleasure though—since Ida's been gone, they're just long walks with her and Jesus."

"I'm glad I remember her Mr. Yarnell. Ida's been gone a long time now—since just after I came to Parma and started my practice. That was what?—almost thirty-five years ago now." Doc continued, "Mr. Yarnell, I'd like you to meet Bruce Dinkle. He wants to learn about farming and where food comes from."

"You don't say. Maybe we can make a shepherd of you, Bruce. We're a dying breed, you know. I reckon we need some new recruits."

"Well, sheep have been around an awful long time, sir. It doesn't seem likely they're about to disappear."

"Well sir, I never thought people would have telephones ringing in their pants neither." Luther Yarnell shook a little with his wheezy laugh, then took a careful step toward the barn, adding, "No telling what surprises the Lord has for us next, no sir." Barney looked back as if to ask Luther if he was coming. "I believe I'll commence toward the barn now and try to get there before you young fellas is finished. There's a dead lamb out there, doctor. I was hoping you could tell me why."

Doc went to his truck for his necropsy knife and a bucket of water while Bruce accompanied Mr. Yarnell on his slow shuffle to the barn.

The lambs were several months old—more than half way to market size. Mr. Yarnell gave them access to a "creep feeder," a small pen with a grain trough that only the lambs could get to. Their mothers, the ewe flock—it looked like there were about twenty of them—had a green hillside pasture to graze. The dead lamb appeared to be one of the largest and fattest of the current crop.

"You know your sheep breeds, Bruce?" Mr. Yarnell asked.

"No sir, I sure don't."

"Well, why would you? Isn't one in a hundred does. These is Shropshires. I always liked them because they's dual purpose, meat and wool, and they's easier to handle than the big meat breeds like Suffolks—they's the ones with the bare black heads. Shrops has got black noses, but they got wool on their faces, and they got shorter ears than the Hampshires—that's how a person can tell them. Hamps is another good breed, a lot of sheep men used to like them too, but I just always liked the Shrops for some reason. Probably because my dad had them."

Bruce noticed big ratty sheets of loose wool hanging from many of the ewes. They appeared to be shedding. He asked, "When do you shear them? It looks like their wool is falling off."

"Well, Bruce, when I was a younger man, I used to shear them myself, but then it got so I couldn't hardly bend over, and if I did I couldn't hardly get back up. Then there was a man from up to Charlotte who used to shear them for me, but it got so it didn't hardly pay to have him do it, and he's quit years ago now anyways. Unless you got yourself good clean Merino wool, it costs more to shear a sheep than the wool is worth."

"So you just let it fall off?"

"Don't seem right, does it son?"

"So why do you keep them? Do you make some money on the meat part?" Bruce asked.

Mr. Yarnell turned his gaze out over the pasture. "I reckon I just like the way a flock of sheep looks on that green hillside of a summer evening. And in the morning, they give me a reason to get out the door. I like the way the lambs run and jump—makes me feel young just watching them. I like the lanolin on my fingers when I handle them. I even like the way they smell—ain't that something?—liking the smell of sheep?" His pale blue eyes looked watery. "I guess I just like having the use of them."

Doc found an old sheep-fitting stand to use for his necropsy table and moved it and the dead lamb out into the sunlight. He laid the lamb on its side, slid his necropsy knife through the skin, disjointed the hip and detached the shoulder with a few quick slices so that the top-side legs were laid over and out of the way. Then he used tree-pruning loping shears to cut the ribs and lay open the chest. In a few minutes all of the thoracic and abdominal organs were exposed. Bruce was impressed by how, revealed this way, the lamb's undisturbed insides looked relatively orderly and almost comprehensible compared to the chaos of the gut piles he had extracted from deer. One-by-one, Doc examined the parts, running his fingers through the gut, opening lengths of it, opening the four stomachs, looking at the color, shape, and size of each organ, feeling the texture of each, and even using his nose to sniff out any abnormalities. After removing what he called "the pluck," which was the heart and lungs, and running his fingers over the lungs—they were heavy and wet and filled with fluid—he cut through the heart sac and took the heart in his left hand. With a quick slice he separated the lamb's heart from its lungs. He turned the heart in his hand.

"I know what this is," he said. Then sliced into the heart muscle where he saw a pale streak on its surface. The paleness extended deep into the muscle. He sliced open the heart's chambers and rinsed it in the water bucket to see its inside surface. More pale streaks and patches. "Yup, white muscle disease, Luther. I bet you didn't give this lamb its shot of vitamin E and selenium this spring."

"It's getting hard to get it all done, Doc."

"Are they getting a mineral mix with selenium?"

"I might a run out of that, too," the old man admitted.

"What's white muscle disease?" asked Bruce.

"It's a nutritional disease caused by deficiencies of vitamin E and selenium. They're both important antioxidants in muscle. Without enough of those things, the muscle dies. It looks white because it calcifies. The soil in Michigan is selenium poor. I got to say, being locavores is tough on animals."

"What was that word?" Luther asked.

"Locavore. Somebody who eats only local food," said Bruce.

"It's that *only* part that will get you Bruce," said Doc.

"Do you do that?" asked Luther.

"I try," said Bruce.

"You should have met my father, son. He's been gone since long before you was born, but he grew up up to Schoolcraft County, up to the U.P. You know, he couldn't button his shirt collar his neck was so darn big. He had a goiter the size of a man's fist. So ugly I'm surprised my mother married him. Kept him out of World War I, though . . . too ugly to shoot—imagine that. I guess that lump probably saved his life. Mine too, if you think about it," said Luther.

"Goiter—I've heard of that. What is it?" asked Bruce.

Doc jumped in, "That's when your thyroid gland can't find enough iodine to make thyroid hormone—iodine is part of the hormone—and your pituitary gland keeps telling your thyroid to make more because there isn't enough to keep your metabolism cranked up to normal. Consequently, the thyroid gets real big trying—that's what a goiter is. Goiter was really common in Michigan before they figured out that they could put iodine in table salt—that was in 1925 up at Dow Chemical as I recall. Now it's easy to get plenty of iodine, but goiter was common in Michigan back then. You know what a cretin is, Bruce?"

"An idiot, right?"

"Close. It's a special form of mental retardation caused by severe iodine and thyroid hormone deficiency, so the brain doesn't develop right. There were places in China up until pretty recently where the locavores—and peasants are always locavores—were all retarded. Not a village idiot, but a whole village of idiots—nobody smart enough to teach school or drive a truck. You talk about a life with no choices, how'd you like to live there?"

"Are you suggesting I'm wrong to want to live on local food?" asked Bruce.

"No, no, it's just me being your mother—all things in moderation, don't go to extremes, don't be too rigid, don't be a cretin," said Doc, softening the last directive with a smile. Adding, "Actually, I think it's a real good idea to support local farmers for a lot of reasons, plus they're keeping me in business and there aren't enough of them left. Just don't be a nut about it."

Doc rinsed his knife in the bucket and dried it on his coveralls. "So, we need to do a couple of things here. Bruce, if you're feeling up to it, could you dig a hole for Mr. Yarnell and bury that lamb? Make it deep enough so Barney doesn't dig it back up."

"I can do that," said Bruce.

"And I'll get a bottle of vitamin E and selenium from the truck and we'll give all these lambs a shot of it. Luther, I'm afraid you're going to have more lambs dropping dead if we don't. Is that all right?"

And so they spent the next hour catching every lamb in the flock—most of Luther's twenty ewes had had twins—and giving each a shot of the life-saving vitamin and trace mineral. They were extra gentle and tried not to chase the sheep any more than necessary. They didn't want to end up with a whole bunch more dropping dead. Luther showed Bruce how to use a shepherd's crook to catch the lambs. Even with the long crook to hook them around their necks as they tried to run away, it was a real effort for Bruce in his weakened state, but he'd already grown so fond of the old man that he didn't consider slacking off. When they finished, Luther asked Doc to write him a bill, and Doc said he'd send it. But he probably wouldn't.

Back in the truck, Doc said, "Well, that took longer than I thought. We're going to be late for the State Vet up at the McNutt place."

"What's this one about?" asked Bruce.

"Neglected horses. Some of those poor people with great big hearts and itty bitty brains."

"What happened?"

"Well, we'll see, but basically we're looking at mass hypogroceriosis."

"What?"

"Highly scientific term for not enough groceries. Too many horses, not enough hay."

"I never cared for horses," Bruce said. Adding, "My wife used to have one—Tilly. Damn, they're expensive."

They arrived at the farm, which was mostly hidden by trees near the road, which partly explained why things had gone so far wrong without being reported, and were greeted by a mismatched pack of four barking dogs. Snot-nosed cats seemed to be everywhere. Cardboard boxes were visible in the dirty windows of the small ranch-style house. Weeds sprouted in its eaves troughs. They saw Sheriff Timmers's car and a State-owned vehicle parked out back by a low pole barn, so they drove out and parked next to them. They saw broken down wire fences surrounding a bare dirt pasture with an area of deep mud up near the barn. Two horses were head to head competing over a few brown stalks of hay, and they kicked viciously at any other horse that came near. Several were lying with their chins on the ground; two appeared to be dead. They all had ribs showing and their withers stuck up like shark fins. Their coats looked half shed, almost as ratty as the unshorn sheep. Several had sores over their hip bones and a lot of them had snotty noses. Bruce figured there must have been twenty-five or thirty horses in the three acre lot. It had been a long time since there'd been a blade of grass there.

"What in the hell were these folks thinking?" asked Bruce.

"Christ, I don't know," Doc said as he got out. Sheriff Timmers was about to introduce Doc to the State Vet, but it was clear that they already knew each other. The State Vet was a tall man, a couple of inches shorter than he might have been if he stood up straight. With the hump over his shoulders and his butt tucked under, he looked like a human question mark. And a version of the same rhetorical question was written on his face: "What the fuck were these people thinking?"

"Hey Larry, what have you learned?" asked Doc.

"No hay, no grain, no pasture. It's a bunch of unbroke rescue horses they collected from some "Save a Mustang" bunch of do-gooders. Then they had some sort of internet scam thing going where they collected money to support their humanitarian mission to save the animals."

"Where are they?"

"Don't know. It appears they took the money and run—probably off in the Caribbean somewhere getting their fat asses sunburned. They left the damned horses to fend for themselves. The whole bunch is starving, they've got strangles, and there isn't a real horse farm in the state that would let a one of them on their place, and I couldn't let them go anyway. I'm afraid we've got to kill the whole bunch of them, Cec."

"Ah, Jesus, I was afraid of this," said Doc.

"What's strangles?" asked Bruce.

"A kind of strep infection. They're automatically quarantined. Can't legally move them—as if there was some place to take them," said Doc.

Sheriff Timmers was busy taking pictures for evidence. The State Vet asked Doc, "Is there somebody with a backhoe around here? We're going to need a hell of a pit."

"Yeah, I'll see if I can get Jack Fitz," Doc answered, and added, "How do you want to do this?"

"Well, being mustangs, I'm sure they're not broke, so we won't be able to lead them to the pit. And it would take a couple days to move the portable corral and chute the State owns, and get it set up down here. And we'd have to find a load of hay and bring it in if there's any more delay in getting this done. Shit, they'd go through a hundred bales a week. I think it's either trank darts and blue juice, or intracerebral lead, Cec."

"I sure don't keep enough blue juice in stock to put down thirty horses, Larry."

"Well, it's back from the road. If we can get it done before we get reporters out here, I think a thirty-eight between the eyes is about the most humane thing we can do," said Doc. "How close are the neighbors?"

"A quarter of a mile, anyway," said Sheriff Lennard Timmers, "But I haven't ever shot a horse."

"The technique is easy enough, Len. You just draw an imaginary X between the bases of the ears and the opposite eyes, and that's your spot—straight in. We can feed them some acepromazine tranquilizer granules to calm them down first. I've got a bucket of that in the truck. The hard part is getting your head around it. I can do it if you can't, Len."

"You know Doc, I've been the sheriff here for seventeen years now, and I've only discharged my firearm twice outside the practice range. Both times it was for deer hit by cars and they were broke up real bad and suffering. I didn't like it, but I did it. Put them out of their misery. But I don't know if I can shoot a horse, let alone thirty of them."

"Yeah, well, we got plenty of misery to be put out of here, Len. How about you, Larry?" Doc asked the State Vet.

"Honestly, I'd rather let you do it, Cec."

So Doc called his friend with the backhoe who promised he could get there that afternoon, and then went to his truck where he had the plastic bucket of acepromazine granules, and the four men spent a somber hour walking among the sick and starving horses, feeding each a handful of the tranquilizer, then watching for the horses' already drooping demeanor to droop further. The sheriff handed his service revolver to Doc, who then walked slowly and calmly from horse to horse, stroking necks and speaking softly to each one before putting a bullet into the X. He had to reload the six-shooter four times before it was all done, but every horse went instantly—just collapsed in its tracks with hardly a kick. By the time Doc dropped the last horse, a piebald downer at the back of the paddock, his face and glasses were heavily spattered with blood and a few soft pink flecks of brain. He trudged out of the horse pen like a soldier returning from battle, the battlefield covered with dead horses, the man wounded by his own acts, however humane and necessary. He smelled of gunpowder and blood. He handed the pistol back to the sheriff and walked to his truck in silence.

"Jesus, Doc. Thanks for doing that," said the sheriff.

"Yeah. Cec . . . thanks man," said the State Vet.

Bruce said, "I just can't believe anybody could abandon all these horses like that."

Doc turned to Bruce and didn't say anything at first. He looked over the top of his bifocals, eyebrows raised, his mouth a hanging noose of incredulity. "Responsibilities. We've all got them. Some of us live up to them." Bruce looked away, fixed his eyes on the dirt, and immediately thought of his kids and the responsibilities he'd pedaled away from. He wondered if Doc had meant to stab him so deeply.

Doc kneeled over his wash bucket and lifted handfuls of cold water up to his face, rinsing the blood away so that he could go home to his wife without scaring her. He needed to be held.

CHAPTER 28

B ruce got out of Doc's vet truck back at Nanny Gate with his mind in more pain than his guts, and his guts still weren't right. The wise words he'd heard from Doc and the old shepherd wore like sanding belts on his locavore convictions and whatever rationalization he'd once had for leaving his family. He was no longer sure why he'd done or believed anything. And he feared visions of the horse killing field would haunt him forever. The long day had taxed his weakened system; his brain felt like a hornet's nest—poisonous, cold, and restless. He wanted to drink.

"Wanda, there's no beer in the house, you want to go over to Miguel's?

"I'm not ready to see people. Just go."

Bruce got on his bicycle and slowly pedaled the four miles over to Miguel and Doris's trailer. Thoughts of his family and visions of the day churned in his brain with hardly an interruption, so that each time his attention snapped-to, he had to remind himself where he was going and figure out where he was. The landscape looked strange—colors too bright, shadows too deep. He'd been down these roads dozens of times in the almost three months since he arrived in Parma, but he felt like he was seeing the place for the first time. Only the most prominent landmarks, like the big pair of white pines in front of the collapsing gray wood farmhouse at the corner of Beaverhead and Bard, kept him oriented. The sight of the falling down house washed a wave of sadness over him. That was replaced by the horror of the horse killing field, then Doc saying, "Don't be a cretin," and the look he'd given him, the incredulous gaze over the top of the wise man's glasses that still felt to Bruce like an accusation. "We all have responsibilities," he had said. Suddenly his children were running through his brain crying, "Daddy, Daddy, Daddy!" And now, he thought, I'm running away from Wanda in her hour of greatest need to go drink beer. I just run . . . I just keep running away—even when I'm so weak I can barely stand. "Don't be a cretin . . . Some of us live up to our responsibilities." He wondered how he could ever have thought that where an apple came from could be more important than providing an apple for his kids, more important than Alice. Where the apple comes from matters, his ideological voice insisted. Compared to what? asked his late developing conscience.

He coasted into Miguel's dirt driveway, rolled around the back, and dropped his bike. That must be Krystal's new truck. Fuck, it is a woodchuck pimpmobile. There's the old Impala. Where is Doris's car?

He wrestled his focus into the present as he made his way to the back door. He knocked and waited. Rhythmic bumps and small screams emanated from the bedroom end of the trailer. Well I'll be damned, he thought, and sat down on the stoop. He knew he didn't have enough juice in his legs to get back to Wanda's—and there wasn't much light left anyway. It was after nine and the sun was dropping behind the woods beyond Miguel's vegetable garden. The golden light of the early evening had dimmed as the western sky pinked and a half moon appeared in the fading blue directly above him. Mercifully, visions of the horse killing field, doubts over his motivations, and the waves of guilt over his family gave way to the lovely sky and imaginings of the sex happening on the other side of the thin trailer wall and open bedroom window. The noises got louder. That lucky bastard. There was a twitch in his jeans—the first since his guts had unloaded on him, and a bit of a surprise considering his exhausted state. You're back, he thought, adjusting himself. You're nothing but trouble.

He heard them finish. Krystal was a screamer—of course he knew that. And he could hear Miguel's Chicano accent in his climactic grunts and howls. Christ, he thought, the bugger even grunts in Mexican.

They'd heard him knock. After a few minutes of breath catching and cleaning up, Miguel got up and checked the window to see whether the interruptus had vamoosed. "It's Bruce; I see his bike," he said.

"You going to let him in?" asked Krystal.

"Pants on first," he said.

"Good idea. I'll be out in a minute."

Miguel opened the back door to find Bruce still sitting on the stoop. "Good timing," Miguel said.

"Yeah, sorry. You got beer?" Bruce adjusted himself as he rose; his jeans were stuck to him like wallpaper with sweat.

"You look like you need couch more than you need beer."

"It's a toss-up; I think I need a beer on a couch."

Bruce drained half a can of Bud on the first slug and it seemed to liquefy him. He melted into the old plaid sofa. For a second his head fell back and his mouth fell open. He could have flown directly to comaland, but roused himself.

"So what happened, man?" Bruce asked.

"I kicked her out."

"But she got you through the prison years."

"*Si*—and she think she own me for it. Like some big favor I can never pay back and she never let go. I want to forget them years, and that's all she talk about, so I don't never forget she wrote me letters when I was locked up. She never even met me before Jackson. She never knew the man I was before I did time. She got her nails in me when I was locked up and she want to keep me there. To hell with her."

Bruce was amazed at how quickly what appeared to be love, or at least a workable truce, could fall apart. To Bruce it didn't seem like Miguel had done enough to save the relationship, but then again, he had no idea what really went on between them. And after all, what had he done to save his own marriage?

Krystal emerged from the bedroom in an alarming pink tube top and dangerously short cut-offs. Damn, it's Daisy Mae, thought Bruce, tipping his can. She'd gotten an expensive haircut and streaky blond dye job and had her nails done a hot pink that matched the top. "Hi Bruce."

"Been some changes going on, eh?"

"I found me a *sweet* man this time." She rubbed Miguel's shoulders over the back of his plaid corduroy recliner. She turned on the TV—the Tigers and the White Sox.

Bruce wanted to talk about his disturbing day but gave the thought a time-out in deference to the batter at the plate. Tiger slugger Miguel Cabrerra dug his cleats into the batter's box and wagged his bat in a low arc, telegraphing an up and out blast. The next pitch was a fast ball—

Cabrerra smacked it hard, a line drive that just kept climbing and passed outside of the foul pole, drilling deep into the left field stands. The crowd jumped to its feet and you could hear twenty-thousand fans all yelling, "Whoa!" Miguel yelled at the TV, "Whoa! Miguel! My main man! Smack this one out, dude!" The count was full.

"Can I get you another beer?" Krystal asked Bruce, ever the waitress.

Bruce didn't respond. He was gone—a curve ball over the left field fence and out of the park.

It was almost mid-June; a short night for the sun. The tireless fiery orb was back on its planet-heating job before five the next morning. Bruce on the other hand remained sucked deep into the couch until ten; by then the heat outside had risen well into the shirts-off range for country boys. Miguel had long since gone to work. He was spraying the Vander Koop corn for weeds today. Krystal was having a cigarette at the kitchen table and flipping through the Victoria's Secret catalogue. Bruce finally stirred and opened his eyes.

"He lives!" Krystal said, as she looked up from the peek-a-boo teddies and blew a stream of smoke toward the open window.

Bruce sat up and stretched. "I just might," he said, flexing his arms behind his head. He could feel his strength returning. "I'm going to go water the garden. Got a cup of coffee?"

"Yeah, but I let the pot go cold. I'll stick one in the microwave for you. It'll be hot by the time you get back."

Miguel's garden was meticulously laid out, every hill in his vine crop area—melons, cukes, pumpkins, squashes—had a stake labeled with the plant and variety name. He spotted "Watermelon, Sugar Bowl." Sugar Bowl Watermelon sounded like something he could get behind, so he decided to bless that hill of four nascent vines with the water and nitrogen fertilizing power of a full bladder. With his back arched toward the trailer for modesty, he backed up one step to adjust the range and trajectory, then lofted a golden stream high so that it broke up into shining droplets before it splashed into the soft garden soil—he didn't want to inadvertently dig a hole under the tender roots. It sprinkled down like warm rain. Peeing in the sugar bowl, he thought. Krystal watched from the trailer and shook her head. "Men," she whispered to herself as she stepped out the door with a steaming mug. Bruce zipped his pants and walked back toward the trailer.

"Those watermelons are going to be extra juicy," he said, pulling up a plastic lawn chair in the sun across from Krystal. Her legs were crossed at the ankles and propped up on the wooden cable spool table. She looked edible, if you like processed food. And who doesn't.

"I can't say I ain't jealous of your plumbing, but I'm darn glad I don't live in your head," she said.

"Men in general or my head in particular?"

"You *and* men in general—and both your heads, too. You ever get tired of being led around by your dick?"

"Not really. I kind of like the adventure." Bruce adjusted the topic: "Miguel got boyfriend status?"

"Yup. No more for you, Brucie. It was fun though. When you going back to Alice?"

"It *was* fun," Bruce smiled, adding, "I really need to call her."

"I don't think he got a chance to tell you, but Miguel said some guy came by the shop with some papers for you. He said he was a real bozo. What do you think that's about?"

"I don't know," he said dismissively. Bruce didn't have much trouble guessing what the papers were, but he didn't let on. "Probably not a job that attracts charmers."

"Yeah, how would you like to go around laying shit on people all day long? Takes a special kind of jerk to want that job."

"Sometimes you take the job you can get." Bruce drained his coffee cup and remembered his job at the power plant. "I think I'll pedal over to the shop and help Miguel. I could use some paid hours."

"It's the road to riches, Brucie. Go turn them nuts and pump that grease, boy."

Bruce smiled. He found Krystal's newfound sassiness dangerously attractive, and knew he needed to be going.

Bruce pedaled over to Vander Koop Farms, Inc., Unit I. He could feel that his strength was almost back. He found Miguel long gone to the fields with the big spray rig. Deb Vander Koop's Buick was there though, and she and her daughter Sarah were just coming out of the house carrying a big plate of frosted chocolate walnut brownies. Several of the goodies had toothpicks rising from their middles to keep the plastic wrap from sticking to the frosting. They greeted each other and Deb introduced Sarah.

"Bruce, this is our daughter Sarah, she's the musical one who lives out in Seattle. I'm so glad she come out to see her daddy—there's always a silver lining isn't there. Anyway, you hungry for a brownie? The nurses probably don't need to eat all of them."

Bruce's appetite was back. "Oh, yeah, twist my arm." He lifted a big moist square from the edge of the plate and sent it straight into his mouth, then found his craw way too full of sweet thick deliciousness to make polite conversation. He mumbled around the goo, "How long you here for?" which came out, "*How ong ooo hee foe?*" He held his hand over his mouth to spare the women the sight of chocolate-covered teeth and half-chewed food.

"Just a few more days. I've got to get back to play a wedding. It's June, you know."

Sarah looked a little like Alice with her light brown hair and unadorned beauty. The way she wore her jeans was hard on a guy. It seemed that everything kept pressing the question: What kind of man was he who could leave, or would leave, a woman like that?—let alone the kids . . . He was lost for a moment, his mouth full of sweet chocolate and bits of walnut, his eyes soaking up Sarah, his mind on Alice.

"Can I give you another one Bruce? You must burn a lot of calories on that bicycle."

"Sure," *Shooo,* Bruce said, still trying to talk around the thick fudgy mix of chocolate and saliva. He didn't think once about where in the world chocolate came from.

"That should hold you till lunch," Deb chuckled. She plainly loved feeding people. "We've got to get back to the hospital. Looks like they'll be moving Ray to rehab in a couple of days. Stop by there if you can. Ray Jr. wants to talk to you about your plans—or maybe you can catch him out here after visiting hours?"

"I'll do that," he said. Bruce's eyes kept involuntarily wandering back to Sarah, who seemed entirely indifferent to his attention. The women got in the car and drove away. Bruce thought: No Miguel . . . time to myself . . . maybe I'll find that legal pad and write something . . . maybe I *could* write a book. It might help make sense of this mess. He went to his room in the shop, found the yellow lined pad and a ball point, and sat down to write. He assumed a thoughtful—writerly, he thought—gaze out the window on the gravel farmyard. It looked almost white in the mid-day sun. The new leaves on the big maple in the Vander Koop's yard turned in the breeze, showing their soft gray undersides. With no thought of ripping off Charles Darwin, he wrote:

On the Origins of Food
by Bruce A. Dinkle

People grow food, find food, feed food to animals to make food animals, hunt food, preserve food, and cook food. Big farmers grow huge amounts of a few things, and small farmers grow small amounts of a lot of different things. Everybody eats, and most Americans eat too much. Food is pleasure, politics, and poison—and you can't live without it.

He leaned back, balancing his chair on its back legs, chewing his pen, and staring into space for a long moment before continuing.

> *In the last three months I've plowed snow, planted three-thousand acres of corn and soybeans, delivered a goat, speared a gunny sack full of suckers and a hell of a big pike, milked a herd of goats, made love to two new women, built a dog kennel, made goat cheese, made rhubarb crisp (with cinnamon!), buried a mean dog, barbequed a goat, had a gun aimed at my bare ass, survived a food fight, and had a horrible case of the shits. I don't know how farmers do it.*

He smiled at the generosity of his prose. He was pretty sure he was just getting started.

> *I've learned to drive a 400 horse power tractor pulling a cultivator thirty feet wide, and to wash a goat's udder. I've learned . . .*

And he might have gotten around to the more important life lessons that were lately dawning on him, but a rust-pocked brown Oldsmobile came flying into the farmyard and skidded to a stop as the rear end slid around to face the shop. A big galoot with a bucket-o-pop got out of the rusted beater with a thick manila envelope. Bruce went out to meet him. He was wearing a tie-dyed T-shirt and saggy cargo shorts. His tattoos were colorful and ubiquitous, but the inky details were too fine for the acre of blubbery canvas they were spread over, so from a little distance he appeared to be assembled of rainbow sprinkle donuts held together by pasty white-man frosting.

"Bruce Dinkle!" he said in his best long-lost-friend voice, tucking the envelope under his pop bucket arm and extending his now free hand. It was how he got people who might not want to reveal their identity to let it out before they thought about it.

Bruce didn't take the bait. "Who's asking?" he said.

"Ed Groening," said Ed Groening.

"You the guy that was here the other day?"

"Yup, that's why they call me Continuing Ed, I just keep coming."

"Aw, Jesus, you use that joke every day?"

"Nope, been saving it all my life just for you—along with these papers." He handed the envelope to Bruce and tried to follow it with a clipboard with a form for him to sign, saying he'd received the item. Bruce didn't take the clipboard.

"I still haven't said that I'm the guy you're looking for."

"Well, you look like your picture, so if it ain't you, could you just sign on this line for your twin brother and I'll be out of here. It's lunchtime, and there's a greasy triple bacon cheeseburger out there somewheres just dying to git in my belly!"

He tried to hand Bruce a pen while keeping the pop bucket level in his left hand and hold the clip board in his right. To free a hand, he lifted the edge of the clipboard to his front teeth—Bruce could see that he spent a lot more money on tattoos than dentistry—then extended his hand with the pen.

Bruce let him continue to struggle with his pop bucket handicap for a few seconds more before saying, "It's alright, Ed, I got one," flashing Ed Groening the pen he had just used to start his book. He took the clipboard and signed his name.

The divorce papers effectively stopped Bruce's creative reflection and started a more urgent one. All the elements of the separation were laid out: essentially, if he could not somehow bend or derail the process, he would lose everything—his share of their modest net worth, including his retirement savings, and, more importantly, his relationship to his children. For the previous three months he had lived without these things, bouncing checks and draining his emotional bank account with Alice and the kids, but now the road home was about to be permanently closed, and it jarred him. A Family Court hearing was scheduled for the week after the Fourth of July in Bay City. He would have to be there. It reminded him that his bike tires were getting thin—a few nylon cords were showing through the worn rubber tread. He would need new bike tires before the trip—a major stress to his finances. Going broke for new bike tires . . . it occurred to him that if it weren't for his room in Ray's shop and Wanda's willingness to share her bed a few nights a week, he would be homeless.

CHAPTER 29

Miguel broke Bruce's reverie when he pulled the big self-propelled sprayer into the farm yard. "Got to get some more Hoedown concentrate for the Unit Three fields," he said as he shut the rig down.

"How much did you get done this morning?"

"Almost three-hundred acres. Man, it goes fast with these booms—ninety feet at a pass. Beats hell out of dragging a four row cultivator around three thousand acres."

"I guess." Bruce sounded unconvinced, adding, "Chemicals make me nervous."

"Yeah, but everybody who done it the old way is out of business, man. This is modern farming—get with the times, dude."

"So all the seed we planted is Hoedown-Ready? I thought Ray said he was going to mix it up a little this year?"

"Yeah, I think he did plant some different varieties, but it's all resistant to weed killer, and Hoedown's the only weed killer we got."

Miguel got Ray's truck. It had a big white plastic tank of concentrated Hoedown in the back. He ran a thick hose from the potent herbicide to the filler hole way on top of the high-wheeled spray rig. "Thirty gallons," said Miguel. He started the truck, then flipped a switch to pump thirty gallons of Hoedown into the twelve-hundred gallon sprayer tank. "Okay, I'm going to the Parma hydrant for water. Follow me with the truck so I don't have to come back here to refill."

They drove to the water terminal and filled the big tank in a few minutes. The high-wheeled spray rig carried Miguel a good nine or ten feet above the pavement at thirty miles per hour with the long booms folded together behind him like the tail of a brontosaurus. By the end of the day they'd killed the weeds on over eight-hundred acres of corn. With lights and the GPS guidance system, they could have gone all night, but the weather looked good for the rest of the week, so there wasn't a big rush. And Bruce needed his sleep anyway. Miguel drove the big rig with its huge wingspan raining herbicide across the fields at the pace of a man running. Bruce snoozed in the truck between sprayer fill-ups and was amazed all over again at the scale of the operation. This was how the few remaining American farmers could overfeed America and still export a third of what they grow. It made milking a goat seem as irrelevant as a romantic poet at a monster truck show.

Early that evening Bruce pedaled into the Jackson hospital to visit Ray Sr. and meet with Ray Jr. He found Ray Sr. dozing in his cranked-up hospital bed with Deb at his side and their offspring crowded around the room. Sarah was reading a novel. Mike and Ray Jr. were locked onto a *Cheers* rerun. Sonia was flipping through a fashion magazine. They all greeted Bruce, causing enough commotion to wake Ray Sr. He saw Bruce and looked frustrated. He made an awkward reeling motion with his good hand. Deb recognized Ray's body language, the spinning thing he did with his finger when he struggled to retrieve a name.

"It's Bruce, he's come to visit you," said Deb.

Ray Senior's expression relaxed into a small, bent smile. "Bruce . . . Working hard?" *Boos . . . Wooin Hah?* The stroke had caused a speech impediment—a lot like having a mouth stuffed with food—but at least he could talk.

"Yeah, I helped Miguel spray the corn today," Bruce answered.

"Which corn?" *whih cone?*

"I don't know, we figured we did about eight hundred acres. All on Unit Three. That's quite a spray rig. Man you can cover some ground with that thing."

Ray Senior's head bowed a little and his brow knotted up again. His head came up. "*Whih pay?*"

"Which spray?" Deb interpreted.

"Hoedown, the only spray you've got."

"*Awww Jeeus,*" said Ray Sr.

"Is that a problem?" asked Bruce.

"What is it Dad?" asked Ray Jr.

"*Nah ahh Ho-ouwn-Eehhe eed,*" said Ray Sr.

"Oh no! Not all Hoedown-Ready seed?! Ray, didn't you tell them?!" asked Deb.

"Oh Jesus! How many acres, Dad?" asked Ray Jr.

"*hee unnud . . . fuh,*" said Ray Sr.

"Three-hundred!? Will crop insurance cover this, Dad?"

"*Fuh . . . I unno.*"

Over the next minutes they figured out that Ray had planted three hundred acres of a different hybrid corn, one genetically engineered to tolerate a different herbicide, a herbicide he had ordered in a bulk tank that was ready to be picked up down in Litchfield, but as yet had not been. He had neglected to tell Miguel anything more than that he was planting a different hybrid in those fields. Over the next week they could count on watching a hundred thousand dollars worth of sprouted seed, fertilizer, time, and energy turn yellow and die. Ray Jr. muttered and stomped around the hospital room, apparently trying to rid himself of frustration through the thin leather soles of his Italian loafers. The rest of them sat or stood in open-mouthed disbelief.

Ray Jr. finally said, "Okay, we're going into the wheat business. It's too late to replant the corn, but we can plant wheat in late August and at least not waste the whole growing season. We'll need a grain drill to get it planted and a grain head for at least one of the combines.

"How much will that cost?" asked Deb.

"Maybe a hundred for the grain head and another fifty for the drill. But if we get Wanda's place, in the next month or two, it would be a way to get that dirt right into production too."

"We can take a hundred grand loss on this year's crop and still put a hundred and fifty grand into new equipment?—and God knows how much into new land?!" asked Mike.

"Wait—what's this "Wanda's place, new land" stuff about?" asked Bruce.

"There's a lot of capital out there looking for a safe investment right now. American farmland looks pretty solid to folks who just lost their shirts in real estate derivatives. I've talked to a few guys in Chicago and Omaha in the last couple of days, and I can put together an investor group that will allow us to grow the farm to a more workable size," said Ray Jr.

"Grow to a more workable size!? You're farming three thousand acres already!" said Bruce.

"Yes, but there are opportunities for scale efficiencies and process integration that we can't fully realize in the current paradigm. And we have too many idle human and capital assets during seasons of the year that could be more optimally utilized by diversification into wheat."

"Fuck, my brother uses the word paradigm without flinching. I think I'm not part of this. I'm going find a bar stool for my human asset, and optimize a couple of beers—wheat beer, I'm thinking. And they don't have Bell's Oberon in L.A.—damn, I missed it. Want to come, Sis?" said Mike.

"I'm coming, too," said Bruce.

"No, stay here for a minute Bruce. I need to talk to you. Let's go sit in the family room," said Ray Jr.

"What is it?" asked Bruce.

Ray Jr. exercised his executive tendencies by keeping Bruce guessing until they found themselves sitting face to face in the cardiac ward waiting area. There was another family at the other end of the room huddled with their own worries. Ray Jr. perched at the edge of his chair and leaned into Bruce using the earnest body language taught in business communications. His starched white shirt cuffs were rolled up, gray tropical-weight worsted wool slacks perfectly creased, tasseled cordovan loafers gleaming. He said,

"We want to increase your responsibilities in the business, but we need some commitment from you." Jesus, he even calls himself *we*, Bruce thought. Ray Jr. continued, "We're prepared to offer you $25,000 a year plus housing and benefits, and a profit-sharing option that grows with seniority."

"That's about half of what I was making at the power plant, but not counting a house. Where would I live?"

"We've got rental houses on several of the farms, I'm sure we could vacate one for you. I just wanted to see if you're interested and find out if you're planning on going back home to your wife."

"I've been thinking about it. But I don't think she'd have me. She's filed for divorce." Bruce found himself answering the inappropriate question before he thought about it.

"How about Wanda? Do you see a future with her? We think she'd make a good farm wife."

"Jesus, what business are you guys in, farming or matchmaking? Why do you think that's your business?"

"It's not exactly, but it's been our experience that men in stable relationships make better employees, and you seem to be a man who needs a woman.

CHAPTER 30

Wanda sat hunched over her keyboard, her reading glasses perched on her nose. She was studying internet listings for small milk pasteurizers, trying to figure out how in the world she could come up with at least five-thousand dollars to buy one—especially now that she had lost all her customers and was pouring her precious milk down the drain. Avoiding the expense of a pasteurizer had been a repressed factor—one she would have denied—in her decision to sell shares in her goats, which had been the legal mechanism that opened the loophole for her to sell raw milk.

As a biology professor, Wanda's interest was in habitat preservation and endangered species. The details of bacteriology and infectious disease had always been a weakness. She'd taken a class or two, but they were never a big part of her focus in biology. She had once known a fellow biology graduate student, a young man with an interest in reproduction, who at many points in his career as a student had to have demonstrated on tests and exams his understanding of genetic mutations, fossils, and all of the mountains of evidence that biological evolution is, in common parlance, a fact. The young man had mentally compartmentalized his belief in the childhood Bible story that God created the universe in seven days just as we find it now, to protect it from his more fully-evolved rational mind.

For him the creation story found in the Bible—as opposed to the creation story of a thousand other pre-literate tribes—was an item of faith, and not subject to critical analysis. Without realizing it, Wanda had done the same thing: she had managed to lock the dangers of raw milk onto a closeted neuron in her cerebral back-forty, and had pretty much forgotten about it. And, having gone for years now without incident, any anxiety she once felt about selling raw milk had faded. She had come to believe her own propaganda.

In the right-brained culture of boutique health-food sellers, where intuition, anecdotes, and heartfelt rants count as data, she had been seduced by the notion that raw is the state that nature intended, and is therefore superior and correct. Among raw believers she felt moderate; she rejected the extremists who extended their belief in the raw all the way to animal flesh. True-believing proponents of the raw had somehow linked cooking and pasteurization to half the modern ailments known to man; in their minds, reversion to rawness was the only cure necessary. Wanda had tried raw meat but didn't like it. She didn't like the taste, and all that chewing made her jaw hurt. So she customized her rationalization to the end she found useful: selling raw milk. And she had correctly predicted that raw true believers would be her customer base—her niche market—and that they would save her a lot of money on an expensive pasteurization unit.

Consequently, she cultivated a raw milk clientele that comprised health food devotees with only the foggiest notions of human biology, conspiracy theorists who believed that the germ theory of disease was invented by big pharmaceutical companies to sell vaccines and antibiotics, and contrarians like Maxine Jurek to whom any irrational argument on any subject might stick. Wanda was suddenly aware that as a biology professor her defense would be tenuous. A good attorney would rip her to shreds on the witness stand. In her mind she took the stand over and over. She played her argument as best she could, but the plaintiffs' attorney who lived in her head kept asking questions that began: "Doctor Caprini, as a biology professor you knew, did you not, that dangerous germs . . . ?" She felt depressed, cornered, and angry. The emotions combined and shot back out of her like the unfocused aggression of a fear-biting dog.

A knock at the door jarred her from her imaginary courtroom. She looked out and saw a heavy man in a tan suit standing on her kitchen porch. His tie appeared to be strangling him. It caused a small roll of flesh to spill over his shirt collar and his face to be the same glistening hue as the pink silk neckwear. The man's balding head was thinly covered by a lacquered mat of blond hair combed forward from a part just an inch above his collar where gray roots were visible. A shiny black SUV was parked and left running in the drive. She smiled slightly for the first time in weeks. "Fucking Donald Trump," she mouthed almost audibly as she went to the door. It wasn't, of course, but the man clearly had Trumpish aspirations. His ridiculousness clicked off the safety on her hair-trigger state of mind.

"Are you Wanda Caprini?"

"Yup I am. Is your car hard to start?"

"No, ma'am, it's a brand new Cadillac."

"Well then shut the fucking thing off. Does this country air smell like it needs your exhaust in it?"

"I can see that you're a woman who speaks frankly."

"Yeah, well, frankly, you're a moron. Go shut that damn thing down, and then you can tell me why you're here."

Wanda watched the man walk sheepishly back to his large luxury vehicle. His suit pants appeared to be trapped in his crack. The midday breeze lifted the hood of his comb over. He turned it off and returned to the house. "It's going be hot as heck when I get back into it."

"And heck's getting a hell of a lot hotter I hear—global warming, don't you know. But you look like a Republican, so for you it isn't happening, right? Anyway, you could go back out and roll down your windows, or you could be quick. I vote for quick—and my vote counts double."

"I don't know that it's quick business we've got, Ms. Caprini."

"Ms. Caprini . . . you a lawyer?"

"No ma'am, real estate." The man extended his hand and forced a smile, "Art Karpinke, I represent a concern that has become interested in your property." He extended his right hand.

"Christ, the vultures are circling. I thought I was the only one who knew I was dying." Wanda looked the man up and down as he continued to offer his hand. She continued, "You can come in. You're probably hungry. Did you know that vultures can eat half their weight at a sitting? That would be what? . . . about a hundred and forty pounds for you . . . of what now? Cheeseburgers I'm thinking. What does a vulture take on its cheeseburger?"

Art Karpinke's expression suggested that he was losing patience with the goat lady, but his heavily armored salesman's demeanor was still winning out by a hair. "Well, Ms. Caprini, you must think I'm a developer, wanting to carve up your beautiful property to plant a crop of houses." His chubby fingers danced across an imaginary plane, a gesture meant to suggest many houses being built.

"It crossed my mind. So what is it you do want to build—a mall? You could start with a Chucky Cheese right over there by the milk house . . . maybe put up a Pet Smart where the empty dog kennel is over there. Oh yeah, and how about a Toy Barn out there—that big red hip-roofed building—just chock it full up to the rafters with plastic crap and whiney kids. Heck, maybe you could put up a Colonel Sanders out by the chicken coop. You could drive in here for a bucket of mashed potatoes to eat in your goddamn Cadillac while you're cruising the countryside looking for more paradise to pave over! And by God I think we need a Bed, Bath, and Bullshit right here where we're standing, don't you, Art?"

Art Karpinke had taken empathy training to prepare himself for dealing with the strong emotions associated with buying and selling homes. He said, "You seem upset, ma'am."

"Fucking-A, Art—you put your chubby little finger right on it."

"I'm here to assure you, Ms. Caprini, that my client does not want to build houses or a shopping mall on your property."

"Well what the hell do they want, Art? And by the way, it's a farm, not a property."

"You'll be happy to know, ma'am, they want to farm it."

CHAPTER 31

Bruce hadn't talked to Alice since he'd had the trots and run up the big hospital bill. More importantly, he hadn't talked to her since the object lessons from the old shepherd Luther Yarnell and Doc Voekle on the perils of absolute locavorism among animals and peasants, and the reminder that he had caused havoc in his family. He had felt like a child scolded by adults who were important to him. At least he was finally feeling physically strong again, but he'd never felt so unsure of his motives or his options.

He was sure of one thing: he missed his children, and he finally admitted to himself that he badly missed what he'd once had with Alice. And with Krystal now committed to Miguel—jeeze, that was fast, he thought, a little overlap would have been fine—and Wanda's sexual favors feeling angry and dangerous, he was getting horny. He had Tom Waits' gravel-voiced musical rambles running through his head. He heard himself repeat Waits' intro to his marriage anthem: *"Christ, I'm so goddamn horny the crack a dawn's gotta be careful around me,"* and the melody had become his musical brain-worm du jour: *All my friends are married, every Tom and Dick and Harry. You must be strong if you're to go it alone . . . .*

Go it alone . . . go it alone . . . that's a hard thing, he thought. I don't know how much longer I can do this. His once longed-for freedom had begun to feel like rootlessness. He had finally begun to sense that he wasn't getting the soul food that should come from belonging to a place. He'd always had roots before. Before he left home they'd felt like lashings, like he was tied to the mast of a domestic ship that he couldn't steer. Now he thought longingly of Alice and the kids every day. He remembered a time playing horse; Mikey sat on his back and Josie led him around the living room rug. Josie then led him to the bathroom to see if she could get her dad to drink from the toilet. They had laughed themselves sick. The memory made him gasp.

But now Ray Jr. was giving him the opportunity to put down new roots right here in Parma—to start over—or maybe, he thought, just maybe he could go back home. He climbed up into the cab of the new John Deere parked in the shop and closed the door. The cab amounted to a big green sound-insulated phone booth with a comfortable yellow seat. It was perfect. He scrolled to Alice and touched send. He was surprised that she picked up.

"Hi . . . I got the papers," he said.

"Good," she said, leaving silence in her wake. If there was conversation to be made, he would have to make it.

"I just wanted to say that, I'm, umm . . . that I'm, umm . . . pretty sorry."

"Pretty sorry? You're about the sorriest jerk I've ever known."

"Alice, please, you know what I mean. Anyway I miss you and the kids."

"So that took, what? Three months? What happened? The goat lady cut you off? How about your little waitress friend?"

"This isn't going so good." He tried to change the subject, "How are the kids? You think they might like to visit their dad for a few days?"

"I wasn't sure they had one . . . but what did you have in mind for them, *Dad*, maybe hang around the shop and climb on the big tractors? No . . . I know . . . you could fill a wading pool with used motor oil and they could splash in it. No . . . wait . . . better . . . they could play hide-and-seek in a pile of pesticide bags! Or . . . maybe . . . do you have a welder in the shop?—I bet they'd love that!—all those sparks!" Alice caught her breath and continued: "I'll tell you what, traveling man, a real dad they could visit in a real home might be nice. But there's no way in hell I'm letting them come down there."

"You could come too."

"Well isn't that sweet. You know what, Bruce?—We're going to have us a little visit with my lawyer and a judge next month. We can discuss all this then. Right now I think it's time to hang up, *Dad*."

"But there's other stuff I wanted to tell you. I just got out of the hospital with—"

Alice cut him off. "With no health insurance!" she said.

"That too. But—"

"Bye, Brucie." Her phone snapped shut.

Bruce closed his phone and passed it back and forth between his hands as he sat in the tractor cab. "That was unsatisfactory," he said to himself. It was several minutes before he opened the door and climbed down to the concrete shop floor.

It was clear that she was right. This farm, Vander Koop Farms, Inc., Unit I, was no place for kids. Nanny Gate—now there was a farm to raise kids on . . . goats, chickens, cats, a garden, a small river running through the woods at the back, even a friendly little dog. He remembered their farmette in Edenville on the Tittabawassee River—the Big Tit was what the locals called it—when they lived there they'd had everything he loved except the long gas-wasting commute to work. It even had a walleye run in the spring. Man, that was a whole lot tastier fish than a sucker. But that was before he'd screwed it all up.

Bruce's cell phone buzzed in his jeans.

"Some asshole wants to buy my farm. You know anything about that?"

"Wanda, hi . . . ummm . . . Ray Jr. let it drop the other night that they might be interested—the Vander Koops I mean. Man that was fast. They're on you already?" asked Bruce.

"So you knew about this? Were you going to tell me about it one of these days?"

"He told me not to, but I expect I would have anyway, if I'd had a chance."

"If you had a chance? What were you waiting for? Something in your pants that made it worth talking to me? I don't like you keeping me in the dark."

Bruce wondered if there were any women in the world who weren't ready to kill him. "I didn't mean to," he said, "I just found out myself. They move awful fast. You thinking of selling?"

"I might have to. I talked to my lawyer and he said I should expect to be sued by Maxine Jurek. Not Maxine exactly, but the insurance company that's got to pay for Amos's medical bills. Even if there was no pain and suffering part, the medical part could be a couple of hundred thousand. Poof . . . there goes Nanny Gate and here comes Vander Koop like the dark angel of death. Jesus, I might have to shoot somebody."

"What about the house?"

"He said he'd rent it back to me "reasonable," but he wouldn't give me a number."

"What would you do with the goats?"

"Dispersal sale. Everything—all my goats, milkers, bulk tank, cheese equipment—everything. I think I might keep Moses."

"So how would that work with all your goat owners?"

"Well, as far as the goats, I'd have to sell them all, subtract the sale expenses, divide up what was left and give it to the shareholders. I'd be lucky to keep five hundred bucks.

Bruce could hear Wanda's voice breaking. "Should I come over?"

"If you want . . . I don't know."

"I'll be over after I finish here."

Bruce didn't hurry to finish his work. After changing the oil on one of the tractors, he steam cleaned the block just to give the angry woman more time to cool. She used it to stew. His main brain told him to stay away from her, but his lizard brain, as usual, had a different idea.

The evening with Wanda was uneasy, but they at least achieved enough peace to have sex, which came down closer to Wanda's "just fuck me" craziness she'd displayed in the truck on the way home from the hospital than any sort of love-making. Foreplay was short, kissing was minimal, and the kitchen table was hard, but they got their sexual tensions relieved, which despite carrying out the act with stark austerity, raised the level of civility between them considerably. When they finished, Bruce reopened a cheap California red that was on the counter and poured two half pint jelly jars to the top and brought them to the table. They sat in the old oak bent-back chairs and drank and talked while the sweat dried. The kitchen screen door let the summer evening air drift over them.

"They offered me full time employment with benefits and a house," Bruce said.

"Which house?"

"I don't know. Ray Jr. says they've got several and he was sure they could vacate one."

"Vacate—there's a nice word for evicting a family. I think I know a few of their houses, but I don't know who lives in them. I hate to think of kicking people out."

"Well, plus, they might own this one if you sell the farm to them," said Bruce, edging toward a suggestion.

"You want to live here?"

"I don't think Alice will have me back; she's filed for divorce."

"So I'm what?—your backup plan? Your second-string blowup fuck doll?"

"No, I didn't mean it like that. Anyway, Ray Jr. said they like their hired men in stable relationships. He asked about you and me."

"So he *wants* us to live together? Did he say anything about us breeding? Do they want to have Doc check my reproductive organs for soundness so we can be sure to raise them up some fine strong field hands?"

"No, he didn't mention that exactly. I don't think they'd own the next generation—although, if the rich keep getting richer, and the poor keep getting poorer, they might. Anyway, I got to admit that I do enjoy breeding you."

"You've got a hell of a way with words for a stud farmhand, Bruce Dinkle. I do believe that's the most romantic thing a man's ever said to me."

"I try," he said.

"Try harder," she said.

At church that Sunday, Deb Vander Koop asked the congregation to pray for Ray Senior. The Reverend Roger Revson had private doubts that it would work very well considering Ray's arm's-length relationship with spirituality. Ray only came to church for weddings and funerals and always seemed mildly amused by the piety of others, including his wife. Of course he was nice about it, in a small Midwestern town you pretty much have to be, but he never really appeared to buy any of it. The Reverend Revson led prayers for Ray Sr. anyway, specifically mentioning the speech center in his brain and his newly revascularized heart muscle as areas where the divine power should be focused. The immediate effect was to make it all the buzz after the service around the row of twelve-quart coffee percolators in the church basement, which was where most local prayers were answered, if they were ever going to be.

Doc Voekle's wife Mattie said to Deb, "I just wish there was more we could do. Ray's given so much to the community. He even had his heart attack while you were having a party for the town."

Deb said, "That's so nice, Mattie, but there's nothing Ray and I really need except more time together. And except for the gazebo and hot tub he's been dreaming about, I don't think there's even anything he really wants."

"I'll mention that to my husband. Don't be surprised if you see men with hammers in your backyard. Is there such a thing as a gazebo bee?" said Mattie.

"I've heard of a quilting bee, a honey bee, a spelling bee, and a bumblebee, but I never heard of a gazebo bee. I doubt it could fly," said Deb.

"Well, if it does we'd better duck."

The women had a great laugh over that, and later that day Mattie put the bee in Doc's bonnet. Doc carried it to the diner the next day, where the remaining silverbacks put together an email list of everybody they could think of who could swing a hammer or bake a pie, and by the end of the week there were close to two dozen workers and feeders committed for a week from Sunday starting right after church. They had a real plumber and a real carpenter, and a bunch of farmers who by definition are all at least half skilled in the trades, although it did also include farmer Floyd Meyers who had once rewired a barn that promptly burned down with two thousand bales of hay in the loft. He suffered a lot of teasing for that; Doc told Floyd that he was putting him in charge of lost and bent nails.

They also got Mike Innert, the man from Ace Equipment Rental who offered the crew a gas powered Ditch Witch to run the water and electric out from the house. Mike always filled his beer belly—at thirty years of age already an impressive vessel—full to the tits at Ray's Memorial Day bashes, and he jumped at the chance to give something back, although at his girth a jump was more of a hop. Deb bought a set of gazebo plans and all the materials from the local lumber yard, and a cedar trimmed four-person hot tub from a place called Hot and Wet in Jackson. Bruce signed on too. Doc told Bruce that he liked the look of his wood butchering skills on Bob Barker's kennel, and assured him that they didn't have to worry about Deb or Ray digging their way out or tearing anybody limb from limb.

Over the next week Bruce and Miguel guided the material drop-offs, and in the middle of the week dug and poured eight footers with embedded anchoring bolts for the corners of the planned octagonal Victorian structure. With the still fresh memory of the Memorial Day storm, no one argued in favor of slighting the structure's connection to the Earth—just setting it on blocks would not do—and Bruce was starting to feel the connection too. When Sunday afternoon came and the Vander Koop backyard filled with workers, several of whom brought their children or grandchildren, Bruce's longing for the full constraining web of his family became painful. He couldn't go home, but maybe he could become part of this community and at least have a place for his children to come visit. The power of two dozen people pitching in on a project for a friend was as close to a miracle as he thought he'd ever seen. Besides the pain of longing, he felt hopeful and uplifted, although that may have been the rhubarb custard pie and black coffee.

As Bruce and Ray Jr. cleaned paint brushes, Ray Jr. asked, "What have you decided? Are you going to come to work for us full time?"

Bruce let the spirit of the present come out. He said yes to corporate farming, although he only meant to say yes to Parma and the community he'd become attached to. In any case, he was flat broke and any job in Michigan was a good thing. Yet again, he'd made an important decision without thinking it through more than once. But when he did get around to thinking about it more deeply, how could he make it turn out better this time? If he made a new home in a new place with his old self, could it turn out differently? Or would it be just another variation on the disaster that had become his life?

CHAPTER 32

I n the weeks that followed, Bruce became a model employee, working much harder, or at least steadier, to please his now full-time employer. He began to think long term about his chances to build a new life in this green rolling farm country, a life in a place to which he might, someday soon he hoped, lure his children if the divorce judge could just see him as a responsible man. He even considered getting a dog like Ishkabibble. Ray Jr. had taken to calling Bruce almost every day from Chicago to check progress on the 'action items'—that's what Ray Jr. called the job list. Without producing an organizational chart illustrating the hierarchy of farm hands, it shortly became clear that since Ray Jr. preferred to talk to Bruce on the phone, Bruce was over Miguel, which irked the hell out of Miguel and put some distance between them.

Art Karpinke had ultimately been successful in convincing Wanda to sell her farm. They were still working out the details of the survey and such. She planned to sell everything, but she would be able to rent back her house at a figure that really was reasonable, along with a few acres that would include the farm buildings. Wanda found it to her advantage not to hold a big dispersal sale with all the expenses associated with an auctioneer. Instead she used eBay and Craig's List, and so almost every day for several weeks somebody arrived at the farm with a pickup truck or a stock trailer, and took away one, or two, or in one case, twenty goats. The Saanen's went to the more serious goat milkers, like the big goat dairy down in Indiana that purchased twenty, while the naturally hornless Nubians with their long floppy ears and colorful coats went mostly for pets. A few were purchased by horse people who wanted a goat to keep a lonely horse company. Wanda arranged for Doc to castrate any young males purchased for pets before they left the farm. The mature billy goats, Sadam, Slick Willy, and Moses, whose testicles were the size of beer cans, were left intact for the time being.

Krystal used three hundred fifty dollars of her new-found wealth to purchase Sadam, then tried to convince Miguel to make a shed for him behind the trailer that they now shared.

"No way, Jose! We ain't having that stinky critter running around here. I have to build a big fence to keep him out of the garden, and he'll eat the bark off my trees, and he'll eat every bush he get to. And he probably break *my* leg if I turn my back on him. Hell no, I am not living with that damn billy goat!"

"But he saved my life—and anyways I already bought him from Wanda today."

"Well you didn't ask me, and we ain't having no damn billy goat here!"

"If you loved me, you'd let me keep him."

"If you love that goat so damn much, you can go sleep with him at Wanda's. Just be sure to take a shower before you come home. He ain't living here and I don't want you smelling like no damn billy goat!"

Krystal tried the seduction card. She rubbed up against Miguel and stroked him, then gazed up and rolled her eyes. "I'll make it worth your trouble, big boy," she said.

Miguel was not moved, "I just got rid of one woman that want to own me. I don't want to have to do it again."

Krystal pouted for a while, it was their first fight, but then she got busy trying to find a home for her stinky, leg-breaking, goat savior. The petting zoo owners she contacted all remembered hearing the story and seeing the pictures of the big handsome long-eared spotted Nubian on the

TV news after the goat saved Krystal from rape and murder. They were excited to hear from somebody as famous a Krystal, but most said, after short reflection, that they couldn't have a dangerous and awfully stinky animal around the school children who came to visit their petting zoos. Two petting zoo keepers said they'd call back, but they didn't. Doc advised Krystal that castration would take care of the odor problem and would make him less aggressive as well, so she spent another sixty dollars to get Sadam nutted, made another round of phone calls, and finally found a petting zoo just south of Kalamazoo that would give the big Nubian eunuch a home. The owner told Krystal she could come visit him any time, free of charge, and she thought that she would.

Art Karpinke had also visited Wanda's neighbor, old Mr. Rogers. His first name was Robert, but he had such a gentle and kindly demeanor, that everybody called him Mr. Rogers. Even his children, now gray-haired with grown kids of their own, tended to give him cardigan sweaters and slippers at Christmas. He'd quit farming fifteen years earlier and put all of his sixty-two acres of arable farmland into the Federal Land Bank so that he could get paid not to farm in his retirement. He was enjoying watching his land from his kitchen window as it slowly returned to its wild state. In the plant succession that is common on abandoned farms in Michigan, after the grasses and various open-land broadleaf weeds have had their day—thistle, goldenrod, ragweed, milkweed, mullet, burdock, and such—his land had been overrun with Russian olive, thornapple, and multiflora rose. Eventually poplar, ash, maple, oak, and hickory would have grown up and shaded out the thorny scrub, but, so far, saplings of the big tree species had sprung up only at the perimeter of the fields from seeds that dropped near the wooded fencerows. For the time being it was a nearly impenetrable thicket, mostly less than ten feet tall, and prime habitat for a wide variety of native birds and mammals. Mr. Rogers' bird feeders were mobbed with all of the local species of woodpeckers, nuthatches, warblers, and finches. Whitetail deer, wild turkeys, mourning doves, squirrels, and rabbits regularly stopped to peck and nibble the seeds the smaller birds spilled to the ground. So while the money that Mr. Rogers received for his seventy-nine acres—he kept an acre with his home—would offer him a higher level of security in the later years of his retirement, the sale was very hard on the land's current inhabitants.

Their hardest day, from the deer, to the nesting birds, right down to the earthworms, came in the first week of July. Bruce and Miguel arrived with chainsaws, a bulldozer, and a big tractor with a front blade and a heavy root-grubbing stump ripper on the back, and began to cut and push all of the tangled vegetation into great piles. They doused the piles with diesel fuel and set them ablaze. The green wood smoldered for days. In two weeks the sixty-two acres were down to bare brown dirt dotted with broad round stains of residual black ash from the burn piles. Literal carbon footprints, Bruce noted. Wanda watched the clearing process from the window over her kitchen sink and breathed the incessant smoke. She discovered that the smell went best with bourbon, so she started keeping a bottle on her kitchen table and began sipping it in her coffee at breakfast. Actually, along with a small stinky wedge of Sadam's Pitchfork cheese, it was her breakfast, lunch, and dinner. She knew that once the survey was done and she signed the deal, her place would be toast, and it was killing her.

Near the end of the clearing process on Mr. Rogers' farm, on a Tuesday morning in the third week of July, Bruce got up early and packed is best clothes—blue jeans without holes and his only button up shirt—into his bike panniers. He put a couple of sandwiches and a bag of double chocolate chip cookies from Deb Vander Koop's kitchen into his handlebar bag, and set out for Bay City with thirty dollars in his pocket. Deb would have loaned him Ray's truck—Ray was still months from driving again—but Bruce wanted to retrace his journey, and didn't want to spend his meager bankroll on gasoline anyway. The weather report looked good: only a small chance of thunderstorms in the afternoon, and a southwest wind that would favor him all the way home. Well, it wasn't actually his home anymore, but it was Alice's home, and Josie and Mikey's home, so home seemed like the right word to call it. He couldn't bring himself to say, even to himself, "my wife's home," much less, "my ex-wife and children's home."

He hadn't come up with the cash for new bike tires. The worn down smooth tread, threadbare in places, was poor protection for his tubes. Consequently, he endured five flats on the trip up. But he had a patch kit and a pump, and so made quick work of the tire changes, never losing more than fifteen minutes. He had thought he might scrounge a place to sleep that night around about the halfway point, somewhere east of Lansing where he'd met Krystal, but midsummer days are long, he had a tailwind, and he was going home, so he hardly stopped except to eat his sandwiches and cookies, and to refill his water bottles.

But he did pass a pick-your-own strawberry place where he ate at least a quart in the field while he picked one. He bungeed the mounded-full box of ripe berries onto his handlebar bag and happily munched the second quart over the next forty miles, easily ignoring the grit he ingested with the delicious unwashed fruit. The manic Ten Years After tune "Going Home" rocked his head and he pedaled like he was in the Tour de France, an illusion helped considerably when, in the heat of the afternoon, the tailwind gusted up to twenty-five miles per hour.

When he reached Gratiot County, the heart of the Saginaw Valley's rich agricultural plain, he saw that the cornfields had far exceeded the "knee high by the Fourth of July" rule of thumb the old timers used. It had been at least waist high by the fourth, and had grown a good foot in the week since. A man could hide in it standing straight up if he wore a green hat, which, given the number of John Deeres he saw around there, he figured most men probably did.

By three in the afternoon he had a hundred miles behind him and only forty to go. He could be home by dinner time. But of course Alice didn't expect him and would not be inclined to make him dinner. Still, the thought powered his imagination and his legs as he glided between the green walls of corn and flat expanses of sugar beets and soybeans.

Kids on summer vacation played in inflatable plastic pools in front yards under the watchful eyes of farm women and their dogs. Bruce suddenly ached for a normal domestic scene like that, one with him in it. He would forget for miles at a stretch that he was going to a place that was no longer home, and he was going there only to endure divorce proceedings.

Whenever the thought recurred to him, the strawberries rose in his throat and he had to sit up, swallow hard against his rising gullet, spit a little red juice, and breathe even more deeply than he already was.

When he passed the first of the McMansion developments on formerly rich farmland at the outskirts of Bay City, his heart thumped in his ears. He felt like his bike might leave the ground. He pedaled the last miles at such speed that he almost laid the bike down in the corners. He guided his old fat-tired black Mongoose with its loaded packs like it was an all-carbon road-racing machine made to carve turns on asphalt like a muscle-powered rocket. When his house came into view, suddenly he was nearly blind. His eyes filled with tears. His heart was bursting with love and remorse. But nobody was home.

Bruce tried his key but Alice had changed the locks. He checked the nail under the porch where they used to hang the extra key, but there was nothing. He checked under the mat and then under the flower pot on the porch. He checked for a new nail in the nearest basement window well. Finally, he gave up and walked his bike around to the back yard.

He could see that the sand box had been getting good use, and that the kids hadn't yet learned to put their things away. Every sort of colorful plastic toy was scattered about, including a Big Wheel, a Whiffle ball and bat, a beach ball, and an inflatable wading pool with a drowned Barbie. There was a Frisbee hung up on a tree branch, and two heavily armed action figures were lined up for trench warfare in the sand box facing a Cabbage Patch Kid leaning on a red plastic sandbox shovel. He surveyed the scene of domestic chaos and couldn't help noticing that it didn't bother him nearly as much as it used to. He was even amused by it.

He stretched out in an aluminum lawn recliner—no doubt the spot from which Alice kept watch on the kids and caught a few rays—and promptly fell asleep. He awoke in darkness feeling chilled, and saw that the lights had come on in the house. He went to the back door and looked in. Alice was at the kitchen table with a glass of wine going through an inch-deep stack of papers. He knocked. She bounced in her chair like she'd been shocked. She came to the door.

"You really should have come to the front door at this hour. You scared the crap out of me."

Bruce's reflex was that he should kiss her. He'd been gone for a long time and now he was home. Alice turned her back and returned to the kitchen table and her papers. "Sorry. Can I come in?" he asked as he came in, adding, "Where were you?"

Alice had taken the kids to McDonald's for dinner and then to a free concert at the park by the river where they'd had chocolate-vanilla swirl soft-serve cones. "None of your business," she said. She turned her eyes back to her papers and added, "And I don't have any beer in the house."

"How have you been?" he asked.

She looked up. "Have you ever been a single parent?"

Bruce hesitated. "It's not easy, I'm sure. You look good though." Actually, she looked tired. He added, "The kids okay?"

"I put them to bed about twenty minutes ago. If they hear you they'll be up, so keep your voice down."

"What have they been doing?"

"Kid stuff. If you cared, you'd know."

"You still going to that painting class?"

"Can't afford it. My asshole husband left us, I've got a half a job, and now he comes waltzing in here and I suppose he expects me to feed him some goddamn politically correct local sprouted-potato casserole."

"I am hungry. A hundred and forty miles is a long day on a bike—but you don't need to fix me anything."

"Thanks for the consideration, biker boy. There's peanut butter and jelly. Knock yourself out. You've got your choice of milk or Kool-Aid to go with it."

Bruce got up and made himself a couple of PB&Js on spongy soft whole wheat bread that was indistinguishable from store-bought white except by its tan color. With grape jelly and smooth peanut butter it was about as bland as a sandwich could get, but apparently that's what the kids were eating these days. He washed the sandwiches down with a glass of milk, then refilled the glass with water several times as he tried to rehydrate after the long day in the saddle. It was a drop in the bucket, but he didn't dare ask for more.

"What happens tomorrow?" he asked as he chewed.

Alice's eyes had gone back to the papers. "I get the kids, the house, and what's left of the money; you get your freedom and a monthly bill for child support that you won't be able to pay, so I'll have to have your ass thrown in the clink." She watched her index finger punch her points into the table. Bruce noticed she wasn't wearing her wedding ring. "You'll be in the slammer, so I'll have my revenge, but I still won't have enough money to raise the kids the way they deserve. They won't be able to afford college and will get surly and depressed in their high school years. They'll never quite understand why their dad left them. They'll blame themselves even though I'll tell them not to. I'll even tell them it's not their fault that their dad's an asshole. Then we'll use them as weapons against each other, and the whole damn family will swirl down the drain like toilet bowl full of hangover shit. Sound about right to you?"

"Jesus Alice, calm down, would you? I want to help."

"Calm down? You're telling me to calm down? Do you know what you've done to this family with your fucking food fetish?"

"I said I'm sorry. I don't know what else I can say."

"Saying sorry doesn't do squat. Saying sorry doesn't pay the bills. Saying sorry doesn't cook or go to the grocery store. Saying sorry doesn't get the kids to school or violin or soccer practice, or . . . shit . . . why do I bother with you!" Alice's anger burst out of her. "Get out! Just get the fuck out of here, you asshole!"

"Alice, please, they've hired me on at the farm full time. I'll be making some money and I'll have a place to live—a real house."

"I want to see Daddy's house!" It was Mikey in the kitchen entryway.

"I want to see Daddy's house, too," Josie said, appearing beside her little brother.

Alice was on her feet pointing in the direction of the kids' bedrooms, "Go!" she stamped.

Bruce was on his knees, grinning and crawling across the kitchen floor toward his children. "Mikey! Josie! Come give Daddy a hug!" His arms spread wide to pull them in. He buried his nose in their hair and breathed deeply. Tears filled his eyes. "I missed you so much," he said, hugging them tightly. "Look how you've grown!" he said, noticing that they were both taller and also a little chubbier. The effects of the new TV and no time to cook had already begun to show.

Alice bit her finger as she watched him gather the children in his arms. She attempted to recover her anger. "To bed!" she repeated, pointing to their rooms.

"You better go kids; your mom and I need to talk," said Bruce, mussing their hair and kissing them both.

Mikey and Josie reluctantly returned to their rooms amid the last words, "See you tomorrow!" from their born-again father, and "And stay there!" from their harried mother.

"You really know how to make a scene," she said.

"I missed them . . . I missed you," he said.

"So you think you can just dance in here without a penny, eat our food—you've got no plans to even come back to town. And you act like we're all one big lovey-dovey family. You think my brain's made of popcorn?"

"I'm trying Alice. Really, I'm trying . . . They hired me fulltime and I'm getting a house on one of the farms."

"So what's this house like?"

"I don't know, they haven't said which one."

"You got a pay stub to prove you're employed?"

"Not since I started full time."

"Well good luck with the judge tomorrow. I'm guessing she'll be about as impressed as I am. Where you planning to stay tonight?"

"I . . . I was hoping I could stay here. I can't afford a motel"

"You can have the couch." Her voice softened a bit. "But don't even think about coming into my bedroom."

CHAPTER 33

D espite exhaustion, Bruce slept poorly. He finally dosed off in the wee hours, and it seemed only a moment later that the TV was on and Mikey and Josie were jumping on him. The feelings of being overwhelmed by parenting, of being beset by the demands of children, of not having his own life in his control came rushing back, but now he had a little distance from his alienation. He managed to locate the source of the frustration in his mind and bury it in favor of a higher purpose.

"What do you want for breakfast, kids?" he asked.

"Captain Crunch!" said Mikey.

"Fruit Loops!" said Josie.

Oh, Jesus, things have changed, he thought. He got up and went to the kitchen, opened the cupboards, and was happy to find a box of oatmeal and a bag of walnuts. In the refrigerator he found a bag of apples—Chilean apples in the summer in North America, but real food, at least—and assembled a pot of oatmeal with sliced apples, walnuts, raisins, vanilla, cinnamon, and nutmeg. Alice emerged from the bedroom to find breakfast simmering on the stove and a hot pot of coffee ready to pour.

"This is good," she said.

Bruce was thrilled to hear a positive word from her. He felt his heart jump. "You're welcome. What time do we have to be in court?"

"Ten. I got to take the kids over to Jazmine's before I drive down there."

"Can I ride with you?" Bruce asked.

"You better ride your bike so you can start pedaling back to Parma afterwards."

"I thought I might stay a couple of days."

"You're not staying here. And I thought you had a job."

Alice seemed determined see this through. He thought she might be softening, but clearly not enough. He resigned. "Yeah . . . yeah . . . yeah, I guess I do."

The kids lobbied hard for Bruce to stay, but Alice held her ground, and shortly they were out the door. In the courtroom Alice sat with her lawyer. Bruce had only himself to represent him. When the judge called their case, Bruce was instructed to sit at a separate table, alone. Alice's attorney laid out the terms of the divorce settlement to the judge. And, just as Alice had said, she got everything. Bruce tried to protest the custody arrangement, which did not allow for visitation due to his lack of a home or evidence of a job. He couldn't produce a W-2 or even a pay stub showing regular employment. He had to sign the divorce agreement, and it was done.

He lifted his leg over his old bicycle to pedal the hundred-forty miles back to Parma. "Have a nice trip," Alice said, her voice dripping with sarcasm. He was gutted. He turned away. He didn't see Alice's face redden and fold into itself as her blue eyes spilled over.

He pedaled away slowly, devastated, gasping against the constriction in his throat and his urge to break down. As he rolled along the edge of the road he looked for a place where he could collapse unseen. He saw a dirt two-track on the left and turned his bike across traffic. A car nearly struck him. He pedaled only a short way down the path leading into the thick woods of the Shiawassee Game Preserve before he dropped the bike and himself to the ground, pulled his knees to his chest, and sobbed. It took several minutes before he could begin to gather himself.

A green pickup with an official seal on the door idled up next to him. The window came down. The conservation officer inside asked, "Can I help you?" He was a bearded man about Bruce's age.

"I don't think so," Bruce said, rising and lifting his bike upright. He blotted tears from under his blood shot eyes with the shoulders of his T-shirt.

"You sure? You look like you're having a hard time."

"Divorce . . ." Bruce said, "my wife just divorced me . . . I lost the kids."

"You're right, I'm sorry, I don't think I can help very much. Where you going now?"

"A little town west of Jackson—Parma—ever heard of it?"

"No. But Jackson's a long way on a bike. I was just headed home for lunch—it's the right direction for you. Why don't you throw your bike in the back and I'll get you a full belly and twelve miles down the road." The man opened his truck door and extended his hand, "Stan Bunker," he said.

Bruce, who had lived in Michigan his whole life, was once again astounded at the generosity a Midwestern stranger could show. He lifted his bike into the back and climbed into the cab.

"You want to talk about it?" Stan asked.

Bruce spilled the whole story with only minimal slants in his favor. For instance, he still thought chickens in the basement had been a pretty good idea. But he owned up to all of it. By the time they'd finished the sandwiches that Stan made—venison sausage and cheddar on rye with lettuce, mustard, and horseradish sauce—delicious—and washed them down with a couple of light pilsners and a pot of coffee, he'd hit all the important points, from selling the cars and the horse and the farmette in Edenville, to his lusty entanglements with Krystal and Wanda. They walked out to the truck and Bruce lifted his bike down.

"Your tires are good and bald—I'm seeing threads."

"Yeah, at least they roll easy that way."

"I bet they do. They look like racing slicks. Hey, I'm a pretty serious mountain biker and I got a tangle of old tires hanging in the back of the garage. I'm sure I could find you an upgrade."

"You've already done a lot, Stan, I couldn't"

"Well, I could," he said, lifting the garage door. Screwed to the back wall of the garage there were two foot-long metal hooks, each with half a dozen bike tires hanging on them. "Here, take these," Stan said as he pulled down a pair. "They've got a fine tread down the middle so they shouldn't roll too bad on the road. They're not new, but they got more life left in them than the skins you're riding on. I believe I've used thicker condoms than those."

Bruce was again taken aback by the generosity of this man. They pulled the wheels off Bruce's bike and each took one. Stan said, "I won the tire changing contest at the Michigan Mountain Bike Association meeting last winter. I'll race you . . . one, two, three, go!"

There was a rush of deflating, bead lifting, tube stripping, and then the whole thing in reverse. Stan was the first to grab the pump, and had the rear tire inflated in less than two minutes, start to finish. Bruce was only a few seconds behind but had to wait for the pump. The flurry and focus on the task made Bruce laugh. It felt so good to laugh.

"You got an awful long road home, buddy. Good luck," Stan said as Bruce rolled out of his driveway, headed south.

"Thanks, I wish I knew if I was on it."

Chapter 34

Bruce retraced the same roads to Parma that he'd come 'home' to Bay City on, the same route he'd taken when he'd left the previous March. It looked a lot different going than it had coming the previous day. And it felt different. Today his legs were leaden from the manic hundred forty mile race back to Bay City. His mind held a hundred times the disappointment and none of the anticipation, however unrealistic, it had held the day before. The southwest wind that had filled his sails on the road home was now in his face. Or was it home he was going to now? The road home—it sounds important, it should mean something, he thought, but he wasn't sure which road that would be. And today it was hot—not just warm, hot—stinking hot and humid—a variety of physical discomfort so much different than the damp cold he'd felt when this had been his escape route four months before. He rode shirtless and finished a water bottle every ten miles or so. But the heat and headwind were the least of his pain. For the first time he understood what it meant that you can't travel the same road twice.

With his late start, the headwind, and his dead legs, even with daylight that lasted until after nine o'clock there was no way he'd make it all the way back to Parma. It was almost nine and the light was fading when he coasted into the same truck stop in Perry where he'd met Krystal, what seemed like a lifetime ago. He found the same table near the window where he could keep an eye on his bike. The waitress brought water and a menu.

"I seen you ride in on your bike, hun. Aren't you the same guy that Krystal run off with?"

"I'm afraid I am."

"How's she doing? We miss her around here. She hasn't called."

"She's doing fine. Better than me, I'd have to say."

"Good to hear that—I mean sorry for you, but good to hear she's doing okay. What can I get you?"

"My usual."

"You'll have to help me on that one, hun."

"Same thing I had last time: meat loaf, mashed potatoes, green beans, and cherry pie."

"Good choices. Cherries are fresh frozen—we started making the pies here. We just got a couple of big boxes of pie cherries from Traverse City."

"I'll have the rest the same, too."

"I don't know what you mean."

"I need a place to stay."

"Well, you're on thin ice on that one, lover boy. But I could probably sneak you into the storeroom since you're a friend of Krystal's. I'm working a double shift, so you'd be good until seven in the morning. Can you sleep on a few sheets of cardboard?

Bruce found that in fact he was tired enough to sleep on a short stack of collapsed cardboard boxes in a truckstop storeroom, but woke up in the pitch black with a crook in his neck, and for a moment had no idea where he was. It took a few seconds to find the sliver of light coming under the door. He got up, felt his way out, used the bathroom, had another piece of that delicious cherry pie with a cup of black coffee, and was on the road again before the sun broke the horizon. A doe and a spotted fawn crossed the blacktop in front of him just as the first golden beams hit the land. The beautiful new day seemed to give him a thread of hope. He made good time in the hours before the heat and southwest breeze rose in his face again, and he was back in Parma by lunchtime. He was glad to see Doc's vet truck out in front of Martha's Kitchen.

"So how was your percyculations?" Doc asked, putting on his comical cowboy accent, and inviting him to sit down with an open hand.

"Percyculations?"

"Like perambulations, only on a bicycle. I just made it up. Can I buy you lunch? You must be starving, probably on the verge of rickets, or beriberi, or maybe even kwashiorkor."

Bruce was too tired to ask what beriberi and kwashiorkor were, but he gathered that they were some sort of malnutrition. "Thanks, I'm starving," he said. More Midwestern generosity, he thought. "It was fast going, slow coming home," he finally answered.

"So you're calling Parma home now?"

"I guess I am. Alice won't have me back and the divorce is a done deal. I need to get a decent place to live if I ever want to see my kids." Bruce suddenly didn't want to talk about it. "What's the news around here?" he asked.

"Ray's home from the hospital, and I think Vander Koops are closing on Wanda's place this morning. I was out there yesterday to check an old lame goat, and Wanda looked like she'd been rode hard and put up wet. Mud in her hair and she smelled like whisky."

"Yeah, I'm afraid she's losing it. Her whole heart was tied up with those goats. Seems like she chose goats over people in her life. The only reason we got together was that I sort of like the smell—well, maybe not the only reason. Anyway, she's a mess."

"Well, I'd venture she'd be glad to see you about now. You had a shower since you left?"

"That's the good thing about riding into a headwind, you don't have to smell yourself. Maybe I'll ride by and check on her before I get over to Ray's."

They finished their lunch and headed out the door.

"You want a ride? I can bungee your bike on top of the vet unit."

"No thanks, I think I'm needing the thinking time I get on the bike."

As Bruce pedaled he found himself pondering the goodness of people, and it made him want to be better, to somehow prove to Alice that he was a man she could depend on. But for now he had a friend who was coming apart, and he wanted to help her. He rolled his bike up to her kitchen door. It was the heat of the day. He wiped the sweat from his eyes and knocked, but there was no answer. He walked down to the milking barn. The bulk tank was gone, the milking machines were gone, and all the goats were gone except for a couple of old nannies that would probably never sell. He wondered what would happen to them.

He walked up to the old hillside barn and down the stairs from the loft. The coolness from the stone foundation felt like lemon iced tea as he stepped below ground level. It took a second for his eyes to adjust to the dim light after the bright summer sun. The young-stock pen was empty. He heard Wanda talking softly, but he couldn't find her with his eyes. He walked down the row of pens. Sadam's pen was empty. Slick Willy was gone too. He found her in the last pen, sitting in the straw next to Moses with her bourbon bottle in one hand, the other stroking the old buck's heavy mane and beard. Moses's horns were enormous, thick and corrugated at their bases, with long S-curves winding to their tips that hung in the air over his muscular shoulders. Wanda was barefoot, wearing a T-shirt and cut-offs. She was filthy. The buck licked at her shirt. Her curly auburn hair had gone tornado wild and there were bits of straw in it. Ishkabibble saw Bruce, barked once, and ran to the stall door with her tennis ball, tail wagging, ears perked. Moses stepped back and emitted a low rumbling bleat as Bruce leaned over the wall of the pen.

"I wish you wouldn't a seen me like this," Wanda said, slurring a bit.

Bruce struggled for what to say. "Me too," he said. He thought he might suggest something everyday normal. "I had a long bike ride and I'm in deep need of a shower. How about you?"

"Me? A shower? Hell no. Ninety-nine and forty-four fucking one-hundredths percent pure. I'll tell you what though, an old goat broad like me could stand to be hosed down once in awhile. You want to hose me down, my little goat boy?"

Bruce was on fresh ground here. He had no idea how to respond to a woman in such a despondent and desperately crazy state. He felt cheerful and well-adjusted by comparison. "Milk house?" he asked.

"To the milk house, goat boy!" Wanda raised her spirits to toast the suggestion.

Bruce reached over the pen wall and offered her a hand up. He put his arm around her and they walked up the barn stairs and across the yard to the milk house. Ishy kept running ahead, dropping her ball in front of Bruce and barking. "Not right now, Ishy," he said. The concrete floor and walls of the milk house felt cool. He helped her undress. With the bulk tank gone, the center of the room empty. But the green rubber hose with the spray nozzle was still there, as was the water heater.

Wanda stood over the drain in the middle of the milk room with her eyes closed and her hands clasped on top of her head, nearly lost in the tangled curls. Bruce carefully adjusted the water temperature before he directed the warm spray at her body. She wobbled and turned like a slow, drunken, disturbed ballerina. The force of the water dimpled and moved her flesh, and she moaned in a way Bruce could not interpret, somewhere between pleasure and despair. He found a bar of soap on the window sill above the utility sink and ran it over her body and through her hair until she was covered with suds. He became excited, though he wished he wouldn't, as his hands slid over her soapy skin. The light from the window was soft and diffused across the white concrete block walls of the room. He couldn't help noticing that a woman's body can be beautiful even when her mind is in chaos. He started her turning slowly again and rinsed the suds and dirt away. He hoped that some portion of her desperation went down the drain with the warm water. She seemed a little better.

"I can do you," she said.

"I don't know if we should do this," he said.

"I want to," she said.

Bruce undressed and took his turn in the middle of the room, and the process repeated. As she sudsed him, her hands began to linger below his waist.

"Let's not. I don't think we should do it while you're like this," Bruce said.

"You're turning me down? Rejecting me?—You son of a bitch!"

"It's not rejection. I just want to wait until you're better . . . and I've got things to sort out myself." Bruce took a step away from her, and took over rinsing himself with the spray nozzle. Wanda began to cry. Bruce dropped the hose and held her. From a distance, you couldn't tell it from love. "When was the last time you had a decent meal?" he asked.

"I don't know," she said.

"Well, what can I make you? Breakfast, lunch, or dinner?"

"Breakfast," she whispered.

They put their dirty clothes back on and walked toward the house. Bruce stopped at the garden for a green tomato and a jalapeno pepper. When he bent to pick the tomato, Ishy dropped the ball in front of him. He threw it as far as he could, and several more times before they reached the house. The little dog was relentless. Ishy needs kids, he thought. He chopped the green tomato with the hot pepper and an onion, then sautéed it all in butter, and finally grated in a chunk of Sadam's Pitchfork. Wanda sat with her face pressed down into her folded arms at the kitchen table. Bruce folded the filling into two three-egg omelets, which he served with buttered rye toast and coffee. It was savory and delicious, but Wanda only ate a few bites. And they had run out of things to say.

"I got to get over to Miguel's," he said.

"I guess we both have to do what we have to do," she said.

Bruce wasn't sure what she meant by that, but she seemed a little better. As he rolled out of her driveway, she found her brown bottle, took another slug, and watched him go.

"Shit . . . he was a good one," she whispered to no one.

CHAPTER 35

Krystal and Miguel were enjoying smoked-pike burritos cooked up by Miguel, along with a couple of beers and a joint at the cable spool table behind the trailer. Bruce was anxious to improve relations with Miguel since the corn spraying mistake that had shifted Ray Junior's managerial favor toward Bruce, so he turned on all the charm he could.

"I'm back! You get anything done without me?" Bruce joked.

"Nothing. Not one damn thing. We crawl around like armadillos without you," said Miguel, smiling and apparently unable to resist the straight line.

"I figured," Bruce said, "I just came over to drink your beer and check on tomorrow's action items."

"That's it!" Krystal said, "You guys is farmer action figures, ain't you? You just need you some combat boots and helmets—and a shiny new pitch fork signed by me!"

"Yeah, well, we just might need to go armed tomorrow," said Miguel. "We start clearing out the fencerows at Wanda's."

Bruce cracked a beer and took a pull on the joint when it came around. "I just came from there. She's a mess. Bourbon and Moses don't help that woman think any straighter. Ishkabibble's about the cutest little dog I ever saw, but even she's not getting through to Wanda."

"You did, though, right my friend?" Miguel chuckled.

"I'm trying to be good," Bruce smiled. "It's not easy."

Bruce felt relieved that he seemed to have his friend back. He thought he'd defer to Miguel on the morning's schedule so he wouldn't seem like the boss. "What time you want to start?" he asked.

"I give you a hour head start on the dozer, then I come get on the tractor."

"You got it, man." Bruce slugged back the rest of his beer. "I better get back to the farm, the sun's going over the edge." He pedaled the few miles back to his room at the shop feeling like he'd made every place he went that afternoon a little happier. It occurred to him that it might just be the intoxicants, but it wasn't a feeling he wanted to wreck by thinking about it too much. As he rolled into the farmyard the western sky was turning red to purple, and a full moon had just cleared the wooded fence row to the east. Across the Vander Koop's back yard in the gazebo he could see the moonlit silhouettes of Ray and Deb up to their necks in warm water in the hot tub out by the edge of the corn, just the way Ray had dreamed. He wondered if they could hear the corn growing. Bruce waved but they didn't notice him, and he didn't want to bother them. It had been a long day. He went down with the sun and slept the sleep of the dead.

He was up at first light and considered the food in his room: a banana and the stale remainder of the factory-boxed powdered road donuts from his trip to Lansing with Krystal weeks before. Quite the locavore menu, he thought. He ate the banana, read the donut package that claimed they were good for another month if unopened, whispered the lord's name in vain, chucked them in the wastebasket, got on his bike, and pedaled into Parma for the farmer's breakfast casserole at Martha's—a concoction of hashbrowns, eggs, two kinds of cheese, diced Canadian bacon, and salsa, all messed up together in a greased baking dish. It was the sort of breakfast that prepared a man for a day on a bulldozer—or possibly a day of being a bulldozer. He ordered it with a glass of grape juice in an attempt to keep it in Michigan. He had just eaten the parsley sprig off the top when Doc Voekle sunk with a grunt onto the stool next to him. Martha was working the morning shift and filled their cups.

"Morning Doc. What can I get you?"

"A bowl of oatmeal with raisons and some O.J. should do it. Thanks, Martha."

"You're out early," said Bruce.

"Had to deliver a dead calf down in Hillsdale County. Backyard beef operation. They had a fat black heifer bred to a Charolais bull trying to pass a hundred and ten pound bull calf. Had to do a fetotomy."

"What's that?"

"You gotta reach inside with a special instrument and cut the calf up in pieces to get it out. She'd probably been in labor for a day and a half, so the calf was already dead, that's why I didn't do a C-section. It's just about the ugliest procedure I ever have to do, and then of course this heifer is a little girl's 4-H project and she was crying her eyes out. Not the best way to start my day. I wonder how much longer I can stay at this job sometimes. Been up since four-thirty and my back is killing me." He sipped his coffee and tried to brighten his face as he turned to Bruce. "And what's got you dining out at this fine establishment at the crack of dawn, my man?"

"Mostly just hungry, but procrastinating too, I guess. We start clearing fencerows up at Wanda's today. She's pretty upset about selling. I hope she doesn't take it too hard."

"She will, you know that," said Doc.

"She is," said Bruce. "You know I saw her yesterday, and she's a mess. But it seems like after having to sell all her goats already, watching the fencerows come down shouldn't make it much worse."

"There's always room for worse, my friend. It's like Jello."

"I thought your job was to be the sage who makes everybody around here feel better?"

"I'm a mite slow to get the cross-hairs on wise and good some mornings."

Bruce had wolfed down his farmer's breakfast casserole with noticing it. His fork wandered the wide white plain of his plate looking for last bits. "I guess I gotta go do this," he said.

"Be kind. Good luck," said Doc.

Bruce swung his leg over his bike and pedaled over to Mr. Roger's farm where they'd left the dozer. He fired it up and started toward the fencerow between the Roger's place and Wanda's, a fencerow that was about to disappear as the arable land of the two farms became one huge hundred-acre field that would be transformed into evenly pulverized dry brown dirt before it was planted to winter wheat in a month or so.

Wanda bolted up on her bare mattress when she heard the diesel roar to life. She looked out the window and saw Bruce steering the bulldozer over the now obsolete property line, uprooting small trees in its path. Bruce's heart jumped and a jolt of adrenalin passed through him as he crossed the fence line. He started down one of the wooden fences that separated the goat pastures, pushing a growing pile of gray boards and cedar posts ahead of the big steel blade. The bulldozer made such quick work of the fence that Bruce consoled himself with the notion that what he was doing was insubstantial. No big deal.

A wave of nausea hit Wanda. She ran to the toilet and retched a few strings of bilious vomit. She squealed in pain and collapsed onto the wooden floor. She curled there and sobbed for several minutes, then suddenly became still for a moment before scrambling to her feet. Her eyes were wild. Ishkabibble sensed that they were going outside and ran to the door and barked. Wanda went to the closet and got her varmit rifle, the Remington .225 with the scope, and carried it down the stairs and out to the old barn, wearing only the T-shirt she'd slept in. She went down the barn stairs from the loft, Ishy bouncing ahead of her, then down the dirt aisle and into Moses' pen. She cooed something reassuring to the old buck as she unlatched his gate and went in.

Bruce was in bright sunlight. She was in the shade with the sun behind her. He would never see her. She worked the bolt action, moving a shell into the chamber. She steadied the rifle on the sill of the open window at the back wall. She found Bruce in the scope on the open seat of the bulldozer pushing down the second wooden fencerow from where she stood. It was a little over a hundred yards—no need to adjust for bullet drop. She waited. He stopped midway down the fencerow and backed the big machine around to change direction. His square shoulders and muscular back now faced the barn as the dozer paused momentarily before going forward again. Wanda had Bruce's spine squarely in the crosshairs, about six inches below the base of his neck; the shot would take his spinal cord and aorta. Even with a small bore rifle he would be dead in seconds. She held her breath and squeezed the trigger at the moment Moses gently lifted the polished corrugated base of a big horn along the smooth cleavage of her bottom. The bump moved the shot a little high and to the right. A red spot instantly appeared on Bruce's T-shirt. He slumped in the seat and the dozer stopped moving. Wanda looked wildly satisfied. She worked the action again, placed the butt of the rifle against the feed trough, put the barrel in her mouth, reached down and put her thumb on the trigger, and pushed herself away.

CHAPTER 36

Mr. Rogers had been enjoying his coffee on his back porch when he heard the shots. Hearing gunshots in the country doesn't automatically mean something bad has happened, the way it does in the city. But he was aware that the only other shots he'd heard from the direction of Nanny Gate in the last eight years were when Wanda had shot Bob Barker six weeks before. Before that, before Doc Caprini died, Mr. Rogers had heard shots almost every weekend as the doctor touched off round after round at paper targets from the shooting bench in his fencerow. Mr. Rogers never understood the pleasure a person could find spending hours shooting a gun, and while he had found Doc Caprini generally agreeable as a neighbor, he wasn't sad when the shooting stopped. He picked up the binoculars he kept for watching birds and walked out for a better look. When he got to a spot where he could see the through the fencerow and spotted the bulldozer, he raised the binoculars to his eyes, gasped, and ran back in the direction of his house as fast as an eighty-one-year-old retired farmer can run.

The dozer was headed almost directly toward him. Bruce had his hands clutched over the exit wound on his chest. The entire front of his T-shirt was soaked with blood and his head lolled back, but he managed to keep a foot on the pedal, and the dozer moved forward. It knocked through the next fence without a sputter. Bruce let go of his chest briefly and pulled back on the right brake lever with a bloody hand, shifting the dozer's path, which now pointed it directly toward Wanda's house. He closed his eyes against the pain and his head bounced as the dozer crawled on its wide steel tracks across the young-stock paddock behind the barn, then flattened the last fence and entered the backyard. He pulled again on the brake lever to miss the fairytale stone house. The big dozer dieseled over the kennel fence that Bob Barker had dug under—the incident that had started Wanda's dominos falling, not counting the day Bruce had come to Parma—and not counting that she had set her own dominos. Then it flattened the cedar dog kennel in an instant, and continued to clatter across the driveway and across the front lawn. Ishy stood at some distance and barked. The dozer dropped into the ditch next to the road and nearly pitched Bruce over the front of the machine, then just as suddenly reared and threw him back against the seat as it lurched up and out of the ditch and onto the road. Bruce pulled his foot from the pedal and slumped back in the seat holding his bleeding chest and gasping.

Miguel had just turned his old Impala onto Beaverhead Road and was cruising easy down the middle of the pavement with his elbow out the window and a marimba band cranked to ear-splitting on his tape player, and so didn't hear the sirens until they were almost on him. Sheriff Timmers swerved wide to miss him, almost causing Miguel to take the ditch. Miguel checked his cracked mirror and saw an ambulance bearing down fast. As it flew past he pulled back onto the road, checked again, and saw still more flashers coming. "What the fuck?" he said to himself.

The sheriff screeched to a halt in front of the bulldozer and said something like ten-four into his handset as he flew out the door of his squad car. He scrambled onto the big machine and placed his bare hands over Bruce's entry and exit wounds and pressed hard. The ambulance was seconds behind. They had Bruce inside and on the way to the hospital in less than three minutes. Miguel watched the whole thing. He yelled at Sheriff Timmers, "Where is Wanda?!"

They followed Ishkabibble's barking lead and found Wanda with Moses standing over her. The old goat licked her blank gray face and nudged her with his nose like a nanny urging a newborn to rise. Ishy licked some blood from Wanda's other cheek and whined. Sheriff Timmers gasped and mumbled an oath. He looked around for something to cover her; all he could find was a feed bag. Miguel groaned and turned away. The sheriff pulled his handset and called for another ambulance. More police and medics arrived, and shortly Wanda took her final leave of Nanny Gate. A volunteer fireman farmer led Moses by the peace symbol down the barn aisle to another pen. He got the old goat a sheaf of hay and a bucket of water. A deputy stretched a yellow ribbon around the crime scene. Miguel took Ishy in his car.

Dr. Bottoms and every available surgical resident and nurse were waiting when the medics ran Bruce through the door and into the ER. Fluid lines were already running. The ambulance medic handed the doctor a tube of Bruce's blood for type and cross match. Type O was the answer they had in less than five minutes. There were four units in the hospital blood bank. He'd need all of it. His right lung was collapsed and the space around it had already filled with blood. He was in the surgical suite before the first bag was up and running full bore. They opened his chest to remove bone fragments from his shot lung and to close the holes on its surface. They drained the blood in his chest cavity and transfused it back to him. The shot had missed major vessels. They declared him lucky. By noon it was clear he would survive.

CHAPTER 37

A lice finished her work for Hunter Sand and Gravel before noon that day. She needed down time—a day at the beach would be perfect. She turned her cell phone off and took the kids to the Bay City State Park, where Mikey and Josie built sand castles and splashed in the waves on the Lake Huron shore. Alice watched them with one eye and read a novel with the other. When the day began to cool she took them for hot dogs and ice cream cones at Mussel Beach before driving home as the mid-summer sun was setting. She was feeling nostalgic and had Crosby, Stills, Nash, and Young in her CD player; they sang, "*Carry on, love is coming, love is coming to us all,*" and she wondered if love ever would come again. Against her will, she remembered when she had been in love with Bruce, how all the hard work had sculpted his body without him ever joining a fitness club, and how incredibly hard he had worked for what he believed was the common good, however selfishly. What an odd thing, she thought, to work selfishly for the common good. "At least he was a man who cared," she heard herself whisper. "Jesus, I must be going soft in the head," she answered herself.

She carried her sleeping children to bed, kissed them, got a glass of wine, and reopened the thick novel she was reading, *A Man in Full,* by

Tom Wolfe, and fell asleep in her chair after turning the page only half a dozen times. She awoke to banging on the door in the wee hours. It was her parents filled with horrifying news.

Alice had thought she was done with Bruce, but of course when there are children involved divorced couples are seldom done with each other. Suddenly she wanted to comfort him. Her mother advised waiting a few days before visiting him with the children, it would be too upsetting for all involved to visit him in the ICU and they might not let her or the kids in to see him anyway.

Alice's father said, "I just wish that damned goat lady could a shot straighter. Anyway, there's no need to visit the son-of-a-bitch, we get to watch his whole stinking life on the TV news."

"I think Mom's right," Alice said, "I'll go down Saturday."

Bruce hadn't expected to see Dr. Georgina Bottoms again after they moved him from the ER to surgery, and then to trauma ICU. But she stopped in every day to check on him. It never occurred to him to wonder why. On Saturday they moved him from the ICU into a regular room. There were flowers there from the Vander Koops and Doc Voekle, even daisies from Big Joyce, and dozens of cards from people he'd never met. Miguel and Krystal stopped in early and sat with him for a while. It was the first he would learn about Wanda. They'd held her on life support, brain dead, for a day in death's waiting room while they determined who would get her organs. Miguel said they had Ishy at the trailer and wondered if Bruce wanted her. Maybe he would, Bruce thought. He thought about the little dog and her tennis ball and smiled as he dozed off into narcotized dreams.

Dr. Bottoms came by about ten. What a babe, Bruce thought as he opened his eyes—and completely out of my league.

"I think they're going to kick you out of here on Monday," she said.

"This seems like the only safe place for me to be these days," he whispered. It still hurt to breathe, although the pain drugs were working pretty well, and they kept his emotions in check. He said, "I just heard about Wanda."

"She saved a lot of lives in the end. Heart, liver, kidneys, corneas, skin, bone—I think they even cut her hair to make a wig for a chemo patient—maybe two," she smiled a little. Then she moved a step closer to Bruce, "I still see little Amos coming in for dialysis every couple of days," she said, her eyes intent on his.

"Is he going to be all right?"

"Long term, no, not without a new kidney."

"Why didn't he get one of Wanda's? That would have been perfect."

"Didn't match—not even blood type."

"What about his family—can't they give one?"

"He's an only child—and Mom's got a prolapsed mitral valve, and Dad caught hepatitis from all his screwing around." Dr. Bottoms apparently still hadn't fully internalized the message on patient privacy.

"So blood type has to match to get a kidney transplant?"

"Yes. That's the first thing that has to match."

"So what am I?"

"Type O . . . universal donor. What does that make you think?"

"That makes me think . . . that you should do the other tests."

"You sure?"

"Sure . . . yes . . . I think I'm sure."

"Fantastic, Bruce. We'll wait a few weeks until the transfused blood is out of your system, and you'll need to heal for a while anyway, then we'll finish the tests. I've got a good feeling about this."

"I thought it was all science with you—none of this touchy-feely stuff."

"It is. But I've got a good feeling anyway."

There was a soft knock at the open door to Bruce's room. It was Alice and the kids.

"Oh my God, what have you done this time?" said Alice. The words were hard, but there was an old softness in her voice that Bruce hadn't heard in a long time.

"I got myself shot," he said, adding, "This is Dr. Bottoms, she saved my life."

The kids stared with wonder at the woman in the white coat. "Why did the goat lady shoot you, Daddy?" Josie asked.

"I was bulldozing her farm . . . I guess I was bulldozing her dream, too. I didn't know it was that dangerous."

"You sure bulldozed mine," said Alice.

"Boy, I did, didn't I. I'm sorry. I am so sorry. I don't know why I do these things. I don't blame you for hating me. I was selfish."

"I have hated you . . . but I'm not sure I hate you anymore. And these two miss you," she said, touching the children's hair. "By the way, that was a good breakfast you made when you were home—that oatmeal. Where does oatmeal come from, Bruce?"

"Who gives a rip," he said.

"It doesn't even say on the box," she said.

"I guess they get it where they find it—I found it in the cupboard at home," he said.

"Home is the best place to find what you need," she said, adding, "Maybe someday you'll have one."

Dr. Bottoms smiled. "Dreams are like body parts. It's painful when you lose them," she said. Then she gave Bruce an opening, "Speaking of body parts, do you want to tell Alice what you're doing, Bruce?"

"I don't think so . . . not yet." Any pride or virtue in the plan was still unearned.

"What are body parts, Daddy?" asked Mikey.

"Things like your heart," Bruce said.

"Is your heart going away, Daddy?" asked Mikey.

"No, I gave it to your mother before you and Josie were born. And now you have it too."

"Okay, fess up—what's the doctor talking about, Bruce?" asked Alice.

"I don't want to say. I don't know yet. There's more tests."

"Tests for what, Daddy?" asked Josie.

"Okay, I guess I'll have to say it . . . tests to see if I can give away one of my kidneys . . . one of my kidneys to a little boy who needs one."

The children needed much explanation concerning what kidneys do, and where they live inside the body, and why one is plenty even though you're born with two, and why Amos needed one. Alice's eyes became wet.

Josie said, "But if Mommy and me and Mikey have your heart, and then you go and give that little boy one of your kidneys, pretty soon there won't be anything left."

The grownups beamed at the children.

Alice touched Bruce's arm. "I think maybe that means there's more of him than I thought," she said.